TORONTO
TERROR

IF YOU Keep ME

NEW YORK TIMES BESTSELLING AUTHOR
HELENA HUNTING

• IF YOU *Keep* ME CAST

FLIP MADDEN

TERROR CENTER
BROTHER TO RIX

SIBLING
BEATRIX (RIX) MADDEN

PARENTS
MUFFY & HOWARD

TALLULAH VANDER ZEE

TALLY, TALLS, KITTEN
COACH'S DAUGHTER

SIBLINGS
TIES & FENNA

PARENTS
ELINE & BEREND

TEAMMATES
CURRENT & FORMER

TRISTAN STILES
HUSBAND TO RIX
BEST FRIEND TO FLIP
SIBLINGS: NATE AND BRODY

DALLAS BRIGHT
BEST FRIEND TO ASH
ENGAGED TO HEMI

QUINN ROMERO
TERROR ENFORCER

KELLAN RYKER
TERROR GOALIE

CONNOR GRACE
HUSBAND TO MILDRED
LOVES HIS MEEMS

ASHISH PALANIAPPA
HUSBAND TO SHILPA (TEAM LAWYER)
BEST FRIEND TO DALLAS

HOLLIS HENDRIX
BEST FRIEND TO ROMAN
BOYFRIEND TO AURORA

ROMAN FORREST-HAMMER
FORMER TERROR GOALIE
MARRIED TO LEXI

BADASS BABE BRIGADE

LEXI FORREST-HAMMER
(ANGEL)
MARRIED TO ROMAN
TERROR ASSISTANT COACH
SISTERS: FEE & CALLIE

PEGGY AURORA HAMMERSTEIN
(PEGGY, AURORA, HAMMER, PRINCESS)
DAUGHTER TO ROMAN HAMMERSTEIN,
GIRLFRIEND TO HOLLIS HENDRIX

HEMI REDDI-GRINST
(HEMI, WILLS, HONEY)
BEST FRIEND TO SHILPA
MARRIED TO DALLAS BRIGHT

MILDRED GRACE
DRED/LITTLE MENACE
MARRIED TO CONNOR
BEST FRIEND TO FLIP

SHILPA PALANIAPPA
(SHILPS)
BEST FRIEND TO HEMI
MARRIED TO ASHISH PALANIAPPA

BEATRIX MADDEN
(RIX, BEAT, BEA)
SISTER TO FLIP MADDEN
MARRIED TO TRISTAN STILES

ESSIE LOVELOCK
(ESS, SWEETHEART)
BEST FRIEND TO RIX
GIRLFRIEND TO NATE STILES

ACKNOWLEDGMENTS

Husband and kidlet, you're my world. Thank you for being mine.

Deb, your insight is always beautiful and I love you.

Becca, thank you helping me create this wonderful world. It is a true honor and a delight to work with you.

Kimberly, thank you for always supporting me.

Sarah, I'm grateful for all the years together, and so thankful for your endless organizational wizardry.

Victoria, you are amazing, and I am so lucky to have you!

Sarah S, thank you for sharing your skill set with me! I am endlessly grateful.

Alpha-Betas your feedback is so instrumental. Thank you for being my first eyes.

BBB, thank you for sharing your creativity with me!

Catherine, Natasha, and Tricia, your kindness and wonderful energy are such a source of inspiration, thank you for your friendship.

Jessica, Erica, Amanda, Julia, and Sarah, thank you so much for working on this project with me. It was a gauntlet, but we tamed the beast!

Kate and Rae, thank you for being graphic gurus. Your incredible talent never ceases to amaze me.

Beavers, thank you for giving me a safe place to land, and for always being excited about what's next.

Kat & Krystin, I am so grateful for your friendship.

Readers, bloggers, bookstagrammers and booktokers, thank you for sharing your love of romance and happily ever afters.

For my BBB. It's an honor to ride with you.

CHAPTER 1

TALLY

"I just want to have sex."

The table goes silent for a moment, and all eyes shift to me.

I'm out for brunch with my Babe Brigade. These women are my friends, though they're all a little older than me, and also almost all affiliated with the Terror, Toronto's pro hockey team, of which my dad is the head coach.

Hemi's eyes flare. "Uh-oh, what happened last night?" She's the head of Terror PR and married to Dallas Bright, a forward on the team.

"The same old same old." I'm the last virgin standing in my university friend group, and I don't see that changing any time soon. "It's so stupid. All these idiot boys just want to fuck the coach's virgin daughter."

A table of dad-aged guys close by looks our way. Hemi stares them down, and their breakfasts are suddenly super interesting.

"It must be frustrating." Essie's expression is all empathy.

Somehow a rumor proclaiming my unsullied status—to counteract the previous one where my ex called me a bad lay—has made its way through the douchebag population of my university. It's become a fun game to play: Who can deflower the precious Terror virgin? Or at least that's how it seems.

"Why can't I find a nice boyfriend who wants to know me?"

Maybe my expectations are too high. Maybe I need to read less LoTR fanfic and omegaverse romance where the heroes are head-over-ass in love with their partner and exceptionally focused on providing unparalleled pleasure. Is that too much to ask?

Dred tents her fingers under her chin in contemplation. "Maybe hockey parties aren't the ideal location to source such a man?" She's married to Connor Grace, the Terror enforcer, who lives to make her happy.

I sigh. "You're right. I know this. But my friends are all connected to the hockey world. There's no escape. Last night some guy waited in line with me for the bathroom, and we got to chatting. He seemed so nice and legitimately interested, but when it was my turn, he asked if I was down to fuck. It's horrifying how predictably horny university boys are."

Rix and Essie make matching icked-out faces. "That's awful."

"Right?" I point my fork at my friends. "There are guys out there capable of a meaningful connection and know where to locate a fucking clitoris."

"Women know where the clitoris is," notes Rainbow, our server, as she tops up my coffee.

"I wish I was attracted to vaginas and not peens." I sigh.

"Peens are fun." Rix bounces a little in her seat.

I keep my cucumber comment to myself.

"So fun." Essie looks all dreamy.

They each have a Stiles brother who is wholly dedicated to their happiness and their vagina. I hang out with the youngest Stiles brother, but we are one-hundred-percent platonic, and he's woefully obsessed with my friend Enid.

Rainbow finishes filling the coffees, humming to herself, and then flounces to the next table.

My rant continues. "I spent all of first year holding out because I wanted it to be with the right person, but it's three-point-five years later and I'm still searching for someone to give my V-Card to! But it's about more than sex," I admit. "Sure, I want my first time to be great, and not some lackluster wah-wah experience with a guy who's afraid of intimacy and needs a map and written directions to find my hot button. But I want my person. Someone I can hang out and cuddle with." I envy the women I'm with because they all have their person. Even some of my university friends have serious boyfriends. I want someone to love, who loves me back.

"You'll find the right guy," Dred assures me.

That gives me pause. It's possible I've already found the right guy. I'm just not on his radar. I probably never will be.

The conversation moves away from my single/virginal status as we finish brunch and head up to Rix and Tristan's penthouse to hang out. Conveniently, they live in the building above the breakfast place. My stomach fills with butterflies as we enter the living room, because the star of all my late-night fantasies, Terror forward Phillip "Flip" Madden (also Rix's older brother), is sitting on the couch, looking far too delicious for his own good. And mine.

He's well over six feet of chiseled, broad hockey player. His thick brown hair curls around his ears, a few weeks past needing a trim. He's wearing a long-sleeved shirt, pushed up to reveal defined forearms. I just want to rub myself all over him and scent him like a cat.

Essie, Rix, Dred, and Hemi are greeted by their significant others, who have also gathered in the living room. I long for that kind of casual affection; to have someone who knows all my secrets.

Hammer and I drop onto the empty love seat.

"Hollis is on the road this weekend?" Quinn Romero, a Terror enforcer, asks. He joined the team a couple of years ago. He has hair the color of fire and a Milky Way of freckles dotting his pale skin.

Hammer nods. "He's coaching the junior team in Ottawa. They should be back later this afternoon."

Flip passes his game controller to Kellan Ryker, the Terror goalie, and his dark-maple eyes shift to me. "How's it going, Talls? You have your holiday dance showcase coming up soon, right?"

"Yeah, it's next weekend." I try not to get overly excited that he remembered, but I also inconveniently recall the way fantasy Flip made me come last night after I'd read a particularly spicy fic update by my friend Cammie. I always replace the heroes in her why-choose stories with different versions of Flip, and of course my stupid cheeks heat.

"Is this one a solo performance? Or are you dancing with your troupe?" Flip leans forward, elbows resting on his thick thighs.

He always asks me about dance, and he always seems genuinely interested. "It's a whole-class ensemble this time, but I have one of the main parts."

His face lights up. "That's fantastic, Talls, and not a surprise since you're magic on the stage. Can you drop the date in our group chat?"

"There isn't a game that night," Hemi says before I can.

"So your dad will be able to go."

"As long as he doesn't have a meeting." My dad can't always make my performances, and when he does, often the Terror show up along with him.

"Right." Flip rubs his bottom lip. "Are there still tickets?"

"I can check for you," I offer, a little lightheaded. To be Flip Madden's girlfriend is the ultimate dream. But he's almost a decade older than me, my dad is his boss, and he's part of my extended friend group.

"That's okay. I can do the legwork." Flip leans back, a warm smile on his perfect mouth.

"I'm so excited to see you perform again!" Rix pipes up, breaking the spell I was under.

A chorus of agreement follows. When their schedules permit, the Babes attend my dance showcases at Tilton U, where I'm a dance major. Occasionally, the guys come too, when they don't have a game. I appreciate that they do what they can to accommodate my events, since we're in different phases of life.

"Are you feeling confident about your routine?" Essie asks. "Cammie said you've been at the dance studio a lot lately."

"Yeah, my troupe has been great about making time to rehearse." Even if we have to take the early-morning studio slot.

Essie's younger sister, Cammie, is one of my closest university friends. My university and the Terror world are hopelessly intertwined. Cammie's boyfriend plays hockey for the university team and is best friends with Brody Stiles, Nate and Tristan's youngest brother.

The conversation shifts, taking the focus off me. I sit back and listen, happy to be surrounded by the people I'm most comfortable with. The Terror crew is like a big extended family.

Well, except Flip. He doesn't feel like family at all.

When I was a teenager, I had a huge crush on him. I still do. But it's shifted in ways I didn't expect over the past year. He's a great guy. He coaches hockey for kids with special needs and plays cards with little old ladies at the retirement village.

He's fun to be around, I'm comfortable with him, and he's always been nice to me. Protective even. Countless times I've imagined what it would be like to be more than just his friend. To be his.

Warmth blooms low in my stomach and works its way up my chest.

Flip's brown eyes meet mine, and he gives me a questioning look. It feels like he's paying more attention to me than usual. Or maybe I'm hyperaware because of the conversation earlier at the Pancake House and his questions about my upcoming showcase. I excuse myself to the bathroom before the heat can reach my cheeks and inspire questions.

I splash cold water on my face and grip the edge of the sink. If things were different. If Flip saw me differently…

Could he?

Would he?

I'm so tired of being a fetish and untouchable at the same time.

I want someone to want me for me. Someone who cares about me and not who my dad is.

Lately the loneliness has been eating at me.

I sigh and pat my cheeks dry before I leave the bathroom.

As I round the corner I nearly run right into Flip.

"Whoa, hey." His wide, warm palms settle on my shoulders, steadying me.

My hand lands on his chest. "Hi. Sorry."

I inhale the mouthwatering scent of his cologne as I lift my gaze, hand still pressed over his heart. I should step back, stop touching him, but he's still touching me, too.

He tips his head, maple eyes searching mine as he drops his hands, fingers gently skimming my arms on the way down. A shiver runs through me. For a moment I believe he's not just my friend. For a moment a spark of something hot flares.

"You okay, Talls?"

Tension builds and swirls, twisting my stomach into a knot. Flip is an amazing person. He knows me. I know him. He cares about me the same way I do him. I've yearned for him for years. Previously innocent fantasies have spun into darker, baser desires over time and merged with my longing for something real. Flip has always been protective of me. He would take care of me. He would make me feel revered. With him, I'd be safe.

Flip Madden would be the perfect man to give my V-card to.

Before I can think it all the way through, I blurt, "I need your help with something."

His eyes soften, and a warm smile tips the corner of his mouth. "Of course. Anything you need, just name it." He's so earnest, his smile so genuine, like he's pleased I would come to him.

I pull in a deep breath. "I need you to take my virginity."

CHAPTER 2

FLIP

Shock leaves me speechless for a moment. I have done everything in my power to *never* think of Tallulah Vander Zee outside the neat, perfect little box labeled *Friend and Forever and for All Eternity Off-Limits.* Despite her being an independent, intelligent, talented, and beautiful woman, I have carefully avoided all landmines that might lead me to think of her in any way that would make her father, my coach, want to bludgeon me with my hockey stick.

I have stopped myself from chasing off other men. I have stood by while Tally has dated idiots, and silently cheered when she realized she could do better. Which was every single time. None of those guys have been good enough for her.

I have not been possessive. Protective, yes, but I have kept my fucking mouth shut even when I haven't wanted to. *Especially* when I haven't wanted to.

So what the hell am I supposed to do when every wrong thing I've tried valiantly, mostly successfully, not to want over the past six months falls into my lap, gift wrapped with a pretty bow?

Definitely not unwrap it and play with it every fucking day

for the rest of my short life—because surely, I'd be dead, and her father would be in prison. The image of her gift wrapped just for me pops into my depraved mind unbidden. I beat back that fantasy with a fucking weed whacker. But it's like a dandelion, growing and duplicating faster than I can mow them down.

I don't know what my expression must be, but Tally squares her shoulders and lifts her delicate chin. Her eyes are alight with so many emotions: determination, conviction, and most, dangerously desire, that echoes through me. The emotion that cuts me off at the knees, though, is hope.

"I'm so sick of university boys and their single-minded incompetence," she explains.

I can't disagree there. The guys I went to university with were pretty damn clueless, and I doubt much has changed. We were all hormones with our brains stuck in our dicks. Still, I keep my mouth shut, trying to figure out how to let her down gently. Because what she's offering, what she's asking…that's a place I should *never* want to go. Based on the scenarios suddenly clogging my brain, I do want to go there, badly. This is what I get for being celibate for almost two fucking years.

"I don't want to have a shitty first time with some guy who only wants to fuck me because I'm the Terror coach's daughter," she continues, making yet another frustratingly valid point.

I'm aware that this has been a problem for her, in part because of her father and her university friend group. Not to mention the fact that she hangs out with all of us. I've spent years watching out for her, she's become a friend, someone I enjoy being around. "Talls, I—"

She cuts me off. "I want my first time to be good, something to remember because I enjoyed it."

I open my mouth to say something wise, something other than, *"Let's have this conversation at my place, in my bed."*

But Tally pushes on, her face growing redder with every

word that tumbles from her soft, plush lips that I will not imagine kissing. Ever. "We're friends, right?"

"Yeah, we're friends, b—"

"Exactly," she cuts me off again. "We've been friends for a long time. You take care of people. It's what you do. You would take care of me. I want to have sex with someone who actually cares about me. You'll know exactly how to make me feel good." Her voice drops to a sultry whisper. "I mean, you might even make me come."

The gut punch is swift and damning in so many ways. And the unexpectedly vicious ache in my chest makes it hard to swallow. My past steamrolls me with ruthless, yet entirely deserved force. She doesn't want *me*. She wants my experience. *Will I never get out from under the reputation I've built for myself?*

Her fingers move to her lips, and her tone shifts, bordering on desperate as she steps closer, tipping her head up, eyes wide and imploring. "Please, Flip."

I swallow past the lump in my throat, hating that for a moment I allowed myself to see her as something she can never be. "Your first time should be with someone you trust—"

Before I can continue, she makes a fresh slice on my already scarred heart. "I do trust you. No one would have to know. It could be our secret," she says. "It probably has to be because of my dad, and our friends, and I wouldn't want to make it weird. But I know you. I'd be safe with you. And you can even teach me—whatever tricks you think I should know so I can make you feel good, too."

If ever there was a time I wanted to erase my past, it's now. The damage my ex, Fiona, did turned me into something I never wanted to be. But here I am. That Tally views me this way is just…devastating. It's one thing for her to want this from me because I mean something to her, because she cares about me and she knows I care about her, too. But to ask because of my extensive history as a fuckboy… It hurts in ways I didn't anticipate.

Maybe because I knew she had a crush and I thought it had progressed beyond the infatuation.

Tallulah Vander Zee is the dream I've never dared to let myself have.

My voice is thick and guttural, but my tone is firm, with no room for argument. "Your first time should be with some who loves you, and who you love back, Tally. And I can't be that guy." I've spent the last decade hiding from love, fearing what could happen if I let someone in again. Tally deserves someone who isn't jaded and broken.

Her shoulders slump, and her eyes dart away for a moment. When they return to mine, they're full of frustration, defiance, and the same hurt I feel. It's like someone reached inside my chest and punctured my heart with a hundred poison-tipped knives. "Please, Flip. It's just this one favor I need help with."

I recoil, and then strike back. "You're not asking me to hang a picture." My teeth grind together. "You only get to have this experience once, with *one* person, and they can never give it back to you. It's supposed to be special."

"But we've known each other for years." Her voice wavers, another stab to my heart. "You would make it special."

I shake my head, desperate to erase the forbidden images trying to form in my mind. In another world, where I wasn't such a mess of a human, I would be so good to her. But it would change everything, ruin our friendship in ways she doesn't understand. Our friends would be appalled. I would never forgive myself. "I can't." *I care about you. I can't take something special that I haven't earned.*

How awful would I feel when she realized down the line that she'd given a precious part of herself to someone who for years had drowned in pleasure to avoid connection? Even if I could give her what she needs, it would be a huge emotional step backwards for me. "You're… I can't do that."

Her eyes fill with tears, and her chin wobbles. "Anyone but me, right?"

My mouth falls open. That's a jagged, raw wound I won't recover from.

She skirts around me and rushes down the hall.

I want to go after her, to tell her she deserves better. I could explain that I can't give her what she wants without losing a part of myself, but nothing I say will soften that blow. And she has no idea she's ripped open a never-healed wound.

I stand in the hallway for a long time, letting the self-loathing seep in. I deserve to feel this shitty. I've hurt people I care about with my past behavior, so this is retribution. I spent my twenties avoiding anything with depth, and I won't go back down that road. Not for anyone, and especially not for my coach's fucking daughter, who I care deeply about. Maybe more than I realized based on the ache in my chest.

When I finally return to the living room, Tally is gone. Dred Grace, who knows me best in this crowd, gives me a questioning look as I sink into the couch. I feel awful for so many reasons. Especially when Hammer mentions how stressed Tally seemed before she left.

I search for the winter showcase at Tilton U. I might not be able to give Tally what she wants, but I can still show her that I care. "Who needs a ticket for Tally's performance?"

"We have ours." Hemi motions to the girls.

"You guys in?" I ask my teammates.

All the guys agree, so I secure our tickets.

Eventually everyone starts to disperse, and I follow my friends to the door.

"You okay?" my sister, Rix, asks as she pulls me in for a hug. "You seem preoccupied."

"Yeah. All good. Just thinking about practice." It's not

untrue. I keep thinking about how dead I'd be if I'd said yes to Tally's request and Coach Vander Zee found out.

Dred, Connor, and I file into the hall and pile into the elevator. I live in the building down the street, while Dred and Connor live in a mansion his Meems owns on the edge of the city. They got married last fall.

"Up for a game of Battleship?" Dred asks as we make our descent.

It's what we play when one of us needs to talk something out.

I glance between her and Connor. "Do you have time for that?"

She turns to Connor. "You're okay to pick up Everly and Victor?"

Dred and Connor adopted teenage twins earlier this year. I've never seen her happier than when she's with him and those kids. The twins were in foster care, just like Dred growing up, and she wanted them to have a home with stability and love.

"Of course, darling. We'll go for cake, and Everly will convince me to take them shopping, where I'll buy them something outlandishly impractical."

"This is why you're their favorite."

"You're their favorite, and mine." He kisses her softly. "Message when you're ready to come home."

We reach the lobby and Connor heads in one direction, while Dred and I go the other. We cross the street and take the elevator to my floor. I let us into my apartment, and Dred sets up Battleship on the kitchen island while I pour us glasses of Tang.

"What happened with Tally?"

I grip the edge of the counter. "She asked for help with something, and I had to say no."

She gives me her full attention, eyes lit up with curiosity. "Would you like to elaborate, or should I guess?"

I drag my eyes away from the Tang. "She propositioned me."

"As in…"

I choke out the words. "She asked me to take her virginity."

Her eyebrows pop. "Oh wow, she's got balls."

"It's not funny."

"I'm not really laughing."

I run a hand through my hair. "She's ready to throw her virginity away like it's an old shirt!"

"She's been holding out for a long time, so that's not quite accurate." Dred props her hip against the table. "Tell me, Flip, how old were you when you first had sex?"

I shake my head. "I'm a—"

"Do not finish that sentence if it ends with some gender-normative stereotype," she warns.

I clamp my mouth shut, because that's exactly what I was about to do.

"I was seventeen," Dred confides. "It was with a guy I'd been dating for a month, and we broke up three weeks later. I was not in love with him, but I was in lust. We had great chemistry, and I thought it would be good. It wasn't the best, but it also wasn't the worst. We were fumbly, and it was awkward, but it did get better after the first time. Could I have waited? Sure. But I liked him, and he liked me, so I made the choice, and I don't regret it." She makes a you-have-the-floor motion. "Now, how old were you?"

I huff. "Sixteen. But it was my ex, and we'd been together for months by that point. We cared about each other."

"You care about Tally," Dred points out.

"It's not the same! I loved Fiona, and I believed that she loved me. We were in a committed relationship." We stayed together for the rest of high school but went to different universities on opposite ends of the province. We reconnected in my last year when she moved back, but that went sideways. Fiona broke more than my heart when we ended the second time. It was gutting to have the person I loved tell me she didn't want me.

But it was so much worse when she dug the knife in deeper, telling me no one would ever want me for me, and that I was only good for two things: money and my ability to make her come. She created unhealable wounds when she left me, and I've spent the years since terrified to give my heart to someone else and find out she was right all along.

"Tally only wants me because I'm good at sex, not because I'd be a good boyfriend."

"Is that what she said?"

"Basically, yes."

Her expression shifts to empathy. "Do you really believe that?"

"She said I could probably make her come." It's gutting to have her see me like that.

Dred blows out a breath and shakes her head. "She's not wrong, though, is she? University guys are not great at that, in her experience."

"I don't want to talk about Tally's experiences with the dickheads she dated!"

Dred arches a brow.

"She's too important to be treated like some bunny I picked up at a bar! I will not indulge in meaningless sex like I used to, I've come too fucking far to go backwards."

She holds up a hand. "What if what you heard Tally say and what she meant aren't the same? She left pretty flustered, Flip. What if she does want you, but she's scared to ask for that?"

I shake my head. "She doesn't." *She can't.* "I have too much baggage."

"Everyone has baggage. And what if she does want you, what then?" Dred repeats.

I swallow. "Her dad is my coach. We're friends. It doesn't matter what she thinks she wants. It's literally the worst idea in the world. All our friends are interconnected. The risk is way too fucking high to even consider. I haven't had a relationship of substance since I was twenty and that ended horribly. I can't afford to entertain these kinds of thoughts about Tally. I've known her since she was a teenager."

The team has always looked out for her. Protected her. I've protected her.

"Do you disapprove of Hollis and Hammer, then?"

"No, but that's different." Although I suppose it was equally complicated. Hollis is twelve years older than Hammer *and* her dad's best friend.

"Do you just want it to be different?" Dred presses.

I pinch the bridge of my nose. "You're worse than my therapist!"

"You can pay me a hundred and fifty bucks an hour to ask you questions you already know the answers to, if it makes you feel better," she offers cheekily, but her voice softens, and her expression shifts to empathy. "I understand that you have always had Tally's safety in mind, and you're probably reeling because you've been trying to keep her inside a space she doesn't fit into anymore. It's also clear that she hit you in a sore spot without realizing it, probably because she was nervous and babbling. I think this is less about the request coming out of left field and more about being afraid of what this could actually mean."

I frown. "She's off-limits."

"She won't be forever." She squeezes my hand. "She's had a thing for you for a long time. When Tally was a teenager, it was sweet. Now she's an adult, and even if you don't want it to change things, it does. We also both know you have two eyes in your head, and a heart in your chest, and you're not immune to her."

I shake my head as I move to the Battleship table. "I need to stay away from her, Dred. She needs time to come to her senses."

CHAPTER 3
TALLY

"Three minutes and we're on." Arya does a full-body shimmy.

"We're going to be amazing." I shake out my hands and do a few deep knee bends. This showcase is worth twenty percent of our final mark this semester. It's another step closer to where I want to be; a graduate on my way to becoming a professional dancer. Top performances tonight mean first choice of studio time in the beginning of semester two, which is huge, so I'm manifesting good things.

"We've got this." Charles and I fist bump.

The rest of the ensemble echoes our excitement.

Tonight we're performing a modernized, full ensemble version of *The Nutcracker*. Every performance is preparation for our final showcase of the year. In second semester, we'll dance as part of a full-class ensemble like we are tonight, as well as with our troupe, plus a solo number.

That my dad is able to attend this time because the Terror doesn't have a game tonight feels special. My mother has never missed a single performance. As a kid, she would even come to rehearsals when she could. She's been my biggest supporter, always encouraging me to pursue my dreams. But it's rare for my dad to make a performance work. I'm excited and nervous to have him here. I always want to make him proud.

I center myself as the current song ends and the other dance class exits to join us in the wings. I squeeze Arya and Charles's hands before we leave the wings, the rest of the class falls into place around us on the stage.

I steal a glance at the sea of faces filling the theater. No seat is empty. I spot my parents with my brother and sister. Ties and Fenna both look bored, which is understandable since they've been dragged to countless performances over the years. The Babes are a few rows back, and my heart stutters and skips a beat as my gaze finds a group of the Terror guys as well. Even Flip is here, looking gorgeous and untouchable. He rejected me, but he still came to support me, which just proves he's a great friend, and I'm an idiot for having asked him what I did.

The first notes of the song filter through the sound system as the lights come up, forcing me back into the moment. I'll panic about Flip later.

But for now, I channel all my emotions into our routine as I move across the stage. This is my happy place, where I get to live in the music and tell a story with my body.

Charles steps in behind me, and his hands find my waist. We move as extensions of each other, synchronized and fluid as he lifts me and I float on air. We hold our position while Arya spins around us, and the rest of our troupe follows, a ribbon of graceful bodies twirling across the stage.

I count the beats, every muscle locked tight so Charles can maintain his balance as he spins, and every time we face the audience, my gaze catches briefly on Flip, whose eyes are fixed on me. My feet touch the ground again, and I leap across the stage, spinning as I weave through our troupe until I'm back in the center with Charles, converging for the final lift. He sets me on my feet and dips me backward, and I arc over his arm, the crown of my head nearly touching the stage as the final notes drift through the auditorium.

It always feels like it's over too soon. We hold the pose for a count of four, chests heaving with exertion. The audience erupts in applause. I'm breathless and high on adrenaline as I join hands with Charles and Arya and the rest of the class, and we step forward to curtsy and bow.

Flip stands and whistles with his fingers. His proud smile makes my silly heart clench. He probably thinks of me like a little sister. Embarrassment hits when I'm in the wings. I can't enjoy the high of our performance because I'm a giant bag of *what-did-I-do?* all over again. For the past week, I've buried that conversation under practice and coursework. But he's here tonight and I can't hide from the sting of his rejection. I don't know how I'll recover from the mortification: the look on his face, his disbelief, his definitive no, all play on an endless loop in my head. As if Flip Madden would ever want more from me than friendship.

And yet, he showed up for me. I don't even know what to do with that.

"The Terror are in the audience!" Charles grabs my shoulders. He has a thing for hockey players. I get it, truly. "What I wouldn't give to be in the middle of a Madden and Stiles sandwich."

"Stiles is married," I remind him. I avoid commenting on Flip, because I don't trust my voice.

"Yeah, but in my fantasy world he's not, and they're both into me." Charles's grin is downright lascivious.

Flip's previous reputation isn't a secret. For a while his exploits were splashed across the internet. But it's been years since Flip has lived up to his fuckboy status.

"I would take Quinn Romero home any night of the week," Arya adds dreamily.

"He does have that strong, silent type vibe," I agree. Of all the guys, he tends to be the quietest. Also, I'm happy to indulge infatuations that don't involve Flip.

"And those freckles." Arya sighs.

This incites an entire whispered conversation about which Terror player everyone would like to take home for a night while we touch up our makeup for the post-performance reception. We're still in full costume as we traipse out to greet our families and friends. I'm reeling with nerves. Will Flip still be here? Did he leave as soon as the show ended?

My dad is the first to find me. He's beaming with pride, and that settles my nerves a fraction. "What an incredible performance! You were wonderful up there." He pulls me in for a hug. "I'm so glad I could be here for this." He presents me with an excessively large bouquet of roses.

I bring them to my nose and inhale their soft scent. "Thanks, Dad. These are beautiful."

He tucks a hand in his pocket, his smile sheepish. "Your mom picked them out."

"I just suggested the color, the rest was all your dad. You were perfect as usual." Mom's smile wavers a little, like she's on the edge of emotion. "I'm so proud of you. You've come so far."

"Thank you for always supporting me and being my cheerleader."

"Always and forever, sweetie." She squeezes me tightly, and I return the embrace.

My mom and I have always been close. With my dad on the road three quarters of the year, it was often her and me looking after Ties and Fenna.

Eventually Mom releases me and I look to my siblings. Ties is on his phone, and Fenna is picking at a loose thread on her cuff.

I tap my sister on the shoulder, and she pulls out one of her noise-cancelling earplugs. She's sensitive to noise in large crowds. "Do you have your scissors in your purse?"

"Yes."

"Why don't you get them out and I'll fix that?" I nod to the loose thread. Usually, Mom would be on top of that.

"Okay." She retrieves them for me. Her face brightens as I trim the thread and pass the scissors back.

"Thanks." Fenna has some sensory issues, and that thread has likely been frustrating her for as long as it's been loose.

"I'm sorry I didn't notice that, honey," Mom apologizes.

"It's okay. Tallulah fixed it for me." She turns to me. "I liked the song choice."

I grin. "I thought you might."

Fenna's in grade nine, plays the cello, and basically lives and breathes classical music.

Ties, who is in his final year of high school, drags his eyes away from his phone long enough to give me a thumbs-up. "Good job." He has a robotics competition next week and being here is probably cutting into his preparation time.

"Once this is all wrapped up, we'll go for dinner." Dad glances at Mom before refocusing on me. "Does that sound good?"

"That sounds amazing." It's rare enough that my dad can make it to a performance, let alone stick around to celebrate after. I haven't seen much of him over the past few months because of school and his schedule, so I can't pass up the opportunity.

My girlfriends step in to give me a huge group hug and a shower of compliments.

"That was flawless." Fee, my roommate and one of my best friends at Tilton U, makes prayer hands and bows. "You are wildly talented."

"What she said. You *are* the music when you're out there," Cammie agrees.

"So awesome." Enid nods her agreement.

I glance around, stomach in knots as I search the crowd. Flip and the other Terror guys are being bombarded by fans, which is not unusual. But he's still here. Did he feel like he had to stay because everyone else was?

He's wearing black dress pants, a pale blue dress shirt, and a dark tie. His hair is still a little too long, curling around his ears. He looks handsome and delicious and remains my favorite fantasy and eternally out of reach. Eventually he makes his way over, a bouquet in his hand.

My mouth goes dry, and my palms start to sweat. It's not like he'll bring up our last conversation in front of all these people, but the residual mortification is overwhelming.

Still, I take a step forward, though I don't know what to do or how to act around him now. "Thanks for coming."

"I wouldn't miss it for the world. You owned that stage," he says.

"Thanks," I croak, and struggle with what to say. He brought me flowers, so maybe we'll be okay. "We worked really hard on that number."

"It absolutely showed." He holds out the bouquet, which is a fraction of the size of some of the other flowers I've been given tonight, but they're stunning blooms in shades of pale blue and white to match my costume. It's like he picked each one with intention and knows all my favorites.

Or maybe I'm projecting.

I bring them to my nose and inhale. "These are beautiful."

"They match you, then."

My eyes flare as he wraps his arms around me. I awkwardly pat his back, and my nose mashes against his armpit because I didn't turn my head in time. He squeezes my waist, chin bumping my temple.

I break out in an anxiety-riddled sweat.

He steps back, his expression is both gentle and amused, but also... "You should be really proud of yourself, Talls."

I'm flustered, and I want to apologize, but we're surrounded by our friends and my family. I wave a hand around in the air, then grip the flowers to stop my flailing. "I had a whole team out there with me."

He tips his head, a smile tugging at the corner of his full lips. Is that empathy or sympathy in his eyes? And which is worse? "Everyone was incredible, but you stole the show," he says. "You're phenomenal to watch."

My stomach is a cement mixer. My stupid heart is all aflutter at the compliment.

But he said no, my helpful brain reminds me.

He's being kind.

He's smoothing things over for the sake of our friend group.

He'll never see me as anything more than his coach's daughter and a friend.

CHAPTER 4

TALLY

At dinner with my family, I can't decide if things feel off because of the Flip situation, or if it's something else. It sometimes feels like Dad is on the outside of things because he's gone so much, but today it's more pronounced. I'm distracted, replaying my post-show interaction with Flip, including the hug. *What does it mean*? I drag myself out of my head and back to my family.

My parents steal a glance at each other over their plates. Mom has been quiet, which is unusual. She typically drives dinner conversation. Fenna is talking animatedly about her upcoming cello performance while Ties stares at his lap because he's texting under the table. Normally he wouldn't be allowed to get away with that. Seems like everyone is preoccupied.

Dad and Mom exchange another look. My stomach twists at their tight expressions, and the wordless conversation they have every time they make eye contact.

"Kids, we have something important we need to discuss," Dad finally says.

"Are we going away for Christmas this year?" my sister asks.

Fenna asks this every year, though it's only happened once.

"I have to work, honey," Dad reminds her.

"You always have to work," Ties mutters.

A few times we've flown out to a game in a sunny destination, but after that it's always been me, Mom, Fenna, and Ties on a short holiday while my dad goes on to the next hockey game. It would be easier now that we're older, but these days I want to spend New Year's with my friends, and so does Ties.

My dad tugs on his tie. He does this all the time during games if he's unhappy with the way a play is going.

Mom fiddles with her napkin, and Dad clears his throat.

Alarm bells sound in my head. "What's going on?"

"We love you all very much," Mom chokes out.

I'm immediately on alert at the unspoken *but*.

Mom looks to Dad, who swallows.

She turns back to us, jaw ticking. "We want you to know how important you are, and that this has nothing to do with you."

My stomach sinks.

"What has nothing to do with us?" Fenna's confusion makes my heart hurt.

She's wildly talented and smart, but she doesn't always read social cues well, or people's emotions, and right now the tension at the table is so thick I'm choking on it.

Then Dad swings the axe. "Your mom and I are getting a divorce."

My heart cleaves in two.

Ties's phone clatters to the floor.

The furrow on Fenna's forehead makes me want to reach out and hug her, but she's not big on spontaneous affection.

Dad looks stoic, and Mom just looks…resigned and sad.

I'm so many things, but shock and anger top the list. "What the fuck?" I look to Mom, betrayal quickly usurping my feelings. She's clearly been keeping this from me. To have this news dropped on me with no warning makes me question everything.

"Honey, language. We're in a public place," Dad chastises.

"Are you *fucking* kidding me?" My gaze swings to him. He must have told her not to say anything. "We're in the middle of a restaurant. Why would you do this *here*, where everyone gets a front-row seat to our family falling apart? Why not at home, where everyone can have their feelings and not worry about the server witnessing them?" I fling a hand toward the poor twenty-something guy holding a jug of water. He does an about-face and rushes off.

I want an explanation. I want my universe not to feel like it's imploding. I'm beyond devastated. I'm hurt, I'm reeling, everything I believe has just shattered.

The resolution on their faces tells me this has been coming for a while. Maybe I missed it because I've been at university, living my life for the past three and a half years. But my mom and I message each other daily, even if it's just one freaking line. We talk on the phone all the time, and not once did she mention being unhappy. Did my dad spring this on her?

"Your father thought it would be better to have this conversation somewhere that wasn't connected to home for all of us," Mom explains gently.

So we wouldn't always walk into the living room and remember how Mom and Dad sat us down and pulled the loose thread of our family, unraveling it. Or sit at the dining room table and recall our devastation over being told everything we ever believed about our parents was a lie.

This isn't our favorite restaurant. It's somewhere new, different, and I'll never return again because it's the place my world upended.

"But why? Don't you love each other?" Fenna asks.

"We do, honey," Mom assures her. "But I'm not *in love* anymore."

"So you want this?" I ask, seeking confirmation.

"Can't you fall back in love?" Fenna asks. "I fall in and out of love with songs all the time."

"It's not the same, Fen," Ties grits out.

"Your dad and I are better as friends." Mom chokes up and sips her water. "Things won't change that much. We'll stay in the house, and your dad will get an apartment."

"But why did you fall out of love?" Fenna presses. "You don't even fight."

"It's hard to fight with someone who isn't home," Mom replies flatly.

Now I understand why Dad didn't take off right after my performance. He's always working, and even when he's home or has time off, he's still half at the arena, with the team. Even now, his phone buzzes, and for a moment, he pats his pocket before dropping his hand, like he thought about answering it.

We might get a few weeks of vacation with him in the off-season, but he still takes calls and schedules meetings. The rest of the year, he isn't around much.

"My schedule made it difficult," Dad explains.

"I've felt like a single parent most of the time." Mom's voice cracks, and her sad eyes shift to me.

She and I were always in it together, taking care of everything. We were a team while my dad was away. Did I set the wheels in motion when I went to university and left Mom on her own? I've been home less this semester with the demands of my courses and dance.

My heart shatters, and I direct my anger at my dad. "You could have tried harder. If you'd been around more, maybe Mom would still be in love with you."

He doesn't disagree. Doesn't tell me to watch myself. Doesn't do any of the things he would if it was the locker room and one of the guys gave him lip. He nods. "I should have made more of an effort to find balance between my career and my home life."

"But you didn't, because you love the Terror more than you love us," I finish for him.

"That's not true, Tally," he argues.

"Isn't it, though? Why not make a change if you knew it was a problem? You had to know how Mom felt before it got to this point."

Mom isn't a pushover. She couldn't be with three kids and virtually no help raising us.

"It's not that simple—"

I cut him off. "But it is. You put the Terror ahead of us, and now you're tearing our family apart." The pain of it makes it hard to breathe. What will the holidays look like? What does this mean for the future? For Fenna, who just started high school, and Ties, who starts university next year? How will I make it through finals when the foundation of my life is suddenly crumbling?

I hate that I'm focused on myself, but couldn't we have gotten through Christmas before they dropped this bomb?

"We still care about each other, Tally, but I need to live my life separately from your father," Mom reasons.

"I don't want Dad to move out!" Fenna pushes her chair back and rushes off to the bathroom.

Mom follows, leaving me with Ties and my dad. My brother looks unsurprised, and Dad looks defeated.

"You pushed Mom to do this. Why couldn't you have put us first? Why did you have to be married to your job instead of your wife and your family?" I mean for it to come out as anger, but instead I sound like I'm pleading, on the edge of tears.

"I know you're upset—"

"You have no idea how I feel," I bark. "You just shredded this family and broke all our hearts in a public restaurant."

Here he thought we couldn't run away from the conversation. Or make a scene. I'm not in the same position as my siblings, though. I don't have to stay and listen to excuses and try to hold myself together. I spent my entire childhood and teen years playing second parent to Ties and Fenna. I helped get them ready for school, made lunches, did all the things Dad might have done if he'd been around. And he praised me for it. Told me how much it meant to him and my mom that I was always willing to step up. They both did. It made me and Mom extremely close. Maybe too close. If he'd just stepped into the shoes he was supposed to wear, maybe we wouldn't be falling apart.

"Fuck you." I push away from the table and sling my purse over my shoulder.

I'm frustrated that I feel guilty for not staying to help my mom take care of Fenna and Ties. But I've done that my entire life, made up for my dad's absence without even realizing it.

"Tally, honey…"

I hug my brother, who continues to sit there woodenly. "I'm sorry," I tell him. "You can come with me, if you want."

A tear leaks out the corner of Ties's eye as he shakes his head. I brush it away—like I'm his parent and not his sister. Which is the problem. I want to rail at my father, but if I do, it'll invariably end up in the papers. Ties and Fenna don't need that any more than I do.

So I leave the restaurant, digging around in my purse with shaking hands. I need support. I need my friends. I finally find my phone and struggle to pull up my contacts through the tears blurring my vision.

Hammer answers on the second ring as I step outside. "Hey, Tally."

"Can you pick me up? My parents just told us they're getting divorced in the middle of a restaurant, and the last place I want to go is home."

She's silent for a beat. "I'm so sorry, Tally. I'll be there as soon as I can."

CHAPTER 5

TALLY

"**I** need shots!" I set the emergency credit card courtesy of my dad on the bar top. We're at the Watering Hole, and my good-decisions button has been flipped to the off position. "Who wants to do one with me?"

Dred wrinkles her nose and shakes her head. She is not a shots girl.

"I could," Rix offers.

"Same," Hammer agrees.

"Just one," Hemi hedges.

"Lemon drops?" I suggest.

I get nods of approval and order six.

No one comments, but Hemi purses her lips, and Dred makes her *are-you-sure-that's-a-good-idea?* face.

"Thanks for coming out." I clink my glass against theirs and down mine, then follow with the remaining two.

I raise my hand to order more, but Hammer pulls it down. "Maybe give it a minute."

"And have a glass of soda." Dred hands me a cola.

I grudgingly accept it. I've already had two margaritas. My

initial disbelief from dinner has morphed into simmering rage, and I need out of my head.

That makes me doubly appreciative that my Babes dropped everything to be here. I love my Tilton friends, but Fee has lost both of her parents, so crying about mine getting a divorce feels insensitive.

"I know this isn't about me, but my parents' timing was terrible." The high of my performance followed by the low of their divorce is a real shock. They probably didn't want to fake it through the holidays.

"I'm really sorry, Tally." Hammer gives me a side hug.

"I don't even know how to process this. Plus, finals begin next week, and then it's Christmas. I don't even know what that will look like this year. I can't imagine I'll feel like celebrating." I'm suddenly buried under the stress of all the unknowns. "Let's talk about something else." I need to get off the merry-go-round of what-ifs and oh-nos.

"How about we plan our New Year's party?" Hemi suggests.

"Connor may have already taken care of this." Dred rolls her eyes, but she's smiling.

"Oooh! Party at Grace Manor?" Rix is obsessed with the chef's kitchen there.

"Well, we are having a party at a Grace property." Dred fiddles with the bracelets on her wrist. "I might have mentioned doing something in Huntsville this year, and Connor may or may not have bought the lodge on the lake—not rented out the rooms, *bought* the entire place."

"I didn't know it was for sale," Hemi says.

"It wasn't." Dred sips her soda.

"Seems like something he would do for you," Essie muses.

"He's ridiculous," Dred replies.

"He's obsessed." How amazing would it be to have someone love me the way Connor loves Dred? But nothing is guaranteed. Anyone can fall out of love. My parents just proved that.

"He really is." She smiles softly. "Will you come? Or do you have plans with Fee and Cammie? They could also come. Lord knows there's enough room."

"Tilton has a tournament that weekend, and Cammie and Fee are driving up with the guys." I haven't made the commitment to tag along, though I've been invited. As much as I love my Tilton friends, spending New Year's with a bunch of guys who want to make the pros is a recipe for disappointment and frustration. The last thing I want is to drunkenly sleep with one of Chase's teammates.

Tristan's youngest brother Brody and I often find ourselves huddled together at such events, trying to avoid the nonsense that comes with our Terror affiliations. Fee occasionally falls into this category, too, because her sister Lexi is an assistant coach for the Terror and is married to their former goalie, Roman, who is also Hammer's dad. But the attention is new for Fee, so she has a higher tolerance than me and Brody.

The bell over the door tinkles, and a gust of cold wind blows in with the Terror boys.

"I told Dallas what was going on and he gathered the rest of the troops," Hemi explains.

"They all came?"

"We want to support you," Hemi says gently.

My heart stutters when Flip appears, dressed in a pair of jeans and a hoodie. He removes his toque and runs his hand through his thick, dark hair. It feels like a year has passed, instead of just hours, since he gave me flowers.

The girls greet their significant others, and I sneakily order another shot while I'm hidden behind Hemi and Dallas.

Flip ends up two stools down, and the woman beside him immediately starts chatting with him. It happens all the time. Usually I let it roll off me, but not tonight. My parents' marriage is ending, my family is broken, my idea of love has been shattered, and I don't even know how to process the betrayal I feel over my mom leaving me on the outside of this with everyone else. My life is spinning out of control and some random woman is flirting with Flip.

His gaze finds mine, and I realize I've been staring. The woman's back is to me, so she can't see us making eye contact over her shoulder. He arches a concerned brow. I arch a defiant one in return.

I shoot my shot, maintaining eye contact. She puts her hand on his arm, dragging his attention back to her. Which, of course, pisses me off. Irrationally.

I push away from the bar, doing my best to walk a straight line to Flip. Based on my slight wobble, the shots are catching up to me. This explains why I don't adjust course and head for the bathroom, instead of proceeding toward the star of my fantasies.

"Hi." Now that I'm standing in front of him, I don't know what to do.

He turns away from the woman flirting with him, and she shoots me a "I was here first" look. She has no idea.

Flip tips his head, furrow deepening as he settles a single finger under my chin. The woman behind him frowns at the intimate contact.

"How many of me are in front of you?"

Triumph emboldens me and I blink a couple of times to bring him into focus. "Just one."

His eyes narrow. "Are you sure about that?"

"I wouldn't lie to you, Phillip." I drag a fingertip between his eyes to smooth the furrow.

"What's going on here, Tally?"

For some reason, I go with blunt honesty. I must have drunk my filter to death. "I'm jealous. I hate the way that woman was touching you, and I want it to be me."

Everything about him softens. "Talls."

The woman who was chatting him up has moved to her friends, her irritation clear in her rigid stance. I climb into Flip's lap and drape an arm over his shoulder. I don't even mind the fresh disapproval slanting his brow, because his attention is on me.

"How drunk are you?" His hand settles between my shoulder blades. I finger the silky strands at the nape of his neck, encouraged by the fact that he hasn't moved me off his lap.

"Not that drunk."

"Are you sure? 'Cause you're sitting in my lap, Talls." His fingers slip under my hair and flex against my neck, sending a shiver down my spine. Something shifts between us, and suddenly I'm hot all over.

"I feel safe with you. Everything is falling apart. I want us to be okay." I follow the neck of his T-shirt with a single finger.

Flip folds my roaming hand in his. It feels good to have him touch me like this, to have his focus on me. "How about I get you some water?"

I don't like that he's treating me like a child, even if I'm behaving that way. "How about you stop acting like my daddy, Phillip?"

"I'm trying to help you make good choices, kitten." The dark look on his face, his gravelly tone, and the surprise term of endearment all send a thrill through me.

So I keep pushing. "What if I don't want to make good choices?"

His nostrils flare. "You're a problem tonight, aren't you?"

"Yeah."

"I'm supposed to protect you from guys like me," he whispers. The DJ cues up a song I like, and another great alcohol-fueled idea forms.

I slide off Flip's lap and move to stand between his legs. He doesn't stop me as I run my hands up his thick thighs. "Then I guess you have to come dance with me."

"Haven't you had enough dancing tonight?"

"Never." I bat my lashes and push my lips out in a pout. "Pretty please?"

His gaze moves over me on a slow sweep. "It's not a good idea."

"Fine. I'll ask Quinn or Kellan. I bet they'd like to dance with me."

He shakes his head. "Not if they know what's good for them."

A shiver skitters down my spine as he slides off his chair. The front of his body brushes mine as he rises to his full height, fingers skimming the length of my arm. It feels intentionally intimate. "You'll be my bodyguard?"

"I'll keep the worst of the wolves away."

He lets me pull him to the dance floor, which is rarely used for its intended purpose. It's mostly full of our friends standing around, chatting. Dred arches a brow at us, but I don't care. All I want is to stay inside this little bubble with Flip and nothing else matters.

The DJ at the Watering Hole usually sucks, but I can dance to anything.

I spin to face Flip, which on any other day I would manage with grace. But the shots finally hit me, and the room spins too. I trip over my own feet, falling into a set of arms.

"Whoa, hey." Quinn Romero rights me, hands on my hips.

"Sorry." I pat his chest. "I'm a little tis-pee. Tippy. Tipsy." I close an eye so there's only one of him and hold my fingers apart.

"That you are." A dimple appears high on Quinn's freckled cheek.

His eyes are a warm seafoam green, and his jaw is angular.

"How are you single?" I blurt.

He laughs. "Oh, you're really drunk, aren't you?"

"Yeah. But seriously, you're gorgeous, and you're nice, so you should totally have a girlfriend." The room is spinning in earnest now, so I clutch his bicep to stay upright. "Prolly time to go home," I mumble.

Quinn's expression softens. "I can take you. I was getting ready to leave anyway."

"No." A strong arm snakes around my waist, and I stumble back into Flip's hard chest. "I've got her."

"I'm fine." My stomach roils dangerously, as reality sets in. "I'll just take an Uber." I don't want to throw up on Flip, or in his car, and I'm worried both options are possible with the way the world has turned into a tilt-a-whirl.

All the things I've done tonight in the name of sidelining the shitstorm that is my life tumble down in a hailstorm of embarrassment. I sat in Flip's lap, and he let me. He let me pull him onto the dance floor. He called me kitten.

Does he feel sorry for me?

Is he placating me?

I'm confused and angry and sad and mortified and growing drunker by the second.

"You're not taking an Uber," he growls.

I look up at his beautiful face and wish I could see inside his head to understand his motives, but I'm too scattered and messy. Flip bends and slides his arm under my legs, lifting me off the ground. I'm all muscle and heavier than I look, but he holds me like I weigh nothing.

"What are you doing?" I drop my forehead to his shoulder and close my eyes to stop the merry-go-round as he crosses the room.

"Taking care of you." He carries me out of the Watering Hole and into the cold December night.

CHAPTER 6
TALLY

lip sets me in the passenger seat and closes the door, blocking out the blustery December cold. He tucks his chin as he rounds the hood to the driver's side.

I'm terrified, not of Flip's disapproval or what all our friends must think—although that will come later, when I'm sober—but I fear I might hurl all over the leather interior of his luxury sports car. It's new. He bought it this summer. It's black and sleek and smells like him. I wish I could appreciate that I'm sitting in it, but my stomach is unhappy with my choices.

Flip settles into the driver's seat and fastens his seat belt. Then he leans across, his hair brushing my cheek, and does the same for me. He backs up, gaze moving over my face. "Shots hitting you hard?"

I nod, but it makes everything spin. "Yeah."

"It's been a rough day, huh?"

"It started out great but went downhill at dinner."

"I'm really sorry, kitten." He opens the center console and passes me a reusable grocery tote. "In case your cookies need to be tossed."

"Thanks."

Being alone in his car with him is high on my fantasy list, but the being-too-hammered-to-function part is not.

He pulls out of the lot and into the sporadic late-night traffic. I stare into the bright green bag from the budget-friendly grocery store. Of course this is where Flip shops. He grew up poor. It doesn't matter that he makes millions a year now. He still remembers where he started.

Too short a time later, he pulls into an underground parking garage.

I glance around, bleary-eyed and confused. I must have fallen asleep during the drive. "Where are we?"

"My place. I wasn't convinced we'd make it to your apartment without an incident. I have a spare bedroom," he explains.

"Oh. Good call." It's all I can think to say. Now my head is reeling just as much as my stomach. *Flip brought me home with him.* It's what I've always wanted, but it's for all the wrong reasons.

He pulls into his designated spot and cuts the engine. It takes me a few seconds to realize I can't get out without some action on my part. It takes several tries, but I finally hit the release button.

When I look up, he's right there, hand extended. I slip my fingers into his open palm, wishing I could appreciate how good it feels to be touched by him. Even with his assistance, I stumble to my feet.

He catches me before I face-plant into his chest. His arm circles my waist, and he cups my cheek in his palm, exactly how I imagine he would if he were about to kiss me. Our faces are inches apart, his brow is slanted. "How much did you drink exactly, kitten?"

That term of endearment again. I want it to mean more than it does.

"Two margaritas, but then there were shots."

"Shots are always the problem." He keeps his arm around me, grabs the grocery tote from my empty seat, locks his car, and mostly carries me to the elevator.

I've never been this drunk before. The ride to his apartment was not good for my already addled brain and unsettled stomach.

I turn into him, pressing my face against his chest, inhaling mint and sandalwood. "I'm really sorry."

"You're okay, Talls. I've got you," he assures me. "I know how tight you are with your family."

"My mom kept this from me, and she never does that. My heart hurts." I'm sure my head will too in the morning.

When we reach his floor, I focus on putting one foot in front of the other. Flip unlocks his apartment, props the door open with his foot, and helps me inside.

A pile of mail sits on his kitchen counter, next to a mostly full fruit basket.

His arm is still wrapped around me, our bodies pressed close. He tucks a finger under my chin. The two versions of him in my field of vision frown.

"You look green."

"I don't feel the best," I say meekly.

"Your stomach is angry?"

"Yeah."

"Let's get you out of these, first." He kneels in front of me, and I settle a hand on his shoulder for balance as he helps me remove my heels.

I absently run my fingers through his hair, marveling at how soft and silky it is. Is this what Flip the boyfriend would be like? Attentive, protective, caring. He lifts his head, emotions swimming in his eyes that I can't catch and hold on to.

"Sorry." I drop my hand to my side, heat rising in my cheeks. I was just petting him like Parsnip, my cat.

"It's okay." He pushes to his feet and guides me to the bathroom. He flicks on the light, illuminating the space. It's clean, but the vanity is cluttered with hair and shaving products, like he got ready in a hurry.

Did he rush to the Watering Hole because of me?

He lifts the toilet seat as I sink to my knees.

"You should leave." I grip the edge of the bowl as my stomach revolts.

"I'm not going anywhere." He has enough time to gather my hair in a makeshift ponytail before the stupid shots come back up.

"I don't want you to see me like this," I say between heaves.

"Too late for that."

I retch again. Flip has been present for two of the top five most embarrassing moments of my life. And they've both been in the past week. "This is so humiliating."

"Connor fucked my sandwich and our entire team knows, you'll be fine," Flip assures me.

He rubs soothing circles on my back when I dry heave. "That's it. Get it all out."

Eventually my body stops rebelling. But I'm sweaty and cold, goose bumps cover my clammy skin. When I shiver, Flip crosses to the shower and grabs his bathrobe. He threads my arms through soft terry cloth and cinches it at my waist. It's six sizes too big, but it smells like him, and at least I'm warm. He picks me up by the waist, sets me on the vanity, and turns on the water in the sink.

I've never had a boyfriend take care of me the way Flip is now. He's so sweet and tender, patient and understanding. He's not even mine and he's being so thoughtful. "I'm really sorry," I say to his chest.

"We've all been there, and you had a hard night." He runs a cloth under the steaming water, wrings it out, and washes my face. "I'm sorry about your parents. And I'm sorry for the way they told you." He hands me a glass of water.

"I didn't see it coming." I take a tentative sip, and when my stomach doesn't immediately expel it, I take another.

"Neither did I, to be honest."

I nod. "You see him more than I do." I roll my bottom lip between my teeth. "I feel so betrayed, like everything I believed has been a lie."

"I get it, better than you probably realize." Flip wraps his arms around me, and I grip his biceps, wishing this night had gone differently, but grateful that he's the one taking care of me.

For now, anyway. Who knows what fresh embarrassment hell waits for me on the other side of this night.

Eventually he pulls back. "You're less green."

I try to brush my hair away from my face, but I'm uncoordinated and sloppy. "I must look awful."

His expression softens. "You're always beautiful, Tally."

A tiny seed of hope tries to blossom at his compliment.

"But you're still my coach's daughter," he mutters.

I can't tell if it's meant for me or as a reminder to him. Regardless, the tiny bud promptly withers.

Flip rummages around in the vanity until he finds a toothbrush, still in its wrapping. He frees it from the package. "Would you prefer mint toothpaste or bubblegum mint?"

"Regular mint is probably better." But I love that he has kids' toothpaste.

He steadies my hand and squeezes a small dollop onto the brush. He's still standing in front of me, one hand resting on the vanity beside my terry cloth-covered thigh. It feels intimate. "Do you need my help with anything else?"

This is how Flip is. He takes care of people. I'm not unique or special. "I bet you do this for all the girls." I don't mean to say it aloud. It's more a reminder not to throw myself at him again like an idiot.

His expression shifts, his sigh heavy. "I know what my reputation is, Tally. It follows me around like a bad shadow, but I didn't realize you thought of me like that, too."

"That's not how I meant it."

"Isn't it?" He steps back. "I'll give you a minute."

The bathroom door closes behind him, leaving me on my own. My stomach twists with fresh guilt over putting that despondent look on his face again.

My thoughts are jumbled and unreliable as I ease myself off the vanity and brush my teeth.

You're always beautiful.

But you're still my coach's daughter.

Tonight, he didn't take me home, where Fee would have played nurse for me. Instead, I'm here, in his apartment.

But he said no.

And now I've upset him. I don't want to be someone who hurts him.

I wish my head was clear enough to connect all the dots.

I finish brushing my teeth and drink another glass of water. My stomach is sore and shaky, but I feel much better than I did half an hour ago.

Flip pushes off the wall when I open the door to the bathroom. "How you doing?"

"Better. Less drunk." I want to apologize again, but they're just words.

He takes me in, assessing, maybe deciding for himself if he believes me. "That's good. You look better." His hand settles on my lower back and he guides me to the spare bedroom.

Two bottles of water and some painkillers sit on the nightstand.

"You're sure you're done throwing up?"

Is he worried about me, or his spare bed?

"Pretty sure. Yeah." I feel awkward and uncomfortable now. The weight of it all too much to bear.

He thumbs over his shoulder. "I'm just down the hall if you need anything."

"Okay. Thank you for taking care of me."

"You're important to me," he says softly. "I care about you."

But only as a friend.

His smile is small and empathetic. "I'll see you in the morning."

"'Night."

He pulls the door closed.

I'm suddenly beyond exhausted.

The sheets are already pulled back, so I climb into bed, turn off the lamp, close my eyes, and wish everything could go back to the way it was a week ago, before my life went up in flames.

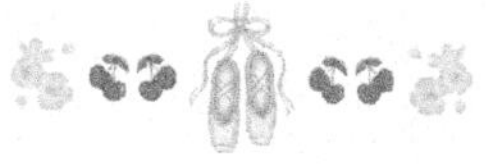

I WAKE UP SWEATY, WRAPPED IN A GIANT PLUSH ROBE. I WRIGGLE out of it and the cool air hits my damp skin, causing a full-body shiver. I smell awful, and I'm hungover as hell. My bladder is screaming just as loudly as my head. *What happened last night?*

My showcase went amazing.

But my parents said they were getting divorced.

I called Hammer.

We went to the Watering Hole.

And then what…?

This bed isn't mine. Panic hits, pushing adrenaline through my veins as I throw off the covers, then groan at the sharp pain slicing through my skull. I'm a mess. I shuffle a couple of steps and nearly trip over my own feet. Then I kick something solid.

A grunt comes from below me as I trip over the lump and hurtle toward the floor. My face doesn't connect with the ground, though. Instead, it mashes against something soft-ish.

"Oh my fuck!" the human groans.

Flip.

Memories of last night pop like bubbles in my brain.

Flip brought me back to his place. He took care of me.

And the tube-shaped thing my cheek is pressed up against is his *dick.*

In all my wildest dreams, this is *not* how I envisioned my first experience with Flip's junk.

CHAPTER 7
TALLY

"**I**'m really sorry." I can't stop apologizing.

"Don't worry about it. I've had a black eye before." Flip's focus stays firmly on the road, hands at ten and two. "And it's not like it was on purpose."

I wish I could evaporate. I'm currently wearing one of his sweatshirts and a pair of leggings that belong to Rix and were accidentally left at his place. Sadly, neither function as armor against my unappealing smell or my embarrassment.

Apparently, Flip was worried about my safety during the night, and the possibility that I might asphyxiate on my own vomit, so he slept on the floor on a yoga mat. I kicked him in the eye when I tripped over him and bagged him with my face. When he flicked on the light, I discovered my dress had ridden up to my waist and my whole ass was on display, including my pink lip-print thong. I will never recover from this humiliation. When I get home, I plan to have a good cry into a pint of ice cream.

"I'm sorry about your parents, and I'm sorry last night was so hard for you," Flip says gently. "But black eye or no black eye, I'm not sorry I took care of you."

More memories from last night surface. I can't get the sad, hurt look on his face out of my head. It echoed the look he wore when I propositioned him.

Flip is just my friend and he's showing up for me more than my dad ever did for our family. It pisses me off and makes me so, so sad.

I'm already embarrassed, so I might as well deal with all my stupidity at once and address the elephant in the back seat.

He pulls up in front of my building.

"I'm sorry," I repeat.

"I've already—"

I hold up my hand. "I'm not talking about last night." I swallow my nerves. "What I asked of you, the way I asked it… was wrong. I know what it's like to always have people want something of you, from you." I'm the Terror coach's virgin daughter, and he's the Terror's notorious fuckboy. We're quite the pair. "I should have thought about what I was asking for and how I was asking for it."

He looks decidedly uncomfortable. "Tally, you don't have to—"

"Please let me finish. It was thoughtless of me, and I'm so sorry I hurt you." I shore up my courage to get out the rest. "I want my first time to be something I remember and feel good about. I don't want to end up with some guy who just wants the notoriety of fucking the coach's daughter any more than you want someone to ask you for something because you're good at it."

I want to throw up all over again, just remembering the nonsense that spilled out of my mouth. And then for other reasons as I finally admit the truth. "But you should know that I asked because I like you, Flip. Not Flip Madden the hockey player. You. The guy who slept on a yoga mat to make sure I was safe. The guy who attended my dance showcase and brought me my favorite flowers even after I hurt you."

I'm afraid and anxious but I turn to face him anyway, because Flip is important to me, and I want to mend our friendship, if I can. "You're an amazing brother to Rix and an excellent best friend to Dred. The way you show up for the people you love is one of my favorite things about you. I know you've made some decisions in the past that you can't escape, and I would never want you to make a choice that you would regret, the same way you don't want me to. I asked what I asked not for the reasons I stated, but for the reasons I didn't. You're a good person, and I care about you, and I'm sorry it came out the way it did." I unfasten my seat belt and open the door.

"Talls—" The ache in his voice scares me.

I cut him off again before he can say anything else. "Thank you again for dealing with me last night, and driving me home, and I'm sorry about your face and your dick and bye." I pull my hood up and scramble out of the car, slamming the door behind me.

I rush as much as I can in my stupid heels. Those I couldn't get out of wearing home. This is the worst walk of shame ever. I'm so grateful when the elevator doors open immediately and it's blissfully empty. I throw myself inside and hit the button for my floor.

I'm barely inside my apartment before I burst into tears.

My adorable, fluffy Maine Coon, Parsnip, trots down the hall, meowing up a storm as he senses my distress. I pick him up, shoving my face into his fur as I carry him down the hall. He headbutts me and licks my cheek. He'd been at the shelter for over year when I decided he needed to be mine. He's a problem and I love him.

He still has dry food, but I plate a small helping of wet food and leave him to scarf it down while I shower away last night's bad choices. Dred was right. Shots are never a good idea. I change into my comfiest clothes, drink two bottles of Vitamin Water, eat a banana while thinking about how Flip's dick was against my cheek this morning, and finally flop down on the couch to check my phone. Parsnip joins me and settles in my lap.

I have several messages from my brother.

TIES

> Can you message when you're home, just so we all know you're safe?

> Mom has tried to call you six times. I said you're probably with your Tilton friends.

> Mom called one of the Terror women called Hammer. Why is her name Hammer? Apparently you were with her so she knows you're safe and so do I. But still message when you get this.

> Tallulah, for fuck's sake, just message.

The most recent one is less than half an hour old.

I call him.

"Tallulah?"

"Sorry I'm only getting back to you now. I didn't mean to make you worry. Are you okay?"

"I'm fine. Well, not really. But you're okay? You're safe?"

"Yeah. How are you? I'm sorry I bailed last night." I feel guilty all over again for walking out.

"I would have done the same if I could. I did once we finally got Fenna out of the bathroom." His voice sounds rough.

"You go to a friend's?"

"Jordan from robotics picked me up from the restaurant."

"You stay the night at their place?"

"Just went to the Hooded Goblin for a while and hung out. When I got home, Dad's truck was gone."

"I'm sorry, Ties." What a gut punch to come home to that.

"Me too." He sighs. "But it wasn't the surprise for me that it was for you. Things have been…strained for a while."

"Why didn't anyone say anything? Why didn't Mom?" That part is hardest to stomach.

"What could she say? That she wasn't happy with Dad? You're in your final year at Tilton, these dance showcases are like, way more involved than I could have realized, and you have courses on top of that, and a life of your own. I don't think she wanted to put more on you."

"She doesn't usually keep things from me."

"I know you two are close, Talls, but it was never your job to be our other parent. I love you for stepping up when Dad didn't, but that shouldn't have been on you, and maybe Mom realized that, too."

I rub my temple. I don't know how to feel about any of this. "How is Mom?"

"Sad. Tired. Maybe a little relieved. She's putting on a brave face, but she has puffy eyes, so she's feeling it like the rest of us."

"How about Fenna?" Maybe I should have gone to the house last night, stayed with my family instead of running away. But it was a bomb I didn't expect.

"Fenna's confused. She's been playing her cello all day. It's the most depressing shit, even if it's flawless." He sighs. "I wish I'd taken the early uni placement instead of waiting until fall."

"I'm sorry this is happening." I can't fix this for any of us. I'm used to manageable problems, like broken bows or a trip to the robotics store.

"Me, too. But we can't make them stay together."

"No. I guess we can't."

"I gotta get ready. I have robotics in an hour, and I still need to shower and eat."

"I love you, Ties."

"I love you, too, Talls."

We end the call, and I rub my chest. My heart hurts for my brother. How much of my slack has he had to pick up? Did he stay back this coming semester because Mom needed the support I wasn't there to provide? I'm angry at her all over again for leaving me on the outside of something so huge, but Ties isn't wrong. I was the second mom of the house, and everyone let me assume that role. And it's the one I'm used to taking on. I send Fenna a text apologizing for leaving last night.

FENNA

I wanted to leave too, but I didn't know the
bus route home.

Poor Fen. She was stuck at home while both Ties and I could escape.

TALLY

Do you want to talk?

FENNA

Not right now. I'm practicing. Maybe later?

TALLY

Okay. I'm here if you need me. I love you.

FENNA

I love you, too.

Fenna takes time to process, so it could be a few days before the reality hits her and she needs airtime.

I move on to the unanswered messages from my friends. I have several from Fee, which started last night, asking if I was coming home. Another one time-stamped half an hour later reads:

FEE

Cammie messaged Essie, who said your
parents are getting a divorce. I'm so sorry.

She also said you did shots and FLIP TOOK
YOU HOME.

> But you are not here, so that means you're
> with him. ●●●●●●

The next one is time-stamped an hour ago:

FEE

> Went for breakfast with Cammie. Message us
> when you get this.

I'll get to that in a minute, because my Babe chat is pinging relentlessly, asking if I'm okay this morning and sending me hugs.

I send a *marching band GIF* and a *crying into my wineglass GIF*.

TALLY

> Hydrating!

I add a photo of my Vitamin Water. There will be no photographic evidence of my face this morning.

My dad has texted and left a voicemail and so has my mom. I'm too upset to deal with them while I'm this hungover. I return to my messages with Fee and Cammie.

TALLY

> I'm home.

FEE

> We are on our way back from breakfast RN.

CAMMIE

> We're speed walking back to the apartment.
> ETA is about eight minutes, but my legs are
> short and I'm not a runner.

TALLY

> Fair. I'll leave the door open for you.

FEE

> How was last night?

CAMMIE

Did you channel your inner Arwen?

TALLY

No inner Arwen. It was…something. I'll fill you in when you get here.

FEE

On our way.

Fee and Cammie arrive ten minutes later. They take one look at me and fold me into their arms. I burst into tears. Again. Parsnip relocates himself to his cat tower to observe from a distance. When I'm calm enough, I relay the whole sordid story.

"I'm so sorry about your parents." Cammie squeezes my hand.

"That was a really shitty way for them to tell you," Fee says.

"I guess it's better that they waited until after the showcase. My performance might have suffered if they'd told us last week." Which had probably been their plan, except I had to bail on family dinner night to rehearse.

I flop back and tip my chin up, but the tears keep falling anyway. My most important relationships are shifting and there's nothing I can do to stop it. But I'm mindful of bemoaning my parental situation when Fee has lost both of hers. Yes, she has her older sister, Lexi, and Roman, Lexi's husband, is the number-one dad in the world, but still.

I switch to my newest humiliation. "I can't believe I smacked Flip's dick with my face."

"Did it feel substantial?" Fee asks.

"Yeah, but this is not how I wanted to find that out." I roll my eyes back to the ceiling. "How will I ever face him again?" Not to mention the speech I laid on him right before I exited his vehicle. Hungover me can't be trusted with words any more than drunk me. Or non-drunk me, where Flip is concerned.

Cammie crosses her legs. "I know it feels horrible right now, but this is Flip Madden we're talking about. It's not like he's made all the best choices in the history of the universe."

"The media definitely does a good job of skewing things," Fee grumbles. She knows firsthand what that's like. Her sister was Roman's coach when they got married mid-season. The rumor mill was churning, and it made Fee's final semester of high school tough. But she had me and the Babes, which helped ease the sting.

"I just wish…everything was different." That my parents weren't giving up on each other, that Flip's answer had been yes, that the way I'd asked him had been less insensitive in the first place.

"I didn't realize you saw me like that, too."

"You're always beautiful, Tally."

"You're also still my coach's daughter."

Reading into the things he said won't change the outcome. I still hurt him, and he still said no.

"We should go to Just Desserts for cake," Fee suggests.

"Yes to this," Cammie agrees.

"You just came from breakfast."

"I always have room for cake," Fee replies.

"Same," Cammie adds.

"Cake it is." That fits perfectly into the eating-my-feelings strategy.

I lie on the couch with teabags on my eyes for ten minutes to take down the redness before we venture outside. It's a cold December afternoon, with the promise of snow in the air.

The walk is pretty quiet, but once we have our treats, the analysis begins.

"So this thing you have for Flip explains why you're always picking these placeholder boyfriends." Cammie digs into her double chocolate fudge torte.

"Placeholder boyfriends?" I parrot.

Fee swallows a bite of white chocolate mousse cake. "Yeah, guys who are okay, but you'll never get attached to them."

I frown as I ponder that. "Shit. Is that what I've been doing?"

Cammie shrugs. "Flip sets a pretty high bar, as far as being a nice guy who is also superhot goes."

"I had a huge crush on him in high school," I admit. It was probably fifty percent of the reason I did the internship with the Terror in grade twelve. The other half being my mom's encouragement and the opportunity to spend time with my dad. "He's always been so nice to me. Kind, thoughtful." And last night he proved he's a stand-up guy once again. He always shows up for the people he cares about, which is a hell of a lot more than I can say for my dad.

"He watched over you last night," Cammie says.

"Because I'm the coach's daughter."

"He would have brought you to the apartment if that was the case," Fee reasons.

I rub my temples. I don't want to read into things. "I know what his reputation was, but I see a different side of him." He's grown so much since I did my internship with the Terror four years ago.

I've grown a lot too. I'm almost through university. I'm not a high school girl with a crush anymore. I'm an adult woman who sees the potential in him and wishes he could see the potential in me, too. Even back then, I crushed on the guy I knew off the ice.

"Maybe things could change with Flip," Fee says. "Maybe you're opening his eyes, too."

CHAPTER 8
FLIP

"What the hell happened to your eye?" Dallas asks as we're suiting up for practice.

"I missed a step coming down from my loft," I lie.

He nods, like this totally makes sense. "Oh man, that's a real design flaw."

"Yeah," I agree. The number of times I've almost fallen down that retractable ladder is unreal. I should consider replacing it with a spiral staircase.

Tristan glances at me, but he keeps his mouth shut and continues lacing his skates.

Not even for one second did I consider driving Tally back to her apartment last night. And that's a huge fucking problem.

So was letting her sit in my lap. The fact that she felt right there is problem number three. Problem four is how fucking territorial I got over her when Quinn offered to drive her home. He's a great guy. And Tally is right, he should have a girlfriend. But no way was I handing her over to him on a silver platter made of my rejection and her emotional turmoil.

Problem five is the churning worry that won't allow my gut

to settle. Tally is under a lot of stress; final exams, her parents getting a divorce, and her guilt over hurting my feelings. I'm a big boy, and it's clear she didn't mean it the way I took it, so the least I can do is make things less awkward when we're with the group. She needs her Terror crew now more than ever.

Once we're on the ice warming up our glutes and quads, Tristan digs in. "Want to tell me what really happened?"

"Not particularly." Because then I have to take a closer look at my actions. Tally's roommate, Fee, is responsible enough to have handled the situation. But Tally was a mess, emotionally and physically. I didn't trust anyone else to make sure she was safe. *And I wanted to be the one to take care of her.*

Tristan raises a brow.

I ignore it and switch to an inner thigh stretch.

"You going to fill me in on the Tally situation?" he presses.

"I drove her home. End of story." That lie is sharp and stupid.

"Dude." He gives me his unimpressed Kermit face. "Your sister is my *wife*, and her best friend is the older sister of Tally's best friend, and Fee is our coach's sister. It's six fucking degrees of separation everywhere you turn, so I already know you drove her home *this morning*."

"Nothing happened," I snap.

"Of course nothing happened. You would *never*. Maybe old Flip if she'd been sober, but that is not you now."

I meet his gaze and guilt cuts through me, swift and painful. We've known each other forever, but I almost imploded our friendship when he first came to Toronto. He's right. Every partner has been sober and willing, or so I believed. But I put Tristan in a position that left little room for his own feelings a couple of times, and I will forever regret that.

I don't want to overshare. "I didn't think she'd make it back to her apartment without hurling."

"So you set her up in the spare room."

"Where else would I put her?"

I shouldn't be this defensive. I haven't done anything wrong. I held her hair while she threw up, put her to bed, then checked on her every fifteen minutes until I gave up and dragged the yoga mat into her room.

But for a moment, I longed to let her cuddle right up next to me so I could hold her while she slept.

Tristan arches a brow. Like he can see inside my fucking head.

I sigh. "I slept on the floor because I was worried. She didn't know I was there and tripped over me on the way to the bathroom. Her foot caused this." I motion to my eye.

"You slept on the floor?" He doesn't sound skeptical, which I appreciate.

"On a yoga mat." It was seriously uncomfortable, and my back is still annoyed, but it was worth it to make sure Tally was okay.

I don't say anything about her face-planting into my dick. Or that I saw her entire ass, thanks to a wardrobe malfunction. I can never unsee it, and I'm pretty sure my future dreams about it will land me a front-row seat in hell.

Tristan rolls his head on his shoulders. "She was pretty flirty with you."

"She was hammered."

"She sat in your lap."

"Again, she was hammered."

"And you let her." He side-eyes me.

I brush it off. Evade. "She had a lot going on."

"You can't lead her on, though, man," he says gently. "Unless there's more to this?"

"That's not...there's not." I shake my head.

"Then you might need to set some boundaries." He claps me on the shoulder. "I get it, though, she was messed up."

I haven't said anything to anyone other than Dred about her proposition, and I don't plan to. Not even Tristan. He's one of my closest friends, but he could accidentally say something to Rix, and it could get back to Tally. She's already embarrassed enough. The speech she gave this morning has been rolling around in my head. I don't know how much of it was fueled by her hangover, but it hit a soft spot. She knows me, and she knows what it's like to be wanted for the wrong reasons, maybe better than I realized.

But last night she was in full-on defiance mode. Hurt. Upset. Devastated and looking for an escape from the shit in her head. And I was the person she came to. Bringing her back to my place, being the one to take care of her, seeing her in my robe, sleeping in my spare bed…is giving me ideas I shouldn't entertain. Can't entertain.

Coach Vander Zee blows the whistle, ending that conversation and dissipating my fantasies.

But my mind is still whirling. I didn't pay much attention to anyone but Tally at the Watering Hole. That doesn't mean other people weren't noticing us, though. Dred sure did. And so did Tristan. I should have let Quinn drive her home, but I couldn't.

I DECLINE THE OFFER TO GO TO THE WATERING HOLE AFTER practice. Instead, I make a stop at the retirement home since it's cribbage hour and I'm always down for cards with octogenarians.

"Stop letting me win, Phillip," Gurdy says after she beats me for the second time in a row.

"I'm not. You have decades of experience on me," I argue as I move the pegs back to the beginning and set us up for round three.

"You're missing points left and right. What's going on?" She covers the cards with her wrinkled, age-spotted hand and tips her head. "Is it woman problems?" She squints. "Or maybe man problems?"

I sigh and flop back in my chair. "It's woman problems."

"Hallelujah. You finally got a girlfriend, didn't you?" She slaps the table and opens her mouth to announce it to the entire room.

"No girlfriend."

Her lips pucker. "Then what kind of woman problems? Did you get someone pregnant?"

"God, no. My coach's daughter has a thing for me," I confide.

"Ah." She nods knowingly. "And you don't feel the same?"

I sip my Earl Grey tea. "That's the thing, I don't know."

She arches a gray, almost nonexistent eyebrow. "You don't know, or you don't want to admit that you have feelings because it would complicate things?"

"My coach would kill me if I dated his daughter."

"You're too important to the team to kill," she reasons.

"She's too young for me," I rebut.

"How young is she?"

"Twenty-one."

She rolls her eyes. "That's hardly too young. She's an adult; you're an adult. You're making excuses. What's the real problem?"

"She deserves better, and I have too much baggage."

Gurdy reaches across the table and places her soft, age-weathered hand on top of mine. "Dear boy, we all come with baggage. What if she's your right person? Don't let her slip through your fingers because you're too afraid to try."

For the time being, I just give her a look and let her win again, but I roll our conversation over in my head on the way home. Gurdy doesn't know my history with women and relationships. She doesn't realize pursuing Tally would be wickedly self-ish. She would have to face all the media bullshit that comes along with me, and eventually I would have to come clean about what really sent me down that dark path. Tally deserves someone who can give her his whole heart, not just a pile of fragments.

When I arrive home, I toss my keys on the counter next to the mail. My first stop is the laundry room. I pull my freshly washed and dried sheets and bathrobe out of the dryer. Immediately after I dropped Tally at her apartment, I came home, stripped the bed, and put everything she'd touched in the wash.

I stupidly thought cleansing my personal space of her presence and her smell would erase the memory of her being here. But the image of her curled up in my spare bed, long wavy blonde hair fanned out across the pillow remains vivid. It's been an eternity since I've felt this kind of…longing for something. *Someone.* She looked so peaceful, like she belonged…

I shut it all down. Compartmentalize it. There's no other choice. Vander Zee would destroy me. Even if he didn't and we did try, I can't risk messing up the friend group because I'm suddenly lonely. Tally needs these people and their support more than I need someone to cuddle with.

I make the spare bed on autopilot, hang my robe in the bathroom, grab a healthy snack made by Rix from the fridge, and park my ass on the couch.

The book I've been reading sits on the coffee table, taunting me. The irony is real, since it's Tally's. She suggested it in the group chat and passed it to Rix, who passed it to me a couple of weeks ago. I flip the book open. But my mind keeps drifting.

Tally's become an integral part of our friend group. I look forward to the nights where she joins us at the Watering Hole. I try to make her dance showcases when we're in town and don't have a game, because she's incredible on stage.

I could convince myself that I feel the same way about her as I do Hammer, Hemi, Essie, and Dred—a friend who's a girl and firmly platonic. But her proposition has altered everything. I don't want to understand, to empathize, but I do. Especially now that she's explained and I've had a chance to reframe it all. But I can't pursue her. Her world is too fragile, and I would be devastated if I hurt her.

I pick up the book and immerse myself in the story, but whenever something funny or interesting happens, I find myself itching to text Tally. Before the proposition, I would have thought nothing of firing off a quick message. But it's not just about the book. I want to make sure she's okay, to tell her everything she said this morning made sense. It's a bad idea, though. Tristan was right, I can't lead her on.

My phone buzzes on the side table.

I flip it over, half hoping it's her. If Tally reaches out first, I can respond.

But it's just an alert from my fan page. There are ten new messages, and all but two are from women who want to hook up.

It's the reminder I need.

Because if I give in, I don't think I could handle it when she continued her life and left me behind. That's what always happens. She doesn't want to keep me; she just wants my help.

CHAPTER 9

TALLY

"Can we all fit in another rehearsal later this week?" I rest my heel on the barre and bend until my cheek meets my knee while scrolling my calendar. Just call me the multitasking queen.

"My schedule is open, apart from Wednesday," Charles says.

"Same, but Thursday is my heavy day," Arya offers.

"What about Saturday?" Exams are on the horizon, and we have an in-class group performance piece that's worth twenty percent of our Contemporary Dance mark this semester.

Charles scrolls through the booking calendar on his phone. "Are we okay with a seven a.m. start? I know it's early, but there's a two-hour block available, and all the afternoon spots are already taken."

"I'm an early riser anyway," I say as I reject yet another call from my mom. I'm in full avoidance mode.

"I can do it," Arya agrees.

We book several more slots, most at the more reasonable start time of nine a.m. Charles sometimes works the late shift at the campus store.

When we've finished booking practice sessions, I drop them

at their apartments on the south side of campus—the perks of having my own car and a parking pass—then drive to my building at the north end. While I drive, I listen to my mom's most recent voicemail, asking if I'd like to come for dinner, and to please call her back.

I'm still processing, and I'm angry at both of my parents. Ties is coping by spending all his spare time at robotics, and Fenna is drowning herself in cello. According to my siblings, Mom has rekindled every single former hobby she's ever had, and Dad is doing what Dad does best: work. I can't deplete what little emotional energy I have with exams around the corner.

Besides, I'm hanging out with my Tilton U crew tonight, so home is a no-go, unless I want to bring a dark cloud with me. That's exactly what would happen if I went for dinner with the fam.

Instead, I soak in the tub for half an hour while I read Cammie's fic update. The chapter is extra spicy, so I end up envisioning my fantasy Flip as the various heroes during my manual stress relief session. In one scene, the heroine sits in hero one's lap (dirty Flip), her back to his chest, riding him while he whispers dirty things in her ear. Her (my) legs are hooked around his, and he spreads her (me) wide while hero two (sweet Flip) kneels between their parted thighs and sucks her (my) clit.

I come twice and am far more relaxed as I pick an outfit. Fee and I step out of our rooms at the same time.

"Did you read the update?" she asks.

"Oh yeah."

"Same."

We nod at each other.

"It's times like these I envy Cammie's prolific love life."

"Also same," I agree.

We pull on coats and tuck our feet into our shoes while Parsnip paws at the door.

"I'll throw the mouse." She picks up Parsnip's favorite toy from the entry table fishbowl.

"And I'll throw the treats." I shake the bag, which gets Parsnip's attention.

He paws at my legs, then rushes down the hall when Fee throws his mouse. I confetti toss treats as she slips into the hall, following behind her. Parsnip yowls his discontent from the other side of the door. He's a complete menace, and the most adorable problem. I'll never regret giving him a home.

Cammie and Chase meet us in the lobby, and we file out into the cold December night. We huddle into our coats as we leave campus and head to one of our favorite restaurants for a bite to eat before we go to the hockey house party.

Chase's teammates Mac, Gage, and Brody are already at the table when we arrive.

"We ordered appetizers," Gage announces as we join them.

"Lots of them," Mac adds.

They're bottomless pits, so this tracks.

The server stops by to take our drink orders. I opt for cola since I plan to study later.

"How you doing?" Brody asks.

My friends know about the situation with my parents, but Brody is the most sensitive of the guys. Probably because his mom bailed on their family when he was four, so he and his brothers were raised by their dad.

"Just keeping my head down so I can get through exams." Mostly I try not to think about the holidays. Otherwise I'll end up in a spiral.

"I get it." Brody nods somberly.

Fee gives me a side hug.

"I'm here if you need someone to cheer you up," Gage offers.

Mac shoves his shoulder. "Don't, dude."

"I mean that in a nonsexual way!" Gage replies defensively.

The table gives him a collective eye roll.

"Seriously, I'm more than just a relentless playboy," he argues.

I rest my chin on my steepled fingers and bat my lashes. "But are you?"

"Occasionally." He shrugs.

This is what I need, friends and some good-natured ribbing to take my mind off everything else.

The server drops off our appetizers. They weren't kidding about ordering a lot of food. Soon the entire table is covered in plates.

Mac turns his megawatt smile on the server. "Thank you, Amanda. I appreciate you."

Amanda blinks at him and stutters out, "You're welcome," while fiddling with her hair.

"We're ready to order now!" Fee's voice is unnaturally high.

Amanda snaps out of her Mac attack and takes our orders.

Cammie does a seat shimmy while waving her phone around. "Oh yay! Enid will be in here in a minute."

Everyone looks at Brody, whose face turns red.

"I need to use the restroom." He hustles off.

"Is he okay?" Fee asks.

"He's probably having a mild panic attack, but repeated exposure is good for him." Mac loads a selection of appetizers onto his plate. "Besides, one of these days he'll get over himself and ask her out, right?"

"Hopefully," Gage muses. "The mutual pining is a lot."

All eyes move to Gage.

"What? It's true. Those two are the king and queen of Pineville."

"We just…didn't realize you recognized feelings beyond the range of lust," Chase quips.

He nudges Chase. "Move over one so they have to sit beside each other."

We reorganize ourselves, and thankfully Enid arrives before Brody returns. She orders herself a mojito when the server brings the rest of our drinks.

"How's everyone doing? Are we decompressing-from-exam-studying-stress, or avoiding-all-the-things?"

Enid is a physiology major and is always studying or working.

"Both?" Cammie asks.

As a creative writing major, almost all her exams are essays, so she's been hunched over her laptop for the past two weeks, which means her fanfic updates are now on pause until the holidays.

"I have a study date with my tutor tomorrow afternoon," Gage offers.

"Study date?" I make air quotes.

"Nah, this one is all business, which is better for my grades, but not my ego or my business end."

"You focus too much on your business end," Mac says.

Brody returns to the table. Enid's back is to him, and his eyes are wide as he looks around the table and fires the double bird at us.

Enid glances over her shoulder, and he quickly runs his hands through his hair to hide the gesture. "Hey, Enid."

"Hi, Brody."

He apologizes when his arm brushes hers as he takes his seat. "What are we talking about?"

"Gage's overused business end," Cammie says.

"Like you're one to talk." Gage flings a hand in her direction. "Chase wears a permanent I-got-laid grin."

Chase frowns. "I don't have a got-laid face."

"If it makes you feel better, Cammie also has a got-laid face," Fee says.

"This is super true," Cammie admits.

I sigh. "One day I'll have a got-laid face."

A couple of guys I've seen at parties before stop by the table to say hi. Apparently, they're also going to this hockey party.

"See you there, virgin." One of them winks at me as they start to walk away.

"Shut your stupid, fucking mouth, dickbag," Gage snaps, surprising all of us.

He holds up both hands. "It was a joke!"

"How about we start calling you virgin and see how cute you think it is," Brody says darkly.

"Sorry, man. Sorry." He bows out, and he and his friend rush off.

"They're assholes, just ignore them," Mac says.

"I'm so tired of being completely untouchable or sexualized by douchebags who just want to say they popped a cherry. Is it too much to want someone to want me for the right reasons?"

Again, I feel bad for the way I approached Flip, because he might say the same thing. In all the years I've known him, he's never had a girlfriend, though, so maybe not.

"I don't want my first time to be some drunken accident. I want it to be special, and I want to be in love."

The table goes silent for a beat at Mac's admission. I guess I'm not the last virgin standing after all. Mac flirts with the world, but none of us has ever seen him kiss anyone, let alone take someone home, or up to his room when he throws a party.

"I love that," Cammie says. "I'm really glad Chase was my first."

"And your last." He kisses her temple.

"Sometimes I wish my first time had been different," Enid muses.

"Me too," Brody blurts. His ears turn red, and he looks absolutely gutted.

I don't know the whole story, but there was a high school party involving Brody and one of Enid's friends, and he's forever regretted it.

The server returns with more plates of food, clearing away some of the empties, and the conversation shifts to holiday plans. It's like my parents can sense me talking about them, and my phone buzzes with a call from my dad, but I let it go to voicemail. Toronto has a home game tonight. Part of me wanted to attend, but then I'd have to deal with my dad and see Flip. I'm taking my cues from Flip, and he's messaged a few times about book-related stuff this week—he's reading one of my recommendations. Things feel closer to normal, but I'm not quite ready to see him in three dimensions yet.

After dinner, we walk over to the hockey party. It's the same old, same old, people getting drunk and stupid. My Terror guys-and-Babes chat is blowing up with messages now that the game is over. I wait in line for the bathroom as I scroll.

ESSIE

I have a spreadsheet for New Year's!

NATE

I helped her with it.

FLIP

I seriously doubt that.

HEMI

I love your spreadsheets.

DALLAS

I love you, honey.

HAMMER

You're sitting right beside her as you type that, Dallas.

Tally, you're still in, right?

TALLY

I am still in.

DALLAS

How did you know? 😳

DRED

Because Hammer's sitting across from you.

Tally! What are you up to? We're at Just
Desserts if you want to join us.

A picture of my Babes and the Terror boys appears in the chat. Flip is missing, though.

TALLY

I'm with my Tilton crew. Eat all the good things in my honor!

ESSIE

If you're with my sister, hug her for me!

TRISTAN

If you're with my brother, tell him I'll be at his game this weekend.

TALLY

I can do both of those things. Or you can just tell Cammie yourself because she's also in this chat, but probably too busy sucking face with Chase to answer.

CAMMIE

We're playing cards in the kitchen. Feel free to join us.

FLIP

I hope you're staying away from the shots 😉

TALLY

Never again. *dies GIF* *shots GIF*

I pocket my phone as the bathroom door opens and a girl wearing a Tilton Hockey hoodie steps out. I trade places with her and lock the door, letting the embarrassment over Flip's message wash through me. At least he's joking around with me again. I wish I could forget everything that happened after I sat in his lap, but my memory of the night is unfortunately clear.

He did use a winky emoji, so maybe he's over the black eye I gave him and the terrible night's sleep on a yoga mat. Analyzing his message will only make me sweaty, so I compartmentalize it until I can ruminate in the privacy of my bedroom.

I avoid making eye contact with random drunk guys as I make my way to the kitchen. I find my friends gathered around the table, playing cards, as is typical.

"I'm heading out. I need to study."

"Do you want me to come back with you?" Fee asks.

Mac is seated to her right, his eyes on his cards.

"Nah. Stay and have fun." I kiss her, Cammie, and Enid on the cheek. "I'll message when I'm home."

"Be safe," they reply in unison.

I duck out the side door to avoid the crowded living room and run into a couple getting it on against the fence. They don't notice me, though, too absorbed in each other.

When I get back to my building, instead of taking the elevator to my apartment, I poke my head in the yoga studio. It's open to students until eleven-thirty, and luckily, it's empty. I text the girls that I'm home, then shed a few layers until I'm in my cropped tee and yoga pants. I do not dress up for hockey parties.

I connect to the sound system, cue up some music, and start with light stretching. I love dancing with Charles and Arya, but the freedom of solo numbers invigorates me. Once I'm warmed up, I give myself over to the heavy bass, trading modern ballet style for contemporary.

There's nothing soft about this music. It's all aggression and emotion. The sadness, fear, disappointment, and embarrassment I've been holding on to fade away as I become a conduit for the sound. A vessel for rhythm. I put the song on repeat and pay special attention to my release technique, because it's the element that needs the most attention for my upcoming performance.

I spiral into a chasse, stag leap, and move to floor work, improvising to make the song my own. I dance until the automatic lights turn off, and then I lie on the wood floor, heart hammering, skin damp with sweat, hair sticking to my neck and temples.

Eventually, when my breathing calms, I peel myself off the floor and head up to my apartment. Parsnip rushes down the hall to greet me, but I close the door in time to prevent his escape. I scoop him up like a baby and rub my face against his cheek. "How is my cute boy?"

He wriggles around, uninterested in the affection.

"I know I need a shower, but you could be less obvious about it." I head for the kitchen first, feed Parsnip so he doesn't become a tripping hazard, and pour myself a glass of water.

I check my messages while I drain the glass. Cammie, Fee, and Enid have sent me a range of gifs.

But a new one from Flip makes my heart skip a beat. It's in our private thread. Mostly it's used for book recommendations.

FLIP

I hope you're staying hydrated. 😉

I didn't drink at the party. I consider taking a selfie with my glass of water, but I'm sweaty and red-faced, so I snap one of the glass, with my bookshelf as the background.

TALLY

H2O for the win. What about you?

FLIP

Not quite as good as you.

A picture of a glass of Tang in his hand appears. He's in his apartment, and the book I suggested in our group chat a couple of weeks ago is open in his lap.

TALLY

Shouldn't you be out indulging in a double chocolate fudge cake with your teammates?

FLIP

I considered it, but this book was calling me.

He's texting me unprovoked for the third time this week. He's home and reading the book I recommended. Is he trying to smooth things over and make things less awkward because I'm joining the group for New Year's? I'm working up the nerve to ask. But for now, I try to reclaim some of the easiness of our previous messages.

TALLY

The nice thing about books is that they'll still be there, waiting for your eyes until after you finish dessert.

FLIP

True. But I'm invested. I need to know what happens.

I click on the photo he sent and magnify the image so I can see where he is in the story.

TALLY

Oh! You're so far already! No wonder you passed up dessert. You're almost at my favorite part.

FLIP

You want to tell me what that is?

TALLY

And ruin the surprise? I would never. 😊

FLIP

Is it in this chapter?

TALLY

No, but it's coming. That's the only hint you get. Otherwise I'll ruin it.

FLIP

Hmm. Good point. I'll be back in a bit with my guesses.

TALLY

Don't stay up too late.

FLIP

No promises. 😉

I'm smiling as I shower and get ready for bed. Parsnip is lying on my body pillow, concealed by my comforter. He meows his annoyance and tries to bite my hand when I pull the sheets back.

"Hi, Flip. Ready for bed?" I barely resist the urge to lean down and kiss his two-dimensional lips. I've had a Flip Madden body pillow since my first year of university. Cammie got it for me as a joke, but I sleep with it every night.

I stretch out next to Pillow Flip and throw a leg over his pillow bottom half. As soon as I stop moving, Parsnip makes himself comfortable against my side. Just as I'm dozing off, my phone vibrates. I groggily check the message.

FLIP

It's the scene where he sends her on a scavenger hunt to all their favorite places.

I grin and hug Pillow Flip. He knows me well enough to pick out my favorite scene. Maybe we're getting back to normal again, which is a relief.

TALLY

That's the one!

It was such a thoughtful thing to do.

FLIP

The little things mean the most, don't they?

TALLY

Exactly.

When you're finished, you can tell me which chapter is your favorite.

FLIP

So far it's the same as yours. But I should be finished in a couple of days, so I'll tell you if it changes.

I'll need another rec soon, though.

TALLY

I'll have one ready for you.

He hearts the message.

FLIP

Back to reading.

Night, Talls.

TALLY

Night, Flip.

CHAPTER 10
TALLY

"Oh my gosh, this room is incredible! Is this why Connor bought you the lodge?" Hammer runs her fingers along the spines on a bookshelf.

Connor and Dred's suite has its very own library overlooking the picturesque frozen lake. It's stunning and romantic and the perfect winter oasis. "Connor can't help but be excessive and extravagant," Dred says dryly, smiling.

I catalogue the titles, noting a few I've read that Flip might like. "Can I borrow a couple of these?"

"Of course," Dred replies.

I select two. How much would I love to read by the fire with Flip? Cuddled into his side, or even my feet tucked under his leg. I'm sad the dream will never be a reality, but grateful things seem better between us again.

Connor pokes his head in the room. "I thought I'd find you here."

"Just showing the girls my favorite room," Dred murmurs.

"Mine, too," Connor replies as he crosses over to her.

The temperature in the room goes up by three degrees as their eyes meet.

"We'll let you settle in." Hammer grabs my hand. "Let's unpack."

We hustle into the hall, and I pull the door closed.

"Did you see the rolling ladder in the corner?" I whisper.

Hammer's eyes light up. "Oh yeah, those two are going to bone *Atonement* style, for sure."

At the sound of her voice, Hollis pokes his head into the hall. "There you are, Princess. Did you know there's a pool and a hot tub on the main floor?"

Hammer smiles up at him. "We'll have to check them out later."

"I'll see you two in a bit." I keep walking, Hammer's giggle floating down the hall after me.

I love being with my friends, but when I'm surrounded by all this love, the loneliness is a lot. It makes me hopeful and scared. They're still madly in love now, but what happens when two decades pass and new love fades in the predictability of routine? Will they endure, or will some of them end up like my parents? How do I know which will be which?

I step into my Nutcracker themed room, shaking off my worries as I check my phone I reluctantly open the one from my mom.

MOM

Please message to let me know you made it to the lodge safely.

I shove down the guilt over my irritation and message back.

TALLY

Here safe and sound! Have fun tonight!

I tuck my phone away before she messages back.

The holidays with my family were awkward and uncomfortable. When I couldn't actively avoid my parents, I divided my time between coaxing a teary Fenna out of her room to play cello for us and helping Ties build a robot—something I'm decidedly terrible at. But both things were better than being cornered by my mom and dad so we could talk about how we're coping. The whole ordeal was exhausting and emotional, and aside from driving Fenna to cello lessons, taking her to the cat shelter, and attending my brother's robotics competition a couple of days ago, I've been successfully dodging my parents.

But now I'm here with my friends, and I'm hopeful that the awkwardness of Christmas won't follow me through the weekend. Along with the Grace twins, Kellan, Quinn, Flip, and I are the uncoupled of the group. Flip has been messaging me every time he thinks he's stumbled upon one of my favorite scenes lately, so I have hope. He's been startlingly accurate, too.

I finish unpacking and head down to the great room. The twins are already there, snacks spread out on the table.

"How much do you love your room?" Everly asks as she pops a peanut butter-filled pretzel into her mouth.

"It's perfect." I drop into a plush chair that could easily fit two.

"Yay!" Everly claps. "I helped Connor and Dred assign all the rooms."

"What's your room's theme?"

"I have the Poe room," Everly replies.

"And I have the Musical Night Sky." Victor stacks cheese and prosciutto on a cracker.

"We can show you later, if you want," Everly says.

"I'd love that." The twins are the same age I was when I interned for the Terror. And in grade twelve, like Ties. Hemi and Hammer never made a big deal about me being younger and immediately folded me into their group. I feel understood by them in a way I often don't with university peers beyond my small circle of friends.

Flip appears in the living room wearing black joggers, a Terror hoodie, and a pair of festive socks. He's carrying my most recent book suggestion, a bookmark tassel marking his spot. He's close to the end.

My heart stutters and then gallops as his eyes find mine.

He grins impishly and sings, surprisingly in tune, "Do you want to build a snowman?"

Everly springs off the couch and bounces toward the door. "Yes! Me! Let's go!"

Victor is right on her heels.

Flip crosses to me and extends a hand, eyes warm and hopeful. "You in?"

My heart aches knowing he'll never be more than a friend, but I accept the peace offering. "Yeah, I'm in."

I slip my hand into his, warmth zipping through my veins as he pulls me out of the chair. His fingers are still wrapped around mine. I try to break the sudden tension by twirling away from him.

His smile widens. "I could watch you dance all day."

"I could watch you watch me dance all day," I fire back without thinking. Before I can apologize for making things awkward, again, Quinn and Kellan come down the stairs.

"Where my party people at?" Kellan calls.

"All the couples are boning, but the rest of us are heading outside to play with snowballs!" I reply. My whole face is now on fire. Flip coughs to cover his laugh.

I pretend that didn't come out sounding suggestive. "You two in?"

"Would you believe I've never made a snowman?" Kellan says.

"How is that possible?" Everly bounds over and hangs off the newel post. She might have a crush on Kellan.

"I grew up in small town California and played the first few seasons of my career in LA, so the whole six months of winter is new to me," he explains.

"Well that's about to change," Quinn replies.

"This will be so much fun!" Everly claps excitedly and bounces back to Victor.

We don our winter gear and head outside. The snow squeaks under our boots as we trudge through waist-deep drifts. It's perfect for packing, and the guys quickly roll several massive balls.

"Wait! Don't stack those!" Everly instructs Quinn and Kellan to roll the balls next to each other.

Victor crosses his arms. "Ev, seriously."

Flip rolls a ball up next to me. Things feel normal-ish, like we're back to being friends. It's a relief, but it also sucks.

He nudges my arm with his. "I bet I know what she's planning."

"What's that?"

"A snow dick."

I snicker. "Oh yeah, that is totally an Everly move. Think Connor will be pissed at us for helping her?"

"If she didn't do it, I would have."

"Fair."

He pats the ball in front of us. "Give me a hand?"

"Sure." Our arms brush as we roll it over to the rest of our crew.

I try not to overthink it, but now the weight of the past few weeks hangs between us. Maybe time will smooth things out and make it less confusing.

It takes all four guys to lift our ball on top of the others. The guys roll more snowballs while Everly and I contour the base.

Kellan and Quinn add another ball, and I help Everly up so she can pack snow around it.

"You want a hand up?" Quinn asks.

"I got her." Flip easily lifts me onto the opposing snowball, making sure I have my balance before he lets go. He bends and gathers snow into a small ball before passing it to me. "It'll be easier to contour this way."

"Thanks." I accept the ball and work on filling in the gaps. Is he being protective? Possessive? I doubt Quinn or Kellan would ever view me as anything but a friend either.

"We need pictures before Connor comes out here and knocks it down," Everly declares.

"Good call," Flip agrees.

I pose while Flip snaps a bunch of pictures, and Victor reluctantly does the same for his twin.

Everly cannonballs into the snow and sinks in so deep she needs Victor's help to get free.

I hop down, but my right foot sinks deeper than my left and I stumble forward. Flip rushes to steady me, but he steps into the same soft drift. We both scramble to right ourselves but end up buried in snow. I'm wedged in, Flip's body half on top of me, one of his knees between mine. Of all the scenarios I've imagined where Flip ends up on top of me, this was not on the list.

I try to wiggle out from under him, but all it does is press me deeper into the snow. I turn my head, and my nose bumps the edge of his jaw.

"I think we're stuck!" I don't know where to put my hands because Flip is *everywhere*.

"Stop moving, kitten," he orders.

I go still.

Flip's hand appears beside my head. When he tries to gain leverage, his arm sinks in all the way to his elbow. Our faces are inches apart. Every part of him is touching every part of me.

I don't breathe. Don't move. His lips part, his tongue darts out. I track the movement, breath leaving me on a whimper. Flip's nostrils flare.

"You need some help over there?" Kellan calls out.

"We're good," Flip grinds out.

Are we?

I don't know what's happening, but it doesn't feel platonic.

Flip's thigh presses against my center and I'm positive I'm a few hip rolls away from a spontaneous orgasm. Which I believed was a gift only Dred possessed.

Flip folds back on his knees, weight lifting off me. I'm not sure whether I'm disappointed or relieved.

He struggles to his feet and extends his hand. "Let's try that again."

This time he successfully pulls me out of the drift.

"Wow, that's some deep snow," Kellan observes.

"For real." The imprint of our bodies is embedded in the powder.

"Nice snow dick," Dallas calls out as he trudges toward us, the rest of the group in tow.

I'm eternally grateful for their arrival.

"Whose idea was this?" Dred points two fingers in opposite directions, one at Everly and one at Flip.

"It was mine!" Everly says proudly.

"I did think about it, though," Flip admits.

"Very classy." Hemi snickers.

"Who wants to go snowshoeing?" Connor asks as a gust of wind blows snow around us and a dark cloud blankets out the sun. He tips his head up and frowns menacingly at the sky.

I shiver and wrap my arms around myself. "Uh, I'm probably heading in." My pants are wet, there's snow in my boots, and I'm pretty sure I have ice inside my shirt.

"Might be better to save that for tomorrow if the weather looks more promising." Dred pats his chest.

"I thought the snow was coming later," Connor grumbles.

"It is later." Quinn holds out his phone. "It's almost four, the sun is setting soon."

We tromp back to the lodge as fat flakes make everything harder to see.

"Hot tub might be a good idea," Quinn suggests.

"Yes!" Hammer agrees.

"I'm in," Flip adds.

I say nothing. I'm not sure I can handle Flip in a bathing suit after what happened in the snow, but I don't want to miss the opportunity either.

I hang my jacket on the heated drying rack in the mudroom, along with my gloves, toque, and scarf—all of which are soaked. Everyone who wasn't outside building a snowman heads to the kitchen for drinks, while the rest of us climb the stairs.

"See you in a bit," Quinn calls over his shoulder.

I disappear into my room, peeling off layers of wet clothes. I was right about the ice down my back. I cross to the dresser and grab my bikini, but I don't make a move to go downstairs yet.

The hot tub would feel nice, but there's new tension with Flip. A blanket by the fire might be the better option. Or I could just go talk to him. I pull on a pair of thermal leggings and an extra sweater, grab the book and step into the hall. I stop outside his door and summon my courage to knock. Bringing him a new book is a good icebreaker.

I raise my hand, but before I can knock, I find myself being tossed over a broad shoulder.

I shriek and drop the book on the floor. "What are you doing?" My cheek bounces twice against Quinn's freckled back.

"It's hot tub time!" Quinn shouts.

Flip pokes his head into the hall and frowns.

I give him a *help me* look.

"Romero! Hold up!" Flip shouts.

"Race you to the hot tub!" Quinn calls over his shoulder.

"My bathing suit is on my bed!"

Quinn darts into my room, grabs my bikini, and hustles back into the hall, Flip on our heels.

"Do not run down those stairs with Tally on your shoulder, Romero!" Flip snaps.

Quinn stops ten feet from the top of the stairs and gently sets my feet back on the ground. I'm lightheaded from being upside down, so when Flip moves in I brace my hand on his shoulder for balance.

"You okay, kitten?" His hand settles on my hip.

"I'm fine." I don't know if that's entirely true. The whole vibe so far is wonky, and I'm pretty sure it's all because I can't get over my stupid mouth.

"Ease up, man. We're just having some fun." Quinn winks and heads for the stairs. "Let's get some drinks!"

I smile at Flip—I'm sure it's slightly manic—and keep my eyes on his chin so I don't accidentally ogle his bare chest. "Seriously, I'm good." I give him the thumbs-up. If Cammie could see me now.

By the time Flip and I make it to the kitchen, Quinn already has a cooler.

"Tally likes cider and margaritas," Flip says.

"Got them right here." Quinn holds up one of each.

"Thanks." I didn't realize Quinn paid attention to that kind of stuff, but then we do have fajita night a lot at Rix and Tristan's.

The three of us head down the hall to the pool and hot tub. "Is Kellan coming?" I ask.

"Yeah, he just had to make a phone call, he'll be down in a bit," Quinn confirms.

I duck into the change room to put on my bikini, which is when I realize I packed the wrong bottoms. "Fuck, fuck, fuck." I stare at the pale blue thong, trying to manifest more fabric. Obviously I fail. "Just cover up with a towel. It'll be fine." I grab one of the huge blue towels, wrap it around my body, and leave the safety of the change room.

Quinn and Flip are sitting on opposite sides of the hot tub.

Both heads turn my way. *Oh Charles and Arya, if only you could see me now.* I'm literally living their fantasy.

"You can hang your towel right there." Quinn helpfully points to the nearby hooks.

"Cool, thanks." I try to angle my body so my entire ass, which Flip has already seen, isn't facing them as I unwrap the terry and drape it over the hook. I quick-walk to the hot tub and step in. "Oh, this feels nice."

"Sure does," Quinn replies, eyes moving over me briefly before shifting away.

I glance at Flip, who doesn't look particularly happy. I wish the vibe wasn't so tense. Or maybe it's me making it that way. I position myself between Quinn and Flip.

Quinn pours me a margarita, then sinks back into the water and stretches his arms along the back of the hot tub. Flip mirrors the movement. I'm slightly closer to him, so his left hand is near my shoulder blade. They're big guys, they need space, and draping their arms over the cool tile would keep them from over-heating.

"How's that friend of yours out in Pearl Lake? The one you brought to Dred and Connor's wedding? She's fair, like our Tally." His fingers brush my shoulder.

I perk up at the *our Tally* reference. His tone isn't possessive. It doesn't hold warning. There is no vibe. It's all in my head.

Quinn glances at me, then looks back to Flip. "You mean Lovey?"

"That's the one. Yeah. You've been friends a long time." Flip takes a swig of his beer.

"Our whole lives, yeah. She's doing great. She's running a charity hockey event this weekend."

"That's too bad."

Does Flip want Lovey here for personal reasons? Why is my brain spinning all these scenarios that now include a Flip-Lovey-Quinn sandwich?

"Yeah, she would have loved it here."

"I'm sure." Flip drains his beer.

"I can get you another one!" I offer. I just want the tension to ease up. I set my drink on the edge of the tub and start to pull myself out of the water, then realize I'm about to flash Flip my ass again.

Water sloshes behind me and Flip's hand is suddenly on my hip, squeezing gently. "I got it, kitten. You stay right where you are."

I freeze, halfway out of the water. His warm, slightly calloused palm is touching my bare skin. Quinn's gaze locks on Flip's hand. He squeezes briefly before reaching around me, his chest brushing my arm as he grabs a fresh beer from the cooler.

Kellan appears, also carrying a cooler. "This place is awesome."

"Right?" Quinn agrees.

Kellan's gaze darts between Quinn and Flip as he joins us. "Everything cool here?"

"Yeah, everything's great." Flip shifts closer to me.

"So awesome!" I chirp.

Hammer and Hollis appear next, followed by Everly and Victor.

"Hammer! Everly! Yay!" I wave both hands manically in the air. "Come join us! The water feels great!" I sound like I'm channeling a Muppet.

Everly jumps right in next to me, and Hammer takes the other side. Hollis squeezes in beside Hammer and wraps his arm around her.

Flip's arm drops into the water.

Hammer leans into me and whispers, "Is everything okay?"

"Everything's great." I sip my margarita.

"You sure?" She wrinkles her nose. "There's a vibe."

I round my eyes.

She rounds hers back.

"There isn't," I whisper.

"There is," she refutes. "Like omegaverse alpha energy vibes."

So it's not all in my head.

And what does that mean for me and Flip, if anything?

The addition of our friends seems to be the magic we need. Although Flip is quiet. Eventually the guys' stomachs start rumbling, though. Flip is first out of the tub and he brings my towel to me, holding it open and wrapping me up like a burrito. Probably so I don't flash everyone my ass.

I shower off the chlorine and check my messages before I head down to help with dinner. Ties is out with his robotics friends, and Fenna is having a sleepover with her best friend at our house.

I call Fenna to check in.

"How's it going?" I ask as I pull on a pair of leggings.

"Great! Abby and I played cello for a while. We're helping Mom make spaghetti and meatballs with garlic bread and cheese because it's our favorite, and we have cake for dessert. We're watching movies after dinner and making extra buttery popcorn."

I smile. "That sounds like a lot of fun."

"Yeah. Will you be here tomorrow to make oliebollen?" she asks, sounding a little distracted. It's been a long-standing tradition that we get together on New Year's Day and make the Dutch treat as a family. I can't say I'm sorry to be missing it this time.

"I can't make it tomorrow. I'm in Huntsville, remember?"

"Right. I forgot. We'll save you some. Do you want to talk to Mom?"

"It's okay, I have to help make dinner. I'll message later."

"Okay, bye, Tallulah."

"Bye, Fenna." I end the call, relieved she's having fun and that my absence tomorrow won't ruin her day.

I message Ties.

TALLY

Be safe tonight.

He sends me a picture of a wrestling ring with fighting robots.

TIES

Take your mom hat off for the night, sis.

TALLY

Have the best time!

TIES

You too!

I move to the message from my dad.

DAD

Hope you're having fun with your friends. Stay safe.

I heart it but struggle to come up with a response that isn't steeped in anger or frustration. I finally type out a generic reply.

TALLY

Having a great time!

I'm sure he's sitting in front of the TV with a stack of paperwork and a hockey game playing in the background, which is depressing. But I didn't make his choices for him.

I switch to my Tilton U chat. Enid had to work tonight, so she couldn't join Fee and Cammie and the hockey guys.

CAMMIE

How's the lodge?

FEE

We miss you!

I smile as a picture of Fee and Cammie appears, heads together, fake tears splashing out of their eyes.

TALLY

Aw. I miss you too! 🩶 The lodge is so cool.

We built a snow peen!

I send photos of me posing on the balls and hugging the shaft. I leave the weird vibe alone. I can fill them in when we see each other.

CAMMIE

😍 😂

FEE

That is epic. 👀

TALLY

Right?! How is the tournament?

CAMMIE

They won their first two games and lost the third.

FEE

We're heading out for dinner now!

TALLY

We're about to make dinner, too. Big hugs! Have the best time tonight!

CAMMIE

You too!

FEE

❤️❤️❤️

I feel bad that I didn't go with them, but it wouldn't have been as fun for me, and I wanted to spend it with the Terror and

Flip, even if he can never be mine. Who knows where I'll be next year. This could be my first and last New Year's with them.

I slide a scrunchie onto my wrist and head downstairs. The whole team is in the kitchen, and I love the way we fall into an easy routine, thanks to our regular fajita and taco nights at Tristan and Rix's.

"You having fun?" Dred asks as we cut carrots into coins.

"So much. Thanks for inviting me to tag along. It's a nice getaway before I start my final semester."

"Are you excited, or is it bittersweet that it's almost over?" Rix asks.

"A bit of both. I love Tilton, but it's very hockey focused and that makes it tricky with my friend group."

"It must have been hard staying in Toronto," Everly muses. "I applied to Tilton, but a bunch of other places, too."

"It's good to keep your options open," I agree.

"There are benefits to commuting," Connor interjects.

Dred hugs his arms and kisses his cheek, whispering something to him.

I love that they've made a family for themselves. Dred grew up in foster care, and so did the twins. Connor's family is filthy rich, but his parents are kind of jerks. Well, his dad is. His mother seems like she's caught in the middle of it with his sisters. A sudden jolt of fear makes my spine hot. What if Dred and the twins finally have the family they've always longed for, and it all falls apart like my parents did?

"You okay, Talls?" Flip's fingers drift down my arm, startling me out of my morbid thoughts.

I shake it off and tuck my worries away. I force a smile, stomach fluttering at his attention. "I'm good."

I end up between Flip and Hammer at dinner. I'm hyper-aware of his proximity, of every brush of elbows, of the smell of his cologne, the warmth of his laughter. And now I can't stop thinking about what Hammer said about the vibe. Flip seems to be orienting himself so he's close to me and Quinn is not.

Afterward, we congregate in the common room with mugs of spiked hot chocolate, and once again, Flip sits next to me. He and Tristan have been exchanging meaningful looks that would be easy to miss if I wasn't so tuned in to Flip.

"We could play a game," Dred suggests.

"We're not playing board games. You kick everyone's ass every time," Flip says.

"What about hide-and-seek?" Everly suggests, then ducks her head. "Or maybe that's too kiddish."

"I'm in," Dallas says.

"Same!" Flip agrees.

"This place is perfect for hiding and seeking," I add.

Everyone else seems excited too, and Everly's answering grin warms my heart. We pick numbers to determine the first seeker. Connor is closest, so the role falls to him.

"You have to stay inside the house, and no hiding in other people's bedrooms." Connor dims the lights on the main floor. "Any other rules we should lay down?"

"You can't steal someone else's spot once they're in it," Rix says.

"Sounds good." Connor turns to face the wall. "I'll count to one hundred. Get to hiding!"

Everyone scatters, the guys yelling after each other. Everly's gleeful giggles bounce off the walls.

"Find your own spot, Dallas!" Hemi calls.

I rush upstairs, along with a handful of other people. I wait until most of our friends have found their spot before I start searching for my own. Sometimes it's best to hide in plain sight.

I peek my head into a small sitting room. A huge barrel chair is set in front of an enormous window. To the left is a small alcove with a door that's been covered in the same wallpaper as the rest of the space, so it's nearly seamless, apart from the ornate knob.

I open it as Connor calls out seventy-nine. Spare bathrobes hang in a neat row. Connor calls out eighty-two. I'm running out of time, so I duck into the closet, pull the door closed behind me, and tuck my body behind the robes.

Connor's voice is muffled, but I finally hear, "Ready or not, here I come!"

A moment later, the closet door opens and another person pushes into the small space. "Fuck, shit." Flip pulls the door closed with a quiet *snick*. The metal hangers clink against each other.

"Flip, shh," I whisper. I don't want to be the first one found.

"Talls?" He bangs his arm against something.

"Shh. Yeah." I tap the rod with my nail. "You have to duck to get under this." His silky hair brushes my fingers as he does.

The hangers tinkle loudly. He mutters more profanity.

The space was cramped with just me, but now it's impossible to move without touching him. My stomach twists with fresh nerves and anticipation.

"Sorry," he says. "I didn't mean to steal your spot."

"It's okay," I whisper. "You're here now. Let's just stay quiet." I try to calm my breathing, but it sounds loud in my ears.

Tension sparks like a live wire between us as his fingers skim my arm. "You okay?"

I nod, then realize he can't see the movement in the dark. "Yeah," I breathe.

His fingers continue to drift up my arm, sending a hot shiver down my spine. They sweep over my shoulder and brush my neck. I don't know what's happening, but I don't want it to stop.

He drops his head, and his cheek brushes mine until his lips are at my ear. I exhale a shuddery breath at the closeness and the contact.

His voice is a barely audible whisper, warm minty breath

breaking across my skin. "Feels karmic to end up in here with you."

"You can't escape me today, can you?" I murmur.

"Or maybe you can't escape me," he counters.

He cups my cheek in his palm, the tension between us visceral.

"Maybe it's me who keeps seeking you out," he whispers. "Even though I shouldn't."

"I don't mind being trapped in here with you," I whisper.

"Fuck, Talls." His voice is a pained whisper as his thumb sweeps along the edge of my jaw. "You're breaking me down."

I suck in a breath as my heart gallops and races. "I'm not trying to."

"Not even with that bikini today?"

"That was an accident. I packed the wrong bottoms."

He chuckles darkly, his lips brushing my hot cheek. "I believe you, your blush is your truth serum."

His other hand finds mine and he laces our fingers. All I want is to feel his lips on mine.

I tip my chin up.

His warm, minty breath breaks across my mouth.

Will he kiss me?

Please kiss me.

"I've been trying to see you the way I used to." His admission is full of the same longing that makes my chest ache. "But I can't anymore." He raises our clasped hands and presses mine against his cheek.

"How do you see me now?" My voice wavers with nerves and excitement.

"In ways I shouldn't." His lips touch the corner of my mouth. "Please, Talls, tell me not to do this."

"But I don't want to." I hold my breath. Will he crack or run?

"Fuck, kitten." His hot palm curves around the back of my

neck. "Why can't I stay away from you?" His lips hover over mine, and time suspends.

I skim the shell of his ear. "Maybe you're not supposed to."

His groan is pained, but before his lips touch mine, the closet door swings open. Flip shoves away from me as the robes part.

"Found you!" Connor's gleeful grin drops as his eyes flit between us.

"Fuck." Guilt laces the word and Flip's expression as he pushes past Connor and disappears down the hall.

"I'm sorry, Tally," Connor says, looking after him.

I shrug and smile, though it feels like my heart just took a right hook. "Curse of the coach's daughter."

CHAPTER 11

TALLY

I've replayed the almost kiss a thousand times over the past week and envisioned endless scenarios where it didn't end with Flip guilt-riddled and me sad. I'm unsure what's worse, knowing the attraction isn't one-sided or that we'll never be more than friends. And now I don't even know if we can be that.

Flip left the following morning before anyone else woke up, and I haven't heard from him since.

My final semester has started, and I'm throwing myself head-first into coursework. I'm focused on dance, getting through the semester, and not fixating on how Flip almost kissed me, or the way my family is in shambles.

I have nearly daily phone calls with my sister, who vacillates between tears of anger and confusion. I hate that I'm relieved that I don't have to manage her feelings for more than half an hour. Ties is coping by spending all his spare time with his robotics team.

The subway stops, pulling me back to the present. I exit the train and join the sea of people heading home from work. I haven't seen my dad since Christmas, and he begged me to have dinner with him. I can't get out from under this anger blanket if we don't talk. I'm also worried about the team and Lexi and Hammer and Hemi, who work in the front office with him. It's not my job to manage everything for everyone else, but I also don't want to make the problem worse. So I'm on my way to the Terror office.

I adjust my toque and step out into the blustery January evening. It's only four thirty, and the sun is already setting. This is my least favorite time of year. The frigid temperatures, the bone-chilling wind, and the short days deplete me. Add in all the other stuff, and the stress is an impossible weight.

I scurry out of the cold and take the elevator to the office floor, but I stop outside my dad's door, and center myself before I alert him to my presence. He's wearing reading glasses, pen tapping against his bottom lip, his focus on the papers in front of him. Despite being over six feet tall and built for sports, he somehow looks older and frailer. Like a regular man, not the super dad I used to believe in. It breaks my heart that my rose-tinted glasses are gone.

He looks up before I knock, and his expression brightens. "Tallulah. Come on in, kiddo."

Roman sometimes calls Hammer kiddo, but it sounds different coming from him. I don't know why it irks me when my dad does it. Maybe because Roman puts so much effort in, and my dad doesn't.

He pushes away from his desk and stands, rounding it to hug me. It's wooden and awkward. I miss the way things used to be, but I don't. I've always been a pleaser, seeking his approval. Maybe because it meant for a few minutes, his attention was on me instead of the team. He's never been present enough for us to be close, and it took my parents separating for me to see that.

He squeezes my shoulders before stepping back. "How are you?"

"Okay." It's not even the truth. I throw the question back at him. "And you?"

He motions to the desk. "Keeping busy."

"So same old same old?" Apparently, I don't feel much like giving grace today.

He sighs. "I'm not good at balance."

"No, you're not," I agree.

"I'm sorry, Tally."

"You didn't even fight for us." We didn't meet at a restaurant, I had to come to his office first.

"Honey, you don't understand," he starts.

"You were never around, and even when you were, you weren't really present. Your whole focus has always been hockey. We were just side dishes." I fling a hand toward his desk. "Why aren't you trying to fix it now instead of burying yourself in work?"

He crosses his arms. "Did you just agree to dinner so you could pick a fight with me?"

"Did you think you could just rip our family apart and expect me not to have feelings about it?"

"I know you're hurting."

"How do you know? Because you've asked me? Because we've had a conversation? Do you just want me to pretend everything is fine?"

"I don't want every interaction we have to be a battle."

"And I want you to be a better dad. I guess neither of us gets what we want." This was a bad idea, I'm not ready for this.

His face falls, but before he can answer, there's a knock on his door.

"Hey, Coach!" Flip appears in the office doorway. "Oh sh— sugar. I'm sorry. I didn't mean to interrupt."

He's wearing black pants, a long-sleeved shirt, and a peacoat. He looks incredible, and it makes my heart hurt even more. Everything I want is out of reach.

"Hey, Talls." He lifts his hand in an awkward wave.

I want to sink into the floor. "Hi, Flip."

"I can come back later." Flip's eyes move between me and my dad. "Or tomorrow."

"It's okay. We can chat now," Dad says.

I'm sure my disappointment is written all over my face.

Maybe this is why my parents' relationship is over. If Dad's default is to jump ship at the first sign of turmoil, how impossible would it be to resolve their issues?

Dad's phone rings.

"Hold on a second." He lifts a finger—for whom I'm unsure—and takes the call.

I glance at Flip, and he glances at me. Then we both look away.

This day could not get any worse.

"Can't it wait until tomorrow?" Dad's brows pull together. "Yeah. I understand." He pinches the bridge of his nose. "No, no, it's fine. I'm on my way." He ends the call and grimaces. "I'm so sorry. I have an emergency meeting. Rain check, honey?"

Or maybe it can get worse. "Whatever." I brush past Flip and head for the elevator. Fuck this bullshit.

"Tallulah!" Dad calls after me.

I keep walking because yelling at him is an embarrassment neither of us needs.

Flip says something, but I don't catch it.

I stab the elevator button until the doors open and throw myself inside. I rocket punch the close doors, but Flip's hand appears before they can, and he steps inside with me. And then it's just the two of us and all of my exceptionally large feelings stuck in a box together.

"That looked tense," he observes.

"Yup." I wrap my arms around myself, as if it will keep me from falling apart.

"Are you okay?" His voice is gentle, piteous.

I hate it. "I'm fine."

"Talls."

I can't decide if I want to scream or cry.

"Do you need a ride home?" Flip asks.

"I'm good." Definitely cry.

I try to brush past him as we step off the elevator.

"Please let me drive you home," Flip says.

I bite my lips together, fighting the stupid tears that threaten to embarrass me. He's already witnessed two of my worst moments, why not add another? "Okay. Thank you."

I follow him to his car.

"Did your dad bail on you?" Flip asks.

"Yup. And he was ready to bail on me for you first, so I guess I know where I sit on his list of priorities."

"He loves you, Tally," Flip says gently.

"He's terrible at showing it. He's used to everyone bending for him. He's always in charge. Except he's not in charge of my feelings, so he's running away from them, and me, and that really fucking hurts." And didn't Flip do the same thing at New Year's?

"I'm sorry." Flip's fingers brush the back of my hand.

I step out of reach. "I don't need your pity, Flip."

Everything about him softens. "That's not what this is."

"Isn't it, though? I came all the way here and my dad blew me off, I feel sorry enough for me for the both of us."

The drive to my apartment is tense. I have so many things I want to say, but I'm too shredded to form the right thoughts. Everything hurts, and I'm too much in my feelings. Flip is taking care of me again, which levels up my anger at my dad.

He pulls up in front of my building and turns to me. "Tally, about what happened at New—"

"Please don't, Phillip. My heart won't survive another hit right now." I can't handle hearing him say he's sorry for almost kissing me. For giving me the wrong impression. "Thanks for the ride."

I leave the car before he can say any of those things.

CHAPTER 12
FLIP

Tally races up the steps to her apartment building. Running away from me the same way I ran from her on New Year's. I can't keep doing this.

All week I've been off. Struggling to sleep, to eat, to not think about how good it felt to spend time with her at the lodge. To not fixate on how close I'd been to finding out how soft her pretty lips are. I miss our text conversations over books, her laugh, the way her face lights up when she's excited about something. I miss *her*.

I can't see her as Coach's Off-Limits Daughter anymore. Not after New Year's. I was territorial, possessive, I wanted her all to myself.

I *want* her all to myself.

My craving for her, *be more to her*, is almost unbearable.

I don't want to shut her out or shut her down. Not again. Seeing her today settled me for the first time since New Year's. I can't let her run away.

Everything I've been afraid of—messing with our friend group, the wrath of my teammates, her dad murdering me—all of it pales in comparison to the pervasive fucking ache that's rooted in my chest. And the idea of someone else stepping in to claim her heart, I can't let it happen. I won't. Whatever shitstorm I bring on, I'll weather it. She's more than worth the risk. And it's about time I showed her.

I park in the closest public lot and follow someone into her building. I helped move Tally into this apartment, along with the rest of the Terror guys and her girlfriends. There's a common space to the right of the entrance, along with a café, a pharmacy, and a couple of fast-food restaurants where students mill around. I keep my head down and wait for the elevator.

I'm joined by half a dozen students, all with full backpacks. A guy who's at least a head taller than everyone else, wearing a Tilton Hockey baseball cap, tips his head.

I glance at him, give him a small smile, and nod.

His eyes flare as he registers who I am.

Thankfully we reach Tally's floor, and I step out before he says anything.

The smell of burned toast, pizza, and something sweet fills the hall. I stop outside Tally's apartment and run my hands down my thighs, suddenly nervous. What I'm about to do will change things again. Not being able to just pull her into my arms and hug her almost fucking killed me back at the Terror office. I want to be the person she comes to when she's hurting. I want to be in her text messages every day. The alternative is unthinkable.

I knock on her door.

The silence stretches on for so long I worry I have the wrong apartment. But eventually I hear footfalls and a muffled, "Oh, God." Followed by, "Just a second!"

Another minute passes before the door swings open.

Tally's eyes are red-rimmed, and her voice is hoarse. "Did I leave something in your car?"

I shove my hands in my pockets so I don't give in and tuck her hair behind her ear—I'm no creep. "No."

"Oh." Her fluffy cat tries to dart between us, but she scoops him up before he can make an escape.

I have a lot of things I want to say but easing into it is probably best. "Would you like to grab a bite to eat?"

She blinks, and blinks again. "With you?"

I nod. "Yeah. I'd like to take you out for dinner, but only if you're up for it." Ordering in is an option, but being alone with her in her apartment will test my personal restraint, and I've come to realize that when Tally is vulnerable, she channels it in one direction, and saying no to her isn't something I enjoy.

"Like to a restaurant?" She looks shocked and hopeful.

"Yeah, exactly."

"Are you doing this because you feel sorry for me?" Her voice is barely a whisper.

"No, Talls. That reason isn't anywhere on the list. I want to spend time with you."

"Why?"

"Why?" I echo.

She nods, still hugging her squirming cat.

"Because I miss you. Because the past week has been awful. Because staying away from you is killing me," I admit.

"Oh," she breathes.

"So what do you say? Want to have dinner with me?"

Her sadness melts away and the most beautiful smile lights up her face. I want to be responsible for making her happy every day.

"I'd love to go for dinner with you, Phillip."

CHAPTER 13
TALLY

I usher Flip into my apartment and close the door so I can release Parsnip, who is clawing my arms in an attempt to escape them. He does a backflip off my chest and promptly rubs himself on Flip's legs. Show-off.

"Do you want to come in? Can I get you anything?"

"I'm good. Why don't you just grab what you need." Flip tucks one hand in his pocket, a smile kicking up the corner of his perfectly luscious mouth as Parsnip continues to rub himself on his shins.

"I'll grab my purse." *And fix my face.*

"Okay."

I walk backwards a couple of steps. "I'll be right back."

"I'll be right here with my new best friend."

"His name is Parsnip, and he loves pets."

"We have that in common, then."

I almost trip over one of Parsnip's many toy mice. "I won't be long."

I rush down the hall and throw myself into my bedroom, making sure Parsnip hasn't followed me before I gently close the door. I grab my Flip body pillow from my bed, run to the bathroom, shut that door too, and scream into the soft fabric. "Oh my God, oh my God, *oh my God*."

I hold Flip's two-dimensional face at arm's length. "We are going out for dinner!"

He smirks back at me.

"Is this a date? Should I call it a date? I don't even know."

What if I'm having some kind of episode? What if I'm hallucinating?

I open the bathroom door and shove my Flip pillow into the closet, in case this isn't a fabrication of my mine, tucking it behind my clothes. I take a deep centering breath, then quietly open my bedroom door, and peek into the hall. Parsnip slips through the crack.

Flip's back is to me, and he's perusing my bookshelf.

Flip is in my apartment, and we are going out for dinner.

Just the two of us.

This is like…a dream come true. It's everything I've ever wanted, and it's happening right now.

I close the door again and slide down my wall, my legs suddenly too unsteady to hold me up. I'm instantly sweaty. Parsnip climbs in my lap. "Holy shit, 'Snip." I cuddle him. "I don't even know what this means."

I do some deep breathing and finally peel myself off the floor and force my unsteady legs to carry me to the bathroom. I cringe at my reflection and set Parsnip on the vanity. "I need to manage these eyes." They're puffy from crying.

Parsnip meows and taps the faucet, unconcerned with my face. I turn the water on, and he sticks his head under the thin stream, letting it run down his forehead like a weirdo as he drinks from the sink.

I fire off a message to my group chat with Fee, Cammie and Enid, because I can't keep this to myself.

TALLY

I have to tell you something, but it must stay under the cone, which means Chase can't know.

CAMMIE

My lips are sealed.

FEE

Same.

ENID

Me three.

TALLY

Flip just asked me out for dinner.

FEE

OMFGGGGGGGG

CAMMIE

FUCK YES! I'VE BEEN WAITING FOR THIS!

ENID

This is the Christmas miracle we've all been hoping for! Or New Year's miracle.

FEE

When? How? We need details!

CAMMIE

^^^This.

ENID

Tell us all the things!

TALLY

Just now. He's in my apartment.

HE'S STANDING IN MY APARTMENT!

I have to get ready. I'll fill you in when I get home, though.

FEE

This is so epic!

ENID

You're my hero!

CAMMIE

Get 'em, girl! Channel your inner Arwen!

TALLY

I love you girls! Wish me luck!

CAMMIE

You don't need luck when you're a smoke show. 🔥

FEE

^^^This, but also ALL THE LUCK.

ENID

confetti GIF

I set my phone aside and do some quick makeup surgery to help with the redness. The puffiness is a problem that will have to resolve itself. I change my sweater from something dad dinner-appropriate to something Flip dinner-appropriate. This one has a V-neck that highlights my modest cleavage. Face and wardrobe managed, I return to the living room.

Flip is leafing through one of my textbooks on the dining room table.

"Ready!" My voice shakes with excitement and anxiety.

He closes the textbook, and his eyes lift. "You look beautiful."

My stomach feels like a blender on full speed. "Thanks. So do you." I cringe. "I mean hot. Or handsome."

He grins, and I blush.

I drop my purse on the table. "I'll just feed Parsnip, and then we can go."

"Sure." He looks too delicious for words.

I quickly spoon some stinky wet food into Parsnip's dish while he meows loudly and weaves between my legs. I barely set the plate down, before he starts chewing noisily.

"You have no manners," I chastise.

"But he's cute."

"Yeah, he is." I grab Flip's wrist and nearly pass out from the contact. "We only have a few seconds before Parsnip realizes we're leaving. Then he'll engage lightning mode and try to make a run for the hall."

"Like a jailbreak?" Flip slips his feet into his shoes while I tuck mine into a pair of heeled boots.

"Exactly." I grab my jacket and put my hand on the knob. "We have to be quick, or we'll spend the next twenty minutes corralling him."

"I have pretty good reflexes." Flip looks highly amused.

"So does 'Snip." I drop my voice to a whisper. "Ready?"

He gives me a thumbs-up. He has no idea.

I turn the knob, yank the door open, and shove Flip into the hall. Parsnip meows and bolts around the corner, rushing toward us at warp speed. "Shit. He's coming in hot!" I grab him around the middle and toss him back inside, pulling the door closed. Parsnip wails mournfully on the other side of the door, nails dragging obnoxiously down the steel. He continues to yowl like he's dying.

"Wow," Flip says.

"Yeah. He needed a home and a lot of love and I couldn't leave him in the shelter for the rest of his adorable, demonic life."

"How long had he been in the shelter?"

Every time I glance at Flip, he smiles at me. "Too long. He can't really be around other animals. He was one more bite away from being put down, so he became mine."

We walk down the hall together, my nerves on overdrive now that I'm not trying to keep my wily cat from escaping. My stomach is behaving like I'm on a tilt-a-whirl. This is literally a dream come true. I'm overwhelmed and I have so many questions.

The elevator comes right away, but it's far from empty. I would suggest waiting for the next one, except it's dinnertime, so it'll be busy like this for the next hour. Flip's fingers press gently against the dip in my spine as we step inside the already mostly full box. This is a student apartment complex, and everyone who lives here attends Tilton.

"Holy shit," some guy mutters.

"What?" his friend asks.

The guy tips his head in our direction.

His friend's eyes widen when they land on Flip and shift to me.

Flip pulls me into his side, and dips down until his lips are at my ear. "We probably should have taken the stairs, eh?"

I giggle and force my knees to lock, since they've turned to Jell-O.

"Flip Madden." The guy's voice is laced with awe.

"Hey." Flip nods his acknowledgement.

Two girls wear confused looks. Another is suddenly very interested. I turn to Flip, and his grip on my waist tightens. Protectively. Possessively, even. He's wearing the same look he was when Quinn slung me over his shoulder at the lodge.

Thankfully we reach the lobby, and he ushers me out of the elevator, arm still around me as he guides me to the front entrance.

We make it outside without causing a scene. I zip my jacket, the heat dissipating quickly in the frigid January evening.

"Dinner rush is probably not the best time for someone like you to take the elevators," I muse. Tilton's hockey team is like royalty here.

Flip shrugs. "I'm used to it. Do you have a place you'd like to go for dinner?" We walk briskly to the public parking lot.

"Wherever is fine with me. We probably want to put a little distance between us and the campus, though."

"Good call. It wouldn't be much fun if we get mobbed." He opens the passenger door for me.

I duck inside and wait until he's behind the wheel before I throw out options. "What about the Pancake House, or the Watering Hole?"

"I like both of those but more when we're going out with friends." He stretches his arm across the back of my seat. "And tonight, I just want to spend time with you."

I'm about to melt into the seat.

"But wherever we end up tonight, this isn't our first date, Tally."

"Oh. Okay. Just friends having dinner," I mutter.

"Friends don't almost kiss friends in closets, kitten." He tucks a finger under my chin and urges me to look at him. "What I mean, is that when I take you on a first date, it will be one to remember, and not because of unlimited salad and bread."

Flip doesn't take me to East Side's. Instead, we end up at an Italian restaurant that looks like a hole in the wall from the outside, but soft lighting and private booths make the interior intimate and cozy.

"This is still not our first date," Flip tells me as he spreads his napkin over his lap.

"It's a pretty nice not-first-date."

"Well, I feel like I have some making up to do, so we can call it apology step one dinner out." He stretches his arm across the back of my chair. "Have you ever had a limoncello spritz?"

I shake my head. God, I'm overwhelmed.

"Do you want to try one?"

His fingers slide under my hair and his thumb strokes absently up and down. It's instantly soothing. "Yes, please."

"God, you're fucking beautiful." He kisses the edge of my jaw.

I could literally die happy now.

Before I can return the compliment, the server appears. Flip tucks me tighter into his side. "I'll take a Peroni and she'll have the limoncello spritz."

The server glances nervously between us. "Um, I'll need to check your ID."

I'm used to being carded, so I immediately reach for my purse.

"She's twenty-one, she'll be twenty-two on August eleventh," Flip says with a practiced smile.

I thrill a little that he knows my birthday so easily. I pat his thigh under the table. "It's okay. It's his job to check." I pass over my license.

The poor server fumbles and nearly drops it. "Thank you, Miss Vander Zee. I'll be right back with your drinks."

"Thanks, buddy." Flip gives him a chin tip.

I wait until he's gone before I turn my attention to Flip, eyes wide with my sort of disapproval. "You can turn your alpha-pack leader down a notch."

He gazes down at me with dark eyes, a slight grin tugging at the corner of his mouth. "Do you think I don't know what that means?"

My eyes flare. I have not shared my love of omegaverse with him.

"Kitten, you are ungodly gorgeous, and I am not the only person who notices this. There are enough boys falling all over themselves to get to you, I won't have our server being one of them."

"He just carded me. It's not like he's flirting with me."

"Not in front of me if he wants to keep all his limbs."

"Oh my God, who are you?"

"The man who can't stop thinking about you." He kisses the inside of my wrist, eyebrows slanting. "I bet he's looking you up on social media."

"He is not." I try to pull my hand away.

"I would if I were him." He gently bites the side of my hand and winks as our poor mortified server drops off our drinks. I'm so flustered.

"Would you like more time with the menus or are you ready to order?" our server asks the candle in the middle of the table.

"How do you feel about an appetizer, kitten?" He's still holding my hand.

"Yeah. Yes. Sure. That would be nice."

"Do you like arancini?"

"I do."

"Me, too." He kisses my knuckle.

"An order of arancini to start. Anything else?" Our server's eyes dart around.

"How about calamari?" Flip's thumb sweeps back and forth along my pulse point.

"I also like calamari."

"Perfect." Flip's gaze stays firmly fixed on me. "We'll take an order of that as well."

"Yes, sir."

"Anything else you'd like, Tallulah?"

I'm pretty sure my panties are trying to grow legs so they can walk off my body and into his pocket. "No, thank you."

"That will be all for now, thank you."

"Of course, sir." The server bows and rushes off.

I turn my attention back to Flip. "You know you don't have to treat every guy like they're a threat."

His eyebrows rise. "What if they are?"

"Like Quinn?" I needle.

He has the decency to look momentarily apologetic, but his expression smooths out. "You've met Lovey Butterson."

"They're like childhood friends," I argue.

"Tristan and my sister have known each other their whole

lives, so have Dallas and Hemi," he points out. "And you and Lovey share some physical attributes."

"Like our hair color," I scoff.

"You're both lean and athletic. You're beautiful, and fun, and easy to be around. Quinn was very friendly with you, and while most of the time I believe he would stay on the right side of the line with you, under the right circumstances, or the wrong ones, he might crack under the pressure."

"Is that what you're doing? Cracking under the pressure?" I ask softly.

He kisses the back of my hand. I feel that point of contact everywhere and all I want is for him to lean in and kiss my lips.

"You opened a door when you asked me for a favor."

"I'm—"

"No apologies. You're done with those," he orders. "You opened my eyes, and I couldn't close them again. Lord knows I fucking tried, kitten. But every time I saw you after that, I couldn't stop seeing *you*." He gently strokes my cheek. "I hated when things were strained between us. I wanted things to go back to the way they were. I wanted text messages and book recommendations. And I sure as fuck didn't want to push you into one of my teammates' arms, or anyone else's, for that matter. I'd never forgive myself if that happened." His jaw works and he swallows thickly, eyes softening. "And then tonight you were right in front of me and you felt a million miles away, and you were hurting and I couldn't just…wrap my arms around you and be the person to tell you it would be okay, and I hated it. I realized there was only one way to fix it. So here we are."

"Here we are," I echo. I'm elated, stunned and just...

"Kitten?" He sweeps his thumb along the hollow under my eye.

"Please don't let this be a dream," I whisper.

He pulls me closer and wraps me in his strong embrace,

surrounding me with his sandalwood and mint scent. "I'm not a knight in shining armor."

"Knights are kind of overrated."

He squeezes me and sits back. "Am I overwhelming you?"

"Not in a bad way." I gather my thoughts. "So much of my life is suddenly in upheaval. What's happening with my family, the way my dad shuffled me to the bottom of his pile is…painful, and then you show up, and I expected it to be more rejection, but it's the opposite, and it's amazing, and I'm scared, and I just don't want to lose what we have, not when I've already lost so much."

"That makes perfect sense." He tucks my hair behind my ear. "We're just going to have a nice dinner, and we're going to hang out and enjoy each other's company, and I'm not going to fight this chemistry because it was making me a miserable, territorial ass."

"I don't mind the territorial part," I admit.

"Good to know, it's tough to get a handle on sometimes." He winks and settles back in his chair as our server brings our appetizers to the table.

"Would you like to order your mains?" he asks.

I turn to Flip. "I haven't even looked at the menu."

"There's no rush, we have lots of time. You can give us a few minutes," Flip assures him.

"Of course." He leaves us with our appetizers.

"Can I serve you?" Flip offers.

"If you want to." I sit back, enthralled with this version of the man I've come to know.

He plates an arancini for me, spooning extra red sauce over it. His eyes stay fixed on me as I cut into the crispy outside, the cheesy inside pooling in the sauce. I cut a small bite and pop it in my mouth.

"Is it good?"

I cut another bite and hold it out for him. "Try it."

His full lips close over the tines.

He hums his approval and takes the fork from me. "Will you let me feed you?"

"Is this like your version of foreplay?" My eyes flare and my cheeks burn hot.

His smile turns downright lascivious. "Head out of the gutter, kitten." He cuts another small bite, feeding it to me. "I like the way you savor things. I think because of the way I grew up, food has always held a lot of power."

"Because sometimes you didn't have enough?" I ask softly.

He nods and pops another bite before cutting one for me. "Things were always tight. Tristan constantly brought food over. Rix learned to cook at a young age. There's something very primal and satisfying about providing for someone I care about."

My stomach flutters and my bruised heart soars.

We finally order mains, I choose the gnocchi and Flip orders the vodka pollo pasta. There are no leftovers, and we finish the meal with a chocolate torte that Flip eats most of. I don't want dinner or the evening to end, but we close down the restaurant, so there's no other option but to leave.

I stop in the bathroom and message Fee to let her know I'm on the way home.

FEE

At Cammie's. Message when it's safe. Brought all the things I need for a sleepover if necessary. *fingers crossed*

Flip is waiting for me at the front door. He links his arm with mine and walks me to his car, holding the door open as I take my spot in the passenger seat. This is literally the most amazing non-first-date I've ever been on, and I hate that it's coming to an end.

By some miracle, the ten-minute spot at the front of my building is open, so he pulls into it and cuts the engine. "I'll walk you up."

"I'd love that." Then I can invite him in.

The atrium is quiet, most people having returned to their apartments for the night. The elevator is empty, and my body hums with nerves as I watch the floors climb.

My mouth goes dry as the elevator doors slide open and all the anxiety I thought I left at the restaurant comes flooding back. Flip's fingers stay pressed against the small of my back on the way down the hall. I fumble with my key fob but manage not to drop it as I swipe my key over the sensor and open the door, but only a few inches so Parsnip can't escape.

What happens now?

"Thank you for taking me out for dinner." I clasp my hands so I don't wring them.

Flip smiles. "Thank you for saying yes."

"I had a really nice time." I bite my lip. *Is it too much to invite him in?*

"I had a great time, too." His palm curves against my cheek, and his thumb sweeps along the edge of my jaw. My entire body sparks with need. Desire. Anticipation. "Can I kiss you good night, Talls?"

"Yes, please," I practically moan.

His warm lips brush over mine.

I grip his shoulders and melt into him as he gently sucks my bottom lip. Then he angles his head, and his tongue is a velvet caress. He tastes like mint and chocolate. My knees go weak, and heat blossoms low in my belly.

It's the perfect first kiss. Soft, sweet, gentle, commanding. His hand curves around my waist, and he pulls me tighter against him, the door at my back and him pressed to my front.

Phillip Madden is kissing me. I'm kissing Phillip Madden.

He walks me backwards into my apartment at the sound of voices in the hall. I nudge Parsnip out of the way so he can't make an escape and ruin a perfect good night kiss.

Flip doesn't stop kissing me as the door falls closed. His lips are soft and sure, his hands firm but gentle. I feel like I'm burning up from the inside. I can't get enough of the taste of him, of the feel of his tongue sliding against mine, or his body pressing me into the wall.

He pulls back and cages me with his arms, gazing down at me with hot eyes. "A kiss is as far as this goes tonight, Tally."

I blink up at him, momentarily stunned and suddenly uncertain. "Did I do something wrong?"

"No, kitten." He kisses my cheek and sighs. "But I have to be honest with you about something."

"Okay." He looks so serious. I swallow down my nerves.

"When you asked me to take your virginity, I thought it was only because of my experience, and that hurt more than I expected it to."

"I'm so sorry," I croak, mortified all over again.

"I know. And I know it wasn't intentional. I have baggage, more than you realize probably. I loved someone once, and she didn't want me for me, and that…broke me for a long time. I spent a lot of years seeking pleasure with no connection, and I can't go there again. Especially not with you. So I need you to let me go at my pace, okay?"

"Okay," I whisper.

"We're going to take this real slow, kitten." He kisses each knuckle and presses my palm to his cheek.

My knees go weak at the sweet affection.

He brushes his lips over mine. "I'm going to kiss you one last time, and then I'm going home."

"Can this one be a little longer then?" I ask.

"One taste of you, Tally, and I'm already addicted." He slants his mouth over mine.

It's better than the first kiss. I'm obsessed with the feel of his lips, the softness of his tongue as he explores my mouth. The gentle way he touches me. He wraps his free arm around my waist and holds me against him as our tongues brush.

It's the perfect good night kiss.

The kind that leaves me aching and needy.

Desperate for more of him.

Eventually he pulls back, and the dark look in his eyes nearly brings me to my knees.

He strokes my cheek one last time. "'Night, Tally."

"'Night, Phillip."

CHAPTER 14

TALLY

The door falls closed behind Flip.

I lean against the wall and debate whether this whole night has been a fever dream. How can this be real life?

I pinch my arm. "Ow." Nope. Not a fever dream.

Flip kissed me. Flip kissed *me*. Flip *kissed* me.

What happens now? Will he call or text? When will I see him again? What happens when I see him again? These are all questions I should have asked, but I was too discombobulated by the kiss. I lick my lips. I can still taste Flip. Feel him. Smell his cologne.

A knock on the door startles me. Maybe he came back. Maybe he wants another kiss. Or more than another kiss.

I throw the door open without checking the peephole first. "Mom? What are you doing here?"

She looks…sad and determined. I'm the spitting image of my mother. We have the same narrow frame, same hair, same eyes. "I wanted to see you." She holds out a cardboard box. "And bring you a care package."

I step aside to let her in, flummoxed and still reeling from the kiss and now my mother's surprise arrival. Parsnip rushes by and slips out the door.

"Fuck! We can't let him make it to the elevator."

"I'm so sorry. I forgot how wily he is." Mom uses the box to prop open the door and I grab his kitty treats.

He's already at the other end of the hall. I shake the treats and call his name, sprinting after him. "You guard the elevators, I'll try to corral him!" When I lived at home, Parsnip believed all doors led to happiness. Usually he didn't make it very far, the gardens too alluring for a house kitty, but here it's just door after door, new smells, and lots of potential new friends who want to give him pets.

"Parsnip! Come back, buddy! I have treats for you!" I shake the container.

The elevator dings. Parsnip's ears perk up.

I glance over my shoulder and hope like hell it isn't Flip coming back and that my mom can prevent my escape artist of a cat from going for a ride. It's happened before. It was a harrowing, endless hour of searching.

I drop the container of treats, which spill out onto the carpet. I narrowly miss grabbing Parsnip around the middle as he darts past me, heading toward my mom. Cammie's apartment door opens and Parsnip corrects course, launching himself through the opening.

"Got 'em!" Fee exclaims.

"Oh, thank God," I heave a sigh of relief and quickly sweep the treats back into the container.

My mom hugs Cammie, who looks over her shoulder with questions in her eyes, which I will have to answer later. After my visit with my mom. I'm sure my friends are dying to find out what's going on.

Mom takes Parsnip, who snuggles into her and starts purring up a storm.

Such a traitor.

"I'll text in a bit," I mutter to Fee and Cammie.

They give me the thumbs-up.

Mom and I return to my apartment with Parsnip. "Can I get you something to drink? Tea? Soda? Water? A cooler?"

"Tea would be nice."

I set water to boil and pull out two mugs.

"Did Dad text you or something?"

"He did, and I'm sorry he didn't prioritize you over work, but that's not the main reason I'm here." She leans against the counter. "We need to talk."

I sigh. I should have expected this. "I'm mad at you."

She nods and her eyes turn glassy. "I know."

"Why didn't you say anything sooner? Why didn't you tell me first?" That hurts the most.

The kettle boils and Mom steps in to pour water into our mugs. "Because I didn't want to put that on you."

I voice the question that's been plaguing me. "Is it my fault you're splitting up? Is it because I moved out for university?"

She sets the kettle down and turns to me. "No, honey. You and your brother and sister aren't the problem. My relationship with your dad is the problem, and I didn't want to make it yours, because for the majority of your life, I did."

"I don't know what that means."

"We have always been close, Tallulah, and you have always been the kind of person who steps in to help and take care of people. You're a lot like me, but I should never have relied on you the way I did. It wasn't fair to you, or your brother or sister, or even your dad. My inability to tell him what I needed and why is the reason our marriage failed. He is a great guy and an amazing friend, but he's not a good partner for me."

"He should have fought for us, he should have put us first."

"I made it easy for him to shirk his parental and fatherly duties by letting you be my coparent. You moving out has been good for our relationship because it allowed you a reprieve from the responsibility that was forced on you. We needed a little space from each other, and Ties and Fenna needed to see you as a sister and not another mom."

"I'm really fucking mad at Dad." My chin wobbles, and tears spill over.

"I know, give yourself time to feel all the feelings. He really fucked it up today. He should have said no to whatever work call came in."

"He was ready to blow me off for Flip Madden before he even took the call. Maybe that meeting would have taken five minutes, but still."

Mom's nostrils flare. "Don't do what I did with your dad. Confront him and make him own his choices. He is not to blame for all of this. If I'd been honest about my feelings, he would have tried to change, but I never gave him the chance."

"And it's too late, now?" I ask, still stupidly hopeful.

"Twenty-five years of being less important than his job is too much to get past." She smiles sadly. "I don't want you to resent your dad, Tally. I was going to do that anyways because I'm the one who lived it the entire time."

"I really hate this," I admit.

"Me, too, baby. But your dad and I are better as friends. Right now there are a lot of hard feelings to sort through, but we'll get there. I promise." She opens her arms and I fall into them.

"I missed you," I whisper.

"Me, too, but I want to work on building a better mother-daughter relationship with you. One where you're not picking up the slack for your dad with your brother and sister."

"I'd like that."

We hug for long minutes until we're both sniffling. I grab us tissues and unpack the care package.

I survey the counter. There are cookies, cinnamon buns, fresh bread, and a whole cake. "Have you been on a baking kick?"

"What would give you that idea?"

We both giggle.

"It's good half my friends play for the hockey team and have bottomless pits."

"Ties said something similar about his robotics friends."

"How's he doing?"

"Okay. Staying busy with robotics and Fenna is focused on cello."

"And you?"

"I'm better now that we've talked. I didn't want to assume you were okay, especially when I knew you probably weren't."

My phone buzzes in my back pocket with a call. My stomach twists as dad's name flashes across the screen. What if someone snapped a photo of me and Flip together and he already knows he took me out for dinner?

"You should answer that. It's late and I need to get home anyway."

"You're sure?"

"Positive. Tell him how you feel, he can and should handle it. I'll make sure Parsnip doesn't escape on my way out." She kisses me on the cheek.

I take a steadying breath and answer the call. "Hey, Dad."

"I'm so sorry I had to cancel dinner, honey. You made it home okay, though?"

"It's been hours, Dad. Have you been working this whole time and just realized you ditched me?"

"I got pulled into a call, and then some emails—"

I cut him off. "I don't want excuses. If you're calling to find out if I made it home okay, I did. Flip is a responsible driver." And an excellent kisser.

Dad makes a noncommittal sound. "Can I take you out later this week? I'll come to you. It doesn't have to be dinner. It can be any meal. I just… I know I've let you down a lot lately."

"That's an understatement."

"Tallulah."

"I came all the way to you, and you bailed on me, Dad. If you want a relationship with me, you can't do it only on your terms."

"I know." He's quiet a moment. "I'm so sorry. I'm learning that I'm really bad at taking care of the people I love." He chokes up at the last part.

I sigh, hating how broken he sounds. Nothing gets fixed if I don't at least try with him. "Why don't you share your calendar with me, and I can give you times and dates that work with my schedule?"

"I can do that. I'll do that right now."

"Did the meeting go okay?"

"Uh, yeah. Sometimes the bureaucratic stuff is a pain in my ass. But you don't need to worry about that." My phone pings, and I check the screen. A notification that Dad's shared his calendar pops up.

"I got the calendar. I'll cross-check it with all my events, and we can figure something out."

Sometimes I forget that he's the one who's alone in all of this. He chose the Terror over his family, but at the end of the day, he returns to an empty apartment. How hard must that be?

"Okay, great," he says.

"But you can't bail on me again."

"I won't. I promise."

"I'm holding you to that."

"Good, I want you to. I love you, Tally, I hope you know that, even if I'm not great at showing it."

"I love you, too, Dad. And it's never too late to stop making the same mistake."

"Isn't that the truth."

Maybe we can find our way through this. Maybe I can have the things I want, and the whole world won't implode because of it.

CHAPTER 15

FLIP

I don't go home. Instead, I message Dred and drive across town to the sprawling Grace mansion, where she lives with Connor, Everly and Victor, and Connor's grandmother, Lucy. Before Dred stepped into her Cinderella story, she used to live across the hall from me. She invited me over to play Battleship and taught me it was possible to have a platonic female friend. She's like family, and my life wouldn't be the same without her.

When I arrive at Grace Manor, Cedrick, one of the full-time staff, answers the door and ushers me inside. "Dred is already on her way down," he informs me.

Hearing Mildred's nickname coming out of this posh man's mouth always makes me smile. "Thanks, Ceddy."

Dred steps out of the elevator—yes, the house is that fancy—takes one look at me and arches a brow. "What happened?"

"I'll have refreshments brought to you." Cedrick bows and disappears down the hall.

"I kissed Tally, and I don't want to take it back."

"Like, kiss-kiss? For real? With tongue?"

"Yes."

"How was that?"

"Everything I wanted it to be and more." Leaving was one of the hardest things I've ever done. I wanted to kiss her until the world turned to ash around us.

"And for her?"

"I think the same?"

She inclines her head to the elevator. "Want to come up to the library, and we can talk it through?"

"Sounds good." I follow her into the elevator. We reach the second floor a few moments later and walk down the hall to the library. "Where's the rest of the family?"

"Connor's in the kitchen with the twins making cookies."

"He's a real sap for those two, isn't he?"

"Oh yeah. He's head over heels. It's beautiful to watch."

"He's having the best season of his career." *Maybe that could be me. Maybe I could have an amazing season* and *the woman I never dared to want.*

"Being settled and feeling like part of his team has definitely changed his game," she agrees.

Cedrick enters with tea and an assortment of other beverages, which he spreads out on the coffee table, along with a snack tray. Of course there's Tang.

Dred pours me a glass. "Want to lay it all out for me?"

I rewind to New Year's Eve and the almost kiss in the closet, vowing to stay away from her, driving her home tonight, being unable to walk away, taking her out for dinner and ending the night with that kiss that's been playing on repeat since I left her. I run my hands through my hair, panic hitting hard now. "What the fuck am I going to do, Dred?"

She settles back in her chair and sips her Tang. "What do you want to do?"

I rub my bottom lip. "I shouldn't want to date her."

"But you do want to date her," Dred affirms.

"It's a really bad fucking idea. Like literally the worst idea in the whole damn world. Vander Zee will bury me in an unmarked grave if he finds out about this."

"He may want to, but it's unlikely that he'll actually follow through," Dred says, unhelpfully.

"I need advice! I'm kind of freaking out here!" I snap.

She raises an eyebrow.

I sigh. "Please help me help myself."

"Let's take Vander Zee out of the equation. If he was a nonissue, what would be holding you back?"

"Beyond the age gap and her still being in university?"

"She'll be done in a handful of months."

I poke at my cheek with my tongue. "I have a past."

"Are you referring to the one everyone knows about, or the one only I and your ex know about?" Dred presses.

"Both." I pinch the bridge of my nose. "It's all going to come back to bite me in the ass if I start dating Tally."

She sets her glass down and shifts to face me. "You have spent the last few years doing a lot of personal work, and yeah, if you start dating the coach's daughter, your previous fuckboy ways will likely be mentioned, but that's not who you are now, and you don't have to let your past dictate your present. I think the thing that you'll need to deal with is the one you've been avoiding for the last decade."

I let my head fall back. My ex is the reason I haven't had a relationship since I was Tally's age. "I just want to leave Fiona in the fucking past with all my other bad choices."

"I get it, Flip. I really do. She did a number on you, but you never really buried that relationship. It's just a secret you've dragged along with you."

"Why is hindsight always twenty-twenty?"

"Because perspective is everything."

"How do I tell Tally I've been married before when I never even told my family?" We'd been high school sweethearts. She came back into my life at a time where I craved stability and I thought I would have it with her. We were married in secret, afraid our parents wouldn't allow it. I understood why after; she only wanted the life I could provide her. It was an expensive, horrifying lesson that left scars. A secret I wanted to keep buried. "What if we start dating, and I tell Tally, and she can't handle it?"

"What if she can?" Dred asks simply.

"There's so much at risk."

"There's always a risk. The bigger question is, can you live without taking it?"

I consider what it would be like if dinner and tonight's kiss was as far as it went for me and Tally. The way my stomach bottoms out and a cold, uncomfortable sweat makes my neck prickle tells me what I need to know. Dinner and the kiss aren't a mistake. "I have a laundry list of reasons why I shouldn't try to date my coach's daughter, but I'll regret it for the rest of my life if I don't at least try."

Dred smiles softly. "Then you know what you have to do."

"I'm going to make her mine."

I send Tally a message:

FLIP

Can't stop thinking about you.

TALLY

Me neither.

CHAPTER 16
TALLY

I have just rolled out of bed and put on a pot of coffee when there's a knock at the door.

Cammie often pops by in the morning because Chase uses an obscene amount of cream in his coffee, and they frequently run out. Parsnip rushes down the hall, meowing excitedly. "No escaping this morning." I scoop him up and throw the door open without looking through the peephole. This is my first mistake.

It's not my pint-size friends standing in the hall. It's Flip.

Flip who took me out for dinner and spent most of it feeding me.

Flip who kissed me and told me he wanted to take it slow.

Flip who I dreamed about last night, and in it, a hell of a lot more than kissing happened.

He looks far more awake and put together in his jeans, hoodie, and winter jacket than I do. He's holding a takeout tray with coffees and a bakery box.

"Hey." His gaze moves over me in a way that warms me from the inside. "Did I wake you?"

"No. I was already up." *Barely.* I'm wearing pajama pants, an oversized long-sleeved shirt, and ridiculous slippers. I probably have lines on my face and a wicked case of bedhead. Parsnip squirms around in my arms, the allure of the hallway a forbidden temptation. I shake off my daze and step back to make room for Flip. "You should come in."

As soon as the door closes, I drop Parsnip, who promptly rubs himself against Flip's legs while meowing loudly.

"You're such a harlot," I scold. I wish I could do that without it being weird.

"A cute harlot." Flip toes off his shoes. "I brought breakfast." He kisses me on the cheek and walks down the hall.

"That was really sweet." I follow him into the kitchen.

I don't know how to interpret this visit. The last twenty-four hours have been surreal.

"Have a seat." He pulls a chair out for me, and I gratefully park my ass because once again, my knees are made of Jell-O.

"Is everything okay?" I'm so anxious. And I really wish I had a mirror and my toothbrush and a different pair of underwear on.

"We need to talk." He opens the box and angles it toward me. It's full of my favorites. I love every single baked good in this box.

"Okay." I wish my stomach didn't feel like it wants to turn itself inside out.

Flip meets my anxious gaze with a steady one. "I had a great time with you last night."

I'm a fluttering, excited mess now. "Me, too."

He tucks my hair behind my ear. "I like you."

I'm at risk of melting into the floor. "I like you, too."

"When the girls go to your showcases, I always try to find a reason to tag along because I love watching you dance. And I love it when you come to games, especially when you come to the Watering Hole afterward so I can find out what you've been up to. I started reading all the books you recommend because it gives me a reason to message you, especially when I think I've found your favorite part."

My mouth is dry, my palms are sweaty, and my heart is pounding. What he's saying is exactly what I always dreamed. And now it's coming true. It seems impossible, but also like this is the best week of my entire life. "I love that you always seem to know exactly what part is my favorite."

"To be fair, those corners usually have a crease in them." His eyebrow lifts.

My cheeks heat. "I knew I should have used flags instead."

"It's been very insightful." Flip has the audacity to smirk and look hot doing it.

I pull my shirt up to cover the bottom of my face. The other scenes I dog-ear are the spicy ones.

"I've been making notes of my own." He winks and covers my hand with his, bringing it to his lips. "I like spending time with you, Talls."

"I like spending time with you, too."

"I want to date you."

I surreptitiously pinch my thigh to make sure I'm actually awake. My heart stutters. "Date me?"

My experience is limited to university age man-boys who want to meet up at some party. Eventually a group movie night ensues, and then a few weeks or a month down the line, dinner at a restaurant off campus.

"I'd like to take you on a real date, one that's planned, where I pick you up, take you somewhere nice, and treat you like a queen," he says with genuine seriousness.

"That sounds..." Perfect. Amazing. Terrifying. "I'd like that." I don't know what to do with my hands, so I clasp them together to keep from fidgeting. Parsnip bumps against my legs under the table.

"I'd like to see where this goes." He laces our fingers. "But you won't be a secret I have to keep."

I swallow my guilt over the way I propositioned him. "I don't want that either."

"Good. That's good, kitten." He nods once. "I know you already get unwanted attention because you're the coach's daughter, and dating me will bring more of that. I have a past that isn't always pretty, and it will likely be dredged up."

"I know what the media is like," I assure him.

"I will do everything I can to protect you, but my past has been pretty prolific," he says gently. "You might read or hear things that make you uncomfortable, and if that happens, I need you to come to me."

"Okay. I will." I breathe through my nerves.

"No brave faces. If something bothers you, I want to know about it," he insists. "I need you to promise me."

"I promise."

"Good girl."

A thrill shoots down my spine at the praise.

"I'll deal with your dad." Flip kisses the inside of my wrist.

"Deal with him how?"

"Talk to him. Explain that I want to date you."

"What if he says no?"

"He won't." He squeezes my hand, reading my nerves. "Do you need time to think this through, Tally?"

I shake my head. "I know the risks and challenges. Not just for me, but for you." That he's willing to put himself on the line like this is humbling and elating.

"That's good." Flip pushes out of his chair and pulls me to my feet. His dark eyes glitter with satisfaction as he strokes the edge of my jaw. "Soon you'll be mine."

My knees nearly buckle.

He bends to press a soft kiss to my lips. But he doesn't deepen it. Instead, he straightens. "Have a good day, kitten."

"Wait. What?" That's it? I'm so confused.

"I have practice in an hour, and you have dance rehearsal." He motions to the whiteboard fixed to the wall with my schedule.

"But, but…I thought…" What did I think? That we'd end up in my bedroom making out after establishing our mutual desire to date? Based on the pinging in all my sensitive spots, the answer to that is yes.

"I can't afford to be late today of all days, and neither can you."

"Wait!" I grab his arm.

He turns back to me, expression amused.

"Aren't you going to kiss me?"

The corner of his mouth kicks up. "I did kiss you."

"I mean a real kiss. Like the one from last night."

He cups my chin in his palm, fingers curving around my jaw as he tips my head back and slants his mouth over mine. I gasp and part for him. He sweeps my mouth on a low groan, and our tongues brush and tangle. When I try to wrap myself around him, he breaks the kiss and pulls back. "Is that what you wanted, kitten?"

"Yes, Phillip." I'm breathless and achy, and he looks completely in control.

"If I let you go, will you be good and not try to wind yourself around me like your cat?"

"Maybe."

He arches a brow. "What was that?"

"I'll be good." I might as well be a puddle.

He kisses my cheek, then releases his gentle hold on my jaw. "I'll message you later. Have a good morning, kitten."

"You, too."

He scoops up Parsnip and passes him to me. "I'll see myself out." He disappears down the hall. The door clicks shut a few seconds later. I glance at the clock. I'm already running behind for dance practice.

"Shit. I don't even have time to handle the fucking pinging in my panties."

I message my group to let them know I'll be a few minutes late and rush to get ready.

There's nothing that can be done about my frazzled state as I sprint across campus to the dance studio. Except when I arrive, my troupe isn't in the studio warming up. Instead, they're huddled in a group with their phones in their hands.

"Is the studio double-booked again?" It's happened before.

Charles looks up from his phone. He gives me a questioning once-over. "Are you okay?"

"Fine. Just had a hard time getting out the door." I'm usually more put together, but it isn't every day that the man of my dreams shows up asking to date me and turns me into a puddle with one kiss.

"Some idiot pulled the fire alarm last night, and the studio flooded. We're trying to rebook, but I think the code is going to your phone because you booked it in the first place," he explains.

"Oh crap, how bad is the damage?" I pull my phone out of my pocket and find the message with the code.

"One of the maintenance guys said they have to replace the entire floor," Arya replies.

"How long will that take?" I input the booking reference code and frown. "All the studios on campus are coming up red."

"How is that possible?" Charles groans. "We just got the email a few minutes ago."

"I can check the yoga studio in my apartment complex." I pull up the booking link. Unfortunately, I'm not the only person with this idea. I secure us an evening spot today and book where I can for the rest of the week, but now we're short on practice sessions.

"We'll have to find somewhere off campus." Arya fiddles with the end of her braid. "I hope it's not too expensive."

Arya is here on a full scholarship and had to take out loans to afford room and board. Charles is in a similar position.

If I'd been on time, they would have had the code, and maybe we wouldn't be scrambling. But I have connections. The Terror office has a gym and a yoga studio. It's not convenient, but it could be an option. "Let me see what I can do."

CHAPTER 17

FLIP

"You all right, man? You seem preoccupied." Tristan passes me the puck during warm-ups.

I glance around, checking for privacy with our whole team out here on the ice. Everyone is focused on their own drills, though. "It's about Tally."

Tristan fumbles the puck.

I snag it and pass it back.

He arches a brow in silent question.

It takes me a few seconds to work up the nerve to spit it the fuck out. Telling Dred and talking to Tally is not the same as asking her dad for permission or telling my teammates. "I want to date her."

"Bea has been waiting for this for fucking ever. The gloating will be next-level."

My sister's name is Beatrix, and he's the only one who shortens it that way. The rest of us call her Rix.

"What?" He's not even remotely surprised, which is really fucking problematic. It's like he expected it. Is everyone expecting it? How long have I been in the dark about my own fucking feelings?

"Timing has really been the thing," he explains as we continue to pass the puck back and forth. "She's graduating university in a few months. She's always had her head on straight, minus the last couple of boyfriends. Bea has not been a fan."

"None of us were." I feel like I'm in the twilight zone. How is this even a casual conversation? It feels fucking monumental.

"Well, we know why you weren't."

"I wasn't looking at her like she had girlfriend potential until recently," I say defensively. He still doesn't know about her propositioning me.

"There's been a vibe. It was particularly strong on New Year's," Tristan says.

I had convinced myself I could be close to her and not do anything stupid on New Year's. Maybe if Quinn hadn't been flirty with her, I would have had half a chance. Maybe if she hadn't worn a thong bikini in the hot tub. Maybe if I hadn't ended up in the closet with her. Yeah, I was fucked regardless. "She's going through it, you know?"

"Yeah, I do."

Tristan's mom bailed when we were twelve, and he helped raise his younger brothers, so he speaks from experience.

"You worried about how Vander Zee will handle it, especially with everything else going on?" he asks.

We both glance at Coach. He's been on edge, and he looks exhausted most of the time. Ending a twenty-five-year marriage is probably the same as mourning.

"Yeah. And Hemi." What happens if Tally and I end up together long-term? What if I fall in love with her and she can't deal with the intensity of my life and leaves? *Why am I spiraling now?*

"She'll have feelings about it, but you're coming to her before the shitstorm, so that should count for something," Tristan reassures me.

"That's what I'm hoping." If Vander Zee trades me or murders me, I'm setting Tally up to be hurt all over again. And I really don't want that.

Coach Forrest-Hammer blows the whistle and calls us in. She's been stepping up more lately. I don't know if Vander Zee is pushing her, or if she's taking the pressure off him.

After practice, I shower and change, then head up to Vander Zee's office. The sooner I rip the bandage off, the better. My palms are damp, my heart is racing, and I feel like vomiting isn't out of the question as I prepare to knock on his office door. The conversation I'm about to have will change everything. But not following through isn't an option. My teammates can shun me, and my coach can rip me a new one, but I won't let either stop me. It would hurt too much to walk away.

Once again, I wish I'd done things differently after Fiona and I ended, that I hadn't let her shake my faith in my ability to find and keep love. But I can't go back and change the past, so all I can do is hope I've done enough work to prove I'm more than my previous decisions. I knock on Vander Zee's door.

"Come on in." He takes off his glasses and motions to the chair across from his desk. "What can I do for you, Madden?"

I close the door most of the way and drop into the chair. "I have something important I want to discuss with you." I run my sweaty palms down my thighs. I hope I survive this.

Vander Zee gives me his full attention. He has circles under his eyes, and he seems to have aged five years since the holidays. "Everything okay?"

"Yeah. Everything's good." I rap on the armrest, then grip them so I stop fidgeting. "You know me well, Coach, and you've seen me grow a lot over the past few years, personally and professionally."

"You're an excellent player. One of the best on the team, and a lead scorer in the league," he agrees, then sits up straighter. "Please tell me another team isn't trying to poach you."

I hold up a hand. "No. Nothing like that."

"Right. Okay. Good. I have enough shit to deal with." He runs a rough hand through his hair. "I can't lose one of my best players, too."

I swallow past my anxiety. He might feel differently about that in a minute. "Tally's been spending a lot of time with us lately."

"I'm glad she has you and the Terror girls to look out for her. She needs people she can lean on," he says. "I know what's going on with me and her mother has been hard on her." He clears his throat. "She mentioned that you drove her home last night. Did she say anything? Should I be worried?"

"She's okay. It's tough when you have an idea of what your parents' relationship is like, and then suddenly everything changes." I shift in my seat. "I, uh…I took her out for dinner."

His brow lifts. "Last night?"

"Yes, sir."

"Oh. I didn't realize. Thanks for doing that. I felt like an asshole for bailing on her. She proved her point about me putting my job before my family." Vander Zee sighs.

I keep my mouth shut about that. It's not my place to tell him how to live his life. "Talls and I have gotten closer recently."

Vander Zee's brows pull together.

I rush to add, "Just in the past few months, really."

"Closer how?" Suspicion clouds his eyes.

"She's a great girl. Woman. She's special." *Just spit it out, man.*

"She is." His tone shifts to warning. "Madden, what—"

I bite the bullet. "I would like to date your daughter, sir."

Vander Zee stares at me.

I don't break eye contact, even though I would like to.

"Repeat that, please."

My mouth is so fucking dry. "I would like to date Tally."

"You want to date Tally," he echoes.

"Yes, sir."

He clasps his hands, and the tips of his fingers turn white. "She's my baby."

"She's twenty-one. She'll be twenty-two this year."

"Her birthday isn't until the summer."

"She's an adult."

"She's still in university."

"This is her final semester. She's very confident in her path, and I'm sure you'll agree she always has been," I counter.

His jaw ticks.

"Her favorite candy is dropjes, specifically the sweeter ones, and her favorite cake is Cherry Chip from Just Desserts. She loves dystopian literature, her favorite genre of music changes depending on her song choice for her showcases, and her favorite color is teal." I avoid mentioning that she likes vanilla lip balm, her shampoo smells like cherry blossoms, and she also likes spicy romantasy and why choose fics.

His eye twitches. "You're serious."

"I am. I care about her, Coach."

"Do not call me Coach right now, Madden."

"Sorry, sir." I feel like I'm tripping around landmines. I haven't asked anyone for permission to date their daughter ever, but these aren't typical circumstances.

His face turns red, and he rubs his bottom lip, chest rising and falling like he's working to contain himself. "She's my little girl." He grinds his teeth.

I avoid mentioning her adult status again.

"You have a really heinous reputation, Madden."

I've been waiting for this. I want to look away. To be someone else—someone like Ryker who's a small-town boy with a squeaky-clean record. The guy is the quintessential Boy Scout. Even Romero, who has a habit of getting into fights on the ice, has never been in the media for bad behavior off the ice. "I've done a lot of personal work over the past few years."

"I can't argue with that." He taps on his desk. "Is this what my daughter wants?"

"It is." Unless she's changed her mind between this morning and now. I really hope not. I would be gutted.

He sighs. His nostrils flare. "If this is what Tally wants." He pinches the bridge of his nose. "Ah fuck." Shakes his head. "I can't believe I'm saying this, but anything is better than the last guy she brought home."

That's not a resoundingly positive approval, but it's better than the alternative, which would be me, six feet under.

Before I can say anything, he pins me with a glare. "But if you hurt her, I'll destroy you, Madden."

"Of course, sir. I promise to treat her with the utmost care and respect." I'll have to prove myself through actions, because that sounds like a whole lot of lip service. But it's been years since I've fed the rumor mill. That life is not what I want anymore.

"Please get the fuck out of my office."

"Yes, sir." I stand and hustle into the hall. "Thank you."

I can't believe I survived that experience with all my teeth.

One down, one to go. I'm not so sure the next conversation will go as smoothly. I chug three glasses of water and say a little prayer before I knock on the head of Terror PR's open door.

Hemi looks up from her computer, and her lips flatten into a thin line. "For the love of all that is good and holy." She tips her chin up and glares at the ceiling. "Lord, give me strength." Her unimpressed gaze returns to me. "You did it, didn't you?"

"Did what?" I don't know why I'm feigning innocence. I've already kissed the girl. Three times. Each one better than the last.

The look she gives me feels like a punch in the balls. "Are you fucking kidding me?"

"I haven't even said anything."

"Get in here and close the damn door."

I do as she says.

She points to the chair across from her desk.

I feel like I'm back in elementary school, and I'm about to get in shit for doing something stupid. Which…is maybe partly true.

She crosses her arms. "Well?"

"I'm going to date Tally."

"You've already talked to Vander Zee?"

"Yeah."

Her eyes narrow. "I don't believe you. Where's your shiner?"

"He said if it's what Tally wants…and also that anything is better than the last guy." Might as well go with the truth.

Hemi shakes her head. "The last guy was about as exciting as chewed gum."

"That's highly accurate." I lean forward. "I'm doing this right. No hiding."

"Damn right you will, because if you fuck this up, I will string you up by your damn balls and let my brothers have at you." Her eyes are fiery with challenge as she waits for my response.

I suppress a shudder. Sam and Isaac are intense on a good day. Dallas also believes that Sam is a finisher, like professionally. It's a legitimate possibility. "Not if Vander Zee gets to me first."

She frowns, apparently unimpressed with my joke.

"She's worth the risk." I would live in a well of regret if I don't try with her.

Hemi nods slowly. "The media might be assholes about this."

"We can try to mitigate the worst of it."

"We may have to highlight some of the volunteer stuff you've kept me out of." She flips a pen between her fingers.

"Can we do that only as a last resort?" Some of my charity work feels intensely personal, and like something I haven't wanted to share with the world.

"Of course. But we can't insulate Tally from your past. There may be some tough conversations ahead."

"I know." It's one thing to talk about it; it's another for her to have to deal with it in real time. "I just have to make the shitty parts worth sticking it out for."

"We'll come up with a plan. And backup plans for those plans."

"Thanks, Hemi. I appreciate you."

"And I appreciate that you're not in the let's-hide-this-until-things-blow-up-in-our-faces club."

"I've seen my friends go through enough shit. Felt like I didn't need to repeat history." But I do have one thing I'm holding on to. Eventually, I'll have to share that with Tally.

"Amen to that."

I leave her office, marveling that I'm still above ground, and head to the parking garage. Once I'm in my car, though, I realize I need bestie support.

On my way to Dred's, I imagine what it would feel like to have Tally at my apartment again. How good it would feel to cuddle with her on the couch. To make dinner together…

I don't allow my imagination to take it further. I want to be more to her than my past reputation.

Once I've parked at Dred's, I slide my phone out of my pocket and pull up Tally's contact.

The message I'm about to send will change everything.

CHAPTER 18

TALLY

My phone buzzes for the twentieth time in as many minutes. Cammie and Chase are picking up drinks, and of course everyone wants something different, and Mac is very particular. The guy is all about craft IPAs.

Except the most recent message isn't from my Tilton friends. Or my Terror/Babe crew.

It's from Flip.

I scream.

Enid's bowl of popcorn nearly ends up on the floor. As it is, much of it spills into her lap. Thankfully she has a blanket draped over her bottom half, so it's fairly contained.

"Did Flip text?" Enid clenches her teeth, as though she's worried she jinxed me by asking.

I hold up my phone. "He did."

"What did he say?" Fee asks.

"I don't know. I haven't read it yet." My stomach is full of fluttery things.

"What are you waiting for? Check it!" Fee grabs my phone and holds it in front of my face to unlock it.

I tap on the new message and suck in a breath.

FLIP

> I hope you had a good day. I talked to your dad, and I'm happy to report that I still have all my teeth. 😅 If you haven't changed your mind since this morning, I'd love to take you on that date.

"Oh my God!" Fee screams.

"Holy shit." Enid moves the blanket full of popcorn off her lap but is considerate enough to keep the mess contained.

I dance around the living room. How is this suddenly my life? "Phillip Madden just asked me on a date!"

"And he talked to your dad!" Enid adds.

"Super swoon!" Fee falls back against the cushions and makes a heart over her chest with her hands.

"This is next-level," Enid agrees.

"Send a reply!" Fee shouts.

I'm suddenly sweaty, and my hands are shaking. "Do I just type yes? No. I should say more than that. What should I say?" I move to the couch because my legs are unsteady.

"That you haven't changed your mind, and you'd love to go on a date with him," Enid suggests.

My palms are damp so my phone slips out of my hands.

Fee sits next to me and scoops it up. "Do you want me to type for you?"

"No, no. I can do this. I have to do this." I take a deep breath. "I honestly never believed this would happen. This feels…huge."

"That's because it is." Enid drops to the cushion next to me. "I think we should take a moment to appreciate how awesome you are."

At my questioning look, she tips her head. "Pro hockey's golden boy just asked you on a date, Tally. You're some hot shit."

"Damn right you are!" Fee puts her hand up for a high five.

I smack it, but my arms are rubbery. "This is like…serious business. All his attention will be on me." I hop to my feet again and pace the living room, which isn't easy because it's a tight space. "I'll be his sole focus."

"That's sort of the point, isn't it?" Enid seems mildly confused.

"Yeah. That's totally the point." When it was just a fantasy, it was easy to imagine. "But I'm still in university, and he has all this life experience. What if I do something stupid? Or say something stupid? What if I'm boring?" *What if I don't live up to the hype in his head?*

Fee holds up a hand. "Can we back this bus up a few stops?"

"The bus is already heading down the mountain, Fee. It's too late to stop it." Why am I panicking now, when everything I've ever wanted is a text message away?

"Do you really think Flip would put his career and his life on the line by asking *your dad* for permission to date you if he thought you were boring?"

"Well, no, but—"

"But nothing. He's clearly into you. He would not take that kind of risk, otherwise. Which honestly, is super fucking hot. Imagine a guy asking Roman if he could date me?" Fee arches a brow.

Enid's green eyes widen. "That's a pants-shittingly terrifying thought."

"I'd be very scared to ask Roman to date you," I agree.

"Right? And Roman isn't half as scary as your dad," Fee reasons.

"Okay, that's true." I've seen Roman pissed before, and I would not want to be on his bad side, but my dad is definitely scarier.

"So we can agree that there are zero chances Flip will find you boring on your date."

"Stop waffling and text him back," Fee orders.

Mac appears, carrying two takeout bags. He frowns when his eyes land on me. "Are you okay?"

"Why would you ask me that?" I grab the closest item, which happens to be a Terror stress puck, and throw it at him.

Annoyingly, he grabs it out of the air. "That's a no, then."

CHAPTER 19

FLIP

I pull my hoodie over my head and toss it on the couch because I'm hot. "What if she says no?"

"What if she says no," Dred repeats.

"Not helpful." I continue pacing. Tally's read my message. But she hasn't responded.

"Dude, sit the fuck down. You're going to wear a hole in the rug. It's Meems's favorite, and it's actually irreplaceable."

"I can't sit down."

"It'll be fine," Dred says in that patient, all-knowing way of hers.

"You don't know that!"

"Don't fucking yell at my wife," Connor says calmly, eyes dark and menacing even as he presses a kiss to Dred's temple.

"Calm down, both of you," she orders.

"I am calm, darling," Connor assures her. "I was merely issuing a warning."

Everly whirls into the living room like a human tornado. Her twin follows like a summer breeze. "What's all the ruckus about?" She hops behind Connor and Dred, puts them both in a headlock and rubs her face on their hair like a cat.

Victor observes the affection with a pleased smile.

"Flip asked Tally on a date, and she hasn't responded yet," Connor explains.

"Tally as in Tally Vander Zee? The coach's daughter?" Everly's eyes light up.

"That would be the one," Dred confirms.

"She's still in university," Victor says.

Connor coughs to cover a laugh.

"She's graduating this semester," Dred explains.

"So she's what, like, twenty-one?" Victor presses.

"She'll be twenty-two this summer." Connor side-eyes Everly.

"And you're twenty-what?" Everly asks.

"I'm thirty." I'll be thirty-one before Tally is twenty-two.

"Ooohhh. The big three-oh." Everly climbs over the back of the couch, wiggling between Connor and Dred. "But that's less than a decade. Hollis is twelve years older than Hammer, and Roman is, like, ten years older than Lexi, right?"

"That's correct." Dred allows Everly to link their arms so the three of them become a human chain.

Victor deposits himself on the other side of Dred and does the same. They make a cute family.

"Why does it feel like less of a difference with Lexi and Roman?" Everly asks. Her head bobs from side to side, touching Connor's shoulder, then Dred's, like she's channeling a windshield wiper.

"Life experience," I suggest.

"Hmm…" She nods, contemplating. "How old is Kellan?"

"Don't even think about it," Connor says.

"Obviously I'm not thinking about it now." Everly rolls her eyes. "But I'm not that far off from twenty. Then can I date a hockey player?"

"Only if you like your boyfriends with no teeth," Connor says flatly.

"You have all your teeth," Everly points out.

"Yes, well, no one has pried mine out with pliers."

"Dred will let me date a hockey player." She snuggles into Dred.

My phone pings with a message.

Everyone goes silent.

I exhale an anxious breath.

"Aren't you going to look at it?" Victor asks.

"Give me a second."

"Nut up, bro," Everly replies cheerily.

"She's definitely yours," I say to Connor.

I open the message.

TALLY

I would love to go on a date with you.

"Well? What did she say?" Victor seems to be on the edge of his seat.

"She said yes."

Dred smiles. "See? I told you everything would be fine."

"Shit, we're playing Nashville tomorrow."

"We're not playing the following night, though." Connor's tone implies that I'm an idiot for not reaching this conclusion on my own.

"I'd like to take her out as soon as humanly possible."

Connor nods to my phone. I flip him the bird.

"I love how sweet you two are with each other," Dred deadpans.

FLIP

I'm glad to hear that. Tomorrow is out because of the game. Are you still coming, and would you be free the day after for a date?

TALLY

> I have night class the next night, and then I volunteer at the cat shelter and have dance rehearsals the following night. But I'm free on Friday.

I can practically hear her biting her lip.

"She's busy until Friday," I inform them, since everyone seems to be waiting for the play-by-play.

"Are you busy that night?" Connor sips his tea. He looks ridiculous holding a china teacup in his massive hand.

I avoid a snarky comeback and type a message instead.

FLIP

> Friday is perfect. Does seven o'clock work for you?

TALLY

> Seven is great!

FLIP

> Perfect. Can't wait.

TALLY

> Me neither.

FLIP

> Have a good night, Talls.

TALLY

> You, too. 🖤

FLIP

> Hey, Talls?

TALLY

> Yes?

FLIP

> In four days, I get to take you on our first official date.

TALLY

I'm very excited for that.

FLIP

Me, too.

TALLY

And for the kiss at the end.

FLIP

Right there with you.

I slide my phone back into my pocket.

"Well?" Everly holds up her hands. "What's the deal?"

"Friday is a go."

"Where are you taking her?" Victor asks.

"Somewhere nice," Everly says. "Connor knows all the best places."

"This is true," Connor agrees. "You should consider buying her a dress."

"I don't know that you need to outfit Tally for your date." Dred side-eyes Connor.

"I buy you dresses all the time."

"You also bought me an entire lodge for Christmas, so it's safe to say you consistently go overboard with the gift giving."

"Connor loves buying things for Dred." Everly hops off the couch. "What about flowers and candy instead of a dress? Something thoughtful and sweet. Like Connor always brings me and Victor treats when he has away games. And he leaves love notes for Dred in the library. One for every day he's gone."

I grin. "Man, you're a sap for my best friend, aren't you?"

"Absolutely." He kisses Dred's cheek.

"I will take all the help I can get with making this the best damn date Tally has ever been on." I might be out of practice, but I'm sure dating is like riding a bike, practice makes perfect.

"And the best damn date you've ever been on, too," Dred says with a smile.

"Exactly."

Our lives are about to get a whole lot more complicated.

I know Tally is worth it.

And I'm going to do everything in my power to make sure I am, too.

CHAPTER 20

FLIP

I'm on edge tonight. Tally has dance rehearsal this evening, but she's coming to the game when she's done. I meant what I said about not hiding this, so I need to be on point tonight. I can't afford to let my team down with the bomb I'm about to drop.

Tristan nudges my knee with his.

"What's up?"

"You're jittery as fuck."

"Ya think?"

Connor pulls his jersey on over his head, covering his many tattoos, which now includes MILDRED scrawled in loopy cursive along his ribs.

Our coaches enter the locker room, and Vander Zee gives us a distracted pep talk. Then Forrest-Hammer steps in with strategy for the first period. I won't be the least bit surprised when she becomes the first female head coach in the league.

"Let's show Nashville who's the better team tonight," Coach Forrest-Hammer says as we file down the hall to the rink for warm-ups.

Grace claps me on the shoulder. "Keep your head in the game and worry about the rest later."

"You got it." If someone told me I'd be getting pep talks from Grace when he first joined the team, I would have laughed in their face. Connor and I had a long history of hating each other from our Hockey Academy days, which carried into our professional careers. When he joined the Terror, we were forced to at least sort of deal with it. And then he married my best friend. We might needle the shit out of each other, but we care deeply about the same people, and that's created a bond neither of us expected.

"You know it's a big deal when your archnemesis gives you a pep talk," Stiles observes as Grace skates off.

"I wouldn't call him my archnemesis anymore, but yeah, clearly there's a lot on the line when *he's* giving me the keep-your-head-down speech."

"I don't see Tally in the box with the girls." Stiles waves to Rix, who blows him a kiss.

"She's coming after her dance rehearsal," I explain.

"Ah." Stiles pats me on the back. "Just stay focused. Everything will be fine."

I set aside my personal shit and, like Grace advised, keep my head in the game. Nashville scores a goal in the first five minutes, making it a rocky start.

I rotate on with Stiles, Bright, Ashish Palaniappa, one of our enforcers, and Grace. We fight for possession, and Ryker deflects shots on net. Grace steals the puck from Nashville, and I rush to intercept the pass at center.

Stiles and Bright flank me as I gain control. Grace and Palaniappa move in to distract their defense. Nashville scrambles to steal the puck, but Bright taps it back to me. I take the shot, but their goalie knocks it away. Stiles grabs it on the rebound and takes another shot, but it goes wide. Palaniappa tips it back to me, and I shoot again as Grace blocks their key defense. This time the puck slides past the goalie's skate, tying the game.

My teammates converge on me, and we're a mass of back pats and *way to go*s. Playing well tonight is essential. I need my team and the media on my side when the news about me and Tally finally gets out.

Stiles scores a goal in the second period with Romero as the assist.

Tally arrives at the beginning of the third period.

"Stay focused," Grace reminds me as I take the ice again, proving once again that he's a reliable ally.

I block out the noise and score again with Bright as the assist. We maintain the two-point lead for the rest of the game. Nashville gets chippy in the last five minutes, and one of their players tries to start a fight with Grace, but he won't engage. Instead, Grace scores a goal during our powerplay, which is the best FU to the guy currently fuming in the penalty box. And we win the game 4 -1.

We stop to give interviews to the waiting media, and I can't tell if Vander Zee is being awkward, or I'm hyperaware of how things will shift once everyone finds out I'm dating his daughter. How our friends react is the first test, and I'm really fucking nervous.

The mood in the locker room is buoyant on the heels of the win. But it's all unknowns once I step outside this room.

Coach Vander Zee seems just as off as me. "Good game, boys. You played with skill and not your balls."

Coach Forrest-Hammer raises an eyebrow.

Coach Arnold coughs.

A few of the rookie players exchange looks.

I can feel Grace and Stiles eyes on me.

Romero's brows pull together.

"Sorry, you know what I mean." Coach looks at me. "You're

doing a great job showing up for each other." He clears his throat. "Keep it up."

I tug on my tie as Coach Forrest-Hammer adds her much more eloquent two cents about teamwork and cohesiveness.

We leave the locker room and head down the hall to where the girls are waiting. Tally is caught in the middle of the group, and my teammates are blocking my path to her. She looks gorgeous in a pair of jeans and a Terror hoodie. Her hair falls in loose waves over her shoulders, and I long to thread my fingers into those soft waves and kiss her pretty, vanilla-lip-balm-flavored lips.

Her ocean-blue eyes meet mine, wide with uncertainty and anticipation, as I nudge Tristan and Dallas out of the way.

Everything is about to change.

Except Vander Zee moves in before I reach her. "Hey, kiddo! I didn't realize you were coming out tonight." He pulls Tally in for an enthusiastic, slightly desperate hug.

She gives me an uneasy look over his shoulder while patting his back.

We should have talked through how this would go, instead of winging it. I don't want to overwhelm her, but I want to make it clear that I'm in this.

Vander Zee steps back, and I respectfully make my move.

"Hey." I run my fingers gently down her arm.

"Hi." She rolls her bottom lip between her teeth.

I lace our fingers and the smile that lights up her face makes whatever shit kicking I'll get from my teammates later worth it. "How was rehearsal?"

"Good." Her eyes dart to her dad and back to me. "You were great out there tonight."

"I had a reason to play well." I wink and her smile widens.

Vander Zee's eyes volley between us.

"Are you coming to the Watering Hole?" I rub my thumb

across her knuckles, hoping the contact eases some of her nerves the way it does mine.

"I can drop Tally off," Vander Zee jumps in before she can respond. He's probably itching for time with her.

Silence has fallen around us, but I stay focused on Tally.

Her cheeks flush. "I won't be far behind you."

"Take your time." I bring her hand to my lips and kiss her knuckles. "I won't go anywhere without you."

"You'll make sure she gets home safely. In the same condition she went out in," Vander Zee barks.

Someone coughs behind me.

I turn to Vander Zee. "Absolutely, sir."

"Okay, cool. I'll see you all soon." Tally threads her arm through his. "Come on, Dad." She leads him away.

"What in the actual fuck is going on?" Dallas looks at Hemi. "And why don't you look shocked?"

"Because I'm not." Hemi pats him on the chest. "And you shouldn't be either."

"Well now." Quinn whistles low. "This explains New Year's Eve."

"I knew that vibe was vibing," Rix says.

"You know you can't fuck this up, right?" Kellan says.

"Like we will all fuck you up if you fuck it up," Ashish, who is the most mild-mannered of all the guys, says.

"Hemi's already threatened me with her brothers."

"They'll get the leftovers," Quinn needles.

"I wouldn't do this if I wasn't serious about her." I glance around the group. "I know what's at stake."

"He does," Connor steps in before anyone else takes a shot at me. "He's been eating up my wife's free time with his existential crisis."

That breaks some of the tension and the girls laugh.

Quinn pats me on the shoulder. "Worst case, you get traded

and spend the final years of your career freezing your ass off and never making the playoffs again."

CHAPTER 21
TALLY

"How long has this been going on?" Dad asks as he collects his things from his office.

"We haven't even gone on an official date yet," I reply.

"He took you out for dinner the other night, though." He steps into the hall, pulling his office door closed behind him.

"That wasn't a date. That was my friend stepping up for me when you prioritized work over me."

"I'm sorry. That meeting was unexpected."

"Surprise meetings usually are." I punch the down button on the elevator, frustrated all over again. Flip keeps showing up for me and my dad keeps letting me down.

He circles back to the date. "Has he asked you out?"

"Yes."

"When did he do that?" he presses.

I side-eye him. "After he talked to you."

"So this has been building for a while."

I sigh. "I've been friends with Flip for a long time, Dad. I hang out with the Terror regularly, and he's been part of that friend group. Over the past year, we've grown a lot closer. He's considerate, thoughtful, ambitious and dedicated. I like him and he likes me. I think it says a lot about him as a person that he came to you first, before he asked me out, don't you?"

"It definitely won him some brownie points," he agrees, albeit reluctantly. "Dating a player won't be easy, honey." The elevator doors slide open, and my dad holds his hand in front of the sensor, waiting for me to exit first.

"Dating anyone as the Terror coach's daughter is never easy. At least we understand each other's lives."

"He has a lot more…life experience than you." He unlocks the truck.

I climb in the passenger seat, thankful the ride to the Watering Hole is short. "Of course he does. He's been alive longer." I know where he's going with this, and it isn't a conversation I'm interested in having with my dad.

He pulls out of the underground parking lot and into traffic. "You know that's not what I mean. Madden is a good guy and an excellent hockey player. He's grown a lot in the last few years, but I witnessed firsthand what he was like before he settled down."

"So did I. I'm not dating Flip from four years ago, I'm dating him now. Please have some faith in my ability to make smart decisions when it comes to relationships."

He rubs the space between his eyes. "I want to be cool about this, but I can't unknow some of the things I know about Flip."

"We can't define people by their worst decisions," I say pointedly.

He sighs. "I just want what's best for you."

"Me, too. And I think that Flip can be that. Look at all the ways he shows he cares. I think his current actions mean a lot more than his past ones."

"I just don't want you to get hurt."

"I know, and I love you, even though some of the things that have happened recently have really hurt."

"I'm sorry. I love you, too." He pulls up in front of the Watering Hole.

"Then keep showing up for me and Ties and Fenna." I lean over and kiss him on the cheek. "Thanks for the ride."

"Of course, honey. Have fun with your friends."

I open the door.

"And please be safe," he tacks on.

"I will. I promise."

I close the door and turn toward the Watering Hole.

My heart rate spikes. I guess now we find out how our friends feel about this.

All heads at the table turn my way as I push through the door. My stomach twists. My palms dampen. Flip is already out of his chair, closing the distance between us.

Anticipation turns my heart into hummingbird wings.

"How you doing?" Flip slips his fingers under my hair, hand curving against my jaw. It's innocent, but comforting and stimulating at the same time.

"Okay. Nervous."

"It's me they want to grill, not you." He wraps his other arm around me and pulls me against him.

He's claiming me. In front of our friends. In front of all these people. He squeezes gently then pulls back, eyes roving over my face. "You're audaciously beautiful."

I laugh and duck my head.

Flip tips my chin up. "You being all shy with me, kitten?"

"Everyone's watching," I whisper.

"Good." His thumb sweeps along the edge of my jaw. "Now they know who I belong to."

My heart stutters and desire, thick and heady, zings through me. He's not just claiming me, he's asking to be claimed. I wet my bottom lip, mouth dry. How is this real life?

Flip's nostrils flare, and he traces the contour with his thumb. He leans down, lips brushing my cheek as he lowers to my ear. "I'm looking forward to tasting those pretty, tempting lips when I drive you home later."

I grip his bicep, knees turning watery at his gravelly tone. "You could kiss me now."

"Not in front of these people, kitten. Only I get to see you melt for me."

I whimper.

His fingers flex on my hip. "I love that sound." He straightens and laces our fingers. "Make it again for me later."

I shake off the haze. "Oh, that was evil."

"I'll make it worth the wait, don't worry." He winks and guides me to the table, where he's already ordered me a cola and a margarita.

Flip helps me out of my jacket, and into my seat.

Quinn breaks the tension. "Anyone need a shot?"

"Never again." I have no verbal filter when I'm drunk.

"Probably again, though," Hammer chirps.

Everyone chuckles.

Connor stretches his arm across the back of Dred's chair. "What does Flip have planned for your date this weekend?"

"Um." I look to Flip.

"It's a surprise," he informs me.

"You better not take Tally to East Side's," Rix warns.

"Like that's where I'd take Talls for our first date."

"I'll have Sam and Isaac on standby just in case," Hemi warns.

"You won't need them," Flip says confidently. "I have a fantastic first date planned, and you can ask Tally all about it after it happens."

"What's the dress code?" Shilpa, the team lawyer, fishes.

"That's actually a good question." And one I haven't asked yet.

"You would look beautiful in a burlap sack," Flip assures me.

"I don't own one of those, so we can't test that theory," I quip.

"You have lots of pretty dresses, though."

"Do not take Tally to glow-in-the-dark mini putt in a dress and heels." Rix points a finger at her brother.

Flip gives her the side-eye. "As if I would do that."

"You suck at mini putt." Tristan smirks.

I jump in. "I don't mind mini putt."

"You can kick my ass in the future, but it will not be on our first date," Flip replies.

It inspires conversation about best and worst dates from our friends. I don't share my worst date, since I don't want Hemi to sic her brothers on the guy, or for Flip to track him down and unalive him.

I down my cola in a hurry, mouth dry from all the anxiety of tonight.

"I'll get you another." Flip squeezes my hand and hops off his chair.

"Okay. Thanks." I'm hyperaware of the way my friends' significant others are casually affectionate with each other, and I don't know what to do with my hands.

"You know we're just giving him the gears because we love you, right?" Rix says.

"And also because Flip hasn't been on an actual date since we were in high school," Tristan adds.

"For real, though?" Quinn seems mystified.

"Pretty much. He had a girlfriend when we were at the Hockey Academy, right?" Dallas chimes in.

"That's right," Tristan confirms.

Before I can ask more questions about the high school girlfriend, Flip returns with my cola.

At the same time a pair of women approach.

I'm immediately on alert as they aim their wide smiles at

Flip. "Hey!" The one with sandy blonde hair throws her arms around him. "It's been forever!"

Flip freezes, jaw tight, along with the rest of his body.

She releases him. "You remember me, right?" She taps over her heart and winks. "Trinity." This draws attention to her ample, enviable cleavage. Then she squeezes her friend's shoulder. "And Tiffany."

"Oh, fuck me." Tristan wraps a protective arm around Rix and drops his head, whispering something in her ear.

My stomach sinks and twists. Flip shifts subtly, putting his body between me and the women.

Tiffany's gaze shifts to Tristan, and she pales. She grabs Trinity's arm and whispers something that makes her eyes flare.

Trinity's smile turns wooden. "Sorry to interrupt," she says. "It was nice to, uh… Have a good night."

The two of them rush off, heads together.

It doesn't take a genius to figure out how Trinity and Tiffany know Flip and Tristan.

Normally, bunnies don't approach the guys when we're at the Watering Hole. It's supposed to be a safe space. Suddenly I feel out of my depth. While I knew eventually it would happen, I didn't expect it tonight.

"I'm taking Bea home," Tristan announces as he pushes his chair back.

Rix lets him help her into her jacket. Tristan seems more upset than she does.

She rounds the table to hug me. "They're no one and you're everything, just remember that."

"Thanks."

"We all have your back."

My stomach is a mess as she moves to hug Flip and murmurs something to him.

A moment later he's at my side, arm stretched protectively

across the back of my chair, finger tucked under my chin. "Are you okay?"

I bite my lip and nod, not trusting my voice, and not entirely sure I'm being honest. But everyone is watching again, and not for any good reason.

His eyes search mine. "Why don't we head out, kitten?"

"Okay." Between our friends, my dad, and those women, I'm at capacity for anxiety-invoking situations.

"I'm taking Talls home," he announces as he helps me down from my stool and into my coat.

I relish each brush of his fingers and the gentle contact.

I hug the girls, who all whisper words of reassurance.

Flip laces our fingers. It's such a simple thing, but it sets me at ease as he guides me to the door.

Once we're alone and the engine is running, he turns to me. "Can I touch you?"

I nod.

"I need you to say it out loud. I need your verbal permission, Tally." He's serious, and on edge.

"I would like you to touch me," I whisper.

We exhale matching relieved breaths as he slides his shaking hand under my hair and curves his wide palm around the back of my neck. "Do you understand why I need permission?"

I shrug. I could guess, but I'd rather hear it from him.

His thumb sweeps back and forth along my pulse point. "I can't make assumptions about how you're feeling after something like that happens. I don't want my touch to be associated with negative situations like those for either of us."

My heart aches at the pained look on his face. "Your touch right now is comforting," I assure him.

"For me, too." He leans in and presses his forehead briefly to mine. "I'm sorry about those women."

"It's not your fault," I whisper.

He pulls back, eyes dark. "Actually, it's totally my fault."

"I know you have a past." It's true. I even witnessed some of it when I was an intern with the Terror, but we're far removed from that, now. This was an unlucky coincidence.

"The Watering Hole should've been a safe place for us."

"You can't control what other people do and say." I cover his hand with mine, feeling like he needs my touch the same way I need his.

"Doesn't change the way it makes either of us feel, though. I want to be worth the risk for you, Tally. So I need you to be honest when things like this upset you. I don't want you to sit on those feelings, okay?"

"Okay," I agree.

He curls his fingers around mine. "You want to tell me how that made you feel?"

I bite the inside of my cheek, parsing through my emotions.

"Talk to me," he encourages. "I need this from you, even if it's hard."

"I was annoyed that they were too clueless to realize they shouldn't approach you at all. I felt bad for Tristan."

His jaw ticks.

I drop my gaze to our clasped hands. I don't know where the boundaries are. "I didn't know what to do."

"What did you want to do?" he asks softly.

"Tuck myself against your side. Pull your arm around me." Show them he's mine. "I knew this would happen, but knowing and experiencing it isn't the same."

"Then next time that's exactly what you should do." He kisses the back of my hand. "I'm going to take you home, okay?"

I try to hide my disappointment. "Okay."

We're quiet on the drive to my apartment. I don't love knowing that women will constantly hit on him wherever he goes. Or that the media will speculate about his sex life. Or that

Flip might externalize his own fears and try to protect me from his past by throwing up walls I don't know how to climb over or knock down.

Flip doesn't pull up in front of my building. Instead, he parks in the visitors' lot.

"I'd like to walk you up."

Relief washes over me. "Yes, please."

He cuts the engine and hops out, rounding the hood as I unfasten my seat belt. He puts his arm around me as we make the short walk to my building. The atrium is mostly quiet apart from a few late-night studiers, as is the elevator.

"I need to hug you." He pulls me against his chest, wrapping his arms around me as we ascend.

I hum contentedly and link my hands at the small of his back while I listen to the heavy thud of his heart.

We stop at my floor and Flip keeps his arm around me as he walks me down the hall. When we reach my door, he pushes my hair over my shoulders. "Can I come in?"

"Yeah, of course. I'd love that."

One side of his mouth quirks up. "Me, too."

My hand shakes as I swipe the fob across the sensor. "We have to be quick," I remind him.

I slip through the door, prepared to block Parsnip's escape as Flip follows me, but instead of darting for the narrow gap, my cat scales Flip's pant leg.

"Hey, gorgeous." Flip gently unhooks the cat from his thigh, which is probably bleeding in several places. Parsnip purrs loudly and headbutts his hand.

"You are such a harlot," I grumble and toe off my shoes.

Flip scratches under his chin before setting Parsnip on the floor so he can do the same. "Is Fee home?"

"She's at a friend's tonight." She had a study session that ran late and didn't feel like walking across campus in the freezing cold.

"So we have the place to ourselves."

"It's just you and me and Parsnip," I confirm.

Flip runs his hands down my arms and lifts them, encouraging me to link them behind his neck.

"Hold on tight, kitten." He bends, gripping high on the back of my thighs as he hoists me up. I wrap myself around him, and he carries me down the hall. But he doesn't head for my bedroom, instead he goes to the living room.

He adjusts my legs as he sits in the middle of the couch, with me straddling his thick thighs. My heart is hammering and my body is humming with anticipation.

Flip runs his hands up my thighs, skims my waist and keeps moving up until my face is cradled in his hands. "Don't be jealous of anyone that came before us." He leans in and kisses the edge of my jaw, sending a shiver down my spine. "No one else gets this part of me, but you, Tally."

I tentatively run my fingers through his silky hair.

"I want to give you everything you need." Flip moves one of his hands to my hip and squeezes. "*Be* everything you need."

His teeth scrape gently along the side of my neck, and I whimper.

"That's the sound I've been waiting all night to hear again," he murmurs.

I slide forward in his lap, seeking some kind of friction, but he circles my waist and holds me in place.

He shakes his head. "Remember what I said."

At my confusion, he smiles darkly.

"We go at my pace." He kisses a path along my neck. "And at times like this it will feel excruciatingly slow, but it will be so worth the wait." He pulls back and cups my chin in his wide palm. "Do you know why?"

"Because you care about me."

"That's exactly right, kitten." He brushes his lips over mine. "And I take care of what's mine."

His fingertips press into my skin as he angles my head and finally, *finally* kisses me.

His lips are satin, his tongue velvet.

I feel special. Important. Cherished.

Flip has spent his adult life avoiding connection.

But with me, it's what he wants most.

CHAPTER 22

FLIP

"Thanks for coming over." I usher Dred into my apartment. It's finally my date night with Tally. I fight a frown as Connor follows her in like an annoyed, threatening shadow. "I didn't realize you were coming, too."

"It's my wife's day off. I go where she goes." Connor's tone implies I'm an idiot for not realizing this.

I plaster on a smile. "If you're hungry, I have everything you need to make yourself a ham and cheese sandwich."

Connor flips me the bird. "Go fuck a T-shirt, Madden."

"Are you offering yours?"

"Stop being a brat. Both of you." Dred kisses her husband's jaw.

"But then your attention won't be on me, darling."

"This won't take long. Then you can go back to being Dred's sole focus," I assure him.

"Untrue. We're taking the twins to the movies tonight, so Mildred's focus will be very divided, much as it is now."

Connor crosses to the fridge and pulls out an ancient Tupperware jug. He opens it, peers inside, and sniffs the contents. Then he rummages around in my cupboards for a glass. Dred could help him if she wanted, since she knows where everything is, but she lets him fend for himself. Probably to keep him occupied for five seconds.

"Let's get you dressed." Dred motions to my bedroom.

"I have two potential suit options. I'm taking Tally to the aquarium and we're having dinner with the sharks."

"Seems fitting," Connor calls.

"Feel free to keep your thoughts to yourself," I retort.

"So happy to see you two getting along," Dred deadpans. "Tally will love the aquarium. She's forever watching the Shark Week documentaries."

"And then regretting it on ocean vacations," I add.

"So true, but she pushed through when we went to Aruba."

"Exactly. And it's a huge step up from keg parties and chain restaurants, without being overwhelming." I want this date to be special, without being over-the-top.

"It's fun, outside the box, and it shows you know what she likes."

"That's the goal." Running into not one, but two past hookups after our last game sucked. We navigated that stressful situation, but I'd like to avoid another one tonight. On the upside, almost all of my previous hookups have been met at bars, so the aquarium seems safe. "I'll just change into my suit and get your seal of approval, yeah?"

"Sounds great."

I change while she and Connor wait in the living room.

"The suit's a little understated," Connor notes.

He wore a maroon tux for his wedding, so I'll take his opinion with a grain of salt.

"Flip doesn't need to piss off his sad, beige parents the way you do." Dred pats his thigh and gives me a thumbs-up. "You look great."

"Cool."

"This stuff reminds me of the orange drink Meems loves from McD's." Connor swirls the liquid in his cup.

"It's Tang." I cross to the cupboards, pull out a packet, and toss it to him. I buy it by the twelve pack, so I feel comfortable parting with one. "You can blow her mind with this. I add an extra cup of water. Otherwise it's too sweet."

"Thanks." He inspects it for a moment, then tucks it into his pocket. "Did you buy Tally a dress for tonight?"

"No. I didn't want to scare her off by coming on too strong." I adjust my tie and check my reflection one last time. "But I did stop by the Dutch Toko for dropjes, and I bought her flowers."

"What are dropjes?" Connor asks.

"Salty and sweet black licorice. They're her favorite," I explain.

Connor seems skeptical. "People enjoy that?"

"Tally does." I prefer the sweet ones exclusively, especially when they're candy coated. "Okay. I'm ready. Any words of wisdom?"

"Tally's used to university boys who think a keg party constitutes a date, so you're already ahead of the curve." Connor removes Dred's glasses, cleans them and replaces them.

"I better be ahead of the fucking curve. Especially where the last guy she dated is concerned."

"No one liked him." Dred wrinkles her nose. "Just be your charming self."

"And keep the focus on Tally," Connor adds. "She's used to being around people who want her for the wrong reasons, or guys who already have too much ego. Whatever she wants, she gets."

"Except for one thing," Dred chimes in.

"What thing would that—" Connor's brow lifts. "—never mind. I already know the answer. Agreed. The only thing you should withhold is your favored appendage."

"Thanks for the solid advice."

"Anytime. I highly advise waiting until you at least get past date five," Connor tacks on.

"Is that how long you and Dred waited?" I hold up my hand when he opens his mouth. "I don't actually need an answer to that."

I gather the flowers and dropjes, and Connor and Dred join me in the elevator.

"You'll be great. You've been friends for years. You're just taking it to the next level now."

I drive across town to Tally's apartment and park in the temporary spot in front of her building, which miraculously opens up the second I arrive. I don't have a chance to go up and get her, because she's stepping off the elevator as I enter the building.

She's wearing a stunning ice blue dress, her jacket slung over her arm, hair falling in artful waves over her shoulders. Her eyes light up when she sees me, then cloud with worry as she takes in the bustling, student-filled space.

I close the distance between us and cup her cheek in my palm. "You look concerned, kitten, is everything okay?"

"Yeah, I just thought I'd meet you outside so you don't have to deal with all of this." She motions to our surroundings.

"I can't see anything but you." I brush my lips over hers and barely resist the urge to deepen it. I step back and take her hand, gaze roving over her. "You're a vision. Is this dress new?"

She shakes her head. "I went shopping in Fee's closet."

"Well, I love this on you." I hold up the flowers. "And it matches these perfectly."

"They're beautiful."

"You're beautiful."

"Holy fuck. I think that's Flip Madden."

"Where?"

"The guy in the suit."

"We should go if you don't want to get mobbed," Tally whispers.

"Let me help you with your coat," I offer as she slides one arm through and I circle her to assist with the other, quickly freeing her hair as she fastens two buttons. I wrap a protective arm around her, and steer her toward the doors, giving the Tilton Hockey guys a chin tip as we pass.

A group of guys check out my ride as I guide Tally to the passenger side and help her in. I use my body to shield her as I adjust her dress to make sure the hem won't get caught in the door, as I close it, protecting her from prying eyes.

"Dude, that's Flip Madden."

"No way. What would he be doing here?" one guy scoffs.

It makes me edgy to think about the questions people might ask once we're public. But this is a first date. One step at a time.

I take my place behind the wheel, closing myself in with Tally. I quickly buckle my seat belt and pull away from the curb before the guys think to swarm my car. It's happened before.

"Did those guys recognize you, too?" Tally inspects the bouquet of blue and white blossoms.

"Yeah. I should probably rotate my cars to keep it fresh," I reply.

"You're also dressed in a suit, so you kind of stand out among the hoodie and jeans crowd."

"And you don't?" I give her a lingering once-over. "Seriously, you're killing me, already."

"I didn't even do anything."

"Stop looking so tempting."

She widens her eyes. "Only if you stop being so devastatingly handsome."

"Is that how you would describe me?" I ask.

"Depends on who I'm describing you to, I guess."

"So it changes according to the audience?"

"Absolutely. Like I'd tell my granny you're handsome, but I'd tell my friends you're fuckhot, one word, not two."

"Is there a dictionary definition to go with that?"

"Yeah, it's the fire and heart eyes emojis."

I laugh and her grin widens.

"I like it."

"It suits you, I think."

"Mm." I set my hand palm up on the center console and she slides her delicate fingers into it. "How was your day?"

"Good. Long because I've been waiting all day to see you. How was yours?"

"The same. I tried to read after practice, but I couldn't focus."

She shifts so she's facing me. "How do you like the new book?"

"It's wickedly addictive."

"Right?" Her eyes light up. "I would have died if I had to wait a whole year between books. Thankfully I stumbled on it when it was complete, so I didn't have to languish in despair over the cliffhangers."

"You didn't say anything about a cliffhanger when you gave it to me."

"Don't worry. I'll have the next one ready for you."

"You should just give it to me now, so *I* don't have to languish in despair," I bargain.

She tosses her hair over her shoulder. "But then I won't have any leverage."

"What would you need leverage for?"

She shrugs. "It never hurts to have a bargaining chip."

"And you think I'm the evil one? You know I live for those dog-eared pages."

She rolls her bottom lip between her teeth. "Are they your favorite?"

"You know it."

"Tell me why."

"Because I get these little glimpses of what makes you tick." I kiss the back of her hand. "They're yours and you trust me with them. They're pieces of you."

Everything about her softens. I want more of these unguarded moments with her.

I turn in to the aquarium parking lot, and Tally's whole face lights up. "Oh my gosh, Flip! The axolotl exhibit! Fee mentioned it last week, and I looked them up and they are literally the most adorable little things in the universe. Plus, sharks! This is so exciting!"

I love that I got it right. "I thought you might like it."

"I love it!"

I pull up to the valet and shift the car into park. I cup her chin in my palm and lean in until her breath breaks across my lips. "Would you like me to kiss you while we still have privacy, kitten?"

"Yes, please," she whimpers softly.

I brush my lips over hers. "Say it again."

She exhales shakily. "Please, Phillip."

"So fucking sweet." I slant my mouth over hers, stroking inside, tasting her, exploring her mouth as her nails bite into my wrist and she mewls softly.

I break the kiss before her hands start to roam. "Wait here."

She blinks at me, dazed as I exit the car and raise a hand, signaling for the valet to wait. I round the hood and he opens the door, stepping aside so I can offer Tally my hand as she rises.

I guide her up the steps and into the building. We head directly for the coat check.

I cover her hands. "Let me."

She tips her head in question.

"I want to savor every minute with you." I bend until my lips are at her ear. "And this is like unwrapping the perfect gift."

CHAPTER 23
TALLY

I am on cloud nine, but also my entire body is pinging with pent-up sexual energy. Everything Flip does and says sends me into a hormonal tailspin. Even just the simple act of holding my hand makes me all melty inside as we watch sea creatures darting through the coral reef.

A sea otter corkscrews in front of us. "That one's flirting with you," Flip observes as it does figure eights against the glass.

"Maybe they're flirting with you." I snuggle into his side as the otter does a full-body wave.

He gazes down at me, eyes heating. "Would you dance for me?"

"Like that?" I nod to the otter.

"However you want, as long as it's just for me."

"I would love to," I whisper.

Before he can reply, a woman calls his name.

Anxiety makes my chest tight as Flip drops my hand and turns toward the voice. *Please don't be another former hookup.* A woman who looks closer to his age than mine approaches. And she's beautiful.

"It's so great to see you!" She hugs him and I immediately want to throw down.

Thankfully she releases him quickly. "What are you doing here of all places? Is there some kind of charity event I don't know about?"

"I'm on a date." Flip steps to the side and slips his arm around my waist, which is when I realize his previous maneuver was meant to be protective. "Tally, this is Laura. I coach her younger brother, Auggie."

"It's so nice to meet you." I no longer want to catfight her. Mostly. I smile and place a possessive hand on his chest.

"Oh! Hi." Her gaze darts between me and Flip. "I'm so sorry to interrupt. Your dress is beautiful."

"Isn't she stunning?" Flip kisses my temple, which I appreciate.

Auggie appears, wiping his hands on his pants. "I'm back! Coach Madden! What are you doing at the aquarium?"

"Checking out the fish, just like you," Flip says.

"I love the sharks the most! Are you still going to be my coach next summer?"

"I sure am. Are you going to be the MVP again?"

"I'm going to try!" Auggie animatedly tells Flip about the last goal he scored for his school team.

"I'm so sorry we intruded on your date," Laura whispers to me.

"Not at all. I love how involved Flip is in the community."

"He's such a great coach," Laura agrees. "He's so patient with the kids."

"He has an incredibly kind heart," I agree.

An announcement comes over the PA that the shark movie starts in ten minutes.

"Oh! We have to go! I want good seats," Auggie says. "See you in the summer, Coach Madden."

"See you in the summer!" Laura waves as Auggie pulls her toward the theater.

"Auggie seems sweet," I note.

"He's a lot of fun. I've been his coach for the past three summers."

"Laura seems like a fan," I observe.

"Of hockey?"

I can't tell if he's being intentionally oblivious. "And you."

He kisses my cheek. "Well, I'm a fan of you." He thumbs over his shoulder at the otter still showing off behind us. "And so is that guy."

I laugh.

"Hungry?"

"Famished, actually."

"Me too, but that shouldn't be a surprise."

Flip leads me to the private restaurant inside the aquarium, which has a 360-degree view of the sharks swimming around us. It feels like we're the ones inside the tank.

"This is amazing," I tell him once we're seated.

"I'm glad you like it." Flip squeezes my hand. "I wanted this to be a date to remember."

"It was already going to be memorable because it's with you," I admit.

"I feel the exact same way." His smile is soft.

The server stops by, and we order drinks and the cauliflower wings to start. The menu is plant-based, and everything sounds delicious.

"Thank you for being accommodating with Auggie and his sister," Flip says once it's just us again.

"You really love coaching those kids, don't you?" He refuses to allow Hemi to use his volunteer coaching as a promo opportunity. Tristan and Brody do it, too.

"I do." He drags his fingers along mine, thoughtful for a moment. "They're just…honest and joyful. They're not caught up in the social media storm, or gossip, or who's the best. It's about having fun, and sometimes I need the reminder there's more to this job than winning."

"Is this something you can see yourself doing professionally later? Coaching?" My stomach twists. I know what that life looks like when it's all-consuming.

"For the pros?" Flip strokes the center of my palm. "It depends on what else is happening in my life. I like playing in Toronto because it keeps me close to my sister and my parents. Ideally, I'd like to finish my career here, but anything can happen." As if sensing my unease, Flip curls his hand around mine. "My future after hockey will be made with the people who are closest to me in mind."

I force a smile and take a breath. We're on our first date. Stressing about what things might look like a few months from now, let alone several years, doesn't make sense. "I just see the way things didn't work out with my parents, and I want to be able to honor what my partner needs, and for my partner to be able to do the same. My mom set aside her needs to make room for my dad's and it didn't work out for them."

"I think that makes a lot of sense, especially with how fresh this all is for you. I've made bad relationship decisions, and I want to avoid repeating those when it comes to you. Which is why I want to do this right and take it slow."

My heart skips a couple of beats. "That makes me feel important."

"You are important, Tally. I care about you."

"I care about you, too." My feelings for Flip already feel bigger than I know what to do with.

Our drinks and appetizers arrive, breaking the sudden tension. We order our mains and dig into the appetizer. "You're not going to try to feed me this time?"

"It feels like we're being watched," Flip whispers as a shark swims by.

I laugh and relax a little.

"When is your next showcase? When do I get to see you on stage again?"

"We don't have a major performance until the end of the term, but we'll have class performances mid-semester and a few smaller individual pieces leading up to our final showcase. All our routines are set, but it's been a struggle to book enough practice time lately."

"Is your schedule too heavy?" he asks.

"No. Our usual studio is being renovated after a flood."

"That's not great. How long will that take?"

"Hard to say." I shrug. "They've been slow with updates."

"There's a yoga studio in my building. I can check availability for you," Flip offers.

"I appreciate that, and if we can't find another solution, I'll let you know, but it's a lot of extra commuting, and they also both have part-time jobs, so we're trying to find something close to campus."

"That's a lot of added pressure with everything else you have going on," Flip notes with concern. "It can't be easy. Courses, dance practice, family stuff."

"We don't have to talk about heavy stuff."

"I want this with you, Tally. I want you to feel safe with me, to confide in me."

"I used to think I wanted a relationship like my parents'," I admit. "I always thought they were happy, now I know they weren't, and everything is reframed."

I see all these great relationships around me with my Terror friends, and with Cammie and Chase, and I want to believe they'll all endure, but who knows what's happening behind closed doors? What if they all fall apart, too? It's terrifying.

"I had my faith shaken like that," Flip says softly.

"With your ex from high school?"

He nods.

"What happened?"

"I loved her and I thought she loved me too." His eyes lift. "But she wanted me for all the wrong reasons."

My heart aches for him. "Because of your career?"

"Basically, yeah." He smiles sadly.

"People always want a piece of you, don't they?"

"Some people," he agrees. "And for a long time I let them take pieces they didn't deserve."

"But not anymore?" He's giving *me* a piece of himself, and I want to protect it, tuck it into my heart, and keep it there forever.

"Not anymore. Now I only want to give pieces of myself to people who will take care of them," he confides. "I used to associate romantic love with pain. I didn't trust my own judgment. So for a long while, I was exclusively pleasure-focused." His gaze lifts. "If it felt good, I did it."

I wait for the jealousy to come, but it never does. None of those women were taken on thoughtful dates. He didn't pick them up and bring them flowers. It was about sex and nothing else. "But that's not what you want now?"

"I want this." He brings my hand to his lips again. "I want intimacy with *you*, Tally. I forgot how good it could feel to share this part of myself with someone."

I can barely breathe. He's so earnest, so honest. "I want to guard all your secrets, Phillip. I want to be safe for you, too."

He cups my chin in his palm and leans across the table, brushing his lips over mine. "You're my dream girl, Tally." He leans back. "Every step we take forward needs to mean something."

"You want me to feel special."

"Exactly. You're a gift. So when I break my two years of celibacy, it will be because I want this experience with you, and you want the same thing for the same reasons." He kisses the inside of my wrist. "But we can have a whole lot of fun learning what makes each other tick while we get there."

Warmth settles low in my stomach. What will it be like when we make it past first base? Will he be soft and sweet? Will we both be so pent-up that we'll come together like a lightning strike?

He bites my knuckle, and I exhale on a needy whimper.

"Are you thinking about all the things that haven't happened yet, kitten?"

"It's hard not to when your mouth is on my skin."

"Tell me what gets you hot."

"You."

He grins. "Have you ever had an orgasm in a public place?"

"Yes."

Surprise flashes across his face and his eyes darken.

"Does that shock you?"

"Pleasantly, yes." He leans in closer, dropping his voice to a whisper. "When and where?"

My foot brushes his shin, and I uncross and recross my legs. "Backstage after a performance."

"Were there other people around?" he asks, eyes lighting up with expectation.

"Other people were performing." We were the first onstage that night. It had been such an adrenaline rush, and hormones added to the high. "We ducked into a dark corner in the wings."

"Who's we?"

"Me and one of the guys from my troupe."

Flip's eyes light up with approval. "How'd he make you come?"

I do jazz hands. I hadn't expected the orgasm, so it had been a real thrill for both of us.

"So the possibility of getting caught turns you on."

"Are you tucking that away for safekeeping?"

His thumb circles the center of my palm. "One day, I'll be making you come in the wings while your friends are performing."

A shiver runs through me.

His answering smile is full of filthy promises.

"What about you?" My voice is hoarse. "What's the most public place you've had sex?"

"You mean other than a night club."

"How did you get away with that?" It's always a pulse of bodies, you can't turn around without bumping into someone.

"Lots of dark corners."

Heat rushes through me at the idea of Flip tucking me into one of those corners, making me come while everyone around us dances. "What's more public than that?"

"I fucked my high school girlfriend on a Ferris wheel while we were stuck at the top."

"Oh my God." A thrill shoots down my spine. "Everyone around you must have known."

He grins. "I'm sure they did. But she was afraid of heights. I was doing my due diligence by distracting her."

I laugh. "So considerate."

He smirks. "I thought so."

"Was it a rush?"

"Oh yeah."

"Maybe you should take me to a carnival sometime."

"When the weather is nice," he agrees.

Like he has plans for us. Like this is the first date of many.

We pause the conversation while the server clears our appetizer plates to make room for our meals.

"Tell me about one of your fantasies," he says when we're alone again.

"In general, or specific to you?"

His eyes darken. "A *me*-specific fantasy, please."

I decide to keep my fanfic-inspired fantasies to myself—for now. I trace the rim of my wineglass. "I was never allowed to have boys in my room growing up."

"Smart parents." Flip nods his approval.

"But were they? Teenagers are resourceful, and I did get fingerbanged backstage after a recital," I remind him.

Flip sucks his teeth, the look on his face sending another shot of heat skittering along my spine.

I run my finger down the stem of my wineglass. This is Flip Madden. He's done it all, and I'm manifesting my dirty hopes and dreams. "Well, sometime in the future, before or after we've taken a ride on the Ferris wheel, I'd like to be fucked in my childhood bedroom. Preferably with the door open."

He makes a low sound in the back of his throat. "While your parents are home."

I shift in my seat as sweat breaks on the back of my neck. "Maybe they have to run to the store."

"Do you really think I would rush when I'm fulfilling one of your fantasies?"

I shake my head and swallow thickly.

He kisses my fingertips. "I would take my time, bring you right to the edge and make sure you didn't tip over until they came back."

I shudder and dark satisfaction sparks in his eyes. "What's your bedroom look like at your parents' house, kitten?"

"An homage to my teen years. Very dance-themed."

"Is it pretty and delicate like you?"

"I guess." I bite my lip and duck my head at the compliment. "I only ever had a single bed."

His nostrils flare. "Daddy didn't want you to have a grown-up bed?"

I shake my head. I'm hot all over and I'm sure that's the point. I've spent years fantasizing about the man in front of me, but nothing I dreamed up comes close to the reality.

"What about your bedroom in your apartment? What's that like?"

I widen my eyes. "You'll have to see it to find out."

"Future me looks forward to that day."

All this talk emboldens me. "Future you has an open invitation to visit my bedroom anytime you like."

He chuckles.

The server stops to refill our waters, breaking the tension.

We spend the rest of dinner talking mostly about how incredible the food is. Flip ordered the dragon bowl, and I have the portobello steak.

Afterward, we drive back to my apartment and Flip parks in the temporary spot. "This is literally never open, except when you're here."

"I manifest it." He winks.

I want to invite him up, but Fee and Cammie were planning to hang out tonight, and our place is often the favored location. I unbuckle my seat belt and shift to face him. "I had the best time tonight. The aquarium was perfect, and dinner was…amazing." And stimulating. Me, pillow Flip, and my vibe have a date before bed tonight.

"I had a great time, too. I learned a lot about you." His eyes caress my face.

"I want to invite you in, but my apartment might be full of my friends," I explain.

"That's okay. I'll still walk you up." He stretches his arm across the seat. "But I'll kiss you good night here, just in case." His fingers slip under my hair, curving gently around my nape. I lean in as he does the same, eyes fluttering closed as his lips meet mine.

He's so soft with me, tender and sweet as he sucks my bottom lip. And then his tongue brushes mine. I whimper as he angles my head and deepens the kiss, exploring my mouth with heady sureness.

"That fucking sound, kitten." He drags me across the center console into his lap. His wide palm drifts up my side.

"Please." I'm ravenous for more of his hands and his mouth and the deep groans that rumble through his chest and across my lips. I moan when he cups my breast and his thumb brushes my nipple.

The touch disappears and he moves to cup my face, separating our lips.

"More, please," I whisper.

"You're fiery tonight, aren't you?"

"You were the one asking me about my fantasies."

"I have no regrets." He kisses my chin. "But we should probably avoid an indecent exposure charge if we want to stay on your dad's good side."

"You're the one who put me here." I wiggle in his lap.

"I did do that, didn't I?" He moves me back to the passenger seat. "I'm still walking you up."

He cuts the engine and comes around to the passenger side to help me out of the car. It's quiet in the atrium, and the elevator is empty except for us. Flip wraps his arms around me, and I settle my head on his chest, comforted by the steady thud of his heart. We reach my floor without running into anyone else.

I pass my key fob over the sensor and crack the door to my apartment. The TV is on, and laughter filters down the hall.

"I'll say good night here." Flip moves closer, until our bodies are flush again.

Parsnip meows and swats at my ankle. The door isn't open enough for him to slip through.

"Thank you for a perfect first date," he whispers.

I melt as he presses his lips to mine, warm, minty, and full of promise.

CHAPTER 24

FLIP

It's fajita night at Rix and Tristan's. We get together once a month for food and drinks. Tally often joins us, but this is the first with her as my date.

"Can you mash these, please?" Rix passes me the flat-bottomed container of avocado halves and the potato masher.

"Chunky though, right? Not holiday-dinner-mashed-potato smooth," I confirm.

"You got it."

Tally is dutifully chopping tomatoes with Hemi next to her, murdering onions while glaring at me. I haven't done anything wrong. At least I don't think I have, but I can picture my balls in place of the onions. Tally has been the little sister of the group for years, and we've all had our skepticism over some of her past boyfriends. Now that I'm dating her, I feel like I'm in the hot seat. And like everyone is waiting for me to fuck it up.

Or maybe that's just me.

I deal with the avocados and move to the sink to rinse the masher.

Tristan gives me a look.

"What?"

"Dude."

"You're going to need to elaborate past a single word."

"Bro." The word drips disappointment. "Is Tally suddenly made of glass?"

"What?"

"You're dating her, be affectionate, man."

"I'm not going to hump all over her." Although the dreams in which I do have been pretty fucking relentless lately.

"That's not—" Tristan shakes his head and looks at the ceiling. "That I'm the one giving advice makes it feel like I'm in a parallel universe." He sighs. "You're making it weird, man."

I rub the back of my neck. "Tally is like everyone's sister. I'm trying to be respectful."

Tristan pokes at his cheek with his tongue. "Or you're being a chickenshit."

Is that what it is? Am I being too cautious? "I don't know how to walk the line."

"Explain."

This is Tristan. We've been friends since we were in diapers. He's seen the worst of me and we're still tight. "Beyond hugs from friends and family, I'm used to affection being a precursor to sex. It's always been all or nothing. I'm struggling with the middle ground. I don't want to fuck it up and default back to old Flip."

"That won't happen. Old Flip doesn't have the power he used to." He squeezes my shoulder. "Before you started dating, you hugged Tally all the time, right?"

"Yeah." But she was in the friend box and now she's in a new one.

"So keep doing that, but add a kiss on the cheek. Just something to show her and everyone else that you're hers."

"Everything okay here?" Rix asks.

"We're good," Tristan and I say at the same time.

"Uh-huh." She gives us a skeptical look. "Flip, can you stir this and a handful of Tally's tomatoes into the avocado mash?" Rix passes me a small bowl with minced garlic, lime juice, and some spices, her expression expectant.

"For sure."

Hemi has put down the knife and is now busy bathing the red onions in ice water. It's a hack to take out the sharpness.

I slip an arm around Tally's waist from behind as she drains the juice from the tomatoes, brushing my lips over her cheek. "Hi."

She relaxes into me. "Hi." Her voice is soft and breathy, exactly like it was when I had to end the kiss the other night before it escalated to criminal proportions. I shut those thoughts down. I'll let them out later, when I'm alone in the shower.

"Can you drop a handful of tomatoes in here for me?" I murmur against her ear.

"Put that tone away." Hemi points a spatula at me. At least it's not a knife.

"What tone?" I glance around. "I asked for tomatoes."

"Yeah, but it sounds like you're offering to service her in front of all your friends," Essie pipes up, unhelpfully.

"You could narrate some spicy audiobooks with that voice," Dred adds with a smile.

I glance at Tristan, who just shrugs. This is harder than I thought it would be.

"Oooh! You should get Flip to read you Cammie's fics!" Hammer's eyes light up.

"I read Dred Cammie's fics." Connor smirks.

"You're so good at it." Dred pats his cheek.

"I'm good at a lot of things." Connor's normally slanted brows tip up.

"Don't be braggy," Dred chastises.

"Pretty sure this is their foreplay," I whisper.

"Oh, it is." Tally's sigh seems a little envious as she drops a handful of tomatoes into the avocado mash.

"Thanks." I kiss her cheek again. I can't learn if I don't try.

"Want help stirring them in, too?" she offers.

"Please." I pass her a spoon, happy to cocoon her against the counter so I can keep huffing her cherry blossom shampoo. "What's the deal with Cammie's fics?"

"I'll tell you more about that when you're ready."

"You don't think I can handle it?"

"Uh no, I don't think *I* can." The flush in her cheeks is revealing.

"Now I'm even more intrigued."

"Excellent. My nefarious plan is working."

"I like it when you're sassy." I wrap an arm around her waist, hugging her from behind.

Tristan gives me a subtle chin dip in approval.

Once the avocado mash is mixed, I add it to the growing spread at the dining room table.

Quinn and Kellan arrive with beer and street corn, completing the meal. Only Ash and Shilpa couldn't make it tonight since Pavin is running a fever.

Gathering around the table, we pass bowls as we doctor up our fajitas. There's a whole carousel of sauces and dips.

"Maybe we need to rotate fajita night locations so you're not always hosting," Hemi says to Rix.

"Oh, this is my happy place. I'm totally living my dream, and getting all our friends together for dinner is the icing on the cake." Rix hugs Tristan's arm.

Tristan beams as he gazes down at my sister. "You're made of magic."

She smiles. "I wouldn't have this without you."

Rix went back to school for nutrition and finished her degree last summer. She finally resigned from her accounting firm and now she handles my, Tristan's, and Dallas's financial portfolios, and spends the rest of her time creating meal plans for many of the guys on the team. She's amazing at it, and she loves it.

Tristan rubs his nose against hers.

"Save it for when everyone leaves, you two," Nate grumbles.

Rix laughs and puts her hand over Tristan's mouth when he tries to come in for another kiss.

I stretch my arm across the back of Tally's chair.

"We're looking at renting Bea a professional kitchen too, and possibly hiring an assistant," Tristan says.

"If you have access to a professional kitchen, will you have room for another client?" Quinn asks hopefully.

"Or two," Kellan adds.

"Once I have an assistant I can," Rix says.

"Awesome," Quinn says.

"I'd even be happy with a meal or two a week," Kellan adds.

Tally rolls her bottom lip between her teeth as she covertly checks a message on her phone.

"Everything okay?" I ask.

"Arya from my dance troupe had to pick up another shift at work, but it conflicts with our scheduled practice, and everything is booked out for weeks," she explains.

"Did you have this problem last semester?" Hammer asks.

"No, but one of the main studios is under construction, and we all need more practice time leading up to the final showcase of the year."

"That's not ideal," Essie says.

Tally smiles, but it's strained. "I honestly thought the floors would be done by now. Hopefully soon, though. In the meantime, we're trying to be creative. I've booked the yoga studio in my building, but other people jumped on that recently, so there's less availability, especially on short notice."

Hemi frowns and turns to me. "What about the one in your building, Flip?"

I nod. "It's an option, but it's a half-hour commute even on off-hours." I've looked into spaces for Tally, but I'm keeping it to myself until I have it locked down.

"The commute eats into study hours," Tally explains.

"I'd offer the Hockey Academy yoga studio, but you'd run into the same commute issue," Roman says.

"I really appreciate it, though. I'm trying to be mindful of Charles and Arya's financial constraints since they're both on scholarship." Tally's phone buzzes again. "It's my sister. I'll be right back."

"The spare bedroom is down the hall on your left, if you need privacy," Rix calls.

"Thanks. I shouldn't be long." Tally disappears down the hall.

"She seems stressed," Hemi says once we hear the door close.

"Her plate is pretty full these days, but I'm working on a solution for the studio." I drop my voice. "I've narrowed it down to two places. One is substantially closer to her apartment."

"You're blocking time for her at a studio?" Dred asks.

"Short-term rental, actually, then her troupe doesn't have to worry about planning around open slots," I explain.

Hemi quiet claps.

Dallas holds out his fist. "That's a top-tier boyfriend move."

Connor starts to open his mouth, and Dred covers it with her palm. "Dallas is right."

"We all know you'd buy Dred the whole strip mall," Roman ribs him good-naturedly.

"It's true." Connor kisses Dred's palm. "I was going to say you've come a long way from fucking a T-shirt."

That gets a few snort-laughs and an eye roll from me.

"Are things okay with Tally's brother and sister?" Rix tugs on the end of her ponytail. "It can't be easy with Vander Zee having moved out."

"Tally was like a second parent before she went to university," Hammer says. "When Tally and I were interning and we'd go away with the team, she fielded lots of video calls from them."

"Yeah, I remember that," Hemi confirms.

"I think it's a little like your situation, Tris," I explain. "Vander Zee is a workaholic, so he's not around much, and there are gaps between all three of them like there are between you and Brodes and Nate."

"I know this relationship comes with risks, but you're really showing up for her in ways that count," Rix says.

"Super swoony boyfriend vibes," Dred adds.

"She's right. I'm super proud of you," Hemi chimes in.

"Same," Tristan says.

"Thanks. I appreciate your votes of confidence." And until this moment, I didn't realize how much I needed them.

Tally returns, and I push back my chair and stand, meeting her halfway across the room. She slips her hand into mine. "Fenna okay?"

"She's stressing about her upcoming cello performance. She'll be okay, though, she just needed to talk it through." I guide her back to the table and tuck her into her seat.

She picks up her margarita and frowns when she realizes it's empty.

"I have a pitcher in the fridge!" Rix starts to stand.

"I got it." I motion for her to stay where she is and grab the fresh pitcher of margaritas, topping up anyone whose glass is low.

"We should play a game!" Hammer declares.

"A drinking game!" Rix adds.

"How about never have I ever, the tequila version!" Essie suggests.

"I thought we agreed that shots were a bad idea," I interject.

"We'll do full margaritas, and it's a sip instead of a shot so we don't end up hating our choices tomorrow," Dred suggests. "And please make mine a zero-proof one."

The women seem to think this is a great plan.

Tristan and I exchange a look.

Connor arches a brow, staring down at his wife. "I'll go first."

"Villain," Dred warns.

"Dredful Menace." He winks and kisses her cheek. "Never have I ever—" He pauses for dramatic effect. "Gone skinny-dipping."

"That is not what I thought you were going to lead with." Everyone takes a sip of their drink, including Tally.

"When?" I ask.

She widens her eyes. "Dance camp."

"You know, it might be time for me and Lexi to go." Roman pushes back his chair and extends a hand to his wife.

"Seriously, Dad?" Hammer rolls her eyes.

"Callie is babysitting Ariel, and we said we'd only be gone a couple of hours. Plus, there are things I just don't want to know," he says.

"Let's be real, Roman. There are also things you don't want your daughter to know." Lexi winks at the table.

That gets a chorus of laughter.

Roman gives Lexi a look, but his ears turn red as he guides her to the door, bending to whisper something to her on the way.

"I bet they're freaky in the bedroom," Dred muses.

"Probably," Hollis says.

Hammer slaps his chest.

"What? There's a good chance. Roman can't be super dad all the time."

"Never have I ever fallen asleep while making out," Dred tosses out, then sips her drink.

"Not with me, you haven't!" Connor says defensively. Then frowns. "Who was this idiot?"

"Dallas actually fell asleep with his face between my thighs," Hemi says gleefully.

"Honey, why you outing me like this?" He holds up a hand. "In all fairness, it was after her brothers came to visit."

"You mean the time they took you on a twenty-kilometer hike?"

"It was a different time, and it was just as fucking awful. I felt like I deserved a real reward for not dying, and I maybe was more exhausted than I realized."

"Half an hour, just sawing logs on top of my pussy."

"You could have moved me at any time."

"You were so peaceful, though."

Kellan almost falls out of his chair he's laughing so hard.

Tally smiles, but she's wringing her hands in her lap.

I try to put myself in her shoes and see it through her eyes. And I get it. Finally. Of course she propositioned me. We have horny friends and we're all open about sex. She's been hanging around with these women for years, and we're a bunch of professional athletes. We do everything at full tilt.

She might not have all of these experiences yet, but I'll be the one to fill every need and fantasy.

"Never have I ever made out with my significant other in an inappropriately public place." I wrap my arm around her shoulder.

"You two need to down the rest of your drinks." Dallas points at Rix and Tristan.

Everyone laughs.

I touch my finger to Tally's chin.

She looks up at me, questions in her pretty, sea-blue eyes. "You don't think my car counts?" I brush my lips over hers. When she doesn't pull away, I suck her bottom lip. Then I move my hand to conceal our faces and stroke inside her mouth.

Someone whistles. Connor starts clapping. Someone throws a balled-up napkin at us, but I don't take my eyes off Tally as I pull back. Her cheeks are red, but she's smiling.

I clink my glass against hers. "Drink up, kitten."

CHAPTER 25

TALLY

I knock, but I doubt anyone can hear me over the whirr of the skill saw. After a few seconds, I poke my head in the studio. I'm holding a tray of coffees and a box of pastries. I don't believe these treats will magically make the studio useable, but Flip suggested it yesterday, so maybe I can at least get an idea of when it will be.

A man in his mid-twenties puts the saw down and approaches. "Hey, how can I help you?"

"I just wanted to stop by with some coffees." I hold out the tray and the bakery box. "And snacks."

"Are you the dance instructor?" he asks skeptically.

I laugh. "No. I'm a student who regularly uses this studio."

"Oh." Understanding dawns. "A lot of you have stopped by to ask when it'll be finished. You're the first to bring snacks, though."

"I'm sorry for the interruption." I look down at the bare plywood floor. "I guess you'll be a while yet?"

He transfers the coffee and snacks to one hand and thumbs over his shoulder with the other. "The prep work is almost done, but the flooring is special order, and it hasn't been delivered yet."

"Ah, okay. So at least a couple more weeks?" I hedge.

"Once the flooring arrives, it should only take a few days to lay, but then it needs to be sealed, so a couple of weeks is optimistic," he explains. "That's probably not what you want to hear, eh?"

I shake my head. "No, but it's easier to plan this way. Thanks for taking the time to explain."

"No problem. Thanks for being understanding."

I can only imagine what other people's reactions have been. A couple of students in my class have broken down in tears over studio time. I've felt the pressure building lately, too.

The final showcase isn't until the end of the semester, but it's not the only thing I need studio time for. I have mini solo and group in-class performances that need my attention as well. I might have to bite the bullet and deal with driving across town to use Flip's yoga studio.

My phone buzzes with a new message.

FLIP

Hey, kitten. How's your morning?

I smile at the term of endearment.

TALLY

I brought the guys working on the studio coffees and pastries. It was appreciated, but it looks like the studio won't be finished for at least another few weeks. I'm worried we don't have enough practice time booked, and the other on-campus studios are waitlist only.

FLIP

I'm sorry. I know this is stressful for you. I'm about to get on the ice, but I'll pick you up when I'm done, and we'll see if we can find a solution.

TALLY

Do you have time for that?

He flies out early tomorrow morning. I'm sure he has things he needs to take care of that aren't me related.

FLIP

I'll always make time for you, kitten.

That hits me right in the heart. I haven't mentioned the studio situation to my family. My mom has recently mentioned getting a part-time job. I don't know how she'll make that work with Fenna's cello practices and performances. And I won't ask my dad. We still haven't managed to find a day that works to make up for the missed dinner.

Flip has taken me on a date, we've gone for fajita night at Rix and Tristan's, and he's driving across town to spend time with me before an away series. He keeps making time for me, and as much as I love it, it shines a bright light on how bad my dad is at putting anything ahead of his job. I shake off the sudden swell of emotion and type out a quick response.

TALLY

Okay. 🩶

I head into my marketing lecture. Ten minutes before the class ends, my phone buzzes with another message. I brace myself because Fenna has been having issues at school lately. Our parents' divorce has become public fodder, which means everyone knows our business. It isn't Fenna, this time, though.

FLIP

Want to pin drop me your location so I can meet up with you?

TALLY

Class is over in a few. I can meet you at my building?

FLIP

I'm already on campus. I'll drive to you.

My stomach churns with anticipation as I share my location.

FLIP

See you soon.

TALLY

Can't wait!

I'm excited that he's here, but so far the media hasn't caught wind of us. That won't last forever. Especially if he keeps showing up on campus or at my apartment.

When class ends, I shove my books in my bag and wipe my damp palms on my thighs as I leave the lecture hall. Flip is easy to spot when I step outside. He towers over everyone. He's wearing dark jeans, thick-soled boots, a black winter jacket, a beanie, and sunglasses.

The whole world disappears as he wraps his arms around me and drops his head, his lips soft and warm. "Hey, beautiful. How you doing?"

"Good. Great. You?"

"Better now that I get to see your gorgeous face." He glances around. "We should probably get out of here before someone recognizes me, eh?"

"Probably a good idea."

He laces our fingers, and we walk to the nearby parking lot. "You're done for the day, right?"

I love that he pays attention to my schedule. "Yeah. I just have studio time this evening." It was the only slot left in one of the less-appealing studio spaces. It's always freezing in there, which makes it tough to be limber.

"We have some time then." He helps me into the passenger seat and rounds the hood. It's bitterly cold today, and a gust of frigid air follows him into the car. He turns over the engine and blasts the heat, then stretches his arm across the back of my seat. "Hi."

I smile. "Hi."

He tosses his sunglasses on the dash. "It's nice to see you."

"It's nice to see you, too."

His maple eyes rove over my face. "You look pretty."

I bite my lip. "So do you."

He laughs. "I look pretty, eh?"

I grin, a flush working its way over my cheeks. "Maybe *yummy* is a better word."

"Mm..." He leans in closer, eyes heating. "You definitely look yummy."

"Want a bite?"

"Yeah. Actually." He sucks my bottom lip. "More than one, if I'm honest." He flicks my top lip with his tongue.

I angle my head and curve my hand around the back of his neck, hoping to keep him close. His tongue sweeps my mouth, gently, sweetly. I savor the feel of his wide, warm palm against the side of my neck. This going-slow thing will probably result in my spontaneous combustion, and I'm pretty okay with that. It's the first time I've dated someone who isn't in a rush to get me into bed, and I like it.

Flip's thumb sweeps the edge of my jaw. "I like you, Tally." He kisses the end of my nose and settles back in his seat.

"I like you, too." I buckle my seat belt. "Where to? Should we grab a coffee off campus or something?"

"I have a surprise first."

"What kind of surprise?"

"It'll be a time-saver, and that's all I'm saying."

"Hmm… Sounds practical." I go with it and stare at his profile while we drive. "How was practice this morning?"

"Good. I think we're solid going into this away series," he replies.

"How's my dad doing?"

"Okay. Lexi's been stepping in to lead a bit lately." Flip glances at me for a moment. "Have you talked to him?"

"The other day, yeah." He threw out a couple of times to get together, but they were both during dance practice or classes.

"Things okay with the two of you?" he presses.

I shrug. "I don't think he'll ever stop being married to his job."

"I'm sorry, Talls." Flip slips his hand under my hair and gently squeezes the back of my neck.

My phone buzzes with a call.

"Do you need to get that?"

"It's my mom. It's like she has a sixth sense." I answer the call and bring the device to my ear. "Hey, what's up?"

"Just thinking about you and wanted to check in," Mom says.

My parents are so vastly different. My mom will call out of the blue, no reason, just to tell me she loves me. I feel like an afterthought with my dad. "I'm good. Are you good? How about Ties and Fenna?"

She chuckles. "I'm good and so are your brother and sister. It sounds like you're in a car."

"I am. I'm not driving, though."

"But you're with friends?"

I glance at Flip who's paying attention to the road. "Yeah, I am."

"Call me later when you're home."

"It might not be until after nine. I have dance practice tonight."

"That's fine. I'll be up until nine thirty."

"Such a night owl," I tease.

"Real partier over here. I love you, sweetheart."

"I love you, too, Mom."

I end the call as Flip turns into a strip mall with a café, a used-clothing store, an independent grocery store, a print shop, and two other businesses that appear closed. This plaza isn't far from the cat shelter I volunteer at.

"Things good with your mom?"

"Yeah, they've been a lot better lately."

"That's good. I'm glad your relationship with her is solid."

"Me, too." I told Flip about her visit after he took me out for dinner and how it helped smooth things out between us a little. Our relationship isn't perfect, but we're working on it.

He parks in an empty spot, and I hop out, meeting him at the hood. I take a step toward the coffee shop, but Flip grabs my hand. "We'll stop there after."

I reluctantly let him lead me away from the decadent smell of freshly ground beans and baked goods. He stops in front of a dark storefront and pulls a set of keys from his pocket.

I glance up at the sign above our heads that reads *Make Your Move* as he unlocks the door. I recognize the name. "I thought this place was closed." I looked up studio rentals in the area, hoping I could find something reasonable. For a few seconds I was excited, until I realized this place wasn't open anymore.

"The owner moved to a new location. Check it out." He flicks on the light.

I step inside the empty studio. It would be the perfect location to practice. "Whose is it now?"

"It's yours," he says.

I frown. "I can't afford this." Based on my research, renting space in a studio off campus is expensive. Before my parents announced their divorce, I might have tossed out the idea, but not when my parents' individual expenses have suddenly doubled.

"You need a place to rehearse, and this is close to campus.

Now you don't have to worry about being able to fit in time around classes, or your troupe's part-time jobs. It's a three-minute drive from your apartment, and it's yours."

"Mine?" I repeat.

"Well, the rental agreement is in my name, but you have it through the end of June."

"You rented me a dance studio?" My voice cracks, and my eyes start to water.

"You were stressed. I wanted to make it easier for you," he says gently.

Tears spill over and track down my cheeks.

Flip frowns and brushes them away. "Is it too much, Talls?"

"No. I mean, yes, but…" I shake my head and bite my lip to keep it from trembling. "No one has ever done anything this nice for me." Flowers and stuffed animals and chocolate are one thing, but an entire dance studio? "This is really expensive."

"I make a lot of money, and I still shop at the no-name grocery stores, so it's well within my budget. More importantly, I want to take care of you."

"Thank you." I throw my arms around his neck. "This is just…thank you." I'm already planning out a schedule. My troupe will have loads of time to practice together and on our own and some of the other groups that are struggling could use this space, too.

"You're welcome." He winds his arms around my waist, and hugs me tightly. "Get used to being spoiled because I plan to do it a lot."

"Charles and Arya will be so relieved." I lean back, fingers slipping through the curls at the nape of his neck. "I don't know how I'll ever be able to thank you for this."

"I have an idea." His eyebrow quirks, along with the corner of his mouth.

I mirror his expression. "It's probably not the same as mine."

He laughs and kisses the end of my nose. "Dance for me."

"Definitely not the same idea as mine," I joke.

"Just for me." He fingers an errant curl, his smile making my stomach twist in the most delicious way.

"Just you," I breathe.

His eyes darken. "Mm. Yes, please."

"Only if there's a cherry on top." I do the wave with my eyebrows.

His grin turns devilish. "You're a problem, you know that?"

"But I'm a cute problem." I love that I don't have to guard myself with him. I can make jokes, and we can flirt and have fun, and I don't have to worry about his motives.

I spin out of his arms, already filtering through potential songs and routines. I know just the one; it's basically mine and Mac's theme song.

I turn on the rest of the lights, looking over the entire space for the first time. The floors are beautiful, bleached wood, the walls mirrored, and there's even a warm-up barre that spans two walls.

Flip turns on the sound system while I shed my coat and sweater and dig my dance shoes out of my bag. I pull my hair up into a high ponytail, then grab a folding chair from the corner and set it in the middle of the room.

Flip holds up his phone. "What's the chair for, kitten?"

"So I can entertain you." I pat the seat.

He snaps a photo and tucks it back in his pocket, regarding me with curiosity as he drops into the chair. I hand him the remote. "I'll tell you when."

"I'm ready when you are."

I move into position on the opposite side of the room and call over my shoulder, "You can hit play."

The music starts, and Flip shakes his head as the song fills the room.

"Really, Talls?"

"It's iconic."

"You're not wrong."

There's nothing quite like classic Madonna. It's been a while since I've performed this routine, but my muscles remember the moves. I spin and twirl and leap, falling into the music. I grip Flip's shoulder instead of the back of the chair, moving around him. His eyes find mine in the mirror, hot and steady as I spin. Like he's my sun. The center of my universe.

The nerves hit me again as I stop in front of him, bracing my hands on his knees. Our gazes lock, our faces inches apart as I kick my leg back and arch until my toe touches my crown. I push away and move into a spin, then drop into his lap for a moment before I roll my body back up. His fingers coast along my hip before I twirl out of reach again. The push and pull between us is addictive. I'm full of longing and desire, and it's echoed back at me in him.

I spin around him one last time as the final lines play out, and I drop back into his lap, stretching my arm across his shoulder, eyes on his as I arc backwards. His hand settles against the small of my back, the other high on my thigh.

We're both breathless as I meet his fiery gaze. "Hi."

"Hi." His voice is all gravel.

"How was that?"

"Fucking incredible." He squeezes my thigh. "I'll be your private audience anytime."

"I'll dance for you whenever you want." I hop out of his lap, in love with the tension flaring between us. "It's your turn."

He runs his hands over his thighs. "For what?"

"To dance for me."

He taps his chest. "Hockey player." Then points to me. "Dancer."

"I've seen you on the dance floor on club nights. You've got moves." He lets me tug him out of the chair and take his place. I cross my legs, pointing to the sound system. "Entertain me."

He leans in to kiss the end of my nose. "Careful what you wish for."

I giggle as he moonwalks to the stereo and cues up a song. He pulls his hoodie and T-shirt over his head, revealing his gloriously cut chest and abs. His six-pack has a six-pack.

I bite my bottom lip, jittery with excitement as he gets into position.

"Ready to be entertained?" he calls over his shoulder.

"So ready." I hit play and nearly die when the first strains of his rebuttal song blast through the speakers. It's been a popular club song since the nineties.

Flip does *not* pull out the anticipated dance-club moves. Instead, he performs a legit striptease, minus the stripping. And while I used him and the chair as props, that has nothing on the way Flip uses it and me.

His muscles ripple and flex as he undulates on the floor at my feet. It's pretty damn obscene, and I can easily envision myself naked under him as he rolls his hips. My mouth waters and then goes dry as he runs his hands up the back of my calves, moving around to push my knees wide. His hot gaze stays fixed on mine, tongue dragging across his lips as his palms slide up the inside of my thighs.

He rises, nose skimming the front of my shirt, lips brushing along my throat, hovering just above mine as he growls the refrain. Time suspends. My body feels like it's on fire, there's a pulse between my thighs, and he's not even touching me. What will it be like when he breaks? I'll be feral for him. I already am.

He spins around, back to my front as he glides down, head resting in my lap for a moment. He grins up at me, and then he's on the move again. He shakes his booty and tosses a saucy wink over his shoulder that makes me laugh.

He pirouettes around me, bending to tuck his fingers behind my knees and press my legs together. Flip straddles my thighs and holds on to the back of the chair, undulating suggestively as the song ends. He kisses the end of my nose and hops off my lap. "How was that?"

"So much thrusting and so many hip rolls!" I say breathlessly, like it was me doing the work, not him.

He smirks. "Haven't you seen hockey warm-ups?"

I have an unreasonable number of video files of Flip humping the ice. Which I've often used as fantasy fodder. "That was a lot more than hockey warm-up inner-thigh stretches."

"Denise, the women's coach, suggested I take some classes for flow and floor work, but I could only go once because I accidentally fucked the instructor," Flip explains.

I give him a look. "How do you *accidentally* fuck the instructor, Flip?"

"Well, you know…" He runs a hand through his hair. "You're twenty-five, and you're horny, and I don't actually need to tell you more about this."

"I've been horny plenty, and I've never fucked one of my instructors," I argue.

"I'm glad I don't have to knock anyone's teeth out." He wraps his arm around my waist and pulls me against him.

A hot thrill shoots down my spine at his dark tone. I loop my arms around his neck, loving that I'm pressed up against his warm, bare skin. "Why is it okay for you to fuck your instructor, but the idea of me fucking one of mine warrants physical violence?"

He gazes down at me, eyes glittering. "I didn't say it was okay that I fucked my instructor, just that it happened. And I couldn't go back to the studio after that." His nostrils flare. "Let's talk about anything other than fucking."

I press myself against him. "You're the one who brought up fucking, not me."

"Stop using the word *fucking*."

"But I like the word *fucking*."

"Kitten." There's warning in his tone and his molten gaze.

I'm sure my smile is absolutely devilish. I make a *fuh* sound.

He narrows his eyes. "What do you think happens to bad little kittens?"

"Naughty things, I hope."

He exhales roughly, jaw flexing along with the fingers gripping my side.

I'm pushing all his buttons. I want him, I want this, but I don't want him to break for the wrong reasons, so I kiss his chin and step back. "Should we check out that coffee shop?"

"We should."

I start to move away but his fingers lap my wrist. I turn back to him, and he gently cups my chin in his palm, gazing down at me with heated longing. "Thank you for dancing for me."

"Thank you for renting me a studio."

He slants his mouth over mine, tongue brushing mine. It's sweet and languid and it makes my knees weak, but it's over too soon. He pulls back, then kisses the side of my neck. "I need to get you out of here now."

"I know." My heart is hammering. My vagina is permanently clenched, and I will definitely need some relief when I get home, but it's so, so worth it to have him look at me like he wants to devour me.

He helps me into my coat, and I watch as he pulls his shirt and hoodie back over his head. We end up driving to another café because the one in the strip mall is full of students, a couple of whom are wearing Terror shirts.

It isn't until we're seated at the too-small table, one of his knees between mine because there's no space for his long legs, and he's playing with my fingers that he says, "I'm sorry."

I look up at him. "For what?"

"For winding you up and leaving you hanging." His eyes are full of apology.

"I like that we can push each other's buttons, though," I say softly.

"You excel at pushing mine."

I roll my bottom lip between my teeth. "I'm wildly attracted to you, and sometimes the yearning is...overwhelming, and I just...forget myself." I gather my thoughts for a moment. It's empowering to have someone like Flip regard me this way: with desire, with reverence. "I also like that you want to treat me with caution and respect."

"You are everything I have ever wanted, Tally." He kisses the back of my hand. "I didn't rent the studio so you'd have somewhere to dance *for me*, I wanted you to have a space that's *yours*."

It's the first time I've been with someone who wants to do things *for* me, not just *to* me. "It's the most amazing gift anyone has ever given me."

The door of the café opens, bringing with it a gust of cold air. I shiver and rummage through my oversized purse. "Crap. I must have left my sweater at the studio."

"Here." Flip stands and pulls his hoodie over his head. "Wear this."

He helps me into it. It's nearly dress length on me, the shoulder seams almost at my elbows, but Flip's satisfied smile makes my heart leap. Especially when he frees my hair and leans in to kiss the side of my neck. "This is yours now."

"It's your favorite, though." It's a constant in his winter-wardrobe rotation.

"I love it on you more than I like it on me."

CHAPTER 26

FLIP

I'm lying on my hotel bed in Colorado, the most recent of Tally's book recs lying next to me. It's open to one of her dogeared sections—it was a particularly descriptive spicy scene—which I've read several times. And now I'm fisting my cock in one hand, and my phone in the other, watching the video Tally sent at my request. She's wearing a pair of shorts that barely cover the swell of her perfect, biteable ass, strong legs on display, and a strappy athletic bra that I want to take off with my fucking teeth.

I stroke roughly, the strains of the song I danced to for her vibrating through my hand. The way she moves, the slow roll of her hips, the flip of her ponytail, how her eyes stay on the camera as she spins around the chair—it all pushes me closer to the edge. I groan as she moves to lie on her stomach, perky ass pressing up, chest brushing the floor. She grins impishly and winks, then she spins, lying on her back, undulating, hands sliding down her chest and over her stomach, easing along the inside of her thighs.

I increase my pace, fucking my hand like a man possessed. I've watched this video half a dozen times since she sent it, and the best part is coming. Tally moves to her knees, legs spread wide, her body rolls as she seems to levitate, landing on her feet. She kicks a leg in the air, balancing on one foot, arm wrapped around the other leg, ankle by her ear as she does the splits standing. She falls forward and I rub my thumb over the crown, wishing for her hand, for her fingers, for her soft, wet pussy, and she hits the floor with grace.

Stroke up. She moves to her back again. Stroke down. She plants her feet on the floor, runs her hands down her thighs, eyes on the camera as her hips pop up, legs spreading wide again. One hand slides up her stomach, the other brushes her cheek as she fucks the air, head thrown back in mock ecstasy.

I can easily envision myself between her parted thighs, coming on her stomach as the orgasm slams through me. I let the video start again as I work to calm my breathing. She was close to breaking me at the dance studio. She knew it, too. And I appreciate the way she backed off. But watching her dance for only me and the way she moves? It's a lethal combination for my hormones. So I asked for a video to take with me on this away series. She sent it right before she went to class so I can't even call her to thank her.

The video pales in comparison to the real thing, but at least it takes the edge off. I've only been in Denver for two hours and I already hate being away from her. I can't smell her lotion or shampoo, I can't drive to her apartment to surprise her with breakfast, or lunch. I can't hug her, kiss her, fight the urge to give in to the raging chemistry between us.

When Tristan messages to say they're on their way to my room, I roll off the bed and head for the bathroom to clean myself up. I take my phone with me, deleting private messages on my professional account as I absently wipe cum off my stomach.

My DMs are full of messages from random women—sometimes Hemi and Hammer will go in and delete them for me when they have time, but they're currently knee deep in gala preparations—our yearly Terror fundraiser, supporting local programs and community outreach—so I've been doing it myself.

The last thing I want is for Tally to see messages from women offering me sex when we've barely made it off the bench.

I finish up in the bathroom, pull a shirt over my head, and flip the safety so the guys can let themselves in. Tristan raps once and pokes his head in before he enters, followed by Quinn, Ash, and Connor.

"Kellan going through the motions?" Goalies are their own breed, and Kellan, like Roman, has his own pregame routine.

"You know it." Quinn glances at the open book on the bed. "Whatcha reading?"

"Tally recommended it. It's the second in the series. It's good so far." Although I've been jumping around, reading her favorite passages.

Connor looks over Quinn's shoulder. "Mildred loves that series."

He never calls her Dred, like the rest of us. Always Mildred, darling, or little menace. The last is particularly hilarious, because there is nothing menacing about Dred.

"Doesn't she usually read domestic thrillers?" I ask.

"Depends on her mood. She'll read just about anything." A faint smile tugs at his mouth. "We read a lot of romance together."

"Like she reads a chapter then you read a chapter?" Quinn asks.

Connor smirks. "When it's dual POV, she reads the heroine's chapters and I read the hero's."

Connor is an interesting guy.

Tristan tips his head. "Huh."

"I wonder if Shilpa would enjoy that," Ash muses.

Quinn sets the book down. "You ready to go?"

"Sure thing." I gather my stuff, and we head out.

The hotel is attached to the arena, so we make the short walk to the player entrance. Photographers snap photos as we head down the hall to the locker room. I haven't started reading about myself, which means the media hasn't gotten wind of my relationship with Tally yet. As much as I want to be open about dating her, I'm not looking forward to the attention it will bring.

I set those worries aside. Marinating in what-ifs won't help me on the ice. I block out everything except for hockey and shift into game mode as I suit up.

Tonight we're playing Colorado. They're fighting to make the playoffs this season, while we're currently one of the top ten teams in the league, but we want to maintain our current position in the rankings.

"How you doing?" Connor asks as we warm up.

"Okay." I move to a chest stretch. "I'm tight here."

"I wonder why," Tristan says dryly from my other side.

"I didn't overdo the workout yesterday," I argue.

Connor claps me on the shoulder. "Do you miss Tally?"

"Well yeah, I'm a three-hour flight away."

"That's why your chest is tight," Tristan explains.

"Welcome to the obsessed partners club. You've earned your first gold star." Connor grins.

"Is this what I have to look forward to during away games now?" I grumble.

"Phone sex helps," Tristan offers.

"Dude." I give him a look.

"He's not wrong," Connor jumps in to defend him.

"Still not things I needed to know."

Warm-up ends before either of them can add to the overshare moment, and the game gets underway. We score a goal in the first period, but Colorado ties it up at the beginning of the second.

The rest of second period we fight for another goal, but

Colorado's goalie is playing tight, and their defensive line is strong.

"I'm going to get dirty so you can make a clean shot." Grace winks as we take the ice again. He steps into his villain role and needles their defense, taking a right hook to the jaw. I use the distraction to steal the puck and pass it to Palaniappa.

"You two are all over each other's jocks." The Colorado player tries to come for Grace again. "You let him fuck your wife, or just you, Grace?"

I get between them before Grace knocks all his teeth out. "You want a piece of me, I'm right here, but leave the wives out of it."

He shoves me and the refs blow the whistle.

"Dred won't be happy with you," I say as Grace and I skate back to the bench.

"I can only hope there are severe consequences." He smirks, rubbing his jaw.

The dirty move gives us the powerplay advantage we need. Stiles scores a goal with Bright as the assist.

The chippy play escalates in the third period, and I end up bodychecked, giving Colorado another penalty. Then Grace and I score a third goal, kicking Colorado down another spot in the rankings.

The win feels good, but we're all sore after the game. I take a long shower, sit in the sauna, and rinse off again. I plan to avoid the bar—I don't need photos showing up online, giving Tally a reason to worry, or Vander Zee motive to trade me. Besides the media is obsessed with my love life. Any time we go to a bar, there's speculation; about my relationship with Dred, who I'm secretly dating/fucking, and past hookups love to throw in their two cents. I want Tally to learn things about me from me, not media conjecture.

I've managed to keep my marriage to Fiona under wraps, but I also haven't had a single girlfriend in that time. That might not continue once my relationship with Tally is public fodder. I don't want people digging into that unhealed wound. Telling Tally will be hard enough. Being used by the woman I thought I would spend my life with left me in pieces. My biggest fear is falling in love again, only to have my heart shredded all over.

I tuck the worries away for later and finish getting dressed. Once we're in our suits, the guys and I walk back to the hotel.

"Why don't you all come to my room?" Connor isn't much for the bar scene.

I nod. "Be there in half an hour?"

"Sounds good." His phone is already at his ear as he steps off the elevator. "I'm okay, darling. No concussion."

When I reach my room, I swipe the keycard over the sensor and text Tally.

FLIP

You around?

TALLY

I am! Nice win tonight. That was an intense game.

FLIP

Thanks. Can I call you?

TALLY

Sure!

I stretch out on my bed and hit the video-call button.

Tally's face appears. "Hey!" I can barely hear her over the background noise. "I didn't realize you were video calling. Give me a second." She moves around someone. "Can I use your room for a few minutes?"

A guy says yes.

She weaves through bodies, saying *hi* and *excuse me* and *I'll be back*. She rushes up a flight of stairs, knocks on a door, then slips inside.

"Where are you?" The anxious jittery feeling makes my spine hot.

"Mac's. It's Gage's birthday, so they're throwing a party. Half the campus showed up."

I may or may not have met these guys in the past. "Who are Mac and Gage again?"

"Chase's friends. They all play for the university team." She drops into a computer chair. "Mac and Gage live with Brody. We're at his house."

"Right. I remember them." Brody has nice friends. I feel better. "Whose room is that?" I note the Terror poster on the wall featuring me, Tristan, and Dallas.

"Mac's. He's Terror obsessed." She kisses my two-dimensional face on the poster while grinning.

"He's a good guy?" I can't see her using his room if he was a douchebag.

"Super good guy," she confirms. "He and Fee are a thing."

"Oh yeah? Has Roman met him?"

"It's only a matter of time. Poor guy."

On the wall behind her is a whiteboard with a class schedule taped to it. The age gap is glaringly obvious right now. When we spend time together, it's with our Terror friends. We have mostly civilized dinner parties, we go to the Watering Hole and exclusive clubs. I'm separate from her university friends. She can't invite me to a house party. I'd be mobbed by the Tilton players and flirted with by the girls.

"Is everything okay?" She bites her thumbnail.

"Yeah, kitten. Everything's good now that I'm looking at your gorgeous face and talking to you."

She tips her head. "I'm sorry I didn't tell you I was going to a party tonight."

"Don't apologize, I don't want you to stop living your life when I'm on an away series."

She spins in the computer chair. "I'd rather be cuddled up next to you than at this party, though."

"When I get home, we will have a serious snuggle session." It's a physical ache to be looking at her, but unable to wrap my arms around her.

"I'm holding you to that." She rolls her bottom lip between her teeth and whispers, almost too quiet to catch, "I miss you."

That feels good to hear. "I miss you too." More than she could know.

She smiles impishly. "Did you like the video I sent you?"

"Oh, fuck me, yeah. I love it. I've watched it an unreasonable number of times. I can't wait to have you dance for me again."

"When you're home," she replies.

"How's the studio?" I ask.

"Amazing. Obviously I'm getting good use out of it." She wraps a tendril of hair around her finger. "Between last night and today, my troupe has spent four hours rehearsing. We all have solo time, and group time and a whole schedule set up. I already feel so much better about the upcoming showcase." Noise makes it hard to hear her for a moment. "I'll be down in a bit," she tells someone off-screen. "You can start this hand without me." She turns her attention back to me. "Sorry about that. I usually end up playing cards with Cammie and the gang at these things. What are your plans for the rest of the night?"

"I'm heading up to Connor's room in a bit."

"So no bar tonight?" She seems relieved.

"Nah. It's a HABs gathering."

She wrinkles her nose. "HABs?"

"Husbands and boyfriends," I explain. "I made that up, by the way."

I'm not sure how to interpret her surprise. "Does that mean I'm a WAG?"

"Do you want to be a WAG?" My stomach knots as I wait for

her reply. I should have done this before I left for the away series.

"Yeah. Yes. Definitely."

"Good." I mirror her smile. "I should let you get back to your friends, but we can talk tomorrow once I'm checked into the next hotel."

"Okay. I'll miss you until then."

"Same. Have a good night, kitten."

"You too, Phillip."

She ends the call, and I lie there for a minute. At her age, I was at the club all the time. But I was nursing a broken heart. If I'd been part of the HABs club then, would it have been different?

My phone buzzes on my chest.

I open the message to find a picture of Tally kissing a cartoon figurine of me on the cheek.

TALLY

Clearly I'm stealing this from Mac.

Good night kisses. 😘

CHAPTER 27
TALLY

Knocking, followed by an incessant buzz, wakes me on Sunday morning. I roll out of bed, not even fully conscious.

"I'm coming!" My eyes haven't adjusted to the light. I bump into the wall as I flip the safety and open the door. Standing on the other side is Flip, looking gorgeous and far more alert and put together than me.

"Hey." His delicious mouth curves into a panty-wetting smile as he slips through the crack, snakes an arm around my waist, and lifts me off my feet. He noses his way through my hair and his lips find the side of my neck. "Fuck, I missed you, kitten."

"I missed you, too." I wrap my arms around his neck. "Where's Pars?"

"Clinging to my leg."

He adjusts his hold on me, grips the back of my thighs and wraps my legs around his waist. My back meets the wall. For a moment I'm worried he'll try to kiss me on the mouth, and I haven't even said hi to my toothbrush yet.

But he just nuzzles my neck.

"Are you huffing me?"

"I missed the way you smell." He jams his nose into my hair. "I'm taking a shirt of yours next away series."

"Only if you leave one of yours for me."

"Deal."

I press my face into his neck and huff him in return. "And I missed the way you smell, too."

Eventually he steps back from the wall and gently sets me on my feet. Parsnip still clings to his calf.

I slap a hand over my mouth before Flip comes in for a kiss. "Give me two minutes."

I run down the hall and disappear into my bedroom. Pillow Flip gets tossed in the closet first. Then I give attention to myself. "Oh shit." My hair is a complete wreck. The rest of me isn't much better. I brush my teeth and pull my hair into a messy bun. I don't change out of my oversized sleep shirt and shorts. The heat in the building can be a lot sometimes, particularly in my bedroom.

Flip is standing in the middle of my kitchen when I return. Parsnip is lying at Flip's feet, grooming himself.

"Okay. I'm a little more presentable and minty fresh." I link my fingers behind his neck. Tipping my chin up, I pucker my lips and close my eyes. After a few seconds of nothing, I crack a lid.

He smiles down at me.

"You can kiss me now."

"Did you run to the bathroom to brush your teeth?"

"Yes."

He presses his lips gently to mine.

I push up on my toes and angle my head, waiting for him to deepen the kiss. Instead, he kisses a path along the edge of my jaw to my ear. "Get dressed so I can take you out for something to eat."

"Just one real kiss first?"

He widens his eyes. "Don't you know kisses are the gateway

drug to getting naked?"

"Total myth," I fire back.

He grins and curves his hand around the back of my neck, squeezing gently as he covers my mouth with his.

Our lips part, and our tongues meet. My knees go weak.

He breaks it, but comes back in for another long, lingering kiss.

"I missed you," I whisper.

"It's good to be home with you." He pats my butt. "Get dressed and let me take you for brunch. Then you can lure me into your bedroom and try to get me to do things to you that your dad will want to bury me for."

Every part of me lights up. "Promise?"

His expression remains serious as he lifts his fingers. "Scout's honor."

"Be right back." I fight not to skip down the hall, but do a little twirl and stag leap once I'm alone in my bedroom.

I return fully dressed and find Flip holding Parsnip like a baby, letting him lick his chin. "Oh, this is too precious." I snap a photo and set it as my wallpaper.

Flip sets a disappointed Parsnip on the floor and helps me into my jacket. We're nowhere near the end of snow season yet, so I bundle up.

Flip tosses a mouse before we leave the apartment, and Parsnip chases after it. Then he yowls forlornly when he realizes he's been duped.

We run into Cammie and Chase on the way to the elevator.

"I just saw you on the ice last night. How are you here?" Chase asks.

Flip tucks me into his side as we join them in the elevator. "I took an early flight home."

Cammie grins and hugs Chase's arm. "That's so sweet."

"We're grabbing a bite to eat off campus, if you want to join us," Flip offers.

"Oh! We don't want to impose." Cammie glances at me, eyes wide.

Chase looks like someone just offered him a contract with the Terror.

"You're not imposing at all," I assure Cammie. This feels like kind of a big deal, especially since he called himself my boyfriend while he was in Colorado, and took an early flight home because he missed me. Now he wants to spend time not just with me, but with my friends, too.

"You're sure?" Chase is already vibrating.

"Totally," Flip and I say at the same time.

We exit the elevator, and Cammie and I climb into the back seat of Flip's car, so Chase doesn't have to eat his knees. Flip drives across town to the Pancake House. It's a favorite, and they know us here, so Flip won't be accosted by fans.

Once we're seated, Rainbow, our usual server, pours us coffees and leaves us to browse the menu.

"That was one hell of an away series. First Colorado, and then Minnesota couldn't keep their shit together," Chase says. "They're having a tough season."

"Yeah, and Minnesota is up against New York this week."

"Oof." Chase shakes his head. "That's rough. Kodiak Bowman is on fire this season."

"Right? He beat his own scoring record four games ago," Flip notes. "Guy is going in the Hall of Fame for sure."

"I love his wife," Cammie says. "I want to be like her when I grow up."

"Oh my God," I agree. "I love Lavender. She's hilarious."

"You have no idea." Flip's arm is draped over the back of my chair, and his smile tells an entire story.

I narrow my eyes. "What do you know that we don't?"

"There was a problem with Tristan's pants at the wedding," Flip replies.

"Oh, I heard about this!" Chase's eyes light up.

Cammie frowns. "Why do you know about this and I don't?"

"Because Brody is Tristan's brother," Chase explains. "And he witnessed it."

"I need the inside scoop," Cammie insists.

"It's cone," Chase and Flip say at the same time. Then they fist-bump each other.

It makes me giddy. My pro hockey player and my friend's boyfriend are bonding over wedding shenanigans.

Cammie and I make a lips-zipped, cross-our-hearts motion.

Chase and Flip have a silent conversation, and then Flip nods. "So Tristan's pants were too small," he explains.

Tristan is a mammoth of a man. He's almost six and a half feet tall, and his hands are stupid huge.

"His business was businessing," Chase blurts.

"And Lavender was called in to fix it," Flip adds.

"Oh my God." Cammie splays her hands on the table. I bet she's planning a scene for one of her fics.

"Did Kodiak lose his mind?" I ask.

Flip nods. "I thought his head might explode when Lavender had to let out the crotch of Tristan's pants."

Cammie and I burst out laughing. "The way he loves his wife is goals."

"He's loved her his entire life," Flip says. "Since they were kids. They're soulmates."

"Their love seems so endless," I muse. My stomach twists uncomfortably. I can't imagine those two without each other. But what if something happened? How devastated would Kodiak be? How broken?

Flip slides his arm along the back of my seat, thumb brushing back and forth along my shoulder blade, maybe sensing my sudden disquiet. I hate how my parents' divorce has made me question even the strongest of bonds.

Flip asks Chase about the hockey season at Tilton, which sparks an animated conversation about where Chase is hoping to be after graduation. I love that Flip is connecting with my friends like this, that he's happy to give advice and gentle guidance.

After brunch, we drop Chase and Cammie at her sister's place and head back to my apartment. Fee is at the art studio, working on a project.

Flip grabs his bag out of the trunk. I'm anxious and excited to have him all to myself as we take the elevator to my apartment. Two guys recognize him, and he signs their hats. It doesn't seem to faze him at all.

"Does that ever get annoying?" I ask once we're in my apartment.

"Being recognized by fans?" He takes off his coat while Parsnip scales his leg.

"Yeah."

"I'm always happy to sign hats and jerseys, but when they get touchy, it can be a lot," he admits.

He doesn't need to elaborate. I've seen plenty of women hanging off him at bars over the years. People assume they can touch him without asking permission because he's a public figure.

Flip relocates my cat to his shoulder so he can take off his boots. Parsnip hops to the floor, then follows us down the hall. My stomach is full of butterflies as I lead him to my bedroom. I push the door open, thankful I remembered to hide my body pillow in the closet.

He steps into my bedroom and drops his duffle on the floor, eyes moving around the space. I try to see it through his eyes. It looks like a regular bedroom, apart from the desk in the corner with my computer, which makes it a decidedly student space.

He walks over to my bed, turns around, and gracefully falls back to stretch out on the teal comforter. He takes up an unreasonable amount of space on my double bed, and I love it.

Flip tucks one arm behind his head and extends his hand. "I promised I would let you *try* to get me to do naughty things."

I slip my fingers into his and let him pull me closer. "Don't think I didn't notice the stress on the word *try*."

"Today we test my self-restraint." He wraps his hands around my waist and lifts me onto the bed with him, moving me to straddle his hips. He's so broad, thick shoulders, heavy biceps, defined pecs, washboard abs, and a tapered waist complemented by a hockey butt and powerful thighs. I settle my palms on his chest and take in his gorgeous face.

His hands curve around my knees. "What are you going to do with me now that you have me in your bed?"

"Admire you." I trace the line of his brow. "Enjoy having you all to myself."

"That's a nice thing to say." He fingers a lock of my hair, then slips his hand under the strands, settling his palm against my nape.

"It's true."

He pulls me closer, until my lips hover over his. But he doesn't make a move to kiss me yet.

He grins, and my heart stutters.

I remind myself that he's accustomed to being used by women. Even the person he gave his heart to a long time ago didn't take care of it properly. I want us to be different.

"Don't be scared." I'm not sure if he's reassuring me or himself, but he taps his lips. "Right here, kitten."

He pulls my mouth to his. The kiss is soft. Sweet. Exceedingly gentle. He tastes like mint and maple. I want to tuck this kiss away in my forever memory bank. That this man is lying in my bed, kissing me, giving me a piece of himself is so special.

His other hand smooths up my thigh and over my hip.

I run my fingers through his hair, letting the silken strands slip through as we kiss.

"Fuck, Talls." Flip groans and his hand flexes, fingers digging in briefly.

One second I'm straddling his hips, and the next I'm on my

back and he's settled in the cradle of mine. I gasp and he pulls back.

"Those little sounds are pure torture." He hooks my leg over his hip. "I missed your lips."

"I missed yours, too." I'm already on fire, desperate for more of his hands on me, of his body pressing me into the mattress.

He sucks my bottom lip, following with the gentle scrape of teeth. Anticipation skitters through me as we make out, kisses deepening, his hands roaming. One moves to cup the back of my head, the other slides under my shirt, skimming my ribs. I follow his lead and run my hand down his back until I reach the hem of his shirt, sliding under the cotton to meet hot, smooth skin.

He groans and bites the edge of my jaw. "You feel so good."

"Oh God." I writhe under him, nails pressing into his back. "I ache."

He kisses my neck. "Do you think you deserve a little relief from all the edging?"

Heat floods my center. My breath catches. "Is this a trap?"

"Does this feel like a trap?" He rolls his hips.

I arch at the feel of him, hard and thick between my thighs, rubbing against the sensitive parts of me. "N-no."

"Does it feel good?" He frames my face in his hands.

"So good." My body lights up in the most excruciatingly amazing way as he rocks against me. "Please, Phillip."

"Please what?" His lips brush mine.

"Please," I beg as I drag my nails down his back and curve my hand around the firm globe of his ass. I'm mindless with want. Desperate and feral. "I need, I need…" *This relentless ache to quell.*

"Tell me." His lips ghost along my jaw, teeth scraping my neck.

"You. I need you."

He brushes his lips over mine. "I want all these firsts with you, Tally."

It's like stepping backwards through time, to the days when first kisses came long before anything else. To the make-out sessions of teen years where bodies rubbed and writhed, every sensation new, the craving growing, the appetite for more insatiable, even as the lack of experience and inhibitions made the idea of moving forward, of doing more, seem awkward. Scary even.

The way he moves over me is an echo of the way he danced, but so much better. One hand frames my face, the other curves around my ribs, just below my breast. And somehow that innocent touch heightens everything. His intense gaze stays fixed on mine as his thick cock rubs against me through layers of clothing.

It shouldn't be enough, but the hot spark of need in his eyes melts my core, turning me molten.

Everything tightens, and I whimper, nails raking down his back.

"I'm going to make you come just like this." He licks my top lip. "Fully clothed." He sucks the delicate flesh. "Without even touching you."

Another soft moan tumbles from my lips. Heat rushes through me, sparking in my veins, an inferno rising.

"Eyes on mine, kitten." He keeps rolling his hips, the pressure steady and even. "Let me see what I do to you."

I move with him, our bodies a wave of need and pleasure.

"That's it, Tally, let go for me." He strokes my cheek. "Show me how pretty you are when you come."

His touch is tender, the demand undeniable. And I shatter, crying out his name, body shaking as sensation ripples through me. It's the most perfect first, and I love that it's here, in my bed.

"You'll only ever make that sound for me," he murmurs, eyes dark with satisfaction.

Because he did this. He made me come fully clothed.

"Only you," I agree.

He slides one palm under me, curving around my ass, tipping my hips up as he grinds against me. And I keep coming, endless waves of euphoria nearly overwhelming me, but I'm desperate for it not to end. I want this intensely intimate connection with him, where I feel safe to show him my most unguarded and vulnerable side.

"Fuck, Talls." His hips jerk, and his jaw tightens.

Pleasure rolls through me again, like it's not just mine, but his too, and I cup his face in my palms, echoing his words, "Show me what I do to you."

He groans and shudders, and I drown in his maple eyes.

Did he come? I think he just came. I'm shaken. I'm floating. I want to lie in his arms for hours and never leave.

He kisses me, unhurried and sweetly for long minutes before he finally pulls back. "Hey."

"Hi."

A lopsided grin tugs at his kiss-swollen lips. "I feel better. Do you?"

I laugh, the movement sending another jolt of pleasure through me, turning it into a moan.

"I'll take that as a yes." He kisses the end of my nose. It seems to be his thing. "I'm going to use your bathroom for a minute."

"Okay." I don't think I could move if I tried.

"We'll snuggle when I come back." He rolls gracefully off me and grabs his bag on the way to the bathroom.

Fee and I both have our own, thankfully.

He pulls the door closed behind him and the water turns on—but it's the shower, not the sink. I bite my lip, grin widening. I made Flip Madden come in his pants. While he cleans up, I change into fresh panties and clean leggings.

A few minutes later, he opens the bathroom door.

The smile slides off my face. He's standing in the doorway wearing black boxers, a pair of loose-fitting shorts, and nothing else. His bare chest and thick legs are gloriously on display.

"What the hell, Flip?"

"What the hell what?" He runs his hand through his damp hair.

"Why not this fifteen minutes ago?" I point to his mostly naked form. "Do you hate me?"

"Of course not." He frowns. "I can put on more clothes if this is a problem."

"Do not put on more clothes."

He smirks. "You want to ogle me?"

"That's a silly question. Of course I do. I would have happily ogled you while we were dry fucking our way to orgasms." I pat the empty spot next to me.

"It was kind of better fully clothed, no?" He arches a brow.

I arch one back. "I can assure you, sir, that it would have been better with your shirt off."

"We'll have to test that theory."

"Now?" I'm sure my face is lit up like a Christmas tree.

He laughs. "You're an insatiable monster."

"That you created."

He stretches out beside me again and slides his arm under me, pulling me against him. "I'm fading." He smells like my bodywash.

"How early did you have to get up to make your flight?" I settle my palm on his bare chest.

"Four." His eyes slide closed.

"You must be exhausted. You need a nap." I kiss the edge of his jaw.

"I do." He sighs sleepily. "Cuddle with me until I pass out."

"Of course." I rest my head in the crook of his arm.

Three seconds later, he's breathing evenly.

It's such a dude superpower. I give it five minutes before I grab my Human Development in the Arts textbook and start reading. Ten minutes later, Flip rolls over, grunting as his head bangs repeatedly into my side.

I set the textbook down. "Where do you want to be, baby?"

"Just close," he grumbles. He settles his head in my lap and moves around until his nose is pressed against my crotch. He wraps his arms around me and sighs contentedly. I snap a couple of photos. Then a couple more when Parsnip stretches out across his side.

Eventually he repositions himself, but it's hard to hold the textbook with one hand, so I move to the floor so I can use my lap pad. Flip shoves his face in my hair and drapes an arm over me, his hand protectively cupping my right breast. Parsnip uses his back as a cat bed.

Two hours later he stretches and yawns, pushing my hair aside until his lips find my neck. "Why are you sitting on the floor?"

I pass him a water bottle. "My textbook was too heavy to hold with one hand."

"Hmm... Fair." He kisses my cheek. "I'm hungry."

"Let's see what my fridge has to offer. Then we can test the shirtless-orgasm theory."

CHAPTER 28

FLIP

Tally often slides these tidbits into our text conversations. I like to think it's on purpose to test my fraying control.

FLIP

You always smell edible. What are you up to now?

TALLY

Lying in bed, reading Cammie's newest fic update.

FLIP

This seems to be a frequent occurrence.

TALLY

She usually updates weekly. It's like waiting for the next episode of your favorite show.

FLIP

Maybe I should read it, too.

TALLY

Maybe. 👀

FLIP

Maybe we should read it together.

TALLY

It's spicy. 🌶️🌶️🌶️

FLIP

How spicy we talking?

TALLY

Ghost pepper level. 💀🌶️

I usually get my toys out and play after I read a chapter.

I can envision her lying on her bed, hair fanned across her pillow, lip caught between her teeth as she waits for my reply. I love that I now have the memory of her lying under me, my name a moan on her lips. The craving for more of her is eating me alive these days. I take the bait.

FLIP

Toys? As in plural?

TALLY

I have a whole collection. 🐗

FLIP

I expect some show and tell in the future.

TALLY

You get to see my toys when I get to see your toy. 😉

FLIP

That can be arranged.

Send me a link to the story.

TALLY

It's why choose. 🫨

A link follows.

I pull it up on my phone and scan the first chapter. It dives right into the action. I watched the movies this story is based on a long time ago, and I remember the characters. But *none* of this happens on the screen.

TALLY

Are you still here?

FLIP

I'm reading.

TALLY

It starts with a literal bang.

FLIP

Oh, I'm aware.

The opening scene is a three-way in which Arwen is getting railed by Legolas and Aragorn. It's exceptionally detailed. And well written. Now I understand why Tally and her friends are always referencing Cammie's fics. But more importantly, I want to know if this is something Tally thinks she wants in real life, or if it's just something she enjoys reading about.

I call her, and she picks up on the second ring.

"I have questions."

"No, Cammie and Chase aren't part of a throuple," she replies cheekily.

"Chase doesn't strike me as someone who shares." He's too singularly focused on Cammie.

"He's not," Tally agrees.

But Chase and Cammie and who they do and don't want to invite into their relationship isn't my concern. "Is this a fantasy of yours?"

"To get it on with Legolas and Aragorn?" Her voice is pitchy.

My chest tightens, and my palms dampen. My experiences far outweigh hers. "To have a threesome," I clarify.

Her swallow is audible.

My heart is beating so hard it feels like it could crack my ribs. This is where things get tricky. I've done it all. Multiple times, with various partners. But the idea of sharing Tally with anyone lights a rage fire in my veins.

"You can be honest." I mean it, even if the truth will gut me.

"Um, well…" Her words blend together in a rush. "Mostly when I picture the scene, and I'm the heroine, I imagine that it's…two of you."

"Two of me?" I repeat.

"Yes," she whispers.

My relief is overwhelming. It's unfair considering my history. "I want to give you all the experiences, kitten. You know that, right?"

"Yeah. Yes. I know that," she whispers.

"Good." I clear my throat. "But I need to be very clear about something, okay, Tally?"

"Okay." Rustling comes through the line.

"Anything you want to try, we can."

She whimpers softly.

"But when it comes to you and me, I want it to just be us. I know that's unbalanced. I don't want to be shared by you, Tally. I want to be yours, and that means there will not be a person who touches you who isn't me," I promise.

"I don't want anyone but you," she assures me.

"Good. That's good." It heals something deeply broken inside me to hear that from her. "I don't want anyone but you either."

"I just want to be what you need," she whispers.

"You're everything, kitten. I can't get enough of you." I'm utterly consumed by her. When I'm not with her, I'm thinking about her. I dream about her constantly. I want to start and end every day with her.

She makes a soft sound, and it echoes my relief. Her sheets rustle again.

"What's going on, Talls?" I crave the intimacy of openness with her. I want her implicit trust, her confidence, so she can share all her secrets and desires.

"I don't know. I'm…achy. I miss you. I wish you were here and I could touch you, instead of being a plane ride away."

"You need some relief?"

She sighs. "You can't dry fuck me from another province."

"No, but I can talk you through it," I offer. "If that's something you want."

"Like…phone sex?" Her voice wavers with excitement and something else. Maybe uncertainty.

"Would you like that? My voice in your ear, guiding you while you touch yourself?"

She inhales sharply, and exhales on a shudder. "I, uh…I haven't…it's not something I've done before," she admits.

"I get another first with you, then." I covet every new experience with Tally. "But only if you want to try it."

"Okay. Yes…yes, please," she whispers.

"If it doesn't work for you, you just tell me, okay?"

"Okay."

I grin and put her on speakerphone, so I have my hands free. "What are you wearing?"

"A tank, your hoodie, and a pair of sleep shorts."

"What about panties?"

"No panties."

"I like that." I can picture my hoodie swimming on her small frame. "You're lying in bed?"

"I am."

"Perfect, put your phone on speaker, then take off the sleep shorts," I order gently.

"Okay." The rustle of fabric follows. "Should I take off the hoodie, too? I'm already warm."

"Leave it on for now, but push it up to your waist." I slide my hand into my boxer briefs and fist my cock. "Are you naked from the waist down now?"

"Yes," she breathes.

"Good girl." I rub my thumb along my weeping slit. "You said you were wearing a tank, too. Describe it for me."

"It's pale blue and cropped."

"No bra?"

"No bra," she echoes.

"Would I be able to see your nipples through the fabric if you weren't wearing my hoodie?"

"Yes."

"Fuck, kitten." I stroke myself roughly. "Would you show up at the door dressed like that?"

"If you wanted me to, yes."

"I'd have you against the wall, with that hoodie pushed up so

I could suck your pretty little nipples through your tank while you rubbed your pussy on my thigh."

"Oh my God," she groans.

"Are you touching yourself, Tally?" I bark.

"I—I—"

"Where are your hands?"

"One is under my shirt."

"And the other?"

"Between my legs," she whispers.

"Did I say you could touch your pussy?"

"N-no."

"So where should that hand be?"

"Not between my legs?" It comes out a question.

"Move the one between your thighs to your stomach," I order.

"O-okay."

"It's hard to be good sometimes, isn't it?"

She makes an affirmative sound. "What about the other hand?"

"That one can stay under your shirt. Are your nipples hard, kitten?"

"Yeah. Yes."

"Good. Lick your fingers and tug on them."

The wet sound of suction follows, and a few moments later she whimpers softly.

"If it was my mouth, I'd use teeth, so tug hard."

She gasps and moans, but the sound cuts off abruptly.

"Is Fee home?"

"No, she's at Roman and Lexi's tonight."

"Good." She'll be less inhibited because she's alone. "Don't be shy with me. I want all your moans and whimpers and sighs, Tally."

She makes a soft, plaintive sound.

"That's it. That's what I want more of. If I was there, I'd eat up all the pretty sounds you make."

"Oh God," she whimpers and the sheets rustle. "Please, Phillip."

"Please what, kitten? Use your words," I taunt.

"Please can I touch myself?"

"You can do better than that," I tsk. "Be explicit."

"I want you," she moans.

"I'm right here," I cajole. "Ask for what you want so I can give it to you."

"I want your fingers inside my pussy," she whispers.

"Good girl," I praise. "Now slip your hand between your thighs and tell me what I'd find if I was there with you."

"I'm wet."

"When I get my hands on you, I'll have you soaking the sheets."

"Yes, please," she groans.

"Circle your clit with your index finger," I order. "Nice and slow, though. We both know I'd tease you."

"So much teasing," she murmurs, then sighs.

"How does it feel?"

"Good. But it would be better if it was you."

"I'd keep you on the edge for a long time. Make you squirm for me." To be able to touch her, see her at her most primal, spread out just for me. "Would you beg for me?"

"Please, yes," she pleads. "I ache for you."

"It's the same for me," I assure her. "Slide one finger into your pussy."

She groans and the sound turns into a low keening.

"How do you feel?"

"Good. Soft." She pauses for a second, then adds in the quietest whisper, "I'm so wet, Phillip."

"You making a mess of your sheets for me?"

Her breath hitches, another low moan tumbling from her lips.

"You're so fucking sexy, Tally. I'd eat you up if I was there. Lick your juices off my fingers just for a taste of you," I promise. "Do that for me. Lick your cum off your fingers and tell me how you taste."

"Oh God."

"Be loud about it, Tally. I want to hear it. Pretend your fingers are my cock."

The liquid sound of her fingers in her mouth and wet suction follow.

"I bet you taste like heaven," I praise. "Add another finger now."

At the next deep moan, I tighten my grip on my cock, and increase my pace. "I'm fucking my hand just like you're fucking yours," I grind out. "But the next time I get you alone, it'll be my cum-soaked fingers in your mouth, my fingers stretching your pussy, me making you come."

Tally swears, and a high-pitched moan fills my ears as she comes. I stroke fast and hard, tipping over the edge right along with her. My heavy breathing and her soft whimpers fill the quiet.

"Hi." I grab a handful of tissues from the nightstand and clean up the mess on my stomach.

"Hi," she whispers.

"How are your sheets holding up?"

"Um. I think they need to be changed."

"Good. Do you feel better?"

"I'm so much more relaxed," she admits.

"Me too, but I still wish I was with you so we could cuddle after we change your sheets and clean you up." I can't handle another four days without her. It's too fucking long. "What's your weekend look like?"

"Studying, rehearsing, hopefully a visit to the cat shelter if I can swing it," she replies.

"When are your rehearsals?"

"I'm still waiting for Charles to get back to me with his work hours on Saturday and Sunday. He won't know until tonight."

"Do you want to come to the game tomorrow?"

"In Montreal?"

"Yeah. Hemi's out here. I can talk to my sister, see if she can come, too, so you have a travel friend. Tristan's always looking for a reason to get her to an away game. And Connor's in the same boat. I can fly you out in the morning, and you can stay for the game. We can go out with our friends, have a night together—"

"Where you'll touch me with your actual hands on my bare skin?"

I chuckle. "You know I can picture your eyebrows dancing on your forehead."

"My eyebrows are very invested in the possibility," she replies.

"You can let your eyebrows know that I plan to actually touch you with my hands."

"Specifically, you will fingerbang me," she clarifies.

I smile and rub my bottom lip. "Yes, Tally, I'll finger fuck you, if you let me fly you to the game."

"And you'll let me jerk you off, too."

"Yeah." My response comes out gruff at the idea of Tally's soft hands on my skin.

"Will you spoon me to sleep after?" she asks softly.

"I'll cuddle you all night." To have her at my game and in my bed will get me through the rest of this away series. I'm gone for her. Obsessed.

"That sounds perfect."

"I can't wait to see you, Tally. I'm counting down the minutes."

CHAPTER 29

TALLY

Fee holds up a slinky blue number I bought on a whim and have never had the confidence to wear. "Pack this."

Cammie holds up a pale blue demi-cup. "And this!"

I have modest cleavage, and the bra in question accentuates everything nicely, but I haven't had anyone to wear it for. Until now.

"Also this!" Enid tosses a blue, mostly sheer teddy into my suitcase.

"I should also pack actual clothes that I can wear to the arena and on the plane and out for dinner." So far, my suitcase contains only lingerie and underwear. I toss in my favorite jeans, a T-shirt, a hoodie, and my Madden jersey (that I've kept hidden in my closet for years).

Fee flops down on my bed next to pillow Flip. "Your boyfriend is flying you out to his hockey game. It's so romantic."

"He's so into you…" Cammie smiles dreamily.

"One day I hope someone is this into me." Enid looks wistful.

Cammie, Fee, and I say nothing. People see what they want to see when they're ready.

"You must be so excited!" Cammie does a full-body shimmy. "Post-game hotel sex is the best!"

"He hasn't touched me," I blurt. I can't keep this to myself anymore. Not when Cammie believes Flip and I will be having swing-from-the-rafters sex in Montreal.

The girls go silent.

Cammie's lips push out in confusion. "But he had his arm around you the whole time we were out for brunch the other day."

"I mean *touched* me." I point to my chest and crotch to clarify.

All three sets of eyes go wide.

"But, but…it's Flip." Cammie is appropriately mystified.

It's legit. Flip's reputation precedes him. I wring my hands, all the anxiety over this trip finally coming to a head. I'm excited to see him, but I'm also so, so nervous. I miss him. I can't wait to spend time with him, both inside and out of our hotel room. The phone sex we had last night was next-level hot, but it will be different when we're together. I'm already so enamored with him. It's terrifying to have these huge feelings that are new, and something I've never navigated before.

"He wants to take it slow," I explain. "Which is like…the opposite of all the other guys I've dated."

"That's so sweet," Enid whispers.

"Like the sweetest," Cammie agrees.

"Right? And I love it." I sit down on the bed and cross my legs. "But it's scary, too."

"What makes it scary?" Fee asks.

I jiggle the Flip bobblehead he sent me to make him nod. "All we've done so far is dry hump—"

Cammie's brows pull together. "Like fully clothed and just… rubbing on each other?"

I nod and swallow thickly.

"It's so hot, right?" Fee jumps in.

"It was so hot. And Flip has these moves that are just." I make a mind-blown gesture. "But it wasn't just about how hot he is or how good his moves are." I wrinkle my nose. "I'm not explaining this well."

"It's the connection you share," Cammie offers.

"Yes! That's it. Like he was so focused on me. It was probably one of the most intense orgasms of my life."

"Amen, sister." Fee holds up her hand for a high five.

"All the eye contact, and the things he says, it's more than that, though. It's the chemistry, but also all the nice things he does for me, too. It's like…he's my dream boyfriend and he's already exceeding all my expectations, but what if I can't meet his?" How did I get in this spiral?

Cammie tips her head. "Did he get off during the dry hump, too?"

I hold up my pinkie. "This stays in this room."

They all swear on our tiniest finger.

"He did."

"With no touching," Cammie confirms.

"Just through-the-clothes friction. But to be fair, he was the one doing all the work," I confide.

"But he wouldn't have come if he wasn't attracted to you, right?" Enid asks.

"Guys are built a little differently, but Flip was definitely into it," I reply. "And me."

Enid tips her head. "Built differently how?"

"They can be erect, and even ejaculate, but not be into what's going on," I explain.

She pales. "Oh."

"But that obviously was not the case with Flip," I assure her.

"Of course he was into it and you." Enid nods emphatically.

"Are you okay?" I ask.

"Yeah." She waves a hand in the air and smiles, but it looks a little off. "I'm good."

"Are you sure?"

"Uh huh. I think if you both got off with a dry hump, he's super hot for you. I mean, Flip Madden came in his pants for you, Tally."

"I just want to be able to give him what he needs. This is the first time I've ever been this into someone," I admit. "And it scares me."

All three of them wrap their arms around me and tell me it's going to be okay.

"Are you falling for him?" Cammie asks.

I bite my lip and nod. "I think so. He's everything I've ever wanted, and he's connected to all my friends, and my dad's team. There's just so much at stake, and now he's flying me out to a game and it feels so real."

"It's big, isn't it?" Fee rubs my back.

"We've been in this bubble and that will break tonight. Once the media sees us together, the speculation will start. All I've ever wanted was to be his and now I am, and I'm afraid of how things will change once we're out in the open." I don't want the pressure to be too much.

As if he can sense me talking about him, my phone buzzes with a call.

"It's him."

"You got this. We will be here on the other side of this trip for whatever you need. Please, have fun." Cammie hugs me.

Enid and Fee join in and then they file out of my room as I answer the call.

"Hey, kitten."

"Hi."

"How you doing? Are you heading to the airport soon?"

"Rix and Dred are picking me up in fifteen." I'm so grateful I'm flying with them.

"I can't wait for you to get here. Not long now and I'll get to hug you."

"I'm really looking forward to that." Just being close to him will make me feel better, I'm sure of it.

"Did you talk to your dad?"

"Yeah. He's taking me for lunch when I arrive." I couldn't fly out to a game and not spend time with Dad.

"That's good. Are you looking forward to it, or are you stressing?"

I laugh. "Why are you such a mood reader?"

"Because I know how hard it's been for you and him lately. I'm glad you're spending some time with him, though."

"I know. I can't repair the relationship by avoiding him."

"No, you can't. And I'll be ready to provide all the stress relief you need after the game tonight," he assures me.

"Promise?"

"Cross my heart, kitten." His tone softens. "I can't wait to snuggle you all night."

"I'm really excited about that, too." To be spooned to sleep by him and wake up in his arms is the dream, even if I'm scared of how much deeper my feelings for him will become once I've had those experiences.

He clears his throat. "We might go out after the game, which means photos will likely be taken."

"I packed a going out dress." I wheel my suitcase down the hall. "The media will know we're dating after tonight."

Parsnip rushes off, probably to hide under my bed. He hates the sound of luggage.

"They will." I can sense Flip's nerves, and they match my own. "Are you ready for that?"

"I am if you are," I reply.

"I am." He's quiet for a moment. "I just don't want to add more stress to your life. We can talk through a game plan when you get here."

"Okay."

"I'll see you soon."
"I can't wait."

CHAPTER 30

TALLY

Dad pulls me in for a lingering hug when I meet him at the restaurant. "Hey, kiddo. How was the flight?"

"It was smooth." I wait until his hold on me loosens before I step back. There's a weird level of guilt attached to spending time with him that I'm trying to parse through. "How was practice this morning?"

Flip messaged that my dad was in a good mood, which took a little of the anxiety out of meeting him for lunch.

"It was great. The boys look good going into tonight's game." He holds me at arm's length for a few more seconds. "Thanks for making time for me."

"I'm glad nothing came up for either of us."

He completely misses the barb. "Me, too."

Flying out to see my boyfriend and not spending time with my dad would put Flip in an awkward position, so here I am.

Dad is all smiles as we check in with the host. We order drinks, then head up to the buffet to fill our plates.

"How are you?" I ask once we're seated across from each other. He looks like he's lost weight, and like he's not sleeping well either.

"Okay. Staying busy, which I guess isn't new." He spears a bite of ginger chicken. "How are you?"

"Okay."

"How's school? I feel like I don't know what's going on in your life."

"You know the highlights. It's my last semester. I'm working hard, and I'm dating someone." All this surface talk is frustrating.

"Madden is serious about you."

"He flew me out here because he misses me, so yeah, I think we're pretty serious about each other."

"Are you being safe?"

"Seriously, Dad. I'm responsible, and so is he. And whether we're being safe shouldn't actually be the thing you're most concerned about. Shouldn't you want to know how he treats me? If he listens? Does he put me first?"

"Does he…put you first?" Dad asks softly.

"He makes time for me before he leaves for an away series. He flew home early from the last one to take me for breakfast with Cammie and Chase, and spent the day with me. I'm here now." My anger bubbles over. "Maybe you could learn something from him."

He sighs. "That's not fair, Tally."

"Why isn't it fair? You've been dedicated to the Terror my entire life. You've seen them through multiple Cup wins. You can do anything you set your mind to, but you can't put the time and energy into being a good partner for Mom? Why don't you want that with her? Why don't you want that with your family?"

He rubs his bottom lip. "Your mom deserves more than I can give her."

"Did you even try? Did you even want to?" I shake my head, frustrated with him and myself and fucking life. "If you really wanted to make it work, you would have found a way."

He nods once. "If this were a decade ago, you would be

right. But I have broken this relationship beyond repair, Tally. I didn't strive for balance, and I didn't put the time and energy into loving your mom the way I should have."

"Why can't you do it now? Why is it impossible to fix?"

"Your mom is tired, Tally. It's years of me not being there enough, of her being the sole source of emotional support for you and Ties and Fenna. Nothing I do now will take away the harm I've already caused. Your mom deserves to be happy, and someone else should have that chance with her. She made her choice and I want to respect that. I don't want to hurt her anymore, and trying to keep her tied to me would do that."

I brush away a tear, sad all over that this is where our family is. I don't want to end up like my parents. What if I give my heart to Flip and he stops taking care of it? How broken would I be?

"I'm sorry, Tally. I know that's not what you want to hear, and it isn't what I want to tell you."

I tip my chin up, fighting to keep more tears from falling. "I'd rather have the ugly truth than a pretty lie."

I'M GRATEFUL FOR DRED, HEMI, AND RIX, WHO HAVE ORGANIZED mani-pedis after lunch. It's a helpful distraction and keeps me out of the panic spiral. Especially since I won't get to see Flip until after the game this evening.

The Terror win 3-2. Flip, Tristan, and Dallas each score a goal, with Connor, Ash and Quinn as the assists. And no one from the media questions my presence at the game since I'm the coach's daughter.

Afterward, the girls and I return to the hotel to change into club attire. I'm a bag of nerves. I've been in Montreal for hours and I haven't even had a chance to hug him yet.

"You okay?" Hemi asks as I adjust my dress and check my makeup for the hundredth time.

"Yes. No. I don't know. This is the first time we've all been out dancing since Flip and I started dating. The media are going to freak out."

"It's okay if you're also freaking out. It's a lot to handle," Dred says gently.

All three of them have been my personal cheer squad since my arrival in Montreal. I vacillate between excitement and excessive nerves.

"How did you handle the pressure? How *do* you handle the pressure?"

"We have each other." Rix motions to the girls. "And we have partners who know it's a lot to be with them and who take care of us and our needs. Flip will be the same for you. He wouldn't have flown you out here if he wasn't ready for this step. He also wouldn't have done it if he didn't think *you* were ready."

"It's getting really real," I whisper.

"It's a statement that you're here," Dred says. "He's claiming you as his."

"People will have feelings about it."

"Fuck the people!" Hemi waves her hand in the air. "You know what I mean. Even when there's nothing to say, they have something to say about Flip's love life. We've already made a plan to counterbalance the nonsense."

"He flew you out here because he doesn't want to be away from you. He made sure you're surrounded by your friends and the people who will watch out for you," Rix adds.

"He's telling the world he's yours, Tally." Dred squeezes my hand.

"And I'm his."

"That's right." Hemi's phone pings. "They're three minutes out. It's go time!"

We shrug into winter coats and head down to the lobby.

My stomach somersaults when I see Flip. Neither of us has any chill as we rush across the foyer. He opens his arms, and I launch myself at him.

His lips find the side of my neck as he lifts me off my feet. "God, I missed you."

"I missed you, too." I feel grounded for the first time in days. It's terrifying.

He huffs me, lips traveling along my neck as he sets me down, takes my face in his hands, and kisses me deeply. Eventually he pulls back. "Hi."

"Hi."

"I'm so glad you're here," he mumbles into my skin.

"Me, too. That was a great game."

"I played better tonight because of you." He kisses me again, eyes moving over my face.

"The media followed you back here, eh?" Hemi inclines her head to the group of camera-toters.

"The limo drew them in," Connor says.

"Or your suit did," Dred says cheekily.

"My suit is awesome." Connor runs his hand down his teal velvet jacket, the maroon piping matches Dred's dress and coat.

"It's definitely a showstopper." Dallas pats him on the shoulder.

"How do you want to handle this?" Flip asks me. "We can stay in if you don't want the attention."

"We knew this would happen." I look to Hemi. "We prepared for this." As much as I want time alone with Flip, I don't want it because we spent the night hiding. I want him to know I'm in this just like he is.

He laces our fingers and kisses the back of my hand. "You stay right next to me, okay? I'll take care of you."

"I know you will." I exhale a nervous breath. Everything will change in a matter of minutes.

"Okay, Tristan and Rix, Connor and Dred, you lead," Hemi orders.

"We'll be your front line." Connor winks.

"Flip and Tally, you follow. Try to stay centered so we can keep Tally as protected as possible. There will be questions, but I'll handle that. Dallas and I will be your tail." Hemi claps. "Okay, team, let's make a statement."

"We got you." Rix squeezes my hand.

"Connor will activate villain mode, if he needs to." Dred winks.

Flip wraps his arm around me and kisses my temple. "You ready, kitten?"

"Ready."

We stay tight to Tristan and Connor's backs, with Hemi and Dallas flanking us. Cameras flash, and there's a collective murmur as their eyes move to me and Flip, his arm wrapped protectively around me. Reporters shout questions, pushing in.

"Are you dating the coach's daughter?"

"Tallulah, does your father know you're involved with one of the players?"

Connor wraps his arm around Dred's waist and spins them toward the reporters. He dips her like they're in the middle of a dance floor and drags his nose along the column of her throat before he slants his mouth over hers. Tristan and Rix step to the side, and Flip moves me ahead of him, helping me into the waiting limo and diving in after. Tristan and Rix follow, then Dred and Connor.

"If you have questions, you can email me regarding interviews," Hemi says. "But I'm off the clock. If you'll excuse us."

Dallas extends his hand and helps her into the limo. "The answer is yes, I'm absolutely trying to get my wife pregnant. Thanks for asking." He ducks in after us.

Hemi slaps him on the chest. "What the hell?"

"I'm manifesting, honey."

"And I thought you were a problem." Dred shakes her head at her husband.

"I am, and you love me for it." Connor kisses her.

"Such a villain." She snuggles into his side.

"Thanks for the distraction." Flip gives him a chin tip and stretches his arm across the back of the seat. "You okay?"

"Yeah. That went pretty well, right?"

Flip nods. "They've seen us together, now they'll work themselves into a frenzy about it, and when they calm down, I can give an official interview." He kisses my cheek. "In the meantime, I'll do my best to be worth the headache."

I squeeze his thigh. "The media have no idea how incredible you are."

It's a short ride to the club. I'm excited to expend some of this anxious energy on the dance floor. The limo drops us off at the VIP entrance, and Flip keeps a protective hand on my lower back as he guides me inside, stopping briefly to show ID.

The bass vibrates through my soles and works its way up my spine as we walk down a black hall. Flip keeps a hand on my waist as we climb the stairs to the roped-off area with table service. We head to our table, where champagne chills in buckets, and Flip helps me out of my coat, his eyes darkening as he takes in my dress.

His lip curls and he pulls me closer. "You know, it'll be tough to make this relationship work if I'm behind bars."

I grin and tug on his tie. "You like my dress, then?"

"Claws out tonight, eh, kitten."

I kiss his chin.

Rix passes me a glass of champagne and grabs my free hand. "Let's dance!"

Flip shoots her a dirty look. "We just got here."

"Find us when you miss us!" Dred kisses Connor on the cheek and spins out of his hold.

Hemi pats Dallas on the chest. "I'll see you in a bit."

We take the stairs down to the dance floor, weaving through bodies until we find a spot we like. I glance up and find Flip leaned against the railing a floor above, watching intently.

Rix follows my gaze. "My brother is intense about hockey and apparently you."

"And KD and Tang," Dred adds.

"Good & Plenty are up there, too."

The girls laugh, and Hemi gives me a side hug. "Let the media do what they do and we'll wait until they've calmed down. Everything will be fine, though."

I nod, and for now I decide to believe her. I push it all aside and get lost in the music, letting the beat flow through me. I love the energy on the dance floor, the hot press of bodies, the freedom of movement.

"Why are they only coming up to me?" I ask after I brush off guy number three.

An arm slips around my waist and warm breath fans across my cheek. I'm about to throw an elbow until Flip's deep voice rumbles in my ear. "Because you're the only one not wearing an engagement or wedding ring."

"Even that doesn't always stop them," Dred says as Connor moves in behind her and presses his lips to her bare shoulder. He follows with teeth, and her lips curve up in a slow, sensual smile. Those two are their own vibe. Tristan and Dallas join us, too.

I spot Quinn and Kellan where Flip was previously standing. I'm not sure when they got here, but they're both being chatted up by women. Kellan seems interested, but Quinn keeps checking his phone.

Flip moves to stand in front of me, blocking out everyone but him.

He pulls me closer, and I link my fingers behind his neck, letting him set the rhythm.

"Having fun tormenting me?"

"You have some strong feelings about this dress."

"I have strong feelings about everything when it comes to you." He tips his head. "It's making me lightly homicidal every time a guy tries to shoot his shot with you." His fingers flex on my hip, sliding lower. "If your goal was to get my attention, you succeeded." He skims the hem of my dress, warm fingers on bare skin.

"Good. Yours is the only attention I care about." I finger the hair at the nape of his neck.

He drops his head, lips ghosting the column of my throat. "I love watching you on the dance floor." He bites the edge of my jaw. "The way you get lost in the music." He kisses my cheek. "All these eyes on you, and you're too busy enjoying yourself to notice." His knee finds its way between my thighs. "So fucking sexy without even trying."

I press up against him, my core aching as I swivel my hips. I want to get closer, lose myself in feeling good and chase away all the worries and fears that keep pricking at me.

He gazes down, eyes hooded, lips parted, a salacious half smile tipping the corner of his mouth. "You move like sex."

I glance around. Most people are vibing, hips swaying, focused on the music or each other, but there's a couple to the right, her back to his chest, his lips on her neck and their eyes on us.

Heat rushes through me, desire thick in my veins. "The end of the night feels so far away." I rub against him, seeking friction.

"Do you need me to take the edge off?"

Everything below my waist clenches. "Right here, in the middle of the dance floor?"

"That's bold." His smile and the heat in his eyes tell me he likes where my head is.

He coaxed me through an orgasm over the phone. I can ask him for what I want when he's right in front of me. "There are plenty of dark corners." I glance around, looking for our friends, but we've migrated away from everyone. Behind me to the right are a few tables lining a curved wall, filled with empty cups and couples making out. To the left is a wide, round column. "Like over there."

Flip's smile turns downright lascivious. "What happens in dark corners, Tally?"

I bite the inside of my lip.

"Talk to me." We're still moving to the music, his thigh between mine, his hand on my hip, fingertips digging in a little. He brushes his lips over mine. "Tell me exactly what you want."

My pussy throbs.

"Was it easier on the phone?" He pulls me tighter against him. "You can close your eyes and whisper in my ear if you want. But you have to ask. It's what I need from you."

I can feel him hard and thick against my stomach. He wants this just as much as I do. Maybe even more. I channel every damn ounce of Arwen I can. "I want you to tuck me away in that corner and fuck me with your fingers."

His nostrils flare, and his lips curve up with pride and dark need. "What else do you want?"

"For you to make me cream all over your hand."

"God, you're fucking perfect." He seals his mouth over mine, tongue pushing past my lips on a low groan.

I'm giddy with anticipation, the thrill of it making my body come alive. And I don't want to wait until the night is over. I want his hands on me. I want him to want me with the same desperation that makes my legs weak and my core ache. I don't want to be a good girl who follows the rules. I want dark corners and the high of getting away with something bad.

"Please, Phillip."

"You're going to lick my fingers clean after you come all over them." His expression turns downright feral. "Say it, kitten. Repeat it back to me."

"I'll lick my cum off your fingers."

He edges me back toward the column, knee between my thighs again. We dance, and his fingers trail unsteadily down my side, skimming the hem of my dress as he peppers kisses on my jaw, but doesn't come back to my mouth.

He glances around, checking the bouncers who stand like statues around the VIP section, looking down on us. But they're focused on the dance floor, not this quiet, shadowed corner. Flip moves me into the empty space, his huge body hiding me away.

He cups my cheek in his palm, and I swear I feel it shaking. "If it's too much, or you don't like it, tell me and I'll stop."

"It won't be."

"I mean it, Talls, if this is uncomfortable for you, or triggering in any way, you say the word, and I'll take you back to the hotel and give you whatever you need."

"I know." I move his hand from my hip back to the hem of my dress. "I want this. I want you to touch me."

He runs the back of his fingers along my thigh, and I whimper when they reach the hem of my dress and slide underneath.

"Is your pussy exactly like the rest of you, Tally?" His fingers skim my panties. "So fucking sweet and pretty."

His mouth covers mine as he slips one finger under the satin, and he swallows a moan as he glides it over my clit. "But when nobody's looking, you like to be bad, don't you?"

I nod, and he sucks my bottom lip, fingers sweeping back and forth, the lightest caress.

"Please, Phillip." I'm already desperate for the feel of his fingers on my hypersensitive skin.

"I'll be so good to you." The words seem heavier, like they're weighted down with other emotions. "I'll always take care of you." He eases a finger inside me, and the sensation, coupled with his low groan, nearly makes my knees buckle. One curl sends a jolt of pleasure radiating through me.

"So soft." He circles my clit with his thumb and rubs inside me again. "Tell me you're mine," he demands.

"I'm yours," I whimper.

"Only my fingers will fuck you." He adds another, stretching me. Like I asked him to. Like I wanted. "Only my mouth will suck this sweet little clit." He rubs it with his thumb, circling and pumping, filling me, fucking me with his fingers like he promised.

The bass vibrates through the floor, the music so loud I strain to hear him. But he's all I can see and feel. If he moved six inches to the right, someone could see us, catch us. The thrill of it pushes me closer to the edge.

He drops his head, eyes on mine, lips close but not touching as he growls, "And mine will be the only cock you ever fuck."

Heat and want rush through me. I grip his arm as my hips jerk and my pussy clenches around his fingers. I moan his name, grateful for the pumping bass and heavy drumbeat that drown me out.

I sag against the column, my legs weak and my body singing. I want him to do that again and again, until I'm nothing but a slick puddle of desire.

Flip slowly withdraws his fingers. The insides of my thighs are wet. He holds his hand up, showing me his slick fingers. "I change my mind. I get to lick them clean this time." He drags his tongue up his palm, then sucks each digit into his mouth, one by one, like he's savoring a decadent dessert.

He gently grips my chin and kisses me deeply. Another surge of desire flares as I taste myself on his tongue. I wrap my arms around his neck, as much to steady myself as to keep him close. I stroke against his tongue, my desperate mewl almost lost in the bass.

Flip breaks the kiss, eyes hot with desire. "How you feel, kitten?"

I should feel sated, eased. But now that he's put his hands on me, all I want is more. "Hungry."

"I'm fucking starved for you." He sucks my bottom lip. "I knew it would be like this with you."

The swell of pride is undeniable. I want it to always be this way. For him to want me so completely.

He kisses the end of my nose. "Let's get your coat."

Flip practically carries me up the stairs, my legs are so wobbly. The oonsing of the music is always an issue for Dred, so she and Connor have already gone. Rix is tucked into Tristan's side, and Dallas is draped over Hemi. Kellan is chatting up some woman, and Quinn is still on his phone.

Everyone but Quinn gives us an eyebrow lift as we arrive.

"What have you two been up to?" Rix asks with narrowed eyes.

"Dancing," Flip replies evenly. "We're heading back to the hotel."

"Keep Tally safe, please," Hemi orders.

"Always." He helps me into my coat and keeps his arm around my waist as we leave the club.

Twenty minutes later, we're back at the hotel and in the elevator on the way to our suite. Flip's jaw ticks as the floors climb. His throat bobs with a nervous swallow and his hand shakes as he brushes my hair away from my face. "It feels good to finally have you to myself."

I wrap my arms around his waist. "I can't wait to spend the night with you."

"I've waited so long for you." He kisses my temple, then my cheek.

I'm the only woman he's ever flown out to a game.

The only woman he's publicly claimed as his.

I press my lips to the edge of his jaw.

He smiles down at me, eyes soft, hand trembling as he curves it around my nape.

I do this to him.

Phillip Madden longs for me the same way I long for him.

CHAPTER 31

FLIP

Take it slow has been my mantra since Tally and I started down this path.

Yet one taste is all it takes to unravel my control. She radiated sensuality on the dance floor. And as soon as I had her in my arms, my reason took a vacation. I can't say I'm disappointed that she and I share similar kinks. The feel of her, the taste, how gorgeous she is when she comes… I'm desperate for more.

Every new first with her replaces a painful memory. It's like we're rewinding time, back to before I married the wrong person for the right reasons, and my views on love and relationships took a dark turn. I need every step forward with her to count, even as I'm agonizing over what that means for me.

My hands are unsteady as I open the door to our suite. I usher her in, toss the keycard on the side table and flip the safety before I turn to her. We both shrug out of our winter coats. I take hers and toss it over a chair. We move toward each other, magnet and metal. I lift her into my arms, and she winds hers around my neck and her legs around my waist.

"God, I love it when you're close to me." I press my face into her hair, breathing her in.

"Me too." She peppers kisses along my neck and the edge of my jaw.

I carry her across to the bathroom. "Thank you for letting me take things slow."

"Thank you for making every new experience feel special." She pulls back, her expression impish as she runs her nails down the back of my neck. "But no rewinding. Fingerbangs in public or private spaces are now on the table, and they can't be taken off."

"I'm already addicted to the way you feel, backtracking would be impossible." I set her on the vanity. "Want to shower with me?"

Her eyes flare. "Fully naked?"

"That's generally how it's done."

She rolls her eyes but smiles. "I get to wash all of you?"

I push her hair over her shoulders, fighting to steady my hands. "And I get to wash you."

"I would love that," she whispers.

"Let me turn on the water, then we can undress each other."

"Okay."

I drag myself away from Tally so I can start the shower.

Tally slides off the counter as I turn to face her again, my nerves resurfacing. *Take it slow.*

I can get naked with Tally and not have sex. I can touch her and make her feel good, and that can be enough. It's about connection, intimacy, being vulnerable with each other.

I close the distance between us. "I can't wait to see all of you."

She shivers and runs her trembling hands up my chest. "Me, either."

I kiss her cheek as she loosens my tie and bend so she can pull it over my head. She runs her fingers through my hair, taming it and calming me, then starts to unbutton my shirt. Her eyes lift as she presses a soft kiss to the center of my chest.

I shudder at the tender affection, exhaling a breath that matches her unsteady hands.

"You're just so beautiful." She pushes my shirt over my shoulders and tugs it free. "Everything about you, Phillip, but especially your heart."

The water hitting tile dims until there's nothing but the sound of our breathing, the staccato beat of my heart and the gorgeous woman in front of me, looking up at me with complete adoration.

"You heal me." I steady my hand and cup her cheek, giving in to the need to kiss her, but I don't deepen it. Not yet.

Tally works my belt free, then pops the button on my dress pants, dragging the zipper down and pushing them over my hips. I step out of them, kicking them aside. Her fingertips rest on my abs as her eyes drop to the outline of my erection, pressing against the fabric of my black boxer briefs.

She skims the waistband, and I catch her hand. "Wait please, kitten."

"I want to touch you." She looks up at me with wide, imploring eyes as her lips brush over my knuckles. "I want to make you feel good, too."

"You already do." My eyes slide closed as I center myself, body already in overdrive. "I want to savor every moment of this." I press her hands to my chest to ground me. "And it's my turn to undress you."

She shivers, goose bumps rising along her skin as I skim the length of her arms, then trace the contour of her body. When I reach the hem of her dress, I follow it with my finger, dipping under to caress the inside of her thigh before I lift the fabric, revealing pale blue satin-and-lace panties.

Inch by inch, I unveil her graceful dancer's body. She raises her arms, and I slide the fabric over her head, leaving her in her panties. She's strong and athletic, with gentle curves. I skim from her ribs to her hip. "You're gorgeous, Tally."

"So are you," she whispers.

I step closer until we're skin to skin. She sucks in a shuddering breath that echoes how I feel inside. It feels good to have her here with me. I run my hands down her back as hers glide up my arms and link behind my neck.

Desire builds as I dip down to capture her lips and our fingers drift and explore.

Eventually I break the kiss and settle my palm against the side of her neck.

For a moment, I'm the one with no experience. Because until Tally, I haven't allowed myself to feel anything but lust and desire. But for her, with her...I want it all, even though it terrifies me.

"You can finish undressing me now." My voice is guttural.

Her eyes shine with excitement as she trails a single finger down my stomach and dips inside the waistband of my boxer briefs. We both take a deep breath as she tugs my boxers down my thighs.

"Oh wow." My erection juts out in the space between us, unapologetically hard. "Okay. That's—" Her eyes flick to mine and drop again. "I expected you to be proportional, but that's a whole lot of something right there."

I laugh and pull her to me, trapping my hard-on between us as I kiss her. "My ego loves you."

"Seriously, though." She settles her hands on my chest and pushes back so she can look down between our bodies. "You are exceptionally above average."

"I'll let you take measurements sometime," I tease.

Her eyes light up. "You said it, and you can't take it back."

We're both grinning as I ease a hand down her side.

The mood shifts as I hook a thumb into the waistband of her

panties. The energy sparks between us. "I think it's time to take these off."

She nods, running her hands down my arms.

I push the satin and lace over her hips and drop to my knees so I can slide them down her calves, unveiling all of her. I run my hands up the backs of her legs, stopping below the curve of her ass, fingers pressing into the soft, smooth skin. She exhales a shaky breath and runs her fingers through my hair.

I press a soft kiss above her navel, then rise and hold my hand out. "Let's get wet."

She laughs. "That was so bad."

"But also accurate." I wink.

I step under the spray first, to make sure it's not too hot before I pull her in with me.

I grab the bodywash, squirting a generous amount into my open palm as I rub them together. "I can't wait to get my hands all over you."

Tally moves so her back is to the spray. I love that she isn't shy or uncertain about her body, and that despite everything, here in this space, we're equal in the newness of it all.

I smooth my hands down the sides of her neck, over her shoulders and collarbones, trailing them across the swell of her breasts before I cup them. Her eyes flutter closed on a sigh.

I brush her nipples with my thumbs and she arches into the touch. "Oh God, Phillip."

It's who I want to be with her.

Not Flip Madden, the hockey player with the slut reputation.

Phillip. Her boyfriend. The man she lets into her heart.

"I love touching you." My lips sweep her throat. "Kissing you." I suck her bottom lip. "Making you feel good."

I pull back, and her trembling fingers trail over my abs, bottom lip trapped between her teeth.

Gripping her by the waist, I spin her around until her back

meets the shower wall. "As soon as you put your hands on me, I'll be addicted to your touch."

My admission emboldens her as she runs her hand down my chest.

"I don't want you to look at anyone else the way you're looking at me now." I brace a hand on the wall above her head.

"It's always been you, Phillip." Her eyes warm. "Only ever you."

"You're all I want, Tally. Just you." She has no idea the power she holds over me. How gone I am for her already.

Tally runs a single finger from base to tip. I shudder at the feel, at the sight, and then groan as she wraps her fingers around my length.

Her pretty blue eyes lift from my cock as it slides through her fist. "Tell me how you like it."

"This is perfect," I grind out, reaching up to skim her bottom lip.

Her tongue darts out to lick the pad of my finger. "Mine," she whispers as her thumb smooths over the head.

"Yours," I groan as she strokes back down.

Her smile is deliciously carnal.

"Does it feel good to fuck my hand, Phillip?" She arches, until the head of my cock rests against her stomach, inches above her navel.

"Like fucking heaven."

"Mine are the only hands that will touch you like this," she whispers the words against my lips, giving them back to me.

I revel in the intimacy of it, at the way she claims me as hers, at the feel of her hand moving over me, at the warmth of her breath on my lips.

"My mouth will be the only one to lick and suck you." She flicks my top lip with her tongue. "And when you're ready for me, mine will be the last pussy you fuck."

I cover her mouth with mine, the kiss possessive. "Tell me you're mine," I demand.

"I'm yours." The words are electrifying and a balm. A promise and a talisman. Every moment with her pulls me in deeper. I want her permanence in my life and my world.

Conviction lights up her beautiful, delicate features. "And you're mine."

"That's right." My fingers tighten in her hair, and I claim her mouth again, just like we've claimed each other.

I memorize this moment, this first for us, replacing a sea of memories that mean nothing with one that means everything.

When she wraps her other hand around me, I lose control and paint her hip in cum. The water washes it away as I drop my head to her shoulder, sated in a way I've never been before. She keeps one hand wrapped around me, squeezing in pulses but not stroking, kissing along my cheek until she reaches my lips. We make out for long minutes, bodies slick and hot.

I ease a hand between her thighs to cup her. "I need to see you come again for me."

"I need to that too." Her eyes are hot with desire.

I stroke her gently, obsessed with the sweet sounds she makes as I fill her with my fingers. She rests her forearms on my shoulders, head bowed, eyes fixed on my hand between her thighs. When her legs start to shake, I cup her chin in my palm.

"Show me how pretty you are when you're coming for me, kitten."

She clutches my shoulder, her mouth falling open, as her hips roll and jerk. I covet the sound of my name when it tumbles from her lips on a moan. We stand under the hot spray, holding each other.

Eventually, I cut the water and dry her off, pulling one of my shirts over her head. "Every time we have a sleepover, from now until the end of time, this is what I want you to wear."

"I will agree to this only if you limit your bedtime apparel to boxer briefs."

"Deal." I kiss her cheek.

We brush our teeth side by side at the vanity. I kiss the edge of her jaw, committing another moment to memory. I'm as enamored with this domestic comfort as I am with everything else about her.

She wraps her arms around my waist, squeezing gently.

I kiss the top of her head. "What's this for?"

"Just because."

I link our pinkies and lead her to bed, tucking Tally against me, big spoon to her little.

I kiss the soft space where her neck meets her shoulder. "'Night, kitten."

"'Night, Phillip."

As I close my eyes, I know I want more of this. More of Tally at my games. More nights with her in my arms. I want to keep her and never let go.

CHAPTER 32

TALLY

I grip the edge of the vanity and repeat my new mantra. "It's going to be great. No one will say shitty things to your face."

My phone buzzes with a call. I glance at the screen. It's my mom. The shit has really hit the fan since my trip to Montreal last week. She knew I was going, but the ensuing social media shitstorm has shed new light on Flip, and my mom is kind of freaking out.

I answer on the third ring. "Hey, Mom."

"Hey, sweetie. You doing okay?" The worry in her tone tells me either she's been online, or my siblings have.

"I'm good. I'm just getting ready for the gala I told you about." It's for the special needs hockey program. A wholesome family event with me on his arm is a lot different than a night out at a club. Hemi's hoping it will mitigate the media heyday around my relationship with Flip.

"Right. Yes. That should be fun."

"Yeah. My friend Rix will be there, and a few of the other hockey WAGs." I rub some anti-frizz serum between my palms and finger comb my curls. "How are you?"

"Good. Okay. Still worried about you."

"You have to stop looking at social media," I say gently. Pictures of Flip and me have surfaced and gone viral—including one strangely angled photo made to look like I was sandwiched between Flip and Quinn. But thankfully none of us in the dark corner.

"It's not intentional, honey. Your sister sees things, and you know kids." She sighs. "I just want you to be in a safe and healthy relationship."

I bite my lips together and roll my eyes to the ceiling. Not because I'm annoyed with my mom. It's the media and their absolute obsession with Flip's love life that's the problem. Not to mention all the women who are happy to slide into my DMs to tell me all about their experience with my boyfriend. The number of accounts Hemi has blocked for me has been unreal and I'm now on a social media hiatus.

"I'm sorry, Tallulah. I don't want to tell you how to live your life," Mom rushes on.

I realize I've been up in my head. "I know you're worried, but I promise the stuff you're hearing about from Fenna and the truth are two different things. Phillip is protective and respectful. I promise." I change gears because this is a hamster wheel I don't need to take a ride on. "Why don't I come for dinner tomorrow?"

"Fenna has cello until five."

"I'll come after. I can meet you at home." I'd go to Fenna's cello practice, but my sister doesn't need the bullshit that will come with that.

"Okay, baby. That sounds great. Will you bring Phillip?"

"He has practice and a game the next night." And he does not need to field Fenna's questions. Or my mother's.

"Of course. That makes sense."

"I'll call you tomorrow, when I'm on my way."

"Okay. I love you, Tallulah."

"I love you, too, Mom."

"Have a good time tonight and be safe."

"I will."

I end the call, swipe mascara over my lashes one last time, and survey my reflection in the mirror. A dress arrived yesterday from Flip. It's pale blue, gauzy, flowy, and modest—nothing like the slinky dress from last week. It makes me feel like a princess. *His* princess.

"You've got this," I tell myself as I slip my feet into my heels and grab my clutch. "Rix will be there. It's a family event. People won't ask inappropriate questions." The number of girls on campus who have asked me if the rumors are true this week has been astounding. Where are people's boundaries?

I compartmentalize all over again and head for the door. Now that the hockey world knows we're dating, it will be impossible for him to stay under the radar. Thankfully I'm done with campus life soon.

I shrug into my coat, grab a catnip mouse, and throw open my door.

Flip is on the other side, poised to knock. "Great timing."

He slips inside as Parsnip comes down the hall, meowing excitedly.

"Am I running behind? I thought I was coming to you." To avoid him being mobbed.

"I didn't want to wait." Parsnip puts his paws on his leg and butts his hand with his head. "Hey, buddy." He gives him a scratch then wraps his arms around me, pulling me against him. "How are you?"

I sink into his embrace, relishing the calm that comes with the contact. "I'm okay. Good. I'm good."

He pulls back, brow furrowed. "Have you been staying off social media?"

"Yeah." I nod fervently.

He arches a brow.

"I promise."

He takes my hand in his. "You seem edgy."

"I'm just nervous."

"About what? Talk to me."

Getting out of this building without him being mobbed or someone asking us an awful question, for starters. I fiddle with the lapels of his suit jacket. "The media will be there, and they'll have questions."

"They'll be focused on the kids and the goals of the program," he reassures me.

"Okay." I exhale some of the worry. "That's good."

"I'm sorry this week has been stressful." He presses his lips gently to mine. "And I'm sorry we haven't had much time together."

Aside from Flip stopping by the studio with coffees a couple of days ago, this is the first time I've seen him since his return from the away series. We've both been busy and time hasn't been on our side. "At least we're together now."

"Mm. I want time where I don't have to share your attention." He cradles my cheek in his palm and drops his head, slanting his mouth over mine.

A few delightfully toe-curling seconds later, I find myself pressed against the wall, Flip's knee between my thighs. My body is already hoping for things that won't happen until later.

"I knew this dress would be perfect." Flip pulls back, eyes hot. There's a slit up one thigh. "I can take the edge off for you."

"By edging me?"

He drags his fingers up the inside of my thigh. "You'll be nice and relaxed when I'm done with you."

"Don't tease, Phillip."

"Not tonight, I won't." He slips a finger inside my panties and skims my clit.

I whimper.

"Such a pretty sound." He pushes my panties to the side and eases a finger inside me.

The relief is almost instantaneous. My shoulders relax against the wall and I arch my back, pushing my hips out. Flip's gaze darts between my face and his hand moving between my thighs.

"If you add another finger, I'll make more pretty sounds for you," I bargain.

"Is that right, kitten?" He withdraws, but before he can suck his fingers, I grab his wrist and bring them to my lips. I keep my eyes on his as I take them in my mouth, swirling my tongue around them, tasting my own desire.

He smiles darkly as he pushes them deeper and kisses my cheek. "That's my dirty girl."

I moan at the praise and suck. He withdraws them from my mouth and slides them back inside me, pumping and curling as he grips the hair at the nape of my neck. His mouth covers mine, swallowing down all my needy sounds.

"I missed you so much this week. It's worse when I'm in Toronto, but I can't be with you," he whispers, almost plaintive as he adds a third finger, thumb strumming my clit.

"It's torture," I agree. "I just want to be close to you." I've been bereft all week. I've lived in his hoodie and slept in the shirt I took home with me from Montreal.

"I can never get enough of you." Heat funnels to my core as he pushes in deeper. "So fucking gorgeous when you're stretched around my fingers."

I moan, and my legs shake as my hips swivel.

"You're so fucking soft, kitten." His eyes darken. "Soon I'll fuck you with my tongue and swallow down all your cream."

I come in violent, desperate waves. His arm circles my waist, and I sink into his hand, moaning his name and ride it out. I never want it to end, but eventually the spasms subside, and my body goes lax.

He withdraws slowly, then brings his fingers to his mouth, licking them clean while humming contentedly. I use the wall to keep me propped up while I calm my breathing.

"Feel a little more relaxed now?"

I nod, still dazed, then glance down at the prominent bulge pushing at the front of his dress pants. "But you look stimulated."

"I'll calm down. Your needs are my top priority." He kisses the end of my nose. "We don't want to be late."

"Shouldn't you wash your hands?" I ask as he helps me into my coat.

"Absolutely not." He opens the door, tosses a catnip mouse, although Parsnip is nowhere to be found, and ushers me into the hall.

I'm grateful the elevator is empty when it arrives, but we pick up a group of students two floors down.

"Flip Madden! Holy shit. Someone said you'd been on campus, and I thought it was total bullshit, but you're here. In like, res."

"Just picking up my girlfriend." He wraps a protective arm around me.

I can't even appreciate the fact that he's called me his girlfriend because I'm terrified someone will say something that makes him want to punch them in the face.

"Right. Yeah." The guy's gaze moves to me. "That's like, wow."

"Want me to sign your hat?" Flip nods to the Terror ball cap he's wearing.

"That would be awesome." He passes over his ball cap, and Flip pulls a Sharpie out of his pocket. He signs stuff for the rest of the guys—with the hand that was between my legs—and by some miracle, we manage to escape my apartment building without another fan run-in.

"You really might need to come up with a disguise now

that we're out in the open," I say once we're in his car and he's navigating Friday evening traffic. "Or I can just meet you off campus or in the parking lot, like I was supposed to."

"I can handle a few fans," Flip assures me. "And the novelty will wear off."

I hope he's right, because spending the rest of the semester being the hot topic on campus does not seem fun. "Things amp up during playoffs, though," I remind him.

"We'll figure it out." He threads his fingers through mine. "There's a treat for you in the glovebox."

"Because the dress that showed up at my apartment wasn't enough for tonight?"

"I wanted us to match and I didn't want it to be something you had to worry about since I know the workload this semester is intense."

"I love the dress."

"So do I." He winks. "Check the glovebox."

I pop it open. "Mini Stroopwafels! Did you go to the Dutch Toko again?"

"I did. But there's more in there. I meant to bring it up with me and give it to you while I was in your apartment, but I forgot."

"In too much of a rush to get to me?" I tease.

"Exactly."

My heart stutters as I pull out a small, wrapped box. "What's this?"

"You'll have to open it to find out."

I carefully peel away the wrapping paper. Inside is a blue box. My stomach tightens as I lift the lid. "Phillip, this is beautiful." Nestled in the cushioned velvet is a pair of jewel-encrusted ballet slippers on a white gold chain.

"I saw it and thought of you," he replies, his smile soft.

"I love it so much." *And you,* I want to say, but it feels too

soon, and too scary a thing to admit. "I'll wear it all the time."
And when I miss him, I'll have a little piece of him with me.

"I'll help you put it on once we're parked."

He pulls into the arena lot and finds a spot. I unclasp the
necklace and move my hair aside so he can fasten it. He presses
his lips to my nape before sitting back. "Let's see."

I finger the delicate charms. "It's gorgeous."

"You're gorgeous." He kisses me softly. "Wait here and I'll
come around and get you." I stay where I am while he rounds the
hood. How did this become my life? I have the most amazing,
thoughtful boyfriend.

Flip links his arm with mine, guiding me inside. The arena is
decorated like a high school prom, complete with balloon arch
for photos. The younger players wear pretty dresses and suits.

I spot Brody and Rix right away, along with Tristan and
Quinn. He's brought a date tonight; the same woman who came
to Connor and Dred's wedding. I didn't have much of a chance
to talk to her, but she seems nice. She's tall with pale blonde hair
and a girl-next-door vibe. I'm grateful to have friends here, so it
won't be totally awkward. Flip takes me over to where Brody
and Quinn are talking to the coaches.

"Hey, Tally." Brody gives me a quick side hug.

"Vander Zee?" A man in his mid-thirties turns to me.

"That's right." I lift my hand in a wave.

"Is this your date?" the man asks Brody.

I swallow my hysterical giggle. I'm pretty sure Brody and I
both want to disappear.

Brody tucks his hand into his pocket. "Uh, no, we're just
friends."

Flip puts his arm around me. "Tally is my date."

"Sh—oot. Right. I saw that and thought maybe it was fake
news."

Rix appears at my side. "Tally!" She hugs me. "Let's get you
a drink."

She guides me away, toward the bar, dropping her voice to a whisper. "What the hell just happened there?"

"One of the coaches asked if I was Brody's date."

"Oh, God." She squeezes my arm. "Are you okay?"

I bite my lips together.

"Do we need to find a quiet space so you can have some feelings about people being obtuse?"

I blow out a breath. "I get why he made that mistake."

"Doesn't make it less awkward. Let Flip deal with it." She rubs my back. "I know it's not easy right now. You're staying off social media?"

"I'm staying off social media," I echo.

"Good." We reach the bar.

"But I have two younger siblings," I add.

She wrinkles her nose. "And they are not."

"Nope."

Rix orders two margaritas. I was going to stick with soda because I have dance practice tomorrow, and I don't want to end up dehydrated, but if this is how the night is going to go, tequila might be necessary.

"How are your parents handling things?"

"Mom is stressing but trying to be supportive. My dad is… letting me live my life, I guess?"

She nods. "How are people on campus?"

"Have you talked to Essie?" I prop my arm on the bar top.

Rix blinks at me, and I blink back.

"So that's a yes," I confirm.

"I know what it was like when my brother was in the thick of things and people would say stuff to me that was super cringe. And then when I started dating Tristan…" She sighs. "It will calm down, I promise."

"Please don't say anything to Phillip."

"Talls, he knows what's going on. You don't have to pretend

it's not hard. Please tell me your Tilton friends have your back like you had Cammie's back in first year."

"They're awesome. And Fee kind of gets it because of Roman and Lexi, and Cammie understands because of Chase, and Brody is Brody. So yeah. I have their support. I don't want Flip to think this is too much for me."

Her expression turns empathetic, and she squeezes my arm. "It's okay if there are moments when it is. Just go to him when it's like that. He needs that from you. He can't protect you from all the idiots, but he can be there when you're struggling, so please let him."

Flip approaches, expression remorseful. "I'm so sorry about that. Are you okay?"

"Yeah. It's going to happen, right?" I force a smile. "He's not the first person to think Brody and I were a thing."

Flip frowns. "Have you been a thing?"

"Okay, I'm going to find my husband." Rix passes me my margarita. "Don't say stupid things, Flip."

I sip my drink. "Brody has a thing for a girl he went to high school with that he doesn't have the balls to ask out, and I've had a thing for you for probably the same amount of time," I inform Flip.

"So that's a no?" He looks relieved.

I narrow my eyes. "Were you jealous for a second?"

"No." He pokes at his lip. "Okay, yeah."

I grin.

"If you weren't already aware, I'm unapologetically obsessed with you." He kisses my cheek. "Let's go get our picture taken under the arch."

I'm not the only person who wants a photo with Flip under the balloon arch. Rix and I spend a good half hour arranging our men while the young players pose next to them. Brody has a few fans and is adorably red-faced through most of the photos.

Cocktail hour is blissfully hiccup and awkwardness free. The media covering the event aren't jerks, and no one else mistakes me for Brody's date. And dinner is fun and easy since I'm surrounded by people I know. All the things I worried about seem silly when I'm insulated by my friends.

After dinner, Flip, Tristan, Quinn, and Brody move to the stage to present awards. Rix leaves because she has to be at the kitchen early to interview assistants, so that leaves me at the table on my own since Lovey, Quinn's date, is helping with the awards backstage.

Two women in their early twenties set up the dessert table behind me.

"What I wouldn't give to be her," one whispers.

"I know, right?" The other whistles softly. "That man has skills."

They both giggle.

I bite the inside of my cheek, frustrated that my relationship is once again reduced to entertainment. People are focused on a narrative that has no basis in the present.

No one but Flip and I know the truth, I remind myself.

It should be a comfort, but all it does is make me feel alone.

CHAPTER 33

TALLY

"I can't wait to be outside," I say to Cammie as I push through the doors of the lecture theater, following the hoard of students toward the exit. It's been a week and a half since Flip flew me out to the game, and three days since the gala. I'd like to say things have calmed down, but that would be a lie.

I'm working hard to block out the whispers from a group of girls as we pass.

"…Flip Madden's girlfriend…"

"…have you seen the pictures…"

"…do you think Romero…"

"Rumors are the gateway to stupidity and opinionless drones," Cammie shouts cheerfully before turning to me. "I vote we find a patch of sun and hang out like lazy cats."

"As long as that patch of sun does not include people churning the gossip mill, I'm game."

Hemi had hoped my appearance at the special needs hockey gala on Friday would replace some of the nonsense, but it went completely under the radar. Probably because it had nothing to do with Flip Madden's sex life.

I pull out my phone and send Fee a message that we're on our way. She replies with a selfie at one of the outdoor tables at the campus café. We're having a warm early-March blip. The temperature is in the mid-teens, which means guys are wearing shorts and T-shirts, and half the girls on campus are in tanks despite there still being snow on the ground. March is a weird month in Ontario.

I show Cammie my phone. "Looks like Fee's already on it."

I tip my face up as we leave the building, welcoming the warmth of the sun on my skin. But my joy is short-lived.

"There she is!" someone shouts.

"What the hell is going on?" a guy to my right asks.

Suddenly Cammie and I are surrounded, microphones shoved in our faces, cameras clicking incessantly.

"The fuck?" I grab for Cammie's hand, panic taking over.

"Tallulah! Tallulah! Is it true you've been secretly dating Flip Madden for years?"

"Tallulah! Are your parents separated because of your relationship with one of the Terror players?"

"Is it true that Flip has been pursuing you since you were in high school?"

"Are you and Flip Madden also involved with Quinn Romero?"

Cammie steps in front of me, acting as a human shield. It would be more effective if she wasn't a head shorter. She points at each of the reporters. "No, no, no, and maybe leave Quinn Romero out of your weird, incessant obsession with Flip Madden's sex life." She takes a step back, forcing me to do the same.

"Are you also involved with Flip and Tallulah?" a reporter asks her.

"Gandalf on a cracker." I can practically hear Cammie rolling her eyes. "No, you creepy weirdo. I have my own hockey player."

Mob mentality setting in like a bad psychology experiment as people pull their phones out and start recording.

"Go back inside," Cammie orders as the reporters shout more questions.

I spin around and push back through the sea of bodies. People close in on me and real terror takes hold. *What if I get trampled? What if I can't reach safety?*

"You're okay. I'm right behind you!" Cammie shouts. "Get out of the way! Emergency!"

We push through the doors, back into the building. Cammie slips in front of me—the perks of being pocket-sized—and grabs my hand. She pulls me down the hall and ducks into one of the gender-neutral bathrooms locking the door behind us.

I slide down the wall and tuck my head between my knees. My head is spinning, and I can't catch my breath.

"Hey, hey. I'm here. I've got you. You're okay, Tally." Cammie's hands settle on my knees. "You're having a panic attack. Just breathe, okay?"

I burst into tears, sucking in lungfuls of air between sobs, the adrenaline rocketing through me. Cammie sounds far away. A phone rings. I can't take a full breath.

"She's here with me. We're in a bathroom. She's safe. She can't right now. Yeah, that's her. No. No. That's a really fucking bad idea. You cannot come here. I'll share her location. I have a plan. I'll get her off campus so you can come to her. I'm hanging up now so I can help her through this."

Hands settle on my knees again. "Tallulah, I need you to look at me."

"I can't breathe," I hiccup and sob again.

"Can you drink this?" Cammie holds out a bottle of water.

I shake my head.

"I'm really sorry for what I'm about to do."

Cold water splashes my face.

I suck in a breath. "What the fuck?"

She blots my cheeks with paper towels. "I'm sorry. I needed to snap you out of it. You were in a spiral," she explains. "I love you and promise that was less than ten percent backwash."

I laugh and then start crying again.

"It's okay." She hugs me. "I'm going to call Chase, okay? We're going to get you out of here and off campus."

"How? The media are everywhere."

"You let me handle it." She calls Chase and puts him on speakerphone. "Hey, babe, are you at the apartment?"

"Sure am. You coming home soon? You want to try that new po—"

She cuts him off. "You're on speakerphone."

"Okay. Cool. What's up?"

"The media mobbed us as soon as we left class."

"They're following Tally again?"

It happened outside the apartment on my way home from rehearsal yesterday, but there were only a couple, and they couldn't follow me into the building.

"Yeah. Someone figured out her schedule."

"This is borderline psychotic. I'm on the way over to the arts building," Chase says. "I'll meet you at the back entrance, closest to Prince Street. Brody's place is only a ten-minute walk from there. I'll escort you."

I wring my hands. "What if there are more reporters at the back entrance? What if they see us on the way to Brody's?"

"There's a hidden path, so we can stay off the sidewalks. I'll message when I get there, stay in the bathroom until then." Chase hangs up.

Cammie and I stare at each other.

"I didn't think it would be like *this*." What if his teammates turn on him? What if my dad freaks out, too? "I don't want Flip to end up traded over me."

"Your dad wouldn't jeopardize the team like that."

"They are his favorite child." I wish I was joking.

"I'm sorry." Cammie hugs me. "Let's get you out of here, then we can deal with whatever we need to."

Cammie and I trade hoodies and I try not to dive back into the panic spiral while she messages with Chase. When we get the all clear, I tuck my hair into her Tilton baseball cap and we slip into the stairwell and descend, popping out at the back of the building.

Chase is the only person there. "You two okay?" he pants and runs a hand through his sweaty hair.

"Slightly traumatized and highly annoyed that we can't soak up some vitamin D in the quad, but fine otherwise," Cammie assures him.

"How did you know about this exit?" I stay pressed against the wall, still anxious that we'll be bombarded again.

"Sometimes Brody uses it to avoid the fangirls who have a class after him," Cammie explains.

"Poor guy."

"It's hard to have a famous brother and be following in his footsteps," Chase says. "I let Brodes know we're coming. He said to stick to the path."

"Okay." I nod, my throat tight as anxiety takes hold again.

"I'll go first, and, Cammie, you fall in behind Tally, so she's guarded, yeah?"

"You got it, babe." She tips her chin up and puckers her lips.

He dips down to kiss her.

Cammie has a black belt in karate, and Chase is a six-four hockey player, so despite my trepidation, we should be safe.

Chase leads us to a trail that runs parallel to the street, through the park behind a few off-campus subdivisions.

"Are there already videos online?" I ask as we speed walk down the path. "I should probably call Phillip. He might worry."

"He's on his way to Brody's," Chase calls over his shoulder.

"How does he know to go there?"

"I had Brody call him." Cammie squeezes my hand. "He called while we were in the bathroom."

"Oh my God." It starts to come together. "He called while I was having a panic attack." What if he thinks I can't handle this? What if he breaks up with me?

"He wanted to come get you, but we thought this would be better. He's worried about you. We all are. The fucking media need a new hobby."

Seven minutes later, Brody lets us into his backyard through a gate I didn't even know existed. His brow is furrowed as he closes it and secures the latch. "You okay?"

I nod. "Just rattled. Thanks for letting us hide out here."

"It's no problem." We follow him through the slush, a few patches of grass showing now.

Gage and Mac are chilling on the back deck.

"The media are really frothing at the mouth over you and Madden, eh?" Gage sets his phone face down on the side table beside his half-finished beer.

"Unfortunately," I agree.

"You all want something to drink?" Brody asks. "We have a cooler of fun stuff and soda, juice, and water in the house."

"And milk," Mac adds.

"No one wants milk unless it's going on cereal or in coffee," Gage mumbles.

"I like chocolate milk." Chase jumps to Mac's defense.

"Water would be great for me, please." My mouth is dry from all the anxiety and the adrenaline.

Chase accepts a beer and Cammie a soda.

We form a circle of Muskoka chairs. I wish I could relax, but I'm paranoid that a horde of reporters are going to ambush me again.

"Where's Fee?" Mac asks.

"She was at the café with Enid," Cammie says.

"We were supposed to meet them until we got mobbed," I croak.

"I'll just invite them here," Mac says with the enthusiasm of a golden retriever.

Brody and Chase return a minute later with drinks.

"Dating a Terror player is a lot when you're still in university, huh?" Mac muses.

"Today it is." I'm emotionally exhausted from this ordeal and the level of attention we've gotten over the past week and a half.

"The prying questions are too much." Mac's voice is full of empathy.

"They're really digging up his past." Gage frowns at his phone. "Some of the pictures floating around are four years old."

"What pictures?" My voice pitches up.

I glance between Brody and Gage, who are communicating through flared eyeballs.

"What pictures?" I ask again.

"They're pre-Rix-and-Tristan old," Brody says, jaw working. "They're irrelevant."

"Why do they feel the need to keep bringing up things that happened years ago?" I hold up a hand when Gage opens his mouth to speak. "I know why. Because they have a strange fixation with his love life, and if I wasn't the coach's daughter, it wouldn't be half as exciting."

"It's frustrating, but true." Brody's tone is all empathy.

"Plus, you're still in university and he's thirty," Gage adds.

Mac kicks his shin.

"I'm not trying to be a dick. I'm just stating facts. You've got this star hockey player with a prolific history with women that may or may not be blown out of proportion thanks to clickbait, and a university student who is the physical embodiment of wholesome and angelic—"

"This is the whole fucking problem!" I argue. "This isn't about how much sex he's had and how much sex I haven't had, or how much sex he and I are or aren't having. We're in a relationship. We have feelings that extend beyond his dick and my vagina!"

"We know that, Tally," Brody says gently.

"I just mean that this sort of presents as an oil and water situation, where he's the oil and you're the holy water," Gage explains.

"Tally?" Flip's deep voice comes from behind us.

"Phillip!" I bounce out of my chair.

He crosses the deck and wraps his arms around me. I cling to him, relieved, terrified, and desperate for the closeness and the comfort.

"Are you okay?"

My bottom lip trembles and fresh tears spring to my eyes as the weight of everything crashes down.

Alarm fills his eyes. "Kitten? What happened, baby?" His thumbs sweep my cheeks, brushing the tears away, but more follow.

"I think she's just a little overwhelmed," Cammie offers.

"Did anyone hurt you? Are you hurt?" He runs his hands down my arms, his panic my own.

"N-no." I suck in a breath. "I was just scared."

"Oh, baby. You need a break from my bullshit." He presses his lips to my forehead and then my lips.

That makes more tears fall. "I don't want a break from you," I whisper.

His expression softens. "That's not what I meant." He squeezes me close. "Those videos." He chokes on the words. "I was fucking terrified, kitten." He cups the back of my head. "You'll stay at my place tonight where I can make sure you're safe."

"I don't have an overnight bag."

"We'll pick up whatever you need." His gaze moves behind me. "Thank you for getting Tally here safely."

I'd forgotten we weren't alone, that my friends are watching this exchange.

"Of course. We always have Tally's back," Brody replies, and Chase murmurs his agreement.

Flip grabs my backpack and slings it over his shoulder while I hug Cammie and say goodbye to the guys.

Flip's SUV is parked in the driveway. He helps me into the passenger seat and takes his spot behind the wheel. His jaw is tight as he backs out of the driveway.

"Are you okay?" I ask once we're on the way back to his place. I just want to curl up in his lap and stay there for the rest of eternity.

"No." He stretches one hand along the back of the seat and finds the nape of my neck. "I'm worried about you. It's my job to keep you safe and protect you."

"They didn't hurt me. They just took me by surprise."

"They need to leave you alone. You're still shaking. This is too much emotional strain. I can't keep my past from surfacing, and I know what people are saying. This is what I was worried about. It was fine when we were flying under the radar, but now…"

More panic hits. What if he thinks I can't handle the pressure? "It'll blow over."

"Dating me shouldn't come with more negatives than positives," he argues as he pulls into the underground parking lot.

"You're not the problem, though. It's all these people who are absorbed with your love life."

"Which I used to broadcast for public consumption, and you're paying the price for it."

"Please don't break up with me," I whisper despondently.

He pulls into his spot and shifts into park. "Hey." He unbuckles his seat belt and then mine, pulling me into his lap. "That's not what's happening." He brushes my hair away from my face.

"But you might. If I can't handle it, you might." My fears spill out.

"I'm worried about you breaking up with me, Talls, not the other way around." He kisses my forehead and my cheeks. "I just hate that being with me has to come at such an emotional cost. I'm going to fix this, okay? I'll make it better."

Once my emotions are under control again, Phillip helps me out of the car and we take the elevator up to his apartment. I haven't been here since the night my parents announced they were getting a divorce. So much has changed since then. I have the one thing I've always wanted, but lots of things around me seem to be falling apart.

Flip pushes my hair over my shoulders, eyes searching mine. "What can I do for you, kitten? What do you need?"

I could ask him for anything, and I'm pretty sure he would give it to me. But I don't want the first time we have sex to be about him feeling guilty and me wanting an escape from the stress. I want to do something normal with him. Domestic. Comforting for both of us. "Can we make mac and cheese and cuddle on the couch?"

"Absolutely." He kisses me softly. "You want to get comfy?"

I finger the buttons on his shirt. "Can we make it together?"

"Rix actually sent over her leveled-up mac and cheese." He waggles his eyebrows. "I can put it in the oven, and we'll get down to cuddling right away while we wait for it to heat up."

"That sounds perfect."

I pour us glasses of Tang while Flip puts the food in the oven. Then he guides me to the couch, and I curl up in his lap. It's exactly what we both need—closeness, connection, and some distance from the stress of everything else. When it's just the two of us, I can believe it will all be okay.

Eventually, the timer goes off, and together we plate dinner. Turns out "leveled up" means homemade white cheddar mac and cheese with peas, tarragon, and baked chicken breasts. We load our bowls and take it back to the couch.

"This is so good," I note a few minutes later as I pop another piece of tender chicken into my mouth. "Rix is a food magician."

"She is excellent at putting together balanced, healthy meals that taste amazing," he agrees.

I spear a spiral noodle. "I'm so glad she went back to school and pursued her dream."

"I should have realized she needed more support."

"You helped her. She lived with you."

"I could've done more, though. I was too busy battling my own demons to see outside myself." His jaw ticks.

I run my nails gently down the back of his neck. "Do you want to talk about that?"

He looks over. "Not tonight. I'd rather focus on you, if that's okay."

Sometimes I wonder if focusing on me is a default. But we've had enough stress today, I don't want to add more by poking at his wounds.

The adrenaline gradually seeps out of my body, leaving me exhausted. I have assignments that need my attention, but I'm too tired to manage them. My eyes keep drooping, and eventually I must fall asleep, because the next time I open them, I'm tucked against Flip in his bed, his arm curved around my waist.

I wish it could always be this easy.

I pray the world won't always feel like it owns a piece of him.

CHAPTER 34
FLIP

Tally throws her leg over mine and nuzzles into me, her nose against my neck. I hated that I couldn't protect her yesterday but waking up with her in my arms is bliss. I haven't slept beside her since Montreal, and I've missed the way she feels tucked against me. I could get used to this. Even though it scares the shit out of me, I don't want to run.

I kiss her forehead, filtering through breakfast options. I can make her pancakes, or bacon and eggs, she alternates between them when we go for breakfast with friends. What would it be like to wake up with her every morning? To start my day with her? To come home to her after away games?

Unfortunately, her alarm goes off, breaking my reverie. It's my song of choice for home hockey games.

She groans and sits up in a rush. Her hair is a wild, untamed, beautiful mess. She glances around, processing her surroundings, eyes bouncing to my bare chest and then the clock on my nightstand.

A slight furrow forms in her brow. "Is that the real time?"

"It's seven thirty," I confirm.

"I have to be at the studio in half an hour for group

rehearsal!" She tosses the covers off and scrambles out of bed. She looks adorable in my T-shirt. She spins around gracefully, then runs from one side of the room to the other. "I won't make it on time from here!"

I slide out of bed. "I'll drive you."

"We needed to leave five minutes ago!"

I cross to her and curve my hands over her shoulders. "Take a breath, kitten."

She sucks in a deep one, but it's wheezy. Her gaze drops to my bare chest, and lower, to where my morning wood salutes her from behind my boxer briefs.

Disappointment pulls the corners of her mouth down. "I don't even get to enjoy your morning wood."

"It happens every day. You'll have plenty of future opportunities." I kiss her forehead. "Get dressed, message your troupe that you're a little behind, and I'll make us coffees to go."

"Okay. Yes. That's a good plan. Thank you." She wraps her arms briefly around my waist, her warm cheek pressing against my chest. When she pulls back, she pats my erection through my underwear. "Sorry, big guy, we'll play another day."

"Leave him alone and put some clothes on."

"Right." She moves to my dresser and I pull on a pair of joggers and a T-shirt and head for the kitchen while she puts yesterday's outfit back on.

Seven and a half minutes later, we're armed with coffee and Rix's famous raisin bran muffins and we're on the way to Tally's dance studio.

"Okay, ten minutes late isn't the worst. Thank you for driving me. The subway would have taken twice as long."

"I'm happy to have the time with you. How are you feeling this morning? Did you sleep okay?"

"I feel better. And I slept like the dead. You're like my own personal body pillow." Her cheeks heat.

"You can use me as one any time you want." I slip my hand

under her hair. "I'm meeting with Hemi later this morning so we can make a plan." And while I'm near campus, I'll talk to their security. I don't like that I can't protect her when I'm not with her.

"Just let me know if there's something I can do."

"Let me handle this." I rub my thumb along the back of her neck.

We arrive at the studio at 8:08, but no one is waiting outside. She plucks a sticky note with *Thank You!* and a heart scrawled on it.

"What's that about?" I ask.

"I offered the space to some of my class who were struggling to find studio time the way we were," she explains as she unlocks the door and lets us in. "We have a calendar that we update weekly. I didn't want it to sit empty when we're not here. I hope that's okay."

"Of course it's okay." It's exactly like Tally to help her peers.

She turns on the light. "They should be here by now. Or maybe they went to the café to wait?"

She checks her phone, rolling her bottom lip between her teeth as her eyes widen. "Shoot."

"What's up?" I arch a brow.

"Sooo…it looks like I'm not late after all."

"Are you a few minutes early?"

"More like almost an hour. I must have put it in my phone wrong." She wrings her hands. "I'm so sorry. I really need the next performance to go well. I made a few stupid mistakes on my last one."

"Did I miss one?" I thought I had all her performances in my calendar.

"It was an in-class performance. It was in the middle of the day."

"Can people who aren't in the class still come and watch those?" I press.

"Yeah, but we have them every month. I don't expect you to make those. Besides, you were at an away game, and like I said, I made some mistakes, so it wasn't my best performance," she explains.

"You know I want to support you, right? I'll always come to your performances, no matter how little of a deal you think they are," I say gently. My stomach twists. "Unless you'd rather I not attend."

"That's not it at all. I've had monthly performances for the past three years and my mom's maybe made a handful and my dad, well...I just didn't say anything because people have busy lives."

"I will always make time for you, Tally. If I am in town and I can make it, I will be there, okay?" I won't be another person in her life that lets her down.

"Okay." She worries her bottom lip. "I'm sorry we're so early. We could have had time together and now we're here."

"I don't mind. And we still have time together. What's stressing you out, kitten?" The past twenty-four hours have been intense.

"I don't know. This performance is a big deal and I don't want to mess it up. All my future prospects sort of hinge on it, and I can't let Charles and Arya down. I don't want to have to work for the Terror because no company in the city wants me."

"Hey, hey." I cup her face in my palms. "Take a breath and step away from the ledge of despair."

She sucks in some air. "I'm sorry. I don't know why I'm so worked up. The in-class piece was only five percent of our grade, and I didn't practice it as much as I have the final-performance numbers."

"You're juggling a lot, kitten," I remind her.

She plays with the aglet on my hoodie. "Everyone has a full plate."

"Your load is heavy." Between her family splitting up, final exams and graduation on the horizon, coursework and assignments, dance, volunteering, and our relationship—she's carrying an impossible load. Especially with the media tailing her everywhere she goes.

"We could have snuggled in bed for another half an hour," she whispers.

"You would have liked that, eh?"

"I like being close to you."

"Me, too." I weigh my options as an idea forms. Last night Tally didn't push for anything physical. I would have given her anything she asked for, and maybe she knew that. We made food together and snuggled; things *I* like. She put my needs ahead of her own. I could give her what she needs now. "I have this fantasy."

Her eyebrows rise. "What kind of fantasy?"

"I haven't been able to stop thinking about you dancing for me. Or rewatching that video clip you sent me." I run my hands down her arms. "Especially the part when you're in the corner on the barre."

Her cheeks flush and her pupils dilate. "It's my favorite part of that routine," she whispers.

"Mine, too. We have some time before Charles and Arya get here." It's eight fifteen. We have at least a half hour. It ticks all her boxes, the potential for getting caught, bringing my fantasy to life. She'll be relaxed going into her day. "Will you let me take care of you?"

She sucks in a shuddering breath and nods.

I cover her mouth with mine, stroking inside as I lift her up and carry her across the room. Tucking her in the corner away from the windows, I set her on the barre.

She makes an annoyed noise when I break the kiss, then gasps when I cup between her thighs. "Should I take your leggings off, or do you want me to get you off like this?" I tease.

She narrows her eyes. "No going backward, Phillip."

"Just checking." I wink and hook my fingers into the waistband of her leggings. She grips the barre and lifts her ass. The soft fabric slides down her thighs, along with her panties, and I hang them over the barre. Tally lowers herself to the bar and presses her knees together.

I run my hands along the outside of her thighs. "Be a good girl and open for me."

Her eyes light up, bottom lip caught between her teeth as she pulls her knees to her chest and twists until her left foot rests on top of the barre. Toe pointed, she extends her leg.

Hot eyes locked on mine, she repeats the movement with her right leg until they're parallel. Her arms strain, muscles tight and corded. She scissors her right leg into the air, sweeping past her face and mine, and brings it to rest on the opposite barre, baring herself to me.

I curve my hands around her ankles and smooth my palms up the inside of her calves, stopping just above her knees. "I'm the only person you'll ever dance naked for."

"Only you," she agrees.

My erection kicks as I ease my hands higher to frame the apex of her thighs. "Everything about you is pretty." I drag my thumb through her slit. "Soft and wet and all for me." I circle her entrance, and we both groan as I ease a single finger inside.

"Oh, God." Her toes curl and her eyes lift, first to mine, and then over my shoulder.

I follow her gaze. "Now that's a stunning view." I shift to the left, my hip pressed against the inside of her thigh. "Anyone could walk by and hear your sweet moans."

I add a second finger, pushing in deep. She groans and swivels her hips, eyes fixed on our reflections. "Does it make you hot, kitten? The idea of someone seeing you like this, spread wide for me, dripping into my palm." I kiss her cheek and find the spot that makes her moan my name. "So gorgeous when you're full of my fingers." I kiss her neck. "Do you want more?"

"Oh God, yes." She props her forearm on my shoulder as she adjusts her left leg, bending her knee and turning her foot so it rests on the barre.

"Tell me what you want, ask me for it." I bite the edge of her jaw. "And don't forget to be explicit."

"I want another finger," she whimpers and rolls her hips. "I want to watch you stretch me so I'm ready for your cock."

"That's my girl." I pull out, circle her clit twice, then add a third finger.

"Oh fuck." Her nails dig into my scalp, eyes locked on the mirrors as her legs start to shake.

I nibble the edge of her jaw. "I think it's time I had a taste."

She groans my name.

I drop to my knees, ease my fingers out, press my forearms against the inside of her thighs, and lick up the length of her on a feral growl. "I could eat you alive."

She pulses against my tongue, her high-pitched mewl filling the room. "Oh my God, oh God."

"Don't I take good care of you, kitten?" I latch onto her clit, sucking softly.

"So good, so fucking good." One leg stays on the barre, and the other foot comes to rest on my shoulder. Tally runs her fingers through my hair, gripping tightly as her hips jerk and roll.

"So damn sweet." I lick up the length of her. "I could feast on you all fucking day and it would never be enough." I fuck her with my tongue. Devour her, lick up every drop of her cum, and suck on her pretty clit until she shudders her way through a second climax.

She slides off the barre into my lap, legs draped over mine. She grips my chin and her hips swivel as she kisses me deeply, moaning into my mouth.

I indulge in a few strokes of tongue before I pull back. She's a glassy-eyed puddle. "It's ten to nine, kitten. We should probably put your pants back on."

"I don't think I can stand up."

"I can help." I grab her leggings and panties from the barre and carry her over to the yoga mats. I unroll one, lay her down, and redress her bottom half while she lies there in a daze.

Her ankles rest on my shoulders, her arms outstretched on the floor, chest still heaving. "That was so amazing. I'm so relaxed. My pussy is so happy."

I laugh and lean forward, hands beside her head as I brush my lips over hers.

"Your whole face smells like my vagina." Her brow furrows, and her eyes flare. "The whole room probably does."

There's a knock on the studio door. Because I locked it when I first let us in.

She shoves at my chest. "They're here!"

I hop to my feet. Tally sits up in a rush, then puts out both hands and folds forward.

"Stay there, I'll let them in."

"They're going to smell my vag on you." Her forehead touches the floor between her legs. She doesn't seem overly concerned.

I scrub a hand over my face before I open the door. Arya and Charles stand on the other side, wide-eyed. "Hey. Talls is just warming up. I'm heading next door to grab coffees. Can I get you two anything special? Latte? Flavored latte?"

"Um, yes, sure, thank you. Please. Flip Madden. Wow. Hi. I'm Charles. I don't really understand the rules, but I am a fan of hockey and especially the warmups." His eyes lift to my hair. I didn't check my reflection before I opened the door.

"Oh my God, Charles," Arya mutters, but her eyes are also on my hair.

I step aside and let them into the studio. Tally's cheeks are red as she turns to face them, hand raised in a floppy wave.

"I'll be back with breakfast and coffees," I call.

But they're no longer focused on me.

"Oh, you naughty girl," Charles says as the door closes. "You're my new hero."

CHAPTER 35
FLIP

I put my phone on speaker as I hit dial. After I dropped off the coffees, I went on a little shopping spree for my girlfriend. I want to surprise Tally with something nice and I'm hoping to get some help from her roommate.

Lexi answers on the second ring. "Is everything okay?"

"Everything's fine," I assure her.

"Fee said you picked up Tally last night. There's a viral video floating around and it looked like utter madness." The worry in her tone hits me hard.

"The girls are okay. They got out safely. How's Vander Zee?" I ask.

"Worried. We all are. What the hell are media doing at a university campus? Where was security?" Lexi asks.

"I'm looking to get some answers this morning. I just dropped Tally off at her dance studio."

"She's okay?"

"She's rattled. It's a lot of stress, but she's safe and that's what's important. I want to surprise Tally with something nice, and I wondered if I could get Fee's number from you." I explain that I'm hoping to bring it up to her apartment so it's there when she gets home.

"Of course. That's sweet of you, Flip."

"Just trying to be a good boyfriend."

"The media sure don't make it easy for you."

"No, they do not," I agree.

Lexi sends me Fee's contact, and I call her as I approach the university campus.

"Flip? What's going on? Why are you calling me? Is Tally okay?"

"Tally's fine. She's at the dance studio with Charles and Arya."

"Okay. Good. That's a relief. What's up?"

"Are you at the apartment?"

"Yeah, why?"

"I have some stuff for Tally. I'm almost at the university. Do you think you could let me in so I can bring it up?"

"Totally. Of course."

"I'll be there in a few."

"I'll meet you at the front doors."

Like magic, one of the ten-minute spots is open as I pull up in front of her building. I barely have the car in park before the fucking reporters are on me.

I dial Hemi.

It doesn't even finish ringing once. "What's going on?"

"I know you've scheduled an interview for later today, but I'm out front of Tally's building and I'm about to be swarmed."

"Is Tally with you?"

"No. She's at her dance studio. I'm dropping something off for her and I'm going to confront these assholes. I just wanted to prepare you since I'm sure it will cause you some headaches."

She's quiet a moment. "Keep the focus on Tally's safety, but you have my blessing."

"That was my plan. I appreciate it."

"Flip."

"Yeah."

"You're really kicking ass at this boyfriend business."

I smile faintly. "Thanks, Hemi. That means a lot." I end the call, summon some fucking calm, and open the door.

"Has Tally gone into hiding?"

"Have you and Tally broken up?"

"Is it true that Vander Zee is planning to trade you at the end of the season?"

"Is Tally moving in with you?"

I round the car and pop the trunk.

Students notice and start to flock toward us. I address their questions, pointing to each reporter. "No, no, no, and that's actually none of your business, is it?"

"Why is Tally the first woman you've dated since you joined the Terror?"

"Have you and Tally been secretly dating for years?"

"For the love of." I pinch the bridge of my nose. "Why is my love life so intriguing? Why are you following my girlfriend around her university campus? Do you have any idea how terrifying it was for her yesterday when you bombarded her after class? And for what? So you can ask her personal questions about our relationship that neither of us will answer?"

"Why are you so secretive about your relationship with Tally?"

"Because she's my girlfriend and it's my job to protect her. If she was your sister or your daughter or your best friend, would you not be disgusted by all of this?" They fire more questions at me.

Campus security arrives and I hold up a hand.

"Look, my relationship with Tally is not for public consumption. She and I have been friends for a long time. She is very aware of my history, just like you are. Unlike you, she's willing to leave my past where it belongs. I care very deeply for Tally. She is my top priority."

"Is she more important to you than your hockey career?"

"My hockey career has a limit. My feelings for Tally do not." I pin the reporter with a glare. "I am asking you, respectfully, to back off. You want access to me, here I am. But you are scaring my girlfriend and you are turning her campus into a circus and unsafe place. Leave Tally alone, or my next step will be hiring her a personal bodyguard. If you have further questions, you can contact my agent or Hemi Bright, the head of Terror PR, and believe me, she's just as protective of Tally as I am, and she will not be nearly as kind with you." I grab the bags from the trunk, use my elbow to close it, and head for her building as security moves in to clear the media.

Fee is standing at the doors with Cammie and the two of them are flanked by Mac, Chase, and Brody.

Fee makes a heart with her hands. "That was amazing."

"Thanks. They probably ruined my fucking surprise, though."

"Worth it for the high-level protective alpha boyfriend vibe, though," Cammie says.

The guys lead, clearing the way to the elevator, which is open and waiting for us.

We get on as a group and no one tries to join us. Once the elevator doors slide closed, I release a tense breath.

"You okay, man?" Brody asks.

"Yeah. I just need them to back off my girl." I sigh. "Thanks again for getting her out of that situation safely. I owe all of you."

"We take care of ours," Brody says and the rest of them echo the sentiment.

Once we reach the apartment, they follow me down the hall to Tally's bedroom.

I push the door open, step inside and freeze.

"Oh shit," Fee says from behind me.

"Dude. That is epic," Brody says.

"I need one of those," Chase says, I'm assuming to his girl-friend. "But of you, not Madden."

"Your birthday is coming up," Cammie replies.

Fee pushes her way through the throng of hockey boys and jumps in front of me, blocking my view of the body pillow in my likeness. "Your face tells me you didn't know that existed."

"I do now."

"I bought it for her," Cammie chirps from behind me.

"Recently?"

"Yup."

I glance over my shoulder at Cammie who stops making wild hand gestures and smiles manically. I decide to leave it alone. "Tally's secret is safe with me." For now.

"Oh thank god, she would die of embarrassment." Fee's shoulders come down from her ears. "I'll just put it away for her." She rushes across the room and shoves my pillow likeness into Tally's closet.

Her friends help me set up the surprise for my girlfriend.

"I'm seriously taking notes here, man," Brody mumbles.

"You think she'll like it?" I ask.

"It's literally all her favorite things. She'll love it," Fee assures me.

Her bathroom has been transformed into a mini-spa, and her fridge is stocked with all her favorite treats, including dinner and dessert for her and her friends.

"Good. I want to be worth the headaches I'm causing." And I'll start by taking care of her any way she'll let me.

CHAPTER 36
TALLY

I stare at the paper in my hands. Fifty-three percent. It's not a fail, but it's close. And it's worth twenty percent of my mark. I should have asked for an extension instead of pushing through. But I didn't, because explaining that I'm having trouble focusing because I'm dating a professional hockey player and my life is public fodder isn't anyone's fault but my own.

I wanted this, even though I knew this would probably happen. But what if it continues indefinitely? What if I fail an assignment? What if I lose my place on the dean's list? I fight the rising wave of panic.

I manage to keep it together, but when class is over, I quickly pack up my bag and duck out of the lecture theater. I pull my hood up and keep my head down. Reporters have stopped trolling me on campus and at my apartment. Flip confronted them outside of my apartment, and later gave a very emotional, heartfelt interview. Both went viral.

It's been more than a week, so I figured it would be safe to check my socials today. I was very wrong. The masses are divided. Half think I should be left alone, the other half still believe they're entitled to a piece of Flip. We made our beds, now we should lie in them.

My phone rings, scaring the crap out of me. I'm jumpy as shit these days. And my appetite is garbage. My mom calls daily to check in. She's caught in the middle, navigating the impact of this on my sister and brother while trying to be supportive. It's a hard line to toe. I don't know how to be just her daughter and she doesn't know how to be just my mom. We're learning under pressure, and it's tricky.

It's my sister calling, which isn't typical. Normally she texts.

"Hey, Fenna. What's up?" I scroll through my calendar to make sure I haven't missed something important.

She hiccups.

"Fen? Are you okay? What happened?"

She sniffles. "Dad came over. I thought he was staying for dinner because Mom made a big chicken pot pie. But I don't like chicken pot pie."

"It's too many textures and flavors at the same time," I finish for her. If Dad came by, it means the team is back in Toronto.

"But Dad didn't stay. I was practicing cello when he arrived and I had to finish the piece, so I didn't even get to see him."

"Was he dropping something off?" Sometimes Fenna gets hung up on the details.

"I don't know. They were fighting, though."

"What were they fighting about?"

She's silent for a moment.

"Fen? What were they arguing about?"

"You and your boyfriend. I didn't mean to listen, but they were being loud. People are saying mean things about you, and I don't want them to be true."

"Are people saying mean things to you about me?" I ask.

"You can't tell Mom, Tallulah. Sometimes she's sad and she cries, and I don't want to make her more sad." She huffs. "And I know that Dad always worked, and wasn't here all the time, but I still miss him. Are you moving home when you're finished university?"

"I don't know yet."

"If you don't, it will just be me and Mom."

"Fen—"

"Will you move in with your boyfriend?"

I'm trying to follow her train of thought, but sometimes it's tough to figure her out. "We haven't been dating that long."

"But you have a whole scrapbook of articles with him in them."

I frown. That scrapbook is hidden in the back of my closet. "How would you know that, Fen?"

"Um… Uh, I was…I was looking for something, and uh… uh…I found the scrapbook. I have to go. I need to get ready for cello. Please don't tell Mom that I told you they were fighting about you."

She hangs up.

"Well, that's great." I tip my head back and scowl at the sky. "I can't even rat her out for being a snoop."

"What?" A girl passing by gives me a funny look.

"Oh my God, isn't she the one who's banging all the Terror players?" her friend whispers, loudly.

"Oh, for fuck's sake!" I throw my hands in the air. "I'm not banging the entire hockey team, you assholes! It's AI-generated nonsense. Get a goddamn clue." There are some new, fun pictures with my face photoshopped all over them.

They rush off, giggling.

It starts to rain.

I want to scream.

It's pouring by the time I reach my apartment building. I didn't check the weather this morning. Otherwise, I would have packed an umbrella. Once I'm in my apartment I can have a nice cry, followed by an eye treatment to manage the puffiness.

I keep my head down as I walk through the foyer, heading for the elevators. But the whispers still reach my ears.

"That's Flip Madden's girlfriend…"

"…Did you see the photos of her with Madden and Stiles…"

"…Weren't those photoshopped…"

"…Or maybe not…"

"…Imagine being in the middle of that sandwich."

I bypass the elevator and take the stairs, so I can start my cry sooner. I'm sobbing and wheezing by the time I get to my floor. I have to wait another two minutes because there's a gaggle at the elevator, and I do not want to run into anyone right now.

The elevator finally comes, and the hall empties. I rush to my door, but I can't find my key fob. It's not in any of the usual pockets. I bang my forehead on my door a few times, but I don't need a bruised face to round out this shitty day, so I dump out my bag and find the key fob stuck inside a textbook.

And because today is the worst, Parsnip escapes into the hall the moment I open the door. I deflate. "I hate my life."

I shove all my shit inside the apartment, flip the safety so I don't have to struggle to get back in, and spend the next ten minutes trying to corral Parsnip. "If Flip was here, you'd be all over him like a freaking catnip toy," I gripe. Eventually he tires of being chased and returns to the apartment.

"You're an asshole," I tell him as he trots down the hall.

He just meows.

My phone rings again with a call from my dad. I let it go to voicemail. I can't deal with my own feelings currently, let alone anyone else's.

But I still listen to the message.

"Hey, sweetie, it's your dad. I'm sure you already know that. I just wanted to check in. Your mom's worried about you. So am I. I know you're an adult, but this uh…it has to be a lot for you. If you need anything, prepared meals, groceries, anything at all,

just call. I miss you. Send me a message when you get this. Love you lots, Tally-Bear."

I drop into a heap in the hall and let the tears spill over.

My phone buzzes again.

It's Flip. They've been away for four days, and I miss him so much.

I hold the phone up in front of my face to unlock it and read the new message.

FLIP

Back in Toronto! Just finished picking up a couple of things and heading to you now. How's it going?

TALLY

Great!!!! 👍

FLIP

👀

What's wrong?

I'm sure the excessive exclamation marks tipped him off.

TALLY

Everything is fine. I accidentally hit the exclamation mark four times.

FLIP

It's the thumbs-up that makes me question your honesty. Do I need to video call you?

If he sees my face, he'll know I'm lying, so I give him some honesty.

TALLY

I got a shitty mark on an assignment.

Which would be fine, but it's worth 20% of the course mark.

FLIP

Can you talk to your professor? Can you make changes and resubmit?

TALLY

Maybe.

I don't know where I'll find the time to revise it, but if I don't, and I get another crappy mark in this class, I could lose my spot on the dean's list.

I should stop texting, but now that I've started, it's like a waterfall of worries pouring out of my fingertips. And I keep hitting send.

TALLY

Fenna called me crying.

She's all my mom has, and Ties is never home, and he's starting university this fall.

She asked if I'm moving home when I'm finished.

What if I don't finish?

What if I tank my exams, and my final assignments? What if my next performance was like my last one and I shit the bed on that too and I have no job prospects?

Like you're going to want to be with someone who doesn't have their shit together.

And why can't people mind their own damn business?

The social media stuff is a lot. I looked and I know I shouldn't have, but it's too late.

Why does everyone need to know everything about our relationship?

> I don't know how you deal with it.
>
> I feel like I'm drowning in all this worry.
>
> I probably shouldn't have said that.
>
> Oh God.
>
> I'm coming off as clingy and needy.
>
> I don't want to be either of those things.
>
> Can you just erase all these without reading them?

I feel sick as I read them over. I'm falling apart, and now Flip has a front row seat through text messages. Why would he want a girlfriend who can't keep it together, not even in text messages? I don't want to be the kind of person who can't handle it when things get hard.

FLIP

> You're not clingy or needy, kitten.
>
> Everything you're feeling makes sense.
>
> OMW. Be there soon. 🖤

Parsnip comes down the hall and curls up in my lap. I let him sit there for a few minutes before I drag my ass off the floor. Flip pokes his head in the door while I'm sweeping stuff back into my bag.

"Tally?" The rest of his body follows, and he flips the latch behind him, letting the door fall closed. Parsnip abandons me to rub himself on Flip's legs. Flip is wearing a suit and holding his travel bag, plus flowers and cookies from my favorite bakery.

He sets the bag on the floor, and the cookies and the flowers on the side table and opens his arms. "You have a rough day, kitten?"

I step into them and press my face against his chest. "I'm a hot mess."

"Sounds like maybe you have a good reason." He hoists me up.

I wrap myself around him and cling to him like a burr and lose the battle against the tears.

He grabs the cookies and his bag and carries me to my bedroom. Parsnip follows on his heels, meowing loudly.

Flip deposits his bag on the floor and the cookies on the nightstand. Then he sits on the edge of my bed with me still wrapped around him. "Let it all out."

"I don't want you to break up with me," I mumble into his skin.

He takes my face in his hands. "Baby girl, sweetness." He wipes my tears away, then kisses both of my cheeks. "Why would you think that?"

"Everything feels like it's falling apart on me," I whisper.

He nods. "Yeah, I'm sure it does." His eyes are so sad. "Can I be honest with you?"

I swallow past the lump in my throat and nod.

"I've been worried you'll be the one who breaks up with me."

I frown. "Why?"

"Because I'm causing you a lot of stress."

"It's not your fault everyone wants a piece of you."

"But it kind of is. My past is haunting both of us, and I hate it." He brushes my hair over my shoulders. "But this." He wipes my tears away. "Where I get to be the one you come to when things are hard, Tally, it's exactly what I want with you. I want to be the person you lean on and confide in. Don't be brave for me. I want all your feelings. I want your laughter, and your dreams, and hopes and fears. I want you to feel safe to cry with me. Okay?"

"I just want to be able to handle this."

"Handle what, exactly?"

"This." I motion between us. "You and me."

"You're telling me how you feel and that it's been hard. You're being honest and open, and to me that's handling things. Add in everything else, and you're a freaking superstar, Talls. I think you're used to being everything for everyone else. You don't have to do that for me. I want to take care of you. It makes me happy when I can do things for you." He kisses me lightly on the lips.

I finger the hair at the nape of his neck. "I've never felt this way about anyone before, and it scares me."

"It's intense, right?" He runs his hands up and down my back.

"Yeah."

"All-consuming?" He strokes my cheek.

"It hurts when you're away," I admit.

"It's the same for me. I couldn't get to you fast enough." Flip kisses me. "Let me be your solid ground."

I nod and hug him, and he hugs me back, like he's holding us together.

I can't hide from the truth anymore. My heart is already his.

CHAPTER 37

FLIP

Quinn sneezes for the tenth time in a row.

"I think you might be allergic to cats," Tally notes. She has a kitten perched on her shoulder, and she's holding another one like a baby. Three other cats sit at her feet, staring up at her like she's their queen.

Hemi organized a promo op with the local cat shelter Tally volunteers at. It's where Parsnip came from and it's run by a woman named Kitty Hart—not a joke. We're here to pose with the wily furballs for a charity calendar. It won't be released until next year, but the plan is to help the shelter raise funds for their hard to home wing, so the long lead time should be fantastic.

Dallas tries to pick up a cat, but it swats his hand and hisses. Tristan is cuddling two kittens, and my sister is looking at him like he's dinner. Kellan is holding a tabby cat who keeps trying to lick his jaw. Connor looks ridiculously regal petting the three-legged sphynx cat perched on his lap. There's a good chance it's going home with him based on the number of photos Dred has taken.

Shilpa is in charge of making sure Pavin, their toddler with an endless supply of curiosity and energy, doesn't try to love the cats to death or use their tails as a leash while Ash juggles two gorgeous Bengal siblings.

We even convinced Roman and Hollis to come out, plus a few of our other teammates, so we'll have a complete calendar.

"You should probably go first, Quinn," Hemi suggests.

"Good call."

He moves to the studio space, and Hemi passes him a beautiful orange and white striped cat who is absolutely in love with Quinn based on the way she's trying to nuzzle him.

Tally pulls out her phone and snaps a bunch of pictures.

"Why are you taking pictures of Quinn?" I murmur.

She glances at me, eyebrow arched. "Don't be jealous."

"But seriously, why?"

"Because Arya has a crush on him and I'm a really good friend." She pats my chest.

"It's his freckles, isn't it?"

"It's definitely part of it."

Quinn sneezes aggressively and the cat does a backflip out of his arms, tail poofed out.

"Okay! Quinn, you're golden. Step outside and get some air. And maybe change out of that shirt," Hemi orders.

He pulls it over his head, hands it to me, and rushes for the exit, still sneezing.

"Does anyone have an antihistamine?" Tally asks.

"I do!" Dallas digs his wallet out of his back pocket. "I'll make sure Quinn isn't going to blow up like a balloon!" Another cat swats at him from his perch as Dallas passes.

We spend the next hour enticing cats into our arms, laps, and onto our shoulders. Several kittens scale my legs in search of treats, which is apparently endlessly entertaining. There's also a floppy-eared bunny named Bubbles who believes it's a cat.

"I want you to pose," I say to Tally once all the guys have had their time in the limelight.

"I'm not a hockey player, though."

"I might want my own calendar." I grab her hand and pull her toward the velvet chaise lounge.

"Hemi, tell him he can't do this!" Tally calls out.

"He actually came up with this idea, so I'll let him do whatever he wants."

I settle Tally on the velvet lounge and pose her like a queen. The cats immediately rush over to her. "You're like the pied piper of kitties, kitten."

"Like I'm alone, look at you!" Two kittens are scaling my legs.

"You two need to pose together," Dallas calls out.

Everyone else agrees.

I join her on the lounge and soon cats are climbing all over us.

I wrap my arm around her, smiling at her delight.

"Thank you for this," she whispers.

"I love seeing you happy." I tip her chin up and press my lips gently to hers.

Once the photoshoot is done, we change out of cat-fur-covered Terror shirts and head to Rix and Tristan's for fajita night.

"I cannot believe how puffy your eyes still are," Ash says as he assembles the ingredients for Rix's famous seven-layer dip.

"I had no idea I was this allergic to cats." Quinn blows his nose for the seven-hundredth time.

"Being in a room full of them is a lot different than just one," Kellan adds.

"Apparently, yeah." Quinn plucks another tissue from the box he's holding, keeping a safe distance from the food.

"Do you need help with that, queen of the kittens?" I press my chest against Tally's back and curl forward until my chin rests on her shoulder.

"I've got it, but you're welcome to continue your human-cape impression for as long as you'd like," she says.

I kiss the side of her neck. "You're staying over tonight."

"Was that supposed to be a question?" A dimple appears in her cheek, so I kiss that too.

I drop my voice and press my lips to her ear. "I have plans for dessert." I stayed at her place last night, but yesterday was emotional for her. I want a night where she's relaxed and everything isn't steeped in stress and worry.

She tips her head up. "Me? I'm dessert."

"All right, you two, save it for when you're alone." Dallas points the salad tongs at us.

Dred grins as she spoons sauces into bowls.

I give Tally some space and move to stand next to her. Later I'll have her to myself and we can spend the night taking care of each other. We only have a few days before the next away series, and I want to make the most of our time.

We bring the food to the table, and everyone takes their seats.

Shilpa puts Pavin into his booster seat. He's positioned between his parents and he bashes his knife and fork against the placemat. The kid is basically outfitted in the equivalent of a raincoat since eating is like a full-contact sport.

Dainty little Ariel is perched in her princess booster between her dad and Hammer. Her eyes are wide and she looks up at Roman like he hung the moon.

Tally hugs my arm and whispers, "They are so cute, aren't they?"

"Ridiculously adorable," I agree. We haven't talked about kids, but she's so good with Ariel and Pavin. I want a family, though. The picket fence, the babies, a house full of love. Will she stay for that? For me?

"Fajita nights are my favorite," Kellan declares, pulling me out of my head and back into the moment.

"I second this," Quinn agrees. "We used to do this in university with my housemates and our friends next door. Lovey always orchestrated it, and at least once a week we'd make a communal meal and hang out like this. Makes me miss those days."

"Is Lovey coming to visit again?" Rix asks. "I wish I could have spent more time with her when she was here for the special needs hockey dinner."

"I'm sure she'll be out this way again soon." He rubs the back of his neck. "I was going to invite her to the gala, but I wasn't sure how that would work with the auction."

"We're shifting it to a night on the ice, so it isn't limited to the single guys, since you're dropping like flies," Hemi says. "And I mean that in a good way."

"It has the potential to be just as successful. Each winner will have their own player, dedicated to them. There will be time on the ice with the team, followed by a fancy dinner," Hammer adds.

"It's so smart!" Dred says.

"We thought it would be a good way to make use of the whole team. Far more opportunities to make community connections that way," Hemi adds.

"I hope the grandmas still bid," Dallas says. "Helga Flourish sends me cookies every year for my birthday."

"Didn't she win a date your second year with the Terror?" I ask.

"Yup. Clearly I made a fantastic impression." Dallas bats his lashes while Hemi rolls her eyes.

Ariel shrieks and tosses a handful of pico de gallo at Roman.

Hammer laughs. "Oh, this is precious."

"It's the onions, isn't it?" Roman asks his youngest daughter in mock seriousness.

"N'onions!" Ariel shouts.

Pavin joins in by bashing his silverware on his tray, sending food flying in all directions.

Both Kellan and Quinn get hit.

"He's all yours. I came out of the womb civilized." Shilpa wipes salsa and corn off her cheek.

"He'll be a drummer or a hockey player," Ash says proudly, while picking chunks of taco meat out of his hair.

Tally hops out of her chair and rushes to wet a couple of baby washcloths. She tosses one to Roman and dances over to Pavin, distracting him enough that she can pass the cloth to Shilpa, who cleans off his hands.

I meet Dred's gaze across the table. Her smile is soft, but also knowing, with a hint of concern. I'm sure she sees the way I look at Tally.

We eat and try to avoid getting hit with flying food. After dinner, Tally takes a quick call from her brother.

"Everything okay with Tally?" Dred asks quietly while we load the dishwasher.

"Yeah. She's good. It's been intense." I don't have to explain.

She nods. "You seem pretty intense about her."

I rub the back of my neck. "I'm invested."

"You both are," she agrees. "Have you thought about when you're going to say something to her?"

"I need things to settle down first."

"Are you using that as an excuse?"

"Yeah. But no." I need to confide in Tally the way she confides in me. "She's under a lot of pressure. School, me, her family. I don't want to put more on her. Not right now."

She squeezes my arm. "Okay. Just know I'm here if you need to talk anything through."

I can't keep this secret from her forever, but telling her also means that I'll have to tell the other important people in my life, too. Like my sister, and Tristan, and my parents. And it will hurt all of us.

"Everything okay, darling?" Connor glances between us.

"Everything is magical, my sweet villain." Dred tips her chin up and he bends to kiss her.

Tally returns, wearing a bright smile.

"Things okay with Ties?"

"Yeah. He was offered a scholarship for Tilton next year. Full ride, plus his accommodations. He's relieved and excited."

"I bet." I hug her. "Didn't you help him with the application?"

"I just read over his essay. He did all the heavy lifting."

"Who wants dessert?" Rix calls out.

Dallas groans and pats his belly. "Me, but I need to make some room first."

"We could play a game and burn a little energy," Tally suggests.

"How about the floor is lava?" Quinn says this straight-faced, with one hand tucked into his pocket. His eyes are finally back to almost normal, and he's stopped carrying around the box of tissues.

"I used to play that with my brothers all the time!" Hemi says.

"Would have been a full-contact sport with those two," Dallas grumbles.

Hemi nods. "Once they broke the coffee table."

"That tracks." Tristan snorts.

"Everyone in?" I ask.

Kellan raises his hand. "I've never played this game."

"Oh, you are in for a real treat." Rix does a hip shimmy.

We toss pillows on the floor while we explain the rules. The first person to make it to the churro cheesecake on the other side of the room gets to take home the leftovers. If there are any. I have my doubts.

Kellan tries to make a beeline for it.

"The floor is lava!" Hemi yells.

Kellan and Quinn fight over the same pillow, shoving each other around. "We gotta hug it out or we'll lose, man!" Quinn wraps his arms around Kellan.

"You're standing on my feet!" Kellan gripes.

"The churro cheesecake, bro."

"Right. Yeah."

Rix finds her own pillow, and Tristan comes in behind her, lifting her off her feet so he doesn't end up out.

Dallas does the flamingo on a doily, and Hemi hops into the occasional chair. Connor fireman-carries Dred so they both stay in.

I'm left with the tiniest throw pillow on earth, and Tally jumps on my back, nearly setting me off-balance.

The next round, Dallas hops onto the coffee table, causing it to groan angrily under his weight. Tally finds one of Dallas's crocheted doilies and adopts a dancer's pose. I get knocked out of the game because I'm too focused on staying close to Tally. I don't mind. She'll share the cheesecake if she wins, and even if she doesn't, the number of great photos I snap are worth losing the game.

Rix is next.

She comes to stand beside me while Tristan tries to fit his giant feet on a small pillow.

"You and Tally seem good," she observes.

"We are," I agree.

"Do you think she's it for you?" she asks softly.

Tally pirouettes to the next cushion, closing in on the cheese-cake. "She's everything my life has been missing."

"I'm proud of the way you take care of her." She hugs my arm. "It was the right time for you."

"It feels like it."

It's terrifying. It's amazing.

But fear scratches the back of my mind.

What if she loses faith in me?

What if one day I'm not enough and she doesn't want to keep me the way I do her?

CHAPTER 38
TALLY

"He's coming over!" I announce. "First he has to shower, though."

Fee and Cammie jump around and squeal with excitement.

"Should we leave now?" Fee's eyes are saucers.

"He'll probably be about forty minutes." It's past rush hour, so the traffic won't be the worst, but it's still twenty-five minutes on a good day, plus shower time.

"Want help with the candles?" Cammie asks.

"That'd be great."

"Thanks for going shopping with me," I say as we each tackle a section of the living room. Yesterday afternoon, we went to the mall for mani-pedis, along with Enid, and they helped me pick new lingerie. Flip has been exceptionally attentive during this away series. Every day he's been away, he's sent me a little something to let me know he's thinking of me. He calls me first thing in the morning and at the end of the day. The evening phone calls are the ones where he tells me how much he misses me and can't wait to kiss every inch of me.

"You know how much I love a good girls' day," Fee says with a soft, wistful smile.

"We all need a break from the studying, and time with friends is so important," Cammie adds.

Once we're finished lighting the candles, they follow me to the bathroom and Fee helps me with my eyeliner because my hands are shaking.

"He's way into you. The flowers, hoodie, and the Just Desserts delivery are all proof. So whatever happens, just remember to have fun." Fee hugs me.

"I will." I'm a bag of excited nerves.

"You've got this." Cammie takes me by the shoulders, her expression serious. "Channel your inner Arwen."

"Channel my inner Arwen," I repeat.

"I'm sexy and I know it," Fee sings while doing the most awkward hip shimmy.

"But seriously, you are sexy," Cammie adds.

"And bendy," I joke. But I'm not really kidding.

They hug me again, and Fee grabs her overnight bag. They wait until I've scooped up Parsnip before they slip out the door.

I boop him on the nose. "No trouble tonight, you hear me? Do not stare into Flip's soul while he's eating my pussy. It's awkward."

Parsnip does a backflip out of my arms and runs down the hall, yowling angrily at the closed door. He gives up a few seconds later, waddles past me with his nose in the air, and hops lithely into his cat tree, curling up in the basket at the top with his back to me.

I don't have time to placate him. I need to get the rest of me ready. Tonight could be the night. Flip has mentioned wanting me to dance for him again. What's better than dancing in sexy lingerie, which he can peel off my body afterward?

I put the champagne in the bucket and set the artfully arranged chocolate-covered strawberries next to it before I return to my bedroom to change. My new lingerie is the same maroon that acts as an accent color on the Terror jerseys, while also being sheer and flowy.

Once I'm dressed, and my teeth are brushed, I grab all but one of my favorite fun-time toys out of my nightstand and arrange them on my bed. I stare at the circle of fun, debating. Now is the time to pull out all the stops. I retrieve the final item and set it in the center.

Parsnip trots in and hops up on my bed, but immediately puffs up, yowls, and does a backflip to the floor, scurrying out of my room. My vibrator always freaks him out.

I shrug into the satin robe that came with my pretty lingerie, cinch it at the waist, and take a deep, calming breath. "You've got this, Tally. You've given Flip plenty of hand jobs, you've dry fucked, and played slip 'n' slide with your fun parts." That was fun. "He tells you how much he wants you all the time. Your mind, heart, and body are all ready for the next step." I shake out my hands and roll my head on my shoulders.

I could use some water.

I'm halfway to the kitchen when there's a knock at the door.

"He's here!" I change directions, expecting Parsnip to join me, but he's probably still traumatized by the vibrator sighting.

I take a steadying breath and throw open the door. I try to adopt a casual, sexy lean, but Parsnip pokes his head around the corner, forcing me to tug Flip inside.

"Hey." He's holding a basket from the Dutch Toko. "I brought you study snacks."

"That's so sweet." I take it from him. It's so big I basically disappear behind it.

He shrugs out of his jacket and hangs it on the hook behind him, brow furrowing. "Is something burning?"

"Just a few candles." Maybe I went a little wild.

"You should unwrap that. There are a few surprises in there." He takes the basket back, and I follow him down the hall, pulling the satin bow at my waist. Except instead of unfurling, it turns into a stupid knot.

Flip comes to an abrupt halt when we reach the living room.

I finally get my robe untied and let it pool at my feet. I prop one hand on my hip and attempt another sexy pose.

"Holy shit, Talls. I thought you meant a candle, singular, not an entire store's worth. What if Parsnip knocked one over?" He starts blowing them out, rushing from candle to candle.

I'm standing here in my sexy lingerie, and he's worried about the fire code.

I blow out a frustrated breath and trudge down the hall to my bedroom. I flop down beside my sex toys, pick up my favorite vibe, and sigh. "He didn't even notice the lingerie."

Flip appears in the doorway, carrying the bottle of champagne. "I'm so—Jesus help me." His mouth drops open. His eyes bounce from the sex toys on my bed to me and darken. He sets the bottle of champagne on my dresser and crosses the room in two long strides.

He runs his hands through his hair and laces them behind his head. "Talls, kitten. Fuck."

"That's sort of what I was hoping for," I mutter.

He moves some of the toys out of the way, eyebrow arching at the last one I added to the mix, and takes a seat on the edge of the bed. Then he circles my waist with his huge hands and moves me to straddle his lap. I stare at his chin. I'm still holding my vibrator like it's a magic wand, capable of transforming this scenario into the one I hoped it would be.

He plucks it from my hand and sets it aside. "You look incredible."

"It took you five minutes to notice." I sound every bit the dejected virgin. Also, that's an exaggeration. It was probably less than two.

"Kitten." He tucks a finger under my chin. "You know you don't have to work this hard to seduce me, right?"

I poke at my cheek with my tongue. "Then why haven't we had sex yet?" I let my eyes fall closed as I blow out a breath. "Sorry. I know it's not about me. I just… all the phone sex lately has been really hot and intense. I thought maybe tonight would be the night."

He cups my face in his hands, nodding slowly. "I know you're ready, Tally."

"But you're not," I finish for him.

"Physically, I'm ready, but emotionally…I'm just…scared, kitten." He wraps an arm around my waist, uses the other to move all the toys aside, and lays me out on my bed, stretching on top of me. "You can feel what you do to me, right?" He rolls his hips, erection pressing against me.

I hook a leg over his. "I can feel you."

"Never doubt that I want you." He kisses the corner of my mouth. "Because I do, desperately."

"What are you afraid of?" I run my fingers through his hair, wanting to understand.

"I don't want to burn too hot, too fast, and risk fizzling out." He traces a line from my temple to my jaw. "It's easy to get caught up, and then it doesn't last. That's the opposite of what I want." He kisses me softly. "I love that we get to take our time. I get to learn your body, to explore you, to have all this time to fall for you." His expression softens. "I'm in so deep with you, Tally. I've never felt about anyone the way I feel about you, and that is as terrifying as it is amazing." His eyes search mine, soft and imploring. "I know you're waiting on me."

He presses his lips tenderly to mine. "It doesn't have anything to do with keeping you pure, or your innocence." He glances at my toys, which scream exactly how not-innocent I am. "But I want our first time to be special for both of us, without any pressure or expectations. Does that make sense?"

"It does." I stroke his cheek.

"I'm sorry I'm not ready yet, kitten."

"It's okay. I understand why."

He slants his mouth over mine. I sink into the warmth of his body, of his unsteady hand on my face.

Eventually he breaks the kiss and glances at the toys now resting against the outside of his thigh. "This is quite the extensive collection."

"I have a healthy libido." And a lot of friends who have exciting sex lives.

"Do you have a personal favorite?" Flip drags a finger along the edge of the bodice, over the swell of my breast.

"Um." I survey my toys. "This one." I hold up my clit sucker. Man, does it ever make my life easier and my wrist less tired.

His grin turns downright devilish. "We should put it to good use tonight."

A full-body shiver runs through me. "I would really love that."

His tongue sweeps out to wet his bottom lip. "Anything here you haven't used but would like to?"

I set the clit sucker aside, summon my inner Arwen, and pick up the last item I pulled out of the drawer.

Flip's fingers flex against my hip, eyes darkening. "Are those for me or you?"

"Me," I whisper.

His nostrils flare and he pushes my hair over my shoulders. "What's the fantasy associated with these?"

A hot shiver of excitement works its way down my spine, and a flush of embarrassment settles in my cheeks.

He skims one with a gentle finger. "Talk to me, kitten. Tell me what's making you blush so sweetly."

I can do this. I can ask for Flip to fulfill the fantasy. "There's a movie from when I was young."

"How young?"

"Like a kid. Animated. I'm sure even you've seen it. Where the princess is captured by the villain, and then he chains her and forces her to serve him."

"This is a kids' movie?" Flip looks doubtful.

"The hero saves her from the villain."

"Do you want me to be the hero or the villain?"

"The villain," I whisper.

"I was hoping you'd say that." A devilish grin turns up the corner of his mouth. His fingers slide into my hair, curling in the strands. He tugs gently, tipping my head back, and bites along the edge of my jaw. "Are you going to be a good girl and do exactly what I tell you?"

I whimper and nod.

"Say it, Tally. Tell me you'll be my good girl," he demands.

Everything clenches below the waist. "I'll be your good girl."

He takes my earlobe between his teeth. "What do good girls do?"

"Exactly what you tell me to." Another shiver of excitement zips down my spine.

"Give me your hands," he orders.

I unlink them from behind his neck and hold them between us. Flip opens the Velcro cuff and slips it on, securing my right wrist, then my left. My stomach clenches at his wicked smile.

He strokes my cheek. "If you change your mind, all you have to do is say the word and we can switch things up."

"I can cuff you?" I ask cheekily.

"If you want, yes."

That sends another thrill through me.

He kisses me softly.

"Can I get on my knees for you?"

His fingers flex on my hip and his jaw ticks. "Is that where you want to start?"

"Desperately." Heat works its way through me.

"Fuck, kitten. We're going to have so much fun together." He kisses me again, rougher and deeper, like he's struggling to stay in check.

He tosses a pillow to the floor at his feet. "Be good for me."

I clamber off his lap, a little awkwardly and with Flip's help since my hands are bound.

Flip regards me with lust-heavy eyes as I sink to my knees. He runs his hands down his thighs and rolls his head on his shoulder as he rises to his full, imposing height.

He steps forward, gazing down as he caresses my cheek and tucks a single finger under my chin, tipping it up. "You are a fucking vision, Tallulah." He bends and kisses my forehead.

When he straightens, gone is my sweet boyfriend and in his place is the villain I asked for.

"Get my cock out," he orders.

My hands are unsteady as I fumble first with his belt, then the button and zipper on his jeans. It's awkward with my hands cuffed, and I'm jittery with excitement.

I free him from his pants, thick and hard. I reach for him, but he shakes his head, so I stop.

"No more hands," he grits out.

I drop mine to my thighs.

Flip fists his cock and strokes roughly. I wait for his next command, nipples tight and pussy already throbbing.

"Are you my good girl?"

I nod, biting back a needy moan.

He presses his thumb against my bottom lip. "Open for me."

I part and he slips his thumb inside, pressing on my tongue.

"Suck."

My cheeks hollow.

He grins, expression devilish. "Treat it like your favorite ice cream cone." He brings the head of his cock to my lips.

I swirl my tongue around the crown, sucking the head into my mouth, releasing with a loud pop, before I repeat the action, but this time I drag my teeth gently over the ridge, eyes locked on his. A slow grin pulls up one corner of his mouth.

I kiss the tip, then run my tongue around him again. "What now?"

"I'm going to guide you."

How often have I fantasized about this exact experience? On my knees, him looking at me like I'm his. "Teach me how to please you."

His lip curls deliciously. "Tap my thigh twice if it's too much or you don't like it."

"Okay." I'm nervous, but excited, because with Flip I'm safe to explore and learn what I like.

"And don't be afraid to make it messy and loud."

He winds my hair gently around his fist and I open for him. He eases inside my mouth, only pushing in a few inches before he shifts his hips back. He takes it slow, praising every new inch I take. I moan and suck and make wet slurping sounds that put a dark smile on his gorgeous, intense face as he gently fucks my mouth.

"Such a good little pet." He pushes in deeper. "I think I'll keep you forever."

I moan softly at the praise.

"Would you like that, kitten?"

I hum my affirmation.

He starts to pull out, and I hollow my cheeks, sucking hard. His eyes roll up and his hand tightens in my hair. "You keep doing that and I'm going to come," he warns.

I channel all the dirty Cammie fic energy I can as I pop off with a wet sound. "I want you sliding down my throat."

Flip grins. "You're a revelation, Tally." He pushes back

inside, and I take as much as I can. His body goes taut and his head snaps back, a shudder running through him as he comes and I swallow him down.

There's real power in this feeling. I do this to him. I make him feel good, turn him on, give him what he needs.

He gently eases me off his spit-covered cock and drops to his knees on the floor in front of me. He wipes the spit from my chin, cups my face in his palms, and slants his mouth over mine, kissing me hungrily.

Eventually he pulls back. "Have you been practicing on Popsicles?"

"Frozen bananas, actually." I can always use the potassium.

He laughs and slides his hands under my arms, lifting me to my feet along with him. "You can practice on me anytime you want."

"I did good?"

"Amazing. Good pets get a reward." He carries me to the bed and lays me out on top of the comforter. He skims the cuffs. "Keep these on or take them off?"

"Keep them on."

A deep groan rumbles through him. "You're literally perfect for me, Tallulah." He raises my hands above my head and hooks them on one of the wrought-iron curls on my headboard. "This comfortable?"

"Yes." I press my thighs together, anticipation skittering through me.

"Where should I start?" He tugs his shirt over his head, discarding it on the floor.

"Wherever you want."

He pushes his pants and boxers down his thighs and kicks them off too, leaving him gloriously naked. He skims my temple, dragging a finger down my body as he takes me in, hands bound, tied to my bed, at his whim.

He climbs onto the bed with me and straddles my thighs,

gazing down at me with hot eyes. He kisses the same path his finger traveled, stopping to suck my nipples through the thin fabric of my negligee. I roll my hips, desperate for more, for contact, for relief from the ache that flares and grows with every teasing touch.

Flip drags my panties down my thighs and runs his hands up my shins, pushing my legs wide. "It's play time, kitten."

"What are you going to do to me?" I whimper.

His eyes lift to mine, full of dirty promises. "Whatever I want."

He grabs my vibrator, but he doesn't start fucking me with it right away. Instead, he turns it on and rubs it over my lips, teasing me, taunting me. He stops the vibrations and presses the head against my clit as he stretches out, holding himself above me.

"Please, Phillip." I roll my hips.

"Please what, pet?" His lips brush mine.

"Please fuck me."

He turns on the vibrator and I bow off the bed at the intensity. And then he's sliding it inside me, filling me, fucking me like I asked him to.

"I think about how good it will feel when it's me inside you," he whispers.

I groan and swivel my hips.

"When I'm surrounded by you. How sweet you'll sound when I'm making you come, how pretty you are when you lose control." He sits back on his heels and grabs the clit sucker.

My eyes flare. All my best orgasms happen with that. He turns it on and positions it over my clit, still fucking me in slow, rhythmic strokes with my vibrator. The sensation is overwhelming, pulling me to the brink. But before I can tip over, he turns it down to the first setting.

"Oh my God, Phillip, please." I tug against the restraints, writhing in need.

"Ask for what you want. Be explicit."

"Please let me come," I beg.

He shakes his head slowly. "Not yet."

I groan in frustration.

He turns the clit sucker back on, ratcheting up the intensity. Again he pulls it away, and again I beg for him to let me come. Around and around we go, always so close to the edge of an orgasm, but never quite reaching the tipping point. Suddenly the vibrator is gone, and so is the clit sucker.

I cry out despondently.

Flip's fingers slide inside me, curling and pumping at a furious pace. He reaches above me and unhooks my cuffs from the bed, then pulls the Velcro free on the right wrist. And then he moves down my body, lowering his head, eyes on me as he latches onto my clit and sucks hard.

I come in violent waves. Dragged into the undertow of sensation, screaming his name. The pleasure is endless, a tide rising and crashing. He wrings three orgasms out of me before he prowls up my body and blankets me with his.

His fingers are gentle on my face. His lips soft when he kisses me. "Hi."

"Hi," I rasp.

"So that was fun." He smiles, eyes warm with satisfaction.

I laugh. "It was."

He kisses the end of my nose. "We should make a list of your fantasies, so when the time is right, I can make them all come true."

CHAPTER 39
FLIP

"First dinner, now this?" Tally hugs my arm, eyes wide with awe and excitement as we move through the foyer.

"You've been working so hard. You deserve a night off."

She's been putting in long hours at the studio and working on final assignments. She even resubmitted the one she didn't do well on a few weeks ago and pulled up her mark by twenty-four percent. I wanted to pamper her and reward her for all the time and energy she's put in this semester. So we started with a romantic dinner, and now we're at the ballet.

"I can't believe you got tickets to this show. It's been sold out for months." She pushes up on her toes to kiss my jaw.

"I might have pulled a few strings." I wink.

"If I could dance anywhere, it would be here. It's hands down my dream company," she says as the attendant scans our tickets.

They direct us to our seats, and I lead the way for Tally.

"We're in a box?" She smiles up at me, eyes shining. "This is just…I can't even. Thank you."

"This is what you've worked so hard for, right?" I motion to the seats filling below us. "You'll be up there soon. Not long now and the world is yours." Watching her this semester has been inspiring. She's dedicated and passionate.

"You are the most amazing boyfriend, Phillip," she says softly. "I'm so thankful for you."

"It goes both ways, kitten." I want to tell her that I've fallen for her, that I can't imagine a life without her by my side anymore, but the lights go down, stealing the moment.

Tally tucks herself under my arm, snuggling into my side as the performance begins. I probably miss half of it because I can't take my eyes off her. She's wholly enraptured by what's happening on the stage—the same way I'm enraptured by her. She provides colorful commentary for me along the way, explaining when certain combinations are complicated and pointing out dancers who attended Tilton's program in hushed whispers.

I would do just about anything to help her realize her dreams, even if it meant leaving the Terror and finishing my career somewhere else. I wait for fear to set in, but all I have is peaceful acknowledgement that she's my right person.

At the end, I stand and clap along with her, heart thundering as she smiles up at me. I want to start and end every day with her smile.

"That was incredible," she says. "Thank you so much for planning such a special night. I didn't realize how much I needed it."

"I needed it too." I kiss her cheek. "There's one more surprise." I link my arm with hers.

Instead of leaving the theater with the rest of the patrons, we wait until most of them have cleared out before I guide her to the wings.

"This isn't the exit," Tally whispers, but she's soaking everything in.

We reach two hulking security guards. They move aside to reveal Hemi's brother.

Sam's usually serious face lights up. "Flip! It's great to see you, man!"

"Sam?" Tally looks confused as he pulls me in for a hearty hug-backslap that might leave a handprint.

He lets me go and offers his hand to Tally. "It's nice to see you again."

When she slips her fingers into his massive, waiting palm, he bows his head, like she's a queen. Thankfully he doesn't kiss the back of her hand, because then I'd have to fight him, and I would definitely lose.

"It's good to see you, too." She smiles, still confused. "I didn't know you were a fan of contemporary ballet."

"I'm a fan of a lot of things." He motions for us to follow him up the steps and through the door leading backstage. "Come with me."

Tally leans into me. "Are we getting a tour?"

I wink. "Something like that."

She grips my arm, explaining all the parts of the stage and pointing out the wings as we follow Sam.

"Costumes are in here." He pauses to let Tally check it out.

"This is so cool. And so much bigger than the costume room at our campus theater," Tally muses. "This is what Lavender does." She runs her fingers across the intricate costume pieces. "She designs and sews costumes for an off-Broadway theater in New York."

"And alters ill-fitting pants in an emergency," Sam tosses over his shoulder.

"I thought Kodiak's head was going to explode." I chuckle.

"Seriously. Those Stiles boys have some good genetics," Sam adds.

"So I've heard." Tally ducks her head to hide her smile.

Voices filter down the hall, and Sam knocks on the slightly ajar door labeled *Dressing Room*.

Tally's breath leaves her on a whoosh as the door swings open.

"Sam! Hey! How's it going?"

"How does he know these people? I thought he was supposed to be a finisher," she whispers.

"He's a mystery," I reply.

"Beautiful performance tonight," Sam says. "I brought a couple of friends to say hi." He steps aside, and one of the lead dancers appears.

Tally's fingers dig into my arm.

"Flip Madden! It's an honor."

"The honor is all mine. You were incredible up there tonight." I put my arm around Tally. "I'd like you to meet my girlfriend, Tallulah Vander Zee. She'll be graduating from the Tilton dance program next month."

"You were amazing," Tally gushes. "I used to go to all your performances when you were a Tilton student. You're such an inspiration."

Sam doesn't have to introduce the cast. Tally already knows them by name and has even met a few of them when they've visited Tilton as guest speakers and dance instructors. Their conversation is easy, and I'm content to sit back and watch my girlfriend work the room.

"Is the final showcase still three pieces?" Kerri, the female lead, asks.

"That's right." Tally nods. "Full class routine, small troupe, and solo."

"What's your solo number?"

"I chose contemporary."

The dancers offer her some pointers on what she could add to make her performance stand apart.

"Have you applied here yet? They'll be hosting auditions mid-May," Kerri asks.

"I've put in an application," Tally affirms.

"Any other companies?" Dalton, one of the other lead dancers, asks.

"A few. Mostly local, though," Tally confides.

"We'll cross all our fingers and toes that we see you at rehearsals after May," Kerri says.

Tally smiles, and I can see her future unfolding. Our future. I want to give her the world, to be the person who supports her, cheers her on. I'll celebrate every win with her and encourage her to keep going despite the losses. If this is where she wants to be, this is where I want to finish my career.

She's the one I've been waiting for.

And I'm through making her wait for me.

CHAPTER 40

TALLY

"Thank you so much for tonight." I'm riding an adrenaline high. "I can't believe I met two of my favorite dancers. I think I was twelve when my mom first took me to see them perform at Tilton."

Flip is all smiles as we step into the elevator and he pushes the button for his floor. "It's a glimpse into your future."

"Is this how you felt every time you went to see the Terror before you made the pros? Or when you were accepted to the Hockey Academy? Learning from all those legends." He truly understands my passion for dance, the way I understand his love for hockey.

"Being coached by Alex Waters and Randy Ballistic and Rook Bowman was a dream come true, not just for me but all the guys who trained with them."

The elevator doors open, and we walk down the hall to his apartment, fingers twined. Tonight feels different. He always makes me feel cherished and special, but taking me to see the dancers who inspired me as a kid shows me how in tune Flip is with my hopes and dreams. I've been pushing extra hard with the end of the semester looming.

"This is exactly the motivation I needed to make sure my performance pieces blow my instructors away."

Flip opens the door to his apartment and ushers me inside. "I'll be your audience anytime you want." He tosses his keys on the side table and flips the security latch.

I loop my arms around his neck. I have the perfect thank you for tonight. "You haven't seen my solo piece yet."

"I haven't." His hands settle on my waist, eyes lighting up.

I wet my bottom lip. "I could show you now."

"Just for me." He takes my hands in his, kissing them. "Before everyone else gets to fall in love with the way you move."

"Just for you," I agree. My heart thrums with anticipation.

"I would love that." He kisses me softly. "Where do you want me?"

I move him to sit at the island, facing the living room. "Here is perfect."

"What else do you need from me, kitten?"

"Just your attention."

"You always have that, even when I'm not with you."

I kiss his cheek and hand him my phone. "I'll tell you when to press play."

He glances at the screen. "This is my favorite song."

"It's one of mine, too." Because of him. We danced to it at Dred and Connor's wedding.

I move to stand in the middle of the room before I kick off my shoes and pull my dress over my head, leaving me in panties and a bralette. I bought them when I went shopping with the girls a few weeks ago and decided to wear them tonight.

"God, you're stunning." Flip's eyes move over me on a hot sweep that I feel everywhere.

I give him my back and toss a wink over my shoulder.

He chuckles. "You're too saucy for your own good."

"You love it." I pull my hair into a ponytail.

"I absolutely do," he agrees.

I move into position. "You can press play, now."

My phone is connected to his portable speaker, so the music fills the room and flows through me. It's such a pretty, soft opening. Awareness makes the hairs on the back of my neck rise. I spin, and our eyes lock. The intimacy of being on display like this for *only* him ignites a deep, primal desire to be his in all ways.

His eyes move over me, reflecting the longing I feel, along with unquenchable desire. Everything changes—the shift irrevocable. I'm falling for him, for what we are, for what we could be. I'm scared, but I've never felt more alive.

He watches me hungrily, as I become the music, the emotions washing over and through me. I could do this all day just for him. I close the distance between us as I shift into an arabesque. He reaches for me, and I adapt the end of the routine, spinning into his waiting arms as the final notes sound.

"How was that?" My heart pounds as I try to recover my breath.

Flip gazes at me with such admiration, my knees go weak. "You are simply exquisite." He stands and lifts me off my feet, wrapping my legs around his waist. "It's an honor to be yours."

I run my fingers through his hair as he carries me across the apartment. My already unsteady breath leaves me entirely as we enter his bedroom. Hundreds of candles illuminate the space (the kind with batteries, lesson learned), and pink rose petals dot the dark blue comforter, which is pulled back to reveal teal sheets.

"Phillip." It's a question enrobed in hope.

He moves to the bed, freeing my hair from the tie before he lays me down and stretches out over me. He traces the contours of my face with trembling fingers. "I don't have expectations, Tally, but I won't deny you anymore." He kisses me. "I can't."

He's so earnest, eyes soft and full of yearning. I press my trembling hand to his cheek. "You want me?"

"Always, Tally. Every minute of every day, you consume me." He turns his head, kissing my palm. "I want you to be mine, and I want to be yours."

The weight of his words settles in my heart. *This is really happening.* "I want this part of me to be yours."

I'll be his in every way. I understand why he was so intent on waiting. It feels right now, like we're connected deeply, wholly and completely. I'm sharing a special piece of myself with him, and he's doing the same for me.

He folds back on his knees, hands sliding up my ribs, fingers dipping under my bralette. "I'm going to take this off now."

"And then I can help undress you?"

"I would love that." He carefully eases it over my head, discarding it on the floor.

I shift so I'm on my knees with him and start on his shirt. He watches me with the same intense desire as he did when I danced. And I savor every moment, tucking each one into my heart as a precious keepsake. We kiss and touch as we bare ourselves to each other. Both of our hands shake, with nerves and desire. I want it, but it terrifies me, too. He already has my heart, and this will connect us irrevocably in the most intimate way.

When we're both naked, Phillip gathers me gently in his arms and kisses me, our tongues gilding, skin pressed to skin. Need courses through me as he eases me back on the rose-petal-dotted comforter. I revel in the weight of his body as he settles between my thighs. His hips press into mine, erection thick against my lower abdomen. His kiss is reverent and unhurried, fingers moving gently over my heated skin.

Soft strains of music float in from the kitchen—my favorite dance playlist. I'll forever associate the music with this special, life-altering night.

He shifts until he's lying beside me. "We're going to take our time, kitten." His fingers glide down my body, skimming sensitive places. "I want every moment of this to be special for both of us."

"I want the same thing." This isn't just a first; he'll be my only, and I'll be his last.

He cups between my thighs and lowers his mouth to mine. I open for him and he strokes between my thighs to the same slow rhythm as our kiss.

I'm heavy with want, and then floating on bliss as the first orgasm rolls through me, and then he's kissing his way down my body, mouth and hands everywhere, bringing me limitless pleasure. His eyes never leave mine as I come apart under his tongue and his touch.

He's so painfully, wonderfully gentle, and I know that this special part of Phillip is reserved for only me. He prowls back up my body, mouth on mine, his bare erection sliding across slick, sensitive skin. My arms tremble as I wind them around him, needing him to ground me in this moment.

Flip pushes up on one arm and caresses my cheek. His eyes are soft and brimming with emotion. "You are so beautiful, Tally." He dips down to kiss me, voice unsteady. "I want you to have all of me."

The weight of his admission settles in my heart. "I want to be yours, and only ever yours."

His eyes slide closed for a moment, and when they open, they're full of deep satisfaction. "And I'll be yours." He brushes his lips over mine. "I'm going to take this real slow, okay?"

I nod and run my hands over his shoulders, craving the comfort of contact. He plucks a condom from the pillow beside my head, tears it open, and rolls it down his length.

He moves between my thighs again, distracting me with soft kisses. "Just relax for me, okay?"

I melt under him.

"That's my girl." He kisses me again, rolling his hips. "We go at your pace, as slow as you need."

I nod, grounded in the moment and his touch.

This is it. He'll be mine and I'll be his.

The head nudges my entrance. "You're sure about me, Talls?"

"I want you, Phillip."

His body trembles as he holds himself above me and pushes in achingly slow. Our labored breaths mingle as he eases in, filling me slowly.

"Oh." I suck in a breath at the sharp burn.

"Are you okay?" He skims my temple. "Do you need me to stop?"

"I just need a second." I relax under him, and the burn fades and turns into something else. Need, thick and heavy, courses through me, enveloping me in a blanket of desire.

"I'm okay." I touch his face. "I want more of you."

He kisses my cheeks and chin, then shifts back, eyes on mine as his hips sink slowly toward mine.

He shudders when our hips meet.

"I feel so full," I whisper.

He makes a noise, lips on my neck, traveling along my jaw. "You feel like heaven, Tally."

I hook my leg over his hip, causing a jolt of pleasure to rocket through me, and my muscles tighten.

"Fuck, kitten." He bites the edge of my jaw in warning. "I need you to give me a second, please."

"Am I tight?" I whisper as I wrap my other leg around him.

He growls and pulls back, the fire in his eyes echoes through me, making my stomach flutter. His cock kicks inside me and I gasp.

He cups my face in his palms. "Good fucking God, Tally. You're squeezing me like a fist, and you aren't even trying. I need you to be good, so I can take this nice and slow." Phillip seals his mouth over mine.

Finally, after what feels like an eternity, he pulls back, one hand anchored in my hair, the other bracing his weight as he starts a slow, sensuous rhythm.

Every stroke takes me higher. Every roll of his hips pushes me closer to the edge. I tuck this moment in my heart. Because this isn't just sex—every emotion and sensation is heightened, like I'm inside him and he's inside me. Like we're an extension of each other.

I never want it to end. I want this to be forever.

Too soon I reach my peak and tip over the edge. I come in waves of bliss, every nerve ending comes alive under his body and his touch. And he falls right along with me, glorious and feral and mine. We're both panting, bodies slick with sweat. He kisses me tenderly before he pulls back, eyes searching mine as we float gently back to earth.

"Hi." He brushes my hair away from my face.

I curve my hand around the side of his neck, the thrum of his pulse a comfort. "Hi."

"How are you?" He kisses my chin and my nose, eyes soft and a little nervous.

"Incredible. You?"

"There are no words, Tallulah." He kisses my lips.

"Best sex of my life," I say playfully.

"Mine too." He gracefully rolls us over, so I'm sprawled across his chest.

I love this easy closeness, how sated I feel not just in my body but my heart, too. "Really?"

"Truly." He kisses me again, like he can't get enough, like he never wants to stop. "I wanted it to be special for both of us."

I press my lips to his throat. "That's how it felt."

"Because the connection we share is right here." He taps over his heart, then wraps his arms around me and holds me tight for a few seconds. "How about I pour us a bath and we can have some cuddle time?"

"That sounds perfect."

Flip sits up and carefully lifts me off him, settling my butt on his thighs. He removes the condom and slides to the edge of the bed, gripping the backs of my legs as he stands. I wrap myself around him and he carries me across to the bathroom. Keeping me in his lap, he sits on the edge of the tub and turns on the water. We kiss as the bath fills, and then he spins us around, helping me in before he positions himself behind me.

We lie in the sudsy water, letting the water wash away the sweat while he kisses my neck and holds me. When we're clean, and I'm sleepy, Flip dries me off and carries me back to bed.

He curls himself around me, tucking me in close.

And in my heart I know I have a different version of this man than anyone else ever has.

CHAPTER 41

FLIP

"That was a rough one," Stiles mutters as he pulls his jersey over his head and tosses it in his cubby.

"Sorry you guys had to work so hard." Ryker unclips his goalie pads.

Grace pats him on the shoulder as he passes. "Anaheim was fucking relentless. Their offensive line has really put in the work this season. We were all fighting to keep the puck away from them."

I shake my head. *And failing about half the time.* We eked out a win tonight, but it was an ugly one. Grace and Romero both ended up in the penalty box, one right after the other. And I took more than one hit into the boards. We'll all be sore and tired tomorrow.

Stiles, Bright, and I are now the veteran players on the forward line, and we need to do better if we don't want to tax our defensive line this close to playoffs. I'm hyperaware of being under a microscope. I have a bad game and the speculation ensues. The media blames my relationship with the coach's daughter, saying my head isn't in the game.

Last night I didn't do myself any favors when I stayed at Tally's. She lured me in with pretty new lingerie and a fantasy-fulfillment request. I can't say no to her. I'm addicted to the way I feel when I'm with her, to the connection we share. Being with her, inside her, is a level of closeness I can't get enough of. It's new for us, which means we crave each other all the time.

But the late-night sex-a-thon with my girlfriend contributed to tonight's lackluster performance. I don't want her to blame herself for my lack of restraint and boundary setting.

The coaches enter the locker room before we can get past taking our jerseys and pads off. "Grace and Romero." Coach Forrest-Hammer's expression is tight. "You spent most of the game helping your goalie keep the puck out of the net, but those penalties could have been avoided. We need clean play this late in the season."

"I know, Coach." Romero bows his head.

"I'm sorry, Coach. I'll do better next game." Grace looks genuinely unhappy about her disappointment.

"I'm counting on you." She scans the faces of my teammates before looking to Coach Vander Zee. He nods for her to proceed. "Some of the offensive line were half asleep tonight." She gives me a pointed look. "That can't happen again. We don't want to be knocked out in the first round. If we keep playing like this, that's exactly what will happen, especially if we're up against New York."

There's a murmur of agreement. Kodiak Bowman continues to blow scoring records out of the water every year, and it's probable that we'll play them in round one. If I can't get a handle on my hormones, it could be detrimental to my team. I don't want to give Vander Zee a reason to trade me.

Coach Forrest-Hammer praises the goals and the solid effort but pushes in on the fact that we're not playing like the playoffs are around the corner.

Vander Zee tips his chin at me. "Can I see you in my office after you're cleaned up?"

"No problem, Coach."

With that, the staff leaves us to change.

"What do you think that's about?" Tristan asks as we finish stripping out of our gear.

"Probably Tally." She talks to her mom daily and makes time to see them every week, even if it's just to attend her sister's cello practice, but things with her dad are strained. She's angry that nothing has changed. He's still a workaholic who has trouble putting his kids ahead of his job. Last week her dad invited her to family dinner at his place, and she's been coming up with excuses not to go.

"Everything okay there?" Tristan asks.

"She's having a hard time forgiving her dad for not making her a priority," I confide.

"But you make her one." Tristan side-eyes me.

Vander Zee and I have similar schedules, but I make time for Tally. He's failing at coming through, and all it does is fuel her anger with him. "I won't let her down the way he has, but I know I need to find the balance, too." I grab my towel. "I don't want to make her a target with my poor on-ice performance."

"We still won the game," he reminds me.

"This time. I have to play better when all eyes are on me."

We shower and change, and I head up to Vander Zee's office. He's sitting behind his desk looking exhausted. I half wonder if he sleeps here some nights, whether on purpose or by accident. I knock on his door, and he startles.

"Flip. Come on in." He motions to the chair across from him.

"Sorry I phoned it in tonight. I know how important every game is between now and the playoffs. It won't happen again." It's not just me and the team it affects anymore.

"We still pulled out a win." He raps on the desk. "I, uh, I wanted to ask about Tally."

"She's pretty focused on exams and her final showcase."

He runs his tongue along his teeth. "But you see her?"

"We make time for each other." When I don't have a game, and I'm in Toronto, we're together.

"I'm worried about how much she's pulling away," he confides.

I grip the armrest so I don't rub my chin or run my hand through my hair. If ever Tally needed me to go to bat for her, it's now. "From you, you mean?"

He swallows thickly and nods.

"Her whole life is a sea of change." I choose my words carefully. "Between me, your family circumstances, and the end of university, she has a lot on her plate"—I rap on the arm of my chair—"but she's working through it."

He rubs his stubbled chin. "She talks to you about this?"

"In confidence, yes," I reply.

He nods a few times, the hope on his face hard to deal with. "Maybe you could suggest she come for family dinner? Her mom is bringing her brother and sister over this weekend. It would be nice if Tally would join us."

Well, this is fucking awkward. "I can mention it to her."

"Thanks, Flip. I appreciate it."

"Can I make a suggestion, though, Coach?"

"Of course."

"Tally needs you to show up for her like you do for your team. It's all she wants from you. Just to feel like she matters as much as we do."

"She's my daughter, of course she matters."

"She needs to hear it and she needs you to show her with actions." I can't make him change, but I can point him in the right direction.

"Right. Yeah." He opens his drawer and pulls out a bag of dropjes. "I got her some study treats. Maybe you could pass them along?"

"I could, but maybe you should hold on to them and give them to her yourself."

He nods and sighs. "Thank you for taking care of her."

"She's my world, sir. I'd do anything for her."

CHAPTER 42

TALLY

I pull into the underground lot of my dad's building. It's the first time I've been here since he moved in. I can't keep avoiding reality. My parents are really over, and I need to come to terms with that.

I find a spot in visitors, park, and pull my phone out of my purse. I wouldn't be here if it wasn't for Phillip. I'd made a thousand excuses not to attend, and he sat me down and asked the hard questions. I told him everything I was afraid of. He held me and promised it would get easier, but I couldn't keep running away from the people I love, because it was just causing me more pain. He was right. But now I'm anxious and I need something to look forward to post-dinner.

TALLY

I feel like I was hoodwinked into this.

By your dick.

FLIP

I mean, if the dick fits...

TALLY

That was a dirty trick.

FLIP

I know.

But seriously, I'll be waiting for you with a bubble bath and cherry chip cake when you get home, and whatever else you need to relax.

TALLY

You better say and do filthy things to me tonight.

FLIP

We will check something off your fantasy list.

TALLY

Promise?

FLIP

Cross my heart. The filthier the better. Maybe a fic related one

TALLY

 I told you the spice was spicing. Okay. I'm going in.

FLIP

Great. Maybe erase the messages that will result in me being buried in an unmarked grave.

TALLY

On it. 🖤

FLIP

🖤

I smile as I delete all the messages that would make me boyfriend-less and my dad a murderer. I wanted to invite Flip today, but I also didn't want the first time my mom and siblings meet him to be tense and awkward.

I check my other messages, pulling up new ones from a few minutes ago.

MOM

I know this isn't easy, but thank you for saying yes to dinner.

I fight the wave of emotion. Our relationship has shifted over the past weeks. We've always been allies, but she's anchored firmly in the mom role lately, and I need that from her. Especially today.

TALLY

I'll be up in a few minutes. 🖤

MOM

I'll be here with a hug when you're ready.

I take another deep breath before I leave the safety of my car. I'm anxious, I miss dinners with my family, and I'm scared of this new normal. I can't get used to this if I don't try, though. And I can't get past my anger at my dad if I don't give him a chance, either.

My heart lurches when I reach my dad's apartment. I don't have a key, so I have to knock. Two seconds later, he opens the door, beaming. "I'm so glad you could make it." He envelops me in a hug.

"Me, too." I'm suddenly choked up. I've been hiding from all these feelings, burying myself in school, focusing on my relationship with Flip so I don't have to manage this. I pat his back as I look over the space behind him. The new living room set looks like it belongs in a university apartment ad.

He releases me and steps back, giving me room to come inside.

"You finally got your recliner, huh?"

He grins sheepishly, but his eyes are sad. "No one to stop me."

"I bet you're in your glory during the nightly news," I joke, even as my heart squeezes. My mom always said recliners were hideous and belonged in retirement homes and man caves. She wasn't wrong.

"It is comfortable." Dad shrugs. "Your brother and sister fight over it every time they stay the night."

It's not meant as a dig, but it still pricks my heart. I'm sure he'd rather have his family back than a recliner, but he can't change the past, and he's right; my mom deserves a chance at real happiness, even if it's with someone else. If I keep putting up walls, I'll never be part of the whole, and I don't want to be on the outside, always looking in.

"Once exams are finished, maybe I can fight over it with them." It's the only way to heal.

"Whenever you're ready." Dad nods. "I know it's been tough."

"It has," I agree.

He inclines his head. "Come on in. You'll be happy to hear that tonight's meal was made by Rix."

"Oh wow! That's great! She's amazing." Rix mentioned that my dad had started ordering from her a couple of weeks ago. He's always been good on the barbecue. It's everything else that's probably a challenge. "And you can't really live on burgers and sausage."

"They get old fast."

"So does ramen and avocado toast."

"But two easy things I can add to my repertoire when I don't have Rix-made meals on hand." We enter the kitchen where the rest of my family preps dinner. "Look who's here!"

"Tally!" Fenna abandons the salad and rushes over to hug me.

It's good to be together like this, but it also makes my heart feel like it's in a blender. The kitchen is too white, the dishes too new, the space too foreign. I made it this way by avoiding dinners, though.

I squeeze my sister tightly. "I missed you."

"Same. I'm so glad you're here."

"Me, too," I whisper.

"It's weird at first, but it gets better." That my sister is reassuring me instead of the other way around tells me she's in a better place about this.

When Fenna releases me, Ties steps in and gives me a quick hug. "Real glad you came, sis."

"Same, same." Even if it is awkward.

Mom is the last to hug me. She doesn't say anything, just wraps her arms around me on a soft sigh.

"It's nice to be all together like this," Dad says.

"It is," Mom agrees, but her smile is a little tight.

"Ties, can I get your help with the steaks?" Dad asks.

"Yeah, for sure." Ties sets his knife down and follows my dad, carrying the seasoning and tongs.

"I want to check the corn to make sure it's not getting charred!" Fenna follows them to the balcony.

"How is this really for you?" I ask my mom. It's a hard habit to break.

"You have to cut your dad some slack, Tallulah," she says gently.

"I'm here. It's progress."

She nods, her smile sad. "I know your instinct is to side with me, and I love your loyalty, but I think it's a little misplaced, honey."

"He was never home," I argue.

"You're right, he wasn't. But I never told him I needed more from him. I said everything was fine, that I didn't mind, that I knew how important his job was. I never told him I wasn't happy. He believed we were okay because I told him we were."

My stomach bottoms out and everything tilts. "But why would you do that if you weren't happy?"

"Because I thought things might change organically. Because when he was home, I didn't want to start a fight. I don't have a good reason, honey, but I don't want you to keep blaming your dad when the fault wasn't all his. He couldn't fix what he didn't know was broken."

"I feel like a jerk." I wrap my arms around myself.

"Don't own this, Tallulah. Your dad and I made mistakes. Big ones. I just don't want you to put all the blame on him, when he wasn't alone in it. I played my part, too."

I want to ask why my dad didn't say anything. But I already know the answer. He didn't want me to be mad at my mom, instead. He'd rather it be him. Reality is a sharp slap; no wonder they never worked out. How can you have a successful relationship when no one is willing to talk about the hard stuff?

"Everything okay in here?" Dad glances between us.

Mom adopts the placid smile I know so well. "Everything's fine. How's the corn?"

"Not charred, so we're winning!" Fenna carries the plate of foil-wrapped cobs in and sets them on the counter.

Ties gives us a thumbs-up and focuses on his phone.

"I thought maybe you'd invite Flip to dinner," Dad says.

"I would have loved to meet him," Mom adds.

I glance between them. "This is the first time I've been here. I didn't want it to be awkward for him."

"It's only awkward if you make it awkward," Fenna says helpfully.

"Or it's always awkward," Ties mutters.

"Maybe next time," Mom says.

And suddenly it's wildly, painfully clear. She's hurt. Of course she is. Dad works with my boyfriend, and my mom has never met him. Not as the guy I'm dating. At first, I just wanted things to calm down and for the media to back off and stop dredging up his past.

"We can make a plan," I hedge.

"That would be nice. I only know the interview side of him. I'd like to meet *him*."

"You mean you'd like to grill him," Ties says.

Fenna snickers.

I point an accusing finger at my sister. "Just wait. You're up next."

"Mom's already met my boyfriend."

"You have a boyfriend?" Dad and I say at the same time.

It sucks that we're in the dark together. But I guess that's how my mom feels about Flip, so I'm getting a taste of my own medicine, and I don't like it.

"It's new," Mom defends Fenna.

"Like, twenty-four-hours new," Ties adds.

"I was going to tell you in person," Fenna assures me.

"Is he nice?"

"So nice. We're going to the movies next weekend."

"But you're only fourteen!" Dad protests.

"They're going with a group of friends," Mom jumps in.

"I had a girlfriend at fourteen," Ties says.

"But—"

Fenna cuts Dad off. "Do not come at me with a gender bias."

He sighs. "You're all just growing up too fast."

Everyone is quiet for a beat, maybe lost in a memory when things were different, but then the oven beeps and pulls us back to the present.

We bring the food to the table. It's familiar but so different—a different table, a different home. Everything is new and modern, nothing like the antiques my mom loves to collect and refinish. It's also missing personal touches, like pictures on the walls. I make a promise to try harder once exams are done.

"You can bring Flip the next time we have family dinner,"

Mom suggests as she passes me the cheesy sour cream and onion potato puffs.

"And Fenna can bring her boyfriend," Ties chimes in, grinning evilly.

"And you can bring Jordan, since you're always studying with them," Fenna tosses back at him.

His cheeks flush. "We're working on a robotics project together."

"We'll have to plan around the playoff schedule, but we can figure something out," I agree, distracting everyone from my brother.

"That sounds great." Mom is all smiles again.

Everything is normal, but it's not. Maybe because nothing has really changed. My mom is still keeping her feelings to herself, and my dad still works too much. I love them, but I don't want to be them.

Flip and I are nothing like my parents. And I never want us to be.

CHAPTER 43

TALLY

"That dress is stunning." Fee is stretched out on my bed next to pillow Flip.

Cammie gives two thumbs-up from the floor beside her. "You look like you stepped straight out of a fairy tale."

"Great. That's what I'm going for." It's a week post family dinner and it's been intense. Final projects are coming due. Exams around the corner. Our showcase right after. Flip decided I needed a stress break, so he planned a night out and sent a dress. I slip my feet into my heels. There's a slit up my right leg and the neckline plunges. This dress hugs my curves, while still being gauzy.

My phone buzzes.

FLIP
How does the dress fit?

TALLY
Like a glove.

It's perfect.

I strike a pose in front of the mirror, making sure my bare leg is on display, and send it to him.

FLIP

You look incredible.

TALLY

Fuckably incredible?

FLIP

You're insatiable.

TALLY

You should see what I have on underneath. 😈

FLIP

Someone's feeling feisty.

First I take you for dinner, then we tick another fantasy off the list. 😉

I'll be there to pick you up in ten.

The fantasy list is my new favorite. The last time I stayed at Flip's, we ate dinner while I wore nothing but a fake diamond collar, and he wore a full suit—a scene from one of Cammie's fics. He was practically feral when he finally fucked me on the dining room table, while still fully dressed. It was hot and messy and filthy, and I would love to do it again.

"You're thinking about sex, aren't you?" Cammie asks, dragging me out of my happy gutter.

"Maybe."

"Definitely," Fee snickers.

Flip arrives a short time later. Now that spring has finally sprung, I don't need a full-on parka to leave the apartment. I pull on a cropped jacket, grab my clutch, and meet him at the door.

His eyes heat as they move over me, and he belatedly sticks his foot out, then frowns at the lack of cat winding around his leg. "Where's my second favorite kitty?"

"Sleeping on Fee's textbook."

"Ah. Sounds about right. Do you have everything you need?"

I pat my clutch. "It's all right here."

An overnight bag is no longer necessary since Flip has stocked his apartment with all my essentials. He even cleared a drawer for me and filled it with comfy clothes. Every time I sleep over, there's another hoodie in his closet, or a pair of shorts or lounge pants in the dresser. I have a toothbrush in his bathroom, my favorite treats have a home in his cupboard, and last week he bought a barrel chair so we can cuddle and read together when the semester is over. It feels serious and real and like we're moving toward something lasting.

"You'll probably be mobbed when we hit the lobby," I warn.

"I don't mind. You look fantastic, and people can take all the pictures they damn well please." He kisses my hand, and we take the elevator down.

The worst of the media shitstorm has passed, thankfully. Between the cat-calendar fundraiser for the animal shelter, the upcoming gala, and his now highly publicized role as a hockey coach for kids with special needs, most of the bumps have smoothed over. It's hard to keep dragging someone through the dirt when it's clear he's an exceptionally stand-up guy.

Flip stops to sign a few hats for fans before he excuses us. He's all PR smile as he guides me to the car and helps me in. Once he's settled behind the wheel, he slides his hand under my hair. "You look ethereal."

I arch a brow. "Ethereally fuckable?"

He laughs. "I've created a monster."

I hold my fingers apart just a bit. "But it feels good, and it's new, and it's the most incredible release." My body warms just thinking about what the end of the night will be like. "It makes me feel closer to you."

"That's my favorite part." His eyes soften. "How open you are with me, how you let me see you at your most primal and vulnerable." He brushes his lips over mine. "Let me wine you and dine you first, kitten, and then we can relieve all your stress."

"And yours, too." I kiss his cheek. "You're so close to the playoffs now."

We drive the short distance to the upscale restaurant.

The host escorts us to our table. Usually, we end up tucked away in a quiet corner, but tonight we're in the middle of the room.

Once we're seated and have placed drink and appetizer orders, Flip holds out his hand, palm up. I slip mine in his. "How are you feeling?" he asks.

Unreasonably horny. I keep that thought to myself. I don't know what's wrong with me tonight, but I feel like a cat in heat. "I think I'm just ready for the next chapter," I say. "The last four years have been fun. I've grown a lot, learned so much, made amazing friends, and gained independence, but I'm excited to fully step into adulthood." I want a regular job with a steady income so I can contribute and be a partner. Being out of university will put us on more level ground.

"I felt the same way when I finished university."

I nod. "You went from university to the farm team." He made more than half a million a year as soon as he graduated.

"I was fortunate to have a contract right away." He sips his water, eyes on our clasped hands. He moved teams twice before he was given a long contract with the Terror.

The server delivers our drinks, and we select our mains.

"Do you think it'll be the same for Brody?" He's a top player for Tilton, and the scouts are always talking to him.

"I would wager, yeah. It'd be best if he was picked up by a team other than the Terror, though."

"Otherwise he's competing with his brother," I finish. "Not that he won't always be compared to him anyway."

"Yeah. Chicago has their sights on him. That would be a great team for him," Flip muses.

"I'm sure he'd love to play there. It's a fun city." But if he's in Chicago, he'll never be able to ask Enid out.

"It is," he agrees. "If we could go anywhere this summer, just the two of us, where would it be?"

My heart skips a beat. "Like a couple's vacation?"

His eyes light up. "Exactly."

I tap my lip. "Are there parameters? Like inside Canada or North America?"

"No parameters. No destination limits. Name your ideal summer vacation."

The server drops off our appetizers.

I ponder the question again while I cut into a pan-seared scallop. "Honestly, Canadian summers are so short. I hate to leave here when the weather is nice. I'd love to go back to the lodge in Huntsville and spend a week enjoying the beach and you shirtless. It's so pretty and peaceful up there."

"I have my eye on a piece of property in that area. We could build a cottage," Flip says.

"Are you taking notes from Connor these days?" I tease. But the fact that he's talking in terms like "we" and building a summer home feels like he's planning a future with me.

"Dallas has a place, now Connor and Dred, so I can see the allure. Especially since you want to stay local and dance in Toronto," he says.

"What about you? You have lots of time left in your career. What's your dream after hockey?" He could do anything, go into sportscasting, work for the Hockey Academy like Roman and Hollis, or be a coach and end up anywhere.

"I want to help you pursue your career goals and find a second career that fits our life." He says this so matter-of-factly.

Like it's the only possibility. *He wants to build a future with me.* My heart soars. Does this mean he feels the same way about me as I do him? Is he falling for me, too?

Is this how my parents were when they fell in love? Did they promise each other the world, and slowly the dreams they imagined faded as life and my dad's career took over? Did my mom just smile and tell him it was fine, but really she was dying inside, alone and wishing for more? What if Flip gets traded? What if I get a job outside of Toronto? What if we make a plan and it all falls apart?

"Hey." He squeezes my hand. "Sorry, was that too much? I don't want to overwhelm you."

"No." I shake my head. "It's not too much. It's just…everything you're saying—" I lick my lips. "—is exactly what I want, but…"

"You're scared?" he asks.

For a moment I want to say no, but then I'm just like my mom. I don't want to say one thing and mean another. "Yeah. I'm scared. I don't want to end up like my parents."

His expression softens and saddens. "I get that. And it's okay to be afraid. I am, too. But as long as we're in it together, we'll be okay."

I love you.

I don't want to lose you.

I bring his hand to my cheek and kiss the back of it.

I don't know why I'm suddenly on the verge of tears. "I need to use the bathroom for a moment."

"Are you okay?"

"Yeah." I clear my throat. "I'll just be a minute." I bend and kiss him on the cheek as I pass, hoping to wipe the concerned look off his face.

I walk down the low-lit hall and push through the door to the bathroom. It's just for one person, so I lock the door and spin to face my reflection. My cheeks are flushed. I don't know what's wrong with me. Maybe it's exam stress, or how certain Flip seems about our future together.

I smooth my hands over my hips and turn to make sure I don't have panty lines, which is the moment I discover why I'm unreasonably horny and my feelings are on fire.

It's shark week.

And not only are my brand-new panties ruined, so is my dress.

CHAPTER 44

FLIP

I almost worked up the nerve to tell Tally about Fiona, but then I thought about how much stress she's already under. It's unfair to put more on her plate just to get this thing off my chest. I also don't want to do it in public, so I kept my mouth shut. But when she's through exams and settled, I'll be honest with her about that piece of my past, even though it scares the absolute shit out of me.

I glance over my shoulder. Tally has been in the bathroom long enough that I start to worry. My phone buzzes with a new message.

TALLY

I have a problem.

FLIP

Do you need me?

TALLY

I need a new dress and new panties.

I frown and push my chair back. *What the hell is going on in that bathroom?*

FLIP

Coming to you.

I weave through the tables and walk down the hall, scanning the row of individual bathrooms. Three are occupied.

FLIP

Which bathroom are you in?

Tally opens the door a crack. Her lips pressed together in a thin line, and she looks like she's barely keeping it together.

"What happened?" I reach out to touch her hand. "Tell me what you need so I can fix it."

She rolls her eyes to the ceiling, chin trembling. "It's embarrassing."

I try to lighten the mood. "Connor fucked a sandwich when we were teenagers to piss me off. It can't be worse than that." That I fucked his T-shirt first is irrelevant under the circumstances.

"I got my period," she whispers, a single tear tracking down her cheek. "And my dress is ruined."

It's pale blue satin with a gauzy overlay. "Let's see what we can do."

"I don't think there's anything that can be done. Not here, anyway." Another tear slides down her cheek, voice laced with panic. "I can't walk out of here like this."

"You won't have to. Can I come in so I can help?"

Tally steps back, and I push through the gap in the door, locking it behind me. I can already see the problem reflected in the mirror. Her panties sit on the edge of the sink. It looks like she tried to rinse them and dry them with the hand dryer.

But the large spot on the back of her pale blue dress is the real problem. It will be impossible to hide. We might be able to rinse it, but without the proper tools, it's unlikely we'll get all the blood out, and it could take a while—long enough for people to notice and ask questions. She doesn't need the negative attention.

"I have a potential solution." I shrug out of my jacket. "Try this on."

Tally slides her arms through it, unfortunately it's a sports jacket.

"It doesn't cover it." I loosen my tie. "My shirt will, though."

"What will you wear?"

I unfasten the buttons. "My jacket." It's not ideal, but it's better than the alternative.

I help her out of her dress, and she puts her panties back on, lines them with toilet paper, and shrugs into my shirt. It's massive on her, but it'll do in a pinch. I take the sash from her dress and cinch it around her waist.

I shrug back into my jacket, adjust my tie, and fasten the buttons. "It's a fashion statement, right?"

She worries her bottom lip. "What if people notice?"

I'm used to the negative speculation, and I'd rather have it aimed at me. "Your comfort is more important." I smooth out her hair and kiss her softly. "You ready to go home?"

She swallows and nods.

I fold her dress to hide the stain and sling it over my arm, then link the other arm with hers. "I'll get you in the car, then manage the bill, okay?"

"Okay. I'm sorry we didn't get to eat dinner."

"There will be plenty of other opportunities." I open the bathroom door. "I've got you." I step out into the hall first and put a protective arm around her. The only way to get to the rear entrance is by going the way we came. Through the kitchen to the service entrance might be our option to avoid the most people.

I pull Tally closer, kissing her temple. "Head down, okay, kitten?"

She makes a noise of acknowledgement.

I walk her briskly down the hall. We almost make it to the kitchen unnoticed, except a random dude rounds the corner, phone in hand, blocking our way for a few precious seconds. His gaze bounces between me and Tally, eyebrows pulling together before popping high. "Flip Madden?"

"Hey, man." We skirt the dude, and I hustle her through the kitchen doors.

Thankfully our server happens to be right there. I explain the situation in the vaguest of terms and he helps us get out with as little exposure to patrons as possible. I'm still worried about the guy in the hall, though.

"Want to take bets on how your dad plans to kill me?" I joke as I help Tally into the car.

"Probably with your own hockey stick," Tally whispers.

"It would be apt."

Once Tally is safely tucked away, I return to pay the bill. People take pictures of me in my suit jacket minus a shirt. Hemi will be pissed, but priority one is taking care of my girlfriend and getting her home and into comfortable clothes.

I join Tally in the car and set our boxed dinners on the back seat. "How you doing?"

"I'm mostly embarrassed and annoyed that Mother Nature ruined a really nice dinner and an expensive dress."

"There's nothing to be embarrassed about. You don't have control over your period any more than you do the moon cycle." She laughs, and I squeeze the back of her neck. "And I'll send the dress to the dry cleaners."

"I thought I had another day to go," she mutters.

"You need me to stop at the drug store to pick up supplies?"

She shakes her head. "I have stuff at your place."

"Okay, good. So home it is." I pull into traffic. "You want me to pick up dessert since we didn't have a chance to order any?"

"Oh, maybe. I would give my left pinkie toe for one of Rix's chocolate lava cakes."

I smile. "You're in luck. I have a few in my freezer. You want me to stop for anything else?"

She folds her hands over her stomach. "I think I'm okay."

"You think of anything, you just let me know."

A little while later, we pull into the underground lot. I'm thankful the elevator is empty and stays that way on the trip up to my apartment, even though most of the people in the building know me and wouldn't post pictures on social media to create drama.

The people in the restaurant are a different story. That's tomorrow's problem, though. I'll message Hemi later, once Tally is taken care of.

I let us into my apartment, and Tally disappears into the bathroom. While she cleans up I pull the lava cakes out of the freezer and turn the oven on. Tally reappears a few minutes later wearing joggers and one of my T-shirts.

"Better?" I run my hands down her arms.

"Much."

"Feel like finishing dinner?"

"Definitely."

We grab plates and cutlery, and I open the boxes.

"So." I spear one of the seven artfully arranged green beans and offer it to Tally. She nibbles the end. "I gotta be honest. The presentation is great, even boxed up." I pop the rest of the bean into my mouth. "And it tastes awesome, but the portions are small." I motion to my cupboard. "I was thinking maybe some spiral KD might be a decent addition."

"That sounds like literal heaven."

"Awesome. I'll break out the good stuff, just for you." I kiss her cheek.

Tally and I make the noodles together and put the lava cakes in to heat while we polish off dinner.

"Why are these always so good?" Tally spears a cheesy

noodle and pops it in her mouth, followed by one of the maple-braised carrots.

"Comfort food? When I was a kid, we used to buy elbow noodles, powdered milk, and cheese sauce in bulk. It wasn't until I went to the Hockey Academy that I learned most people just used the KD packets and bagged milk."

Her expression softens. "Bagged milk was more expensive."

"By a lot, yeah." We were always trying to stretch grocery money. "And my appetite was endless."

"It must have been so hard."

I shrug. "It was all I knew."

"Is it difficult to go out for a nice dinner like we did tonight? Places like that are super expensive." Tally strokes the back of my hand.

"It used to be. At first, I worried it was all going to disappear." My upbringing, coupled with what happened with Fiona when I signed my contract, exacerbated my fears for a long time. Again, I'm tempted to tell Tally the real reason, but tonight has already been hard enough on her. "Rix has been great about helping me invest," I explain. "And I have security after nine years in the pros, which makes it easier."

"It's wild that you've been doing this since you were my age." Tally rubs her abdomen and winces. "I should have taken a painkiller as soon as I got here."

"You getting sore?" I push my empty bowl away.

"Yeah. Nothing a couple pills and a heating pad won't solve."

"There are other ways to remedy that problem." I want the closeness that comes with taking care of her.

She narrows her eyes. "I'm not going for a walk right now."

"I'm not talking about a walk, kitten."

She frowns.

"Orgasms help alleviate cramps," I explain.

"I'm bleeding."

I shrug. "Natural lube."

"You're serious." She blinks up at me. "Are you serious?"

"I'm a hockey player, Tally. I'm not scared of blood, and my libido is always at a level ten." I turn her to face me and push her legs apart. "You want a natural analgesic? I can help with that." I run my hands up her warm thighs. "You were pushing my buttons earlier, let me push yours."

She rolls her bottom lip, cheeks flushed. "It'll be messy, though."

"I have plenty of dark towels, and I would love to make you feel better."

She runs her hands over my chest. "I would love that, too."

I stand, pick her up and pause to turn off the oven before I carry her through the apartment. On my way to my bedroom, I grab dark towels from the bathroom closet and wet a couple of washcloths.

Once we're in my bedroom, I strip her out of her clothes and me out of mine, lay a soft towel over my navy sheets, and lift her into bed, climbing up after her. She reaches for me as soon as I'm stretched out beside her. I kiss her softly, fingers trailing over her collarbones, moving lower to skim her nipples.

She arches and moans. "Everything is so sensitive."

I focus my attention there for a minute, gentle caresses, followed by a light pinch. "Just think about how good it will feel when I'm filling you up, kitten."

She shudders and sighs. "Every time is better than the last."

"I'm addicted to your pretty moans." I kiss her neck, dragging my fingers lower, circling her navel, eliciting one of those sweet sounds.

She catches my hand in hers just before I reach the apex of her thighs. "What are you doing?"

I lift my head and meet her wide, slightly panicked gaze. "Getting you ready for my cock."

"But—"

I kiss her. "Stop worrying about the mess we're about to make, kitten. That's what showers and the washing machine are for."

She releases my wrist, and I cup her, soft and warm under my palm. Then gently I stroke along her seam, going low to tease her entrance before I circle her clit.

"Oh, fuck me." She shudders, and her eyes flutter closed.

"Soon." I cover her nipple with my mouth and lap gently as I ease two fingers inside her, quickly finding the place that makes her arch and moan my name.

"Oh God, Phillip, that's—" She writhes under my touch.

"Tell me how I make you feel," I demand.

"So good. Every time," she whimpers, toes curling against my thigh. "Everything is heightened."

I add a third finger, stretching her, eyes lifting as I swirl my tongue around her nipple, before I use teeth and suck hard. Her head snaps back on a deep groan and she goes rigid as the orgasm slams through her. I know how to make her body sing, how to take care of her. *I'm* what she needs.

When she's boneless and panting, I kiss my way over her chest until my lips brush hers. "I have an idea."

She runs her hands over my shoulders and grips my biceps. "What kind of idea?"

Tally's on the pill. She takes it religiously, at the same time every day. If ever there was a safe time, it's now. "Would you like me to go bare?"

Her eyes flare with surprise. "No condom?"

"I'm safe, and I know you are too."

"I could feel all of you?" she whispers.

I nod and stroke her cheek. "And I'll feel all of you."

"I want that." She licks her lips. "I—yes, I want that."

"If you change your mind, or you get nervous, you tell me, and we'll stop and I'll put a condom on, okay, kitten?"

"Okay, but I won't change my mind."

I fit myself between her thighs. "I'll bring you right to the edge, kitten." I roll my hips, shaft rubbing against her clit. "And right when you're just about to come, I'll fill you up so I can feel you squeeze my cock. No barriers."

"Oh God." Her nails dig into my shoulders.

I adjust her right leg, hooking under her knee to draw it up and tuck it against my ribs as I move over her.

"You're so soft and wet." I roll my hips again. "So perfect."

"I'm so close," she whimpers.

"Right where I want you." I curve one hand against her cheek, holding her gaze as I push inside.

She moans, the sound primal and needy as I fill her, body quaking as she spasms around me.

Sensation threatens to pull me under and fray my control. "God, you feel so fucking good, Tallulah." My hips press her into the mattress. "Warm and soft and *mine*," I growl.

"Yours." She threads her hands through my hair, gripping tightly. "It's so intense."

Her head kicks back when I stay deep and roll my hips.

"Look at me. I want your eyes on mine," I demand.

Her hazy gaze returns to me.

"Good girl."

She shudders and I grin.

"Do you like being my good girl, Tally?" I pull out to the ridge. "My sweet little kitten."

I slide back in, and she clenches around me on a moan. "Yes, oh God."

"Me, too." I bite the edge of her jaw as I start a slow, steady rhythm. "But I like it best when you want to be dirty with me."

Her eyes flare and she trembles, coming violently. I focus on her glassy, lust-drenched gaze and fight the desire to just fuck into her, to get as deep as possible.

"So fucking beautiful when you're milking my cock," I growl in her ear.

"I can't stop." She rakes her nails down my back. "Oh fuck, I can't—"

She keeps coming, wave after wave of sensation sweeping through her. No one else will ever have this part of her but me.

I fold back on my knees and grip her hips.

"Oh, my sweet hell." Tally props herself up on her elbows, eyebrows pulled together, eyes wide with shock. The insides of her thighs are slick with blood and cum.

"I have to pull out now, kitten," I warn, pumping into her one last time before I leave the blissful warmth of her body and fist my cock.

"Oh that—" Her eyes flare and her pussy clenches. "—should not be hot." It's phrased more as a question than a statement.

"Why not?" I grunt as I fuck my own hand, fast and hard, coming on the inside of her thigh.

She covers her mouth with her palm. "This looks like the scene of a shark attack." A slightly hysterical laugh bubbles out of her.

I cock a brow. "But would you do it again?"

She falls back on the mattress, one hand covering her face as she grins. "Yeah." She peeks through her fingers, shaking her head. "I would do it again."

I lean in and kiss her cheek. "Good. Me, too."

"We're a little depraved, aren't we?" she whispers, still smiling.

"As it should be." I tip my chin up. "Come on, let's shower."

"Then lava cake and bedtime snuggles?"

"Sounds perfect."

CHAPTER 45

TALLY

I'm in a fantastic mood the next morning, until Flip drops me off at my first class and the whispering begins. Then my phone starts blowing up with messages from my dad.

Anxiety makes my mouth instantly dry. My first instinct is to ignore my dad's messages and look at the internet, but I know better on both counts. I address my dad's text with facts and logic.

And Flip is your lead scorer. You can't send him to Winnipeg.

Especially not with the playoffs around the corner.

DAD

YOU ARE WALKING OUT OF A RESTAURANT BATHROOM WEARING HIS DRESS SHIRT AND HE IS WITHOUT A SHIRT.

TALLY

I'm aware. I was there. Please cease with the SHOUTY CAPS.

DAD

You have better sense than this.

TALLY

This will be a conversation. I'm in class. We'll talk later.

I shove my phone in my bag. I'm sitting in the middle of the row, in the middle of the lecture theater. Leaving halfway through the lecture will only shine a bigger spotlight on me, so I'm forced to suffer through an hour of whispering and giggles. My phone buzzes relentlessly in my bag the entire time.

I don't have a chance to check it at the end of class because Fee and Cammie push their way into the lecture theater—it's literally like salmon swimming upstream—to escort me out. They flank me, each hooking an arm through one of mine, and guide me into a gender-neutral bathroom.

Cammie crosses her arms and leans against the door. "We're hanging out here until the next class is firmly underway."

"Okay. It's really bad, isn't it?" The incessant chatter around me during class answered that question.

"I mean, your smutty fanfic didn't get posted all over your residence building with your picture on it for the university to see.

But there are some photos of you and Flip walking out of a bathroom together. You're dressed in his shirt, and he's minus one, so assumptions are being made." Cammie doesn't sugarcoat things.

"I got my period in the middle of dinner and bled through my dress," I explain.

Cammie and Fee both gasp. "Oh no."

Fee's hand goes to her chest. "So he gave you his shirt?"

"Yeah." I nod.

"That is so swoony." Fee's eyes are all dreamy.

"So swoony," Cammie echoes.

"But the whole world believes he fucked me in a super classy restaurant bathroom. We were in there for all of two minutes." Maybe three, but still. "It would have been the shortest, quietest sex in the universe." I rub my temples. "This is so bad. My dad is threatening to trade him to Winnipeg."

How will I continue to function if this goes viral? The potential is there. *Coach's Daughter Gets Railed by Player in Public Bathroom* is exceptionally click-worthy, even if it's the furthest thing from the truth. Tears prick at my eyes. Things were finally settling down and now this.

Cammie's phone pings. It's Chase.

I need to check my messages, but I'm terrified of what I'll find.

"Chase is waiting for us at the same exit as last time. Media have swarmed your apartment building and are waiting at the front entrance of this one."

"The Groundhog Day vibe is strong."

"You'll be safe at Brody's," Cammie assures me.

"And I'll bring your car over, so you have wheels," Fee adds.

"Can you grab my dance stuff and some extra period supplies? I have practice tonight." Getting into my apartment later will be a feat, but I can only afford to worry about one thing at a time.

"I'll bring you a ball cap and a plain hoodie or something so you can be incognito." Fee kisses me on the cheek, checks to make sure the coast is clear, and steps into the hall. She gives us the thumbs-up when she reaches the end.

Chase is waiting at the back of the building, and we take the trail to Brody's place and slip through the hidden gate.

Brody's jaw is tight, eyes sharp. "You okay?"

"It's not what it looks like."

"I know." He squeezes my shoulder. "Flip wouldn't do that to you."

I drop into one of the chairs on his back deck.

The sliding door opens and Gage peeks his head out.

Brody pins him with a look. "Do not say anything stupid."

"I wasn—"

"Shut it." Mac flicks his ear.

My phone buzzes again. I finally pull it out of my bag so I can check the damage. My Babe Brigade is on fire.

RIX

Stay off socials, please.

HAMMER

All socials.

HEMI

Flip should have messaged me about this last night so I could get ahead of it, but I'm running interference now.

ESSIE

I'm sorry 

DRED

I'm seeing what kind of strings my husband and his endless-pool-of-wealth family can do. I'll report back when I have information.

TALLY

Aunt Flo made an untimely visit and ruined my dress, and my reputation. So fun.

Another slew of messages follow, all with hearts and empathy. I wish it made this suck less. I exhale my anxiety and switch to the ones from Flip.

FLIP

Are you okay?

I need you to message me as soon as you see this.

I'm taking care of this now.

I'll pick you up as soon as practice is over.

My fingers hover over the keys. I don't even know what to say. I'm scared, I'm anxious. How will I make it through the end of the semester if I'm the hot topic on campus again?

TALLY

I'm at Brody's. Fee is bringing my car here.

FLIP

I will fix this, kitten. And I will be there as soon as I can.

TALLY

Okay. I might be at the dance studio later.

The humping dots appear and disappear a few times before another message pops up.

FLIP

Make sure the studio is clear before you go.

TALLY

I will. I'll share my location.

FLIP

Stay safe, please.

I hope that's not a lie.

"How bad is the stuff online?" My stomach is in my throat.

Cammie and Brody exchange a look.

Mac kicks Gage when he opens his mouth.

"They're digging into Flip's past," Cammie says gently.

"So all the old stuff is resurfacing?" I clarify.

"Yeah." Chase runs his hands through his hair. It's a tell.

"What else?" I glance between my friends.

"There are a lot of rumors floating around. They've gone all the way back to his university days."

"What does that mean? What kind of rumors?"

"Just that he had a serious girlfriend at one point," Mac says quickly.

"It's hard to know what's real and what's not." Brody's expression is empathetic. "I'm sure when you see Flip, he'll be able to smooth it all out."

I feel like they're talking around something, but my stress levels are through the roof, and I can't process anything.

Fee finally shows up with my car. Despite my friends' repeated attempts to get me to message my troupe and cancel, I go to dance practice. I understand why they made the suggestion once I'm there, because I get to explain the situation and how things have been taken out of context to Charles and Arya. Rehearsal does not go smoothly. I'm distracted, and my timing is off.

It does nothing to ease my worries or anyone else's.

What if this one stupid mistake tanks the rest of my semester?

What if I fail my finals? What if no company wants me?

What if Flip decides I can't handle the pressure of being his girlfriend and he breaks up with me? How heartbroken will I be then?

An hour into practice, there's a knock on the studio door. I half expect it to be a reporter, so Arya opens it while I hide in the bathroom.

"You're safe," Arya calls out.

I poke my head out.

Arya is holding a box.

"It's from Flip," Charles explains. "There's a card."

I glance inside the box, which contains lunch from my favorite local bakery, chocolate, and a note:

> *I don't regret taking care of you for a second, even if the media wants to twist it into something ugly. I promise I'll fix this for us.*
> *Xx Phillip*

Arya and Charles group hug me.

"At least my dad hasn't traded him." Yet.

CHAPTER 46

FLIP

"Give me one good reason why I shouldn't trade your ass," Vander Zee grinds out.

My stomach is a mess, my mouth is dry, and all I want is to get back to Tally to make sure she's okay, but I'm here, sitting across from her dad, because he's my boss and I made a huge fucking mistake. "Because it's not what it looks like."

He glares at me.

"Do you honestly believe that I would deflower your daughter in the bathroom of a high-end restaurant? And then exit the bathroom with her wearing my shirt and me not wearing a shirt so every single person in the restaurant would know?"

Vander Zee doesn't need to know what happens behind closed doors with me and his daughter, or in dark corners. My goal was to save her from public humiliation, which backfired spectacularly.

"If that's not what happened, then what did?" Vander Zee compulsively squeezes a stress ball. His face is worrisomely red. I better not give him a heart attack.

"Tally got her period in the middle of dinner and bled through her dress."

He blinks a couple of times, like this was the last thing he expected. "And you didn't think to give her your jacket instead?"

"We tried that. Her dress was blue and my jacket didn't conceal the spot. She was already embarrassed and uncomfortable. I wasn't going to make her wear a dress covered in period blood home. So I gave her my shirt because it solved the problem."

"You have to know how this looks."

"I do, thanks to the way the media is spinning this."

"There are pictures of the two of you all over the fucking internet, Madden. They are making my daughter look awful, and they certainly aren't painting you in a positive light." The stress ball pops out of his hand and bounces across the floor. "I warned you."

"Don't think for a second that you're more upset about this than I am," I snap.

"I'm her father."

"And I'm her boyfriend. It's my job to take care of her and protect her from shit like this. Now she's in the middle of this nightmare, all because my love life is clickbait fodder. I'm doing everything I can not to mess this up because of the choices I made before Tally. I am very aware that she isn't the only person being dragged into this. Hemi and I are working through a strategy."

Every woman I've ever spent the night with who posted a photo is getting new airtime, thanks to this. And worse is how close they're getting to my relationship with Fiona. If it becomes public knowledge, I'll have everyone else's unhelpful perspectives on why that relationship imploded the way it did.

And so will Tally. She's already stretched to the breaking point and this won't help. I don't want Fiona to be the thing that pushes her over the edge.

"You talk about showing up for my daughter, well now's the time, Madden. You better find a way to shift the media's attention."

"I know how high the stakes are."

"Do you though, Phillip? Because I'm not sure you thought through the consequences of your actions." He runs a rough hand through his hair. "I should have said no. I shouldn't have allowed this."

"With all due respect, sir, Tally and I are both adults—"

"Don't," he snaps. "Don't tell me you can make your own choices. She's my baby. You knew you'd be under a microscope. You said it yourself, your job was to protect her and show the hockey-watching nation that you'd grown up and changed, that you could handle the responsibility of dating your coach's fucking daughter. Instead, you've turned her into the worst kind of gossip. How do you think it will affect her job prospects when she's splashed all over the internet like this?" Vander Zee looks like he's two seconds away from punching me in the face.

I wouldn't stop him. He's right about all of it.

"I will fix this, sir."

"You better, or you'll be uninvited to family dinner next weekend and you'll be warming a bench in Winnipeg next season. If they'll even take you. Get the fuck out of my office."

I feel sick all over again as I push out of his chair. What if I ruin her future? What if he does trade me? I need to make this better.

My next stop is Hemi's office again.

She and Hammer are sitting at her conference table, heads bowed. Dallas is lounging in the executive chair behind her desk.

"Close the door," Hemi says without looking up.

"Want me to leave, honey?" Dallas asks.

"No, actually. You're good at cleaning up messes, so you might have something valuable to contribute." She closes her laptop. "Judging from your expression, your conversation with Vander Zee didn't go as well as planned."

"Not really, no."

"You did make it look like you had sex with his daughter in a public bathroom," Dallas says, unhelpfully.

"Thanks for the reminder I didn't need."

Dallas ignores my angry glare. "You should tell the media the truth."

"And embarrass Tally more by telling the world she got her period in a restaurant and bled through her dress?"

"It's a hell of a lot *less* embarrassing than everyone believing she got screwed in a public bathroom after a nice meal, isn't it?" Dallas picks up a crocheted peach from the basket on Hemi's desk and rolls it between his fingers. "And you can helpfully point out that while in the past you made some choices that had questionable consequences, you sure haven't made a habit of it in the past few years. You could also mention that you're a grown-up, and that your goal was to protect your girlfriend from embarrassment, but thanks to the way things get twisted around, she's forced to endure more of it instead. Also, no one wants to talk about periods, even though they're part of life, so shoving that at the media will shut them up real fast. Women are badasses for dealing with that every freaking month."

Hemi and Hammer clap.

Dallas grins.

After a moment, Hemi clears her throat. "Dallas makes a good point. If you run with the truth, they will back off, which is what we want. A ruined dress is a whole lot more appealing than a ruined reputation. Plus, it paints you as the boyfriend who literally gave his girlfriend the shirt off his back to save her from the humiliation the media is happy to shower her with."

"This could work," I muse. "Whatever I can do to make it easier for Tally. How soon can you get me an interview?"

Hemi reaches for her phone. "I can have someone here in half an hour."

"Make the call. That will give us enough time to prep."

Hemi secures the exclusive interview.

"Anything I need to know about the journalist?" I ask once she's off the phone.

"She went to Tilton and her brother plays pro hockey in Chicago. She's been following your story and is on our side, so it'll be a fair interview."

Connor appears in the doorway, hand poised to knock. He rests it on the jamb instead. "I'm glad to see you're still alive." His gaze falls on me. "My wife would be exceptionally sad if Vander Zee unalived you to death for having sex with his daughter in a public bathroom."

"That's not what happened."

"I'm aware. My wife filled me in. So why haven't you released a public statement?"

"We're working on that now," I grumble.

"You should work faster. Your girlfriend getting her period is far less scandalous." Connor inspects his nails. "They should have had supplies in the bathroom for her."

"It was too late for that."

"Oh my gosh! I have the best idea!" Hammer slaps the table.

Everyone startles.

"Sorry." She wiggles around in her chair. "But hear me out." She holds up both hands. "What if we have a tampon toss?"

Hemi wrinkles her nose. "The visual on that is not appealing."

"Like the teddy bear toss, but we do it with period supplies. Let's spin this around on the media and do something good with it. There are all kinds of women's shelters looking for feminine hygiene products."

"And the group homes," Connor adds. "We had a similar incident with Everly."

"Poor thing."

"I've learned a lot about tampons in the past couple of years."

"I love this idea, and we will run with it." Hemi points at me. "And you will be the one to promote it during this interview."

"I'll get started on graphics and T-shirts!" Hammer says.

"I'll go on a coffee run," Dallas offers.

"I'll have Meems threaten to pull advertising funding from the networks who are incessantly posting those pictures of you and Tally," Connor says.

"Because you don't want your wife to be sad if I end up traded?" I ask.

He blinks steadily at me. "I never want my wife to be sad, but I also don't enjoy watching the media create unnecessary drama."

"Thanks."

"You're welcome. Good luck with the interview." Connor leaves us to it.

Hemi, Hammer, and I spend the next twenty minutes talking things through.

"I want to make sure the focus stays on the present, on me and Tally." I've seen a couple photos of me and Fiona floating around out there, and I really don't want that to come up now.

"I think we all want the same thing." Hemi taps her pen on her desk. "Is there anything else we need to know?"

"No." I lean back in my chair. "We're good."

The journalist from the Tribune arrives. She's a tiny thing with dark curls, thick glasses, dressed all in black. The only pop of color is her patterned flats.

"Marietta! Thank you so much for coming." Hemi rounds her desk, and they shake hands before she introduces her to Hammer, Dallas, and then finally me.

"Flip Madden, your reputation precedes you."

"Hard to get out from under."

Hemi coughs. "Maybe keep that off the record."

Marietta arches a brow but motions to the table. "Shall we start putting things on the record?"

"Right to the point. Sure."

"I'd like to get this article in the evening edition if possible." She pulls out her device. "I'll record this and send it to Hemi as soon as we're done."

"Sounds good." I take the seat across from her.

Hemi sets a bottle of water in front of me. I take a long swig. "Can we keep the focus on my current relationship?"

"I'll do my best." She hits record. "Your relationship with Tallulah Vander Zee has gotten a lot of attention recently."

"To be fair, I always get a lot of attention. But yeah, there's been a heavy focus on us this season, despite the Terror being in a strong position going into the playoffs."

"This has been true for the past several years, so hockey watchers might have come to expect it. You, however, haven't publicly dated anyone in that time. It's doubly interesting when you're dating the coach's daughter."

I cross my arms. "You're not wrong."

Hemi gives me a look.

I uncross my arms and try to keep my posture relaxed.

"Recently you took Tallulah out for dinner."

"It's not the first time and it definitely won't be the last."

"That's good to hear. Chop has great food." She smiles.

"You're not living if you haven't had the scallops," I agree.

"Is that your favorite dish?"

"One of. Tally likes their burrata salad."

"Also an excellent choice." She meets my gaze. "There are some pictures from the restaurant."

"I know. I can't open social media without seeing them. Neither can Tally."

"That must be hard. Especially since she's still in university and her school is highly hockey-focused."

"I can't protect her, and I hate it. Especially since the conjecture is inaccurate. I would not do what I'm being accused of to my girlfriend."

"But you know why you are."

"Imagine the world having a front row seat to some of your worst decisions, and then having them played on repeat so you can't get past them."

"That would be difficult."

"I've been dealing with this for years. But Tally hasn't. It's the first serious relationship I've had during my entire career. I get that people are interested. I went from commitment averse to fully committed."

"People can't help but be intrigued. The untamable Flip Madden has finally settled down." Marietta says.

"Hard to believe with the rumors floating around, though," I add.

Marietta leans forward. "What's the real story?"

"My girlfriend got her period and bled through her dress."

Marietta sits up straighter and glances at Hemi, who nods.

"Her dress was pale blue. And she looked incredible, by the way. Ethereal. Gorgeous." I tent my fingers, pressing the tips together. "I wasn't going to make her wear the dress out of there. She's had more than enough attention on her these past few months. So I made a choice. Maybe it was the wrong one. But if I hadn't given her my shirt, if she'd walked out of there wearing a blood-stained dress instead, what would the narrative have been then? Would it have been better or worse? We'll never know, because that's not what happened."

"So you gave her your shirt?"

"Yes."

"You gave your girlfriend the literal shirt off your back," she repeats.

"Of course I did. I l—" I stop short.

Hemi and Hammer look like they're holding their collective breaths.

Marietta leans in. "You what?"

"She's my girlfriend. She's the most important person in my world. I would do whatever it takes to protect her."

She reaches across the table and hits pause. "Does she know?"

A cold spike of fear shoots down my spine. "Does she know what?"

She looks briefly at Hemi before her gaze returns to me. "How you feel about her."

"I'd appreciate it if she hears those words from me first."

"Fair. I do think your actions speak volumes." She unpauses the recording. "Is there anything you'd like to say, Phillip Madden, the man who gave his girlfriend the shirt off his back to protect her?"

"In honor of my girlfriend, and the fact that the hockey-watching nation now knows she gets a period, we're asking our fans to give back to the community by donating a box of tampons, pads, or any other helpful period-related items, which will go to local women's shelters and to group homes in the city. Anyone who brings a donation to the next home game will automatically have their ticket added to a lottery for seats at our first playoff game in Toronto."

"I love it. Thank you for being so candid and honest. Tally's a lucky young woman."

"I'm the lucky one."

She ends the recording and sighs. "Well, you're nothing like I expected and everything I hoped you would be."

"Thanks. I think." I rise as she does.

"Thank you so much for coming on such short notice." Hemi shakes her hand.

"Honestly, it's my pleasure. I sincerely appreciate the opportunity. Love covering hockey, but I'd never want to date one of the players."

"Yeah, me either," I joke.

CHAPTER 47

TALLY

Flip's interview with Marietta from the Tribune went live last night. Coupled with his Tampon Toss video, they reached viral status within a few hours. Apparently, my period makes an excellent headline. At least we've found a way to turn my monthly cycle into something positive.

The amount of attention I've received over the past forty-eight hours, has made it hard to focus. It's stress on top of stress because I have final assignments to hand in, exams to prepare for, and a showcase I can't afford to flub.

But tonight, I'm with my Babes at the Terror game. I want to be a supportive girlfriend. The anxiety is hard to handle, though. I keep waiting for someone to yell something vile. It happened relentlessly after the pictures of Flip and me leaving the restaurant went viral. But after Flip's interview, the tone changed, and I've been on the receiving end of empathy. And everyone wants Flip Madden to be their boyfriend. The whiplash is intense.

Once again, it feels like all eyes are on me. Hammer had special jerseys made featuring a smiling cartoon tampon for the Terror's newest community outreach initiative: The Tampon Toss.

For every box of women's feminine products donated, Connor's family is matching it with a monetary donation to local women's shelters. One lucky person will win box seats during the first home playoff game.

So, hockey and community support are the main focus again, aside from one hockey blogger who is on a mission to dig up every skeleton in Flip's walk-in closet.

"How are you feeling?" Hammer hugs my arm.

"Okay. Anxious. Nervous."

"We got you," Rix says from my other side.

"No one messes with our Tally." Hemi squeezes my shoulder from behind me.

"It's nice to feel insulated here," I admit.

"It's been tough on campus?" Hammer asks.

"Depends on the day and the headline." My Tilton friends have been amazing, and Cammie and Fee both understand the challenge, but no one can pluck the things people have said to me out of my ears. I know it will stop, and that people's attention span for drama is fleeting, but when the drama is me, it's inescapable. "Sometimes I just feel buried underneath it all," I admit. "It would be fine if it was just one thing, but it's school and dance and the future and family and blah." I exhale a heavy breath.

"It's a lot. More than you need," Rix says gently.

"You and Flip need some space to just be a couple without the constant attention," Dred says softy. She understands what it's like to be under the microscope. She and Connor were always a headline from their engagement announcement until their wedding.

"Not long and most of it will be behind us, though." I try to infuse that statement with some positivity. This is equally stressful for Phillip's with playoffs looming.

"You're almost through it," Rix agrees.

I want to be excited about what's next, but the only thing I feel certain about is my relationship with Flip.

We settle in as the game gets underway and I'm happy to have my focus somewhere other than myself.

"Offense is playing smooth tonight," Hemi says.

I nod in agreement. Last night Flip came over and reviewed plays on his tablet while I studied for my Marketing for Creatives exam. "Flip said Connor, Ash, and Quinn have been working with Kellan on their defensive strategy," I say.

"The four of them were hanging out in our living room with a whiteboard yesterday," Dred confirms. "Everly made sure they never ran out of refreshments."

"Because Quinn is cute?" Hammer asks.

"She has her eye on Kellan."

Everly is almost eighteen, and Kellan is twenty-seven. "Something about those older boys, huh?" I quip.

Hammer grins. "Seems that way."

"I'm hopeful college next year will help distract her for a while," Dred says.

"It didn't really work for me, but maybe it'll be more successful for Everly," I mumble.

That earns me some chuckles.

We shift our attention to the game as Toronto gains control of the puck and carries it to Boston's net. I follow Flip down the ice, as he and Dallas pass back and forth, looking for an opening, but Boston steals it back. His shoulders tense for a moment, but he rushes after Boston's center, snatching it back and tipping it to Tristan. I grip my armrest, the pressure of the game just as heavy as everything else. If Flip doesn't play well tonight, there will be more questions about the impact of our relationship on the team this season.

The net is open, so Tristan takes his shot, but it bounces off Boston's goalie's pads. "Fuck," I mutter.

"It's okay." Hammer squeezes my hand.

I exhale a tense breath as Connor catches it on the rebound. He flips it into the air and taps it. The puck sails past the goalie's glove and into the net.

"Hell yes!" I'm out of my seat, fist pumping as the arena follows in a wave, screaming and clapping. The relief that the Terror are on their game tonight is overwhelming. It means fewer whispers on campus tomorrow.

The goal puts Toronto up by two points. They maintain the lead but don't increase it through the end of the second period and the third, giving us another hard-earned win.

The high of the victory spills over into the crowd, and the girls and I agree to wait until things die down before we leave the box. Connor's face appears on the jumbotron. His brows are slanted, his expression severe as he answers questions about his goal and how he feels as the team approaches the playoffs. This has been his best season yet, and he credits his coaches, team-mates, and the support of his family.

I center my full attention on Flip when he appears on the screen. He didn't score a goal tonight, but he helped make both of them happen.

The sportscasters ask the usual questions about the game and how he feels going into the playoffs, especially since it's been a tumultuous season.

"Being in a relationship with the coach's daughter must put pressure on your game," one reporter says.

"That's not a question," Flip bites out, his frustration obvious.

"There are some rumors floating around about your past relationships. Would you like to debunk them?" another tosses out.

Flip sighs and runs a hand through his wet hair. "Haven't I done that enough this season? This has nothing to do with the game."

"Does your girlfriend know about your ex-wife?" another reporter asks.

It feels as if ice has been injected into my veins. Ex-wife? I laugh shrilly at the preposterousness. "Oh, come on, this is next-level ridiculous." My stomach bottoms out as the color drains from Flip's face. "That's impossible." I glance at my friends, hoping to see my disbelief reflected at me.

"This is bullshit," Rix says with certainty. "I would know if my brother had been married."

I glom onto Rix's conviction and try to make it my own.

Hemi, Hammer, Essie, and Shilpa all look as shocked as I feel and Rix sounds, but it's Dred's face I lock on to.

Because she doesn't look surprised at all.

"No comment," Flip grinds out.

Dred's eyes slide closed, and she sighs, despondently.

"Dred?" I croak.

All eyes move to her.

"You should let him explain," she says softly.

"So it's true?" Flip was married. He fell in love, committed himself to someone, and ended it. *Why? Who? When?* Why is Dred the only person who knows?

"That's not possible." Rix's disbelief mirrors my own.

"Was it *you*?" I feel sick.

"No, it was long before me. It's not my story to tell," Dred replies.

Dred has always been Flip's strongest ally. His best friend. The one person he trusts more than anyone else.

More than me.

Flip was married and divorced, and he never shared it with me. Even he doesn't believe in lasting love. It's devastating in a way I can't quite process to learn this about him in such a public way. To find out this secret along with everyone else.

He was my first.

I'm supposed to be his last.

Why wouldn't he tell me?

Why did he give his heart to someone else and take it back?

Does this mean he can never give me his?

CHAPTER 48
FLIP

I feel ill. And like my life just blew the fuck up. I'm crushed under the weight of everything I should have said and done but didn't.

Coach Forrest-Hammer handles the post-game team talk, probably to keep Vander Zee from murdering me. It's exceedingly brief and chilly. And then she leaves the room.

"Kind of a big secret to keep from the people who care about you." Tristan's hurt is written in the slant of his brow. "Does Rix even know?" He holds up a hand when I open my mouth. "You know what, don't tell me. I'll find that out for myself when I see her."

I don't argue. What can I say? Rix will be hurt. Tristan will be relieved that I didn't make her keep the secret from him. No one really wins.

And Tally. What must she think now? How does she feel? Betrayed? Angry? Confused? Hurt? *Will she break up with me over this*? I wouldn't blame her, even though it's the very last thing I want.

I wait until my teammates finish showering before I go in. I don't want to be around me, so why would anyone else?

Connor stops in front of me, the last to leave. "You must have had a good reason to keep this from everyone."

"Dred is the only person who knew. Please don't hold it against her." I won't be able to live with myself if I come between my best friend and her husband.

"I wouldn't do that to my wife. Her loyalty is one of the most miraculous things about her, and there are many, considering everything she's been through."

I lift my gaze. "She's a rare and precious gem."

"Very." He nods and cants his head, his serious expression making his features sharp. "I didn't understand it before."

"Understand what?"

"Why my wife is so abjectly loyal to you, but I do now. Someone broke you." He claps me on the shoulder. "Whatever this was, be honest with Tally about it. She deserves it, especially from you."

He leaves, and I shower and change.

I expect to find Vander Zee outside the locker room, waiting to shred me, but it's Tally leaning against the wall, eyes red.

"Kitten." I reach for her.

"Don't." She holds up a hand. "No pet names and no physical contact. We're not having this discussion here. Take me home and explain it there."

She's willing to talk, that's something. "Your place or mine?"

She sighs. "Fee's home tonight, so yours."

"Okay." We're silent on the walk to the parking garage. All my words are trapped in my throat. I'm terrified I'm about to lose her. Is that what I deserve? To finally have someone I can see a future with again, only to have it disappear.

The drive home is silent. Painful. I'm afraid I can't fix this.

We reach my building and I park in my spot. Tally doesn't wait for me to open her door. It feels like the space between us is unbreachable as we walk side by side to the elevator. She tucks herself in a corner, arms wrapped around her body.

We arrive at my floor and I let us into my apartment. She turns to me, eyes hard.

"I planned to tell you—"

"I didn't deserve to find out this way." Her voice cracks. "Not at the same time as most of our friends, including your sister. Don't you trust me? Don't you trust anyone?"

"Of course I trust you." I want to close the distance between us, put my arms around her, make her stay.

"That's obviously not true if you couldn't share this part of your past with me. I thought we were starting a future together, Phillip. You were talking about building a cottage in Muskoka. You said you wanted to support me and my career goals, but you don't trust me enough to share this part of you?"

"You're the only person I've let into my heart like this since Fiona." I wish it hurt less to admit it.

"Fiona." She crosses her arms. "That's the first time you've ever said her name. Right now, she feels like the person standing between us."

"I am long over that relationship."

"Really? How can you say you've let me into your heart when this is the first time you've said her name and I'm just learning what she was to you?"

"I've told you about her," I admit.

"This is the high school girlfriend?" Her eyes flare and she rolls her shoulders back. "The one who broke your heart? You gave me pieces, Phillip, not the whole. She wasn't just a long-term girlfriend. You committed yourself to her. You planned to spend your life with her. To be blindsided like this… You had so many opportunities to tell me yourself, so why didn't you?"

"I was protecting you," I explain. "I wanted to tell you when the time was right."

"When was that going to be?"

I give her the answer I've been giving myself this whole

time, and Dred. "You already had so much going on. Dating me was already a stressor for you. I didn't want to add to it."

"And you think somehow this situation isn't stressful?" She dashes away more tears. "Are you sure you were protecting me and not yourself?"

I run an anxious hand through my hair. "I don't want you to leave me."

"And you think I would because you were married at one point?" she presses.

"Your parents are in the middle of a divorce." I don't want her to question my ability to stick it out.

"I know. I'm living through it." She threads her hand through her curls and tips her head up, eyes on the ceiling. "My parents' relationship ended because my dad didn't show up for Mom or our family. He always put us second, but my mother didn't tell him their relationship was broken and needed to be fixed. And maybe my dad should have seen the writing on the wall, but my mom just kept saying everything was fine." Her eyes meet mine, her bottom lip trembling. "You show up, every time, but you do the same thing with me that my mom did with my dad."

"That's not—" I shake my head, not wanting her to draw those kinds of parallels.

"But you do. You've always got it, everything is always great, or good, or you have it handled, but clearly that's not true if we're having this conversation." She takes a steadying breath. "You can't use the excuse that you're protecting me so you don't have to talk to me about the things that hurt you. I don't need you to rescue me all the time. And I don't need you to be the perfect boyfriend."

"I'm far from perfect, Tally. I'm trying to make up for the shit being with me puts you through—"

"—By keeping parts of yourself from me." She shakes her head and wipes away another tear. "I will not repeat history. I can't be in a relationship where we're protecting each other, but we don't communicate out of fear. I want to be your best friend and your lover. I want to be the person you confide in. You want to be my rock, you want me to share all my worries and fears, but you won't do the same. What *really* kept you from telling the truth?"

I lace my fingers behind my neck and hang my head. My throat is tight, my chest the same.

Tally moves into my personal space and settles a shaking hand on my chest. "I have given myself to you completely. You have all of me. You can't just give me the pieces you want and think it will be enough. Why didn't you tell me you were married?"

"She didn't want me," I grind out.

"What part of you didn't she want?" Tally whispers.

"This." I motion to myself. "Me. She didn't want me. She wanted a lifestyle. I fucking loved her. I handed over my heart and she acted like she was doing the same, and then she took it all back," I choke out.

"How? What happened?" Tally's voice is gentle, but unsteady.

"Fuck." I grit my teeth. Shake my head. My stomach is twisted up, my mouth dry. "You won't want me either." And that's what this is really about. Revealing this part of me threatens everything, but if I can't be honest, I'll lose her anyway.

She takes my face in her hands. "I have seen every side of you, Phillip Madden, the good, the bad, and the broken, and that has never stopped me from wanting you. Please let me in. Please have faith in my ability to handle your truth."

There isn't another choice, so I nod. Tally takes my hand and guides me to the couch. She doesn't let go once we're seated, and I'm grateful for the contact.

"This is really hard for me to talk about, Talls. With anyone."

"I know. But I need this from you."

I scrub a hand over my face, choking on the memories I've been running from for years. "Where do you want me to start?"

"What happened to break your faith in love?"

"So many things." I sigh. "We were accepted to different universities, so we broke up at the end of grade twelve. Between the distance and hockey, we knew it wouldn't work. It hurt, but it made sense."

She nods. "What brought you back together?"

"She moved back in my fourth year, and we reconnected. She'd been part of my life before the scouts and the promise of a contract after I graduated."

"You had history."

"We did," I agree. "And you know what it's like in university."

"It's a lot of fun when you're a hockey player," Tally says without judgment.

"After three years, I'd had enough. I wanted…someone I could trust, and I thought Fiona was that person." I exhale the agony of what comes next. "I didn't want distance between us again. There were restrictions with my housing because it was connected to the university, but I learned if we were married, the problem would be solved."

"But why keep it a secret?"

"Our parents would have wanted us to wait, and her parents would have wanted her to move home. I knew my mind. I was in it with her. I thought she felt the same."

Tally's eyes hold deep sadness. "But she didn't?"

I shake my head. "The scouts were all over me. I was so excited. We were planning this life. I thought I had it all figured out."

"What happened after you got married?"

"Things were good for a couple of months. She didn't have a job yet because we thought it made more sense for her to wait until we knew where I'd end up." I put a hand on my leg to keep my knee from bouncing, as the memories bring up old anxiety. "She didn't grow up the same way I did. Her parents helped her with tuition. She had her own car in high school. They were comfortable. She was used to having things."

"And you weren't," Tally finishes for me.

"Not at all. And especially not in university. The pros are a long shot for most of the guys on the team. Maybe a couple will get called up every year. Some guys make it and choke. Some guys play a few years and end up back on a farm team. I didn't know where I'd land. I had promise, but I could injure myself and be out of the game like that." I snap my fingers. "Fiona was spending money we didn't have yet. She racked up credit card debt, took out loans. She knew how hard my life was growing up, but she had a YOLO attitude." I lick my lips. "We started fighting a lot. Every day there would be another purchase. My grades started to slip. I had a few bad games. I was under a lot of stress."

"Of course you were, that's a lot of pressure to put on you," Tally says gently.

I nod, remembering the day things ended. "One day I came home from practice, and her bags were packed. She told me this wasn't what she signed on for. That she didn't want to be trapped in a marriage where she was monitored all the time. She didn't want me anymore and that the only thing I was good for was money and sex."

"I'm so sorry, Phillip. What a horrible thing to tell someone you're supposed to love," the ache in her voice matches the one in my chest.

We were in the middle of the season. Midterms were around the corner. I was devastated. My entire future was suddenly upended. "I didn't want to start my career with that hanging over me. I talked to a lawyer, had an NDA written up, and I basically signed over my first-year salary to erase the mistake." And then spent the better part of a decade avoiding any kind of connection out of fear I'd give my heart to the wrong person again.

Tally is shrouded in sadness. "You had to do all of it alone, without support. All of these years. That's so heavy to hold on your own. Why not tell your family? Why keep it from everyone?"

"I just wanted to bury it." I felt like a fucking idiot for not seeing it. The woman I gave my heart to hadn't seen any value in me as a person. It shattered me. "I didn't want to spend my entire hockey career living it down. But then I made it so much worse." I sigh, and force myself to continue. "After the divorce, I didn't trust my instincts, and I didn't trust women to want me for anything other than my fame and money. I didn't want to hurt, so I drowned myself in pleasure, and I splashed it all over the internet as a fuck-you to Fiona. I wanted her to believe I'd moved on, and she didn't matter."

"You were in a lot of pain."

"So much. I didn't ever want to hurt like that again." I let my eyes fall closed and bring Tally's hand to my cheek, pressing it to my skin. "I have so much baggage and so many scars, Tally." What if all my unhealed wounds infect her, too? What if I'm intrinsically flawed? "I didn't want you to see the same things in me."

Tears track down her cheeks. I hate that I'm responsible for making her feel this way again. "You didn't protect either of us by keeping this secret from me. I know this hurts you, but it hurts me too. I need you to keep letting me in. How would you feel if I always told you what you wanted to hear? If I said everything was fine, but really it wasn't?"

"Not good."

"Exactly. You can't ask me to share myself and not do the same. There's no balance in that. How can we be partners if you hide your feelings from me?"

She's right about all of it. I have been protecting myself,

hiding feelings behind fear. Telling her everything is fine so she doesn't worry. But if I'm not vulnerable with her, how can I ask her to do the same? "I didn't want to give you a reason to leave me."

Her sadness makes my chest ache. "Sharing your painful secrets won't make me leave, Phillip." She skims the edge of my jaw with gentle fingers. "But keeping me in the dark, placating me, not showing me all of you unbalances us."

"I get it. I see it. I'm so sorry." I kiss the palm of her hand. "Please stay tonight." It's a selfish request. She probably needs time to process, but I'm terrified if I let her go, she'll have time to think it through and decide she's done with me.

"Phillip." Her eyes slide closed.

"I know you're hurt and upset. I know I've fucked up." *I love you, don't leave me.* "Please keep me," I whisper.

A tear tracks down her cheek as her eyes flutter open and search mine. She kisses the edge of my mouth. "I'll stay."

CHAPTER 49
TALLY

I'm beyond exhausted the following morning when Phillip drops me off at the dance studio. I'm emotionally wrung out. I don't want to break up with him, but now that I see the pattern, I can't unsee it. I don't want to end up like my parents. I don't want Phillip to think he has to be the perfect boyfriend every moment of every day. I want him to feel as safe with me as I feel with him.

What if he never does?

What if we love each other but he can't be vulnerable with me the way I need him to?

What if we get married and have a family, and it all falls apart?

What if what if what if.

"You going to be okay today?" He has dark circles under his eyes.

"Yeah. I'll manage. Go easy on yourself." No one else will, and I worry about that, too.

"You'll stay off social media?" His jaw works.

"I will. You should let Hemi handle things."

"Yeah." He nods woodenly and sighs. "I'm sorry."

I settle my hand on his cheek and force him to look at me. "Just because we are not okay right now doesn't mean we won't be."

"You'll have time to think," he whispers.

"So will you." It's all too heavy. Like we can't get out from under Phillip's past. Maybe because he's never truly dealt with it. "We will be okay. It will just take time."

He nods, eyes still weighed down with sadness and exhaustion. "I know."

"I have to go." He's clinging to my hand like it's a lifeline. "And you need to talk to Tristan and your sister." It will be a hard morning for both of us. After dance, I have to talk to Fee, Cammie, and Enid, and then my mom is coming over. At least I've already dealt with my dad. He tried to rein his temper in, but my tears and his inability to console me made him angry.

"Can I kiss you?" he asks softly, expression forlorn.

Despite spending last night in his arms, the only kisses were the ones on the back of my neck when he curved his body around mine. "You can."

He slides his hand into my hair, fingers shaking as he leans in and presses his lips gently to mine. He makes a pained sound, and despite the conflict and fear raging inside me, I tilt my head and part my lips. This part is easy with him. We can always fall back on the chemistry. Avoid difficult topics by succumbing to desire. Ironic that he wanted all the connection but couldn't give himself over the way he wanted me to.

He strokes inside, fingers tightening in my hair as he deepens the kiss. It turns from tentative to desperate in a matter of seconds. I want to get lost in this, but I can't. I have responsibilities and so does he. So I pull back. He tries to bring me back to him, but I touch the back of his hand.

"I have to go and so do you."

He presses his forehead to mine, releases a shaky exhale. "Okay. I'll call you later."

"Okay." I extricate myself from his hands, grab my backpack from the floor, and exit the car.

Charles and Arya are already in the studio warming up when I arrive.

"Are you okay?" Charles asks.

"I'm fine." I do not have time for an emotional breakdown.

"I would feel better if you're *not* actually okay," Arya says.

That's enough to turn on the eyeball faucet. They wrap me in a hug from both sides. We might not spend a lot of time together outside of the studio, but we've been dancing together for four years, and we share a strong bond. They don't ask me to explain, or dig for information, they just let me get my feelings out until I'm ready to put them aside and dance.

Rehearsal isn't smooth, but it is a good and necessary distraction. Afterward, I return to my apartment, grateful for the plain black ball cap and hoodie that help make me less identifiable. Exams are on the horizon. I need to study and stay focused.

Fee, Enid, and Cammie meet me at the door and fold me into another group hug.

"This semester has been a roller coaster ride for you," Fee says.

"That's the truth," I agree. The ups and downs have been legendary.

"Are you okay? Are you and Flip okay?" Cammie asks.

"Not really." I understand Phillip's motivations now, and why his past has kept such a tight hold on him all these years. To have the person he loved reduce him to an object would be heart shattering. But my own hurt and fears won't disappear. Now we both need to do triage with our loved ones, again. He has to explain this to his friends and his entire family. He's kept this to himself for a decade. Now it's out in the world and he has no choice but to deal with it.

Fee wrings her hands and glances at Cammie.

"Do you want to talk about it?" Enid asks gently.

"Yeah." I need an impartial sounding board, people who won't be hurt because they didn't know about my boyfriend's secret ex-wife.

We convene in the living room with bottles of Vitamin Water, and I tell them the parts of the story that feel okay to share. Not the personal, private stuff, just the basics.

"Oh wow, I can't believe only Dred knew," Cammie says.

"It's a big secret," Fee agrees.

"It's *why* he did that I'm having the hardest time with." I explain the realization I came to. "He's thoughtful, kind, attentive, we have amazing chemistry, but he wants me to be completely honest and vulnerable with him, and he won't do the same." I dash tears away. "I can get over the fact that he was married, but I can't spend the rest of my life wondering if he's just telling me things are fine because he's too scared to be honest about his feelings." I let my head fall back. "I know my parents' divorce is making this worse."

"I'm so sorry," Cammie says softly.

"You're carrying a lot right now," Fee murmurs.

"It's reasonable that you're overwhelmed," Enid agrees.

"I just need a break from the noise. The media always being in our faces doesn't help." The tears are free flowing today and they're exhausting.

My friends pull me in for another group hug.

"I don't even really have time to fall apart. Exams are almost here. Everything is changing and I'm terrified I'll fuck it all up because all my feelings are made of lava."

"Deep breaths." Fee inhales with me.

"Do you think he can learn how to be open with you about how he feels now that he knows it's a problem?" Cammie asks.

"Last night he was but only because he was forced to be." I can't get out from under the mountain of worries. "I don't want to end up like my parents."

"That won't happen," Enid says quickly.

"Phillip does exactly what my mom did with my dad, though," I whisper.

"But now you know why, and so does he. You won't spend two and a half decades letting him get away with it."

"You're right." I dab at my swollen eyes. "Phillip hasn't just been living up to the fantasy boyfriend I built in my head; he's been exceeding it. But he's human and imperfect, and he has damage."

"At least now you know what it is," Fee says.

"Yeah." She's right. And sitting here stewing about the future isn't helpful. "I think I'm just hypersensitive to all of it because of what's happening with my parents." As if on cue, there's a knock on the door. "And that's my mom."

"We'll be at my place. Just come over when you're ready." They help me to my feet and disappear into Fee's room to grab her backpack while I let my mom in.

She's holding a bag from the Dutch Toko by our house. They have the best selection of dropjes in the city.

"Pars is coming for you!" Fee yells.

I nab him before he can escape. He yowls and writhes. My mom comes in and quickly shuts the door, but not before my cat scratches the hell out of my arm and launches himself off my chest.

And because I'm a hot mess, more tears fall.

Mom drops the bag and hugs me.

I can't hug her back without bleeding on her, so I just rest my head on her shoulder and let her squeeze the sadness out of me.

Eventually she pulls back. "You're really having a rough go, aren't you?"

My arm is bleeding in several places. "Yeah."

She ushers me down the hall. "Let's get those disinfected since Parsnip steps in his own poop."

"Good call." I don't need an infection to go with the rest of the shit heap I call my life at the moment.

Fee, Cammie and Enid pass us in the hall.

"Oh no! What happened?"

"Pars tried to escape."

"Do you need us?"

"We've got it," Mom assures them.

Fee chastises Parsnip as we disappear into my bedroom.

Mom's gaze lands on my Madden body pillow, but she doesn't say anything. I'm too sad to be embarrassed.

She closes the toilet seat and pats the top.

"I can disinfect these," I say.

"I know, but let me be your mom, please."

I take a seat and direct her to the first aid supplies.

"Do you want to talk to me about how you're feeling?" she asks as she wets a washcloth with warm water.

"Sad. Confused. Scared."

She nods. "It's a big secret to keep."

"He kept it from everyone except Dred."

"How do you feel about that?"

"I'm not jealous that she knew and I didn't. His childhood best friend and his family didn't even know. But if I'm his person and he's mine, I need him to share all of himself with me, not just the good parts."

"Did you tell him that?" she asks.

"Yeah. Last night we talked."

"Did that go okay?" She dabs gently at the wounds. They're just surface scratches.

"I think so. It's just...a lot. There's so much going on. My head is so messy," I admit.

"You've had a lot thrown at you the past few months. And you haven't had the luxury of a relationship without interference. They're hard when you're not in the spotlight, but they're infinitely more difficult when everyone else believes they have an opinion that counts." She wets a cotton pad with hydrogen peroxide and applies it to the scratches.

"Is that why you always told Dad everything was fine?" I ask.

She meets my gaze. "It's possible. Your dad's job has always been public and maybe that impacted my choices. But you've grown up in this world. Phillip won't always play professional hockey."

"I know." I roll my bottom lip between my teeth. "The media stuff has been hard, but that's not what I'm most worried about."

"Does the fact that he's divorced scare you?"

"I just…I love him. I've never felt this way before. He has my whole heart. And what if we build this life together and it all falls apart? I don't want that."

"Oh, my sweet girl." Mom smooths her hand over my hair, her expression sad and knowing. "We can't predict the future, but you can take what you've learned, good and bad, from me and your father, and do your best not to make the same mistakes we did."

"I'm trying."

"Does he know how you feel?"

"I haven't told him. I don't know if he feels the same."

"It's hard to put your heart on the line. Especially when it's been broken before. He wouldn't be this scared if he didn't have deep feelings for you."

"I just need him to feel safe enough with me to admit them."

CHAPTER 50
FLIP

Tristan and I are meeting at the Pancake House in a couple of hours, which means I can either stew in my own self-loathing, regret and fear, or I can make a trip to the retirement village. I'm long overdue for a Gurdy visit. I sign in with Jerico at the front desk.

"Boy, you've been a hot topic the last few months," he notes as I scribble my name, who I'm visiting, and my phone number and email on the sheet.

"Yeah."

"Gurdy will be happy to see you're alive. There were some bets floating around about you maybe disappearing and your coach being the reason."

"It's still not out of the question. If I go missing, have them search his house for the murder weapon. But it'll probably be my hockey stick and he'll likely put it through a woodchipper."

"That's oddly specific."

"It was last night's nightmare." I hold my fist out. "Stay cool."

"As a cucumber."

I leave him and go in search of my favorite retirement home

grandma. Mine are long passed, so Gurdy is a beautiful stand-in. I feel shitty that I haven't been keeping up my regular visits.

I find her in the common room, which is typical. Gurdy is a social butterfly and loves being in the middle of all the action. She knows all the tea. Who's dating who, who gave who chlamydia, who the hound dogs are.

"I was wondering when you'd show up." Gurdy holds out her hands and I help her to her feet. She's all of five foot one and could probably fit in one of my pant legs.

Her white hair is permed. Her gnarled fingers soft, the skin thin and delicate. I try to picture Tally as an old lady. She'll have sore feet, and all my joints will ache from hockey. We'll need a hot tub. If she stays. If she doesn't break up with me.

Gurdy doesn't let go of my hand once she's standing. I bend so I can link our arms.

"I'm sorry I've missed a couple of dates."

"You've been busy."

"It's no excuse."

"It's every excuse. You're young and you should be living your life, not hanging out in retirement homes with people who smell like they're two weeks away from being underground."

"I love hanging out with you," I argue. "You have insight and perspective I don't."

"I've had a lot of time to make mistakes."

"What does that say about me since I've been making so many lately?"

"Seems like your mistake was made a long time ago, based on everything I've been reading. Also seems like that ex-wife of yours maybe broke her NDA."

"I don't know that I want to pursue that. It would mean dealing with her again."

"The problem with the skeletons in the closet is that eventually those doors get opened and they fall out."

"I'm learning that the hard way."

Gurdy makes a hard right. "Your girlfriend is beautiful."

"Isn't she stunning?" My heart swells and then aches.

"Is her heart just as beautiful?"

"Yeah. She's incredible. I'm afraid she's going to leave me," I admit.

She makes a noise and hands me her key. I unlock the door and hold it open for her. She heads for the table where the cribbage board is already set up. Like she was expecting me. "There's some contraband scotch in the bottom cupboard. Get out two glasses." She waves to her tiny kitchen and sits in one of the cushioned chairs. "What makes her incredible?"

"Everything. She's smart, driven, talented, compassionate, fun."

"You love her."

"I love her."

"But you didn't tell her about the ex-wife."

"I didn't tell her about the ex-wife," I agree.

"Because you were scared."

"Yeah." I pull out two lowball glasses and find the scotch—it's dusty—and pour us both a shot.

"That's a weak-ass pour. Do better."

I add more. Then another splash when she purses her lips. I also pour us both glasses of water and set them all on the table, then join her. The chair is tiny and groans under my weight.

"What are you scared of?" Gurdy asks.

"I'm a headache. I've brought Tally nothing but drama."

"To be fair, Tally knew there would be drama. She's the coach's daughter." She raises a pointed, drawn-on eyebrow.

"She can't escape my past and neither can I," I say.

"Stop trying to run away from your shadow, Phillip. It's attached to you, it won't leave you alone because it's part of you. You still haven't answered the question. What are you afraid of?"

I pick up the deck of cards and shuffle them. "Repeating history."

"Is Tally anything like your ex, apart from them both being women?"

"No. They're nothing alike." I set the deck between us and she cuts, then I cut and we show our cards. "Your deal."

She shuffles the deck. "So why would you believe that?"

"Because I'm the common denominator. I'm the unchanged variable. What if six months down the line the shine wears off and she decides I'm not the one for her?"

"What if six months from now it's the opposite? What if you're exactly right for each other? What if you're hiding all of her favorite parts of you? Everyone makes mistakes, Phillip. What if you're making the biggest one by not giving her the true version of you?"

"I should have come to see you sooner."

She waves the comment away. "You were busy wooing your future wife."

"I'm so in love with her."

"Have you told her yet?"

I glance up from my cards. They're shit.

"Phillip." She puts two cards in her crib and gives me her full attention. "What the hell are you waiting for?"

"The right time," I mumble.

"Is that the same reason you didn't tell her about the ex-wife?"

I purse my lips and play a six.

"Fifteen for two." She lays a nine. "Stop sabotaging your own future."

"Twenty-four for two." I match it with my own nine. "I need to make sure we're stable before I put it out there."

She plays a seven and takes two points. "Nut up, bro."

I almost spray my scotch on the cards. It's good stuff. "Who taught you that saying?"

"Nate and Essie were here last week. They brought his younger brother. The young Stiles. He has secrets, that one."

"You think?"

"Oh yeah. Dark cloud over that boy. Looks like he's afraid of hugs, and also desperately needs one. But really, Phillip, put your big boy pants on and tell her how you feel. If she's the one for you, she'll be able to handle all the downs, just give her a chance. And yourself."

Gurdy beats me three times, not for my lack of trying. I walk her to lunch and hang out with her friends for a bit before I make my way to the Pancake House to meet with Tristan. I know he won't stay mad at me, but he's married to my sister, so that means he'll have to handle her emotions over the secret I've been keeping all these years.

He's already there when I arrive, two beers on the table. He shifts in his seat as I take mine. It's a practiced move so both our legs fit under the table.

"How's Rix?" We've been messaging, but I haven't seen her since last night. We don't have practice until later, which is when I'll have to face the rest of the team.

"Okay. She'll be here in about forty-five minutes, but she had to go into the kitchen this morning to get out meals for a few of the guys." He pushes a beer toward me. "How are you?"

"Wishing I made different choices at the moment."

Rainbow, our usual server, stops by to take our order. Tristan gets the hungry man, and I order a regular breakfast because my appetite is trash.

He waits until we're alone before he digs in. "That's a big secret to hold onto."

I've hurt him. Again. I complicated our relationship when he was traded to Toronto and moved in with me. We're okay now, but we'll never be the same. Not just because he's married to my sister, but because we crossed some lines that can't be erased. It altered our friendship, and I hope this new revelation doesn't change it in another irreparable way.

"Telling people meant owning the mistake. She ruined me for a long time."

He nods slowly. "Did she leave or did you?"

"She did." I roll the bottle between my hands. I tell him what happened, how it happened, why she decided to leave, and what I gave up to get her out of my life.

"Shit, man." Tristan drags a hand through his hair and shakes his head. "That's…she's a terrible person. I mean, I wasn't ever really a huge fan in high school, and when you broke up again, I was kind of relieved, but I didn't realize it had been this serious."

"I didn't want it to be the thing I was dealing with at the beginning of my career," I explain.

"Yeah, man. There's enough pressure without that noise, too."

Rainbow drops off our meals. She's chipper as usual and probably doesn't concern herself with the hockey gossip.

"This just explains…a lot." Tristan accordions a slice of bacon into his mouth and chews thoughtfully.

He doesn't need to elaborate. I already know what *a lot* encompasses. "I'm sorry I didn't tell you, Tris."

"Look, I know you have it coming at you from all sides, and everyone will have feelings and opinions, but we were in different cities for a lot of years before we ended up here. I can't even be upset that you told Dred because it's fucking Dred. She's a damn saint and I'm sure she compelled it out of you over Battleship. Dredging up the past sucks, and you have it done to you often. You're forgiven, Flip. For whatever you think you've done wrong, let it go, okay? We're good."

He means it. "I appreciate it, Tris. More than you can know." Now I just need my sister's forgiveness. And my parents', my teammates', and my coach's. It's an upward climb.

Rix slides into the booth next to me like she was summoned. "I'm so glad you're not dead."

"Vander Zee might still take me out." I wrap my arm around my sister. "I'm sorry."

She tips her head up and regards me with empathy. "You must have had a good reason to keep such a big secret for so long." I start to tell her the same story I told Tristan, but she puts her hand on my arm. "What caused it to fall apart?"

"She didn't want me, she wanted the life I could afford her."

Sadness washes over her. "I'm so sorry you had to carry that hurt with you for so long on your own. You can let it go now, though."

All this fear has been weighing me down, holding me back.

I keep expecting everyone's anger, but all I get is compassion.

Maybe I should extend a little of my own to myself.

CHAPTER 51

TALLY

I'm anxious. Bringing my pro-hockey boyfriend who plays for my dad's team to family dinner was already going to be awkward, but post ex-wife reveal, it's unlocked a new level of anxiety. Everything between me and Phillip feels off. I'm used to him being doting, but all our interactions seem steeped in uncertainty. We're walking on eggshells. I'm hyper-alert and hypersensitive to everything he says and does. Is he being honest? Is he protecting me? How does he feel? How do I feel?

It's only been a couple of days, and he leaves on an away series tomorrow. Spending the evening under my parents' microscope isn't what I want, but there's no getting out of it, so here we are. I run my hands down my thighs and take a deep breath as we pull into the driveway of my childhood home. It's not just the Phillip situation weighing on me. My family isn't a whole anymore, but we're all together in this space, and it makes me feel even more unbalanced.

"You okay?" Phillip shifts the car into park.

I consider lying, but then I'm doing what I've accused him

of, and what's the point in that? "No. I'm nervous. They're going to grill you, and it probably won't be an easy dinner."

Phillip squeezes my hand. "I've been grilled plenty. I can handle it."

"This is a little different than the media, though," I hedge.

"It is, but I want to put your mom at ease. It'll be okay." He kisses the back of my hand. "Your mom is important to you, and you're very important to her. I've already made a lot of bad impressions, so tonight I'd like to make some good ones," he admits. "What are you most worried about?"

"I want my family to like you." It's not nearly that simple, but it's all I can give him right now. I need them not to make this harder than it already is, and Fenna can be very blunt sometimes.

"Me too." He leans over and kisses my cheek. "I think your sister is watching us through the window."

I spot her peeking through the living room curtains. "We should go in."

Phillip grabs the bottle of wine for dinner and the flowers for my mom before we exit the car.

I knock, but let myself in, calling out as we leave our shoes at the front door. Hubert, the rescue dog they recently adopted, barrels down the steps and bounces around. Mom follows, commanding him to sit. He immediately complies, looking up at her as she pets his head.

Phillip smiles, but it's not the one he gives the media, it's a little nervous and hopeful. "Hi, Mrs. Vander Zee, thank you so much for inviting me over. These are for you, and this is for dinner." He holds out the flowers and the wine.

"How very thoughtful, these are lovely." Mom takes the flowers and wine. "Thank you. It's nice to finally meet you outside of the news outlets and the hockey games."

I give my mom a look. She ignores it. Phillip runs his fingers down the back of my arm.

"I'm sure you have a lot of questions and I'm happy to answer them."

Mom gives him her practiced *yes you will* smile.

My stomach churns with fresh nerves as she guides us through the living room to the kitchen.

Fenna is waiting expectantly, and Ties has his phone in his hand. He slips it in his pocket as we enter the room.

"Hey." Phillip raises a hand. "You must be Fenna and Ties."

"You're Flip Madden," Fenna says.

Ties elbows her.

"What?" Fenna rolls her eyes at our brother. "He is."

"You don't have to use his last name," Ties mutters.

"Everyone does it with Connor Grace," Phillip offers.

Dad comes in, wearing an apron that reads GRILLING IS MY SUPERPOWER. "Tally-Bear, when did you and my personal PR nightmare arrive?" I think he means for it to come out as a joke, but his tone lacks humor.

"Why don't we pour some drinks and get comfortable in the living room?" Mom suggests.

"I'll open the wine!" And possibly just add a straw to the bottle.

"There's a bottle of white in the fridge," Mom says.

Phillip opens the red while I retrieve the white wine, and we fill glasses and move to the living room.

Fenna seats herself in the chair closest to Phillip. "You're thirty. I read that in an article the other day."

To his credit, he doesn't even flinch. "That's correct."

I have no idea where she's going with this since Phillip's age hasn't been a secret the entire time we've been dating.

"And you were married when you were Tally's age," she tacks on.

"Fen," I caution.

"What? It's true." Fenna leans in. "Why did you get divorced, anyway?"

"Seriously, Fen." I wish I could die.

"It's okay. I know everyone has questions." He stretches his arm across the back of the couch. "I thought my ex and I wanted the same things out of life, but I was wrong."

Before Fenna can lob another question at Phillip, Mom interjects. "Fenna, honey, why don't you set up your cello in the music room so you can play for us before dinner?"

"Okay!"

"Ties, help her please," Mom directs.

Ties sighs but leaves the room.

"Fenna can be quite direct," Mom explains. "I'm sure this is a sensitive subject, but I'm also sure you understand that as Tally's parents, we have some concerns about the secretive nature of your previous marriage."

"We're adults and this is our relationship, not yours to manage."

"It wouldn't matter how old you are, Tally. We'd still be worried, and we would still have questions five years from now if you brought home someone who had been previously married and failed to disclose it," Dad says. "You can understand how concerning it is that you've been on my team this entire time and no one, not even Stiles, knew about this."

"It's okay, Tally, I'd rather get things out in the open now." Phillip squeezes my hand.

Phillip explains, concisely, what happened with Fiona and why they divorced. He's had to tell this story multiple times over the past few days. It's hard for me to hear it again, so I can't imagine it's easy for him either. "I realize my keeping it a secret wasn't good for anyone, least of all, Tally, but it wasn't done out of malice." He tucks me into his side, maybe sensing my unease, or maybe it's because of his own.

"Why keep it a secret at all," Dad presses.

"It was a very difficult time in my life, and I didn't want to drag it with me into the present." He runs his thumb along my shoulder. "I always planned to tell Tally, but dating me has brought a lot of new attention to her, and I didn't want to add more stress on top of what she was already dealing with this semester. That was a mistake, and one I won't make again."

"Secrets put a lot of strain on a relationship," Mom says.

Dad crosses and uncrosses his legs.

Phillip nods. "I'm not perfect, and I'm learning how to navigate this relationship along with Tally. I don't ever want to blindside her like this again."

I'm overwhelmed, this feels too fresh and like the wrong time to deal with all of this. I don't want to cry in front of my parents, or for this dinner to turn into family therapy time.

Fenna appears with her bow in hand. "You can all come to the music room now."

I'm grateful for the interruption to the interrogation. My head is spinning and so is my stomach. I want everything Phillip is saying to be true, but we haven't had much time to process and it's all been triage. Besides, he'll tell my parents what they want to hear. He might be sincere, but he hasn't had much time to prove he can be honest and open about his feelings with me.

We move to the music room, and Fenna plays one of her favorite pieces flawlessly, which is always the way.

Afterward, everyone helps put dinner on the table.

Phillip asks my brother and sister questions about school, and the conversation is surface and light post living room grill session.

"How are you feeling about exams and your upcoming showcase?" Mom asks.

"I feel good."

"You had some problems earlier in the semester with studio practice time, didn't you?" Mom presses. "Did that issue resolve itself?"

"Um." I pause with my fork halfway to my mouth. Everyone's eyes are on me. Including Phillip's. Which is the moment I realize I never told them about the studio. "Sort of."

Mom's eyes narrow. "What does that mean?"

Phillip answers for me. "I rented a studio close to campus for Tally and her troupe so she wouldn't have to struggle for practice time."

The table goes silent.

I can't look at my boyfriend as his knee presses against mine under the table.

"You rented my daughter a dance studio?" Dad asks.

"It's leased until the end of June. There were issues with one of the main studios and I wanted to make it easy for Tally," Phillip explains. "All the other available spaces required a commute."

"That was generous of you." Mom's eyes bounce between me and Phillip.

"It was a stressor I could alleviate." He kisses my temple.

My parents seem to ease up after that, which is a relief, and the rest of dinner is a little less tense. After we clear the table, Mom follows me to the cold cellar to retrieve dessert.

"Why didn't you tell us about the studio?" Mom asks.

I shrug. "I didn't want to stress you and Dad out. He'd just moved into the apartment, things were…unsteady. Then Phillip solved the problem, and I didn't need to make it yours and Dad's to worry about or handle."

"He really cares about you," Mom says gently.

"I really care about him, too."

She tips her head, eyes roving over my face. "Are you two okay?"

I roll my bottom lip between my teeth. If I voice my worries, I'll break down again, and I don't want to return to the dining table with puffy eyes. "Yeah. I think so. I was stressed about tonight."

Mom hugs me. "He's devoted to you."

"I know." But is that enough?

"I'm sorry my relationship with your father is making things difficult for you."

"It's just everything." I wrap my arms around her and absorb the comfort, wishing I felt stronger and steadier.

"You've been through a lot over the past six months, honey. Be gentle with yourself and with him, okay?"

"I'm trying."

We hug it out before we bring dessert upstairs.

Phillip moves to my side the moment I'm back in the kitchen, offering his assistance. I desperately crave the contact and tuck myself under his arm.

Fenna rushes to the freezer, then props her hands on her hips. "We're out of ice cream."

"That's my fault." Ties grimaces and rubs the back of his neck. "I could walk to the store."

"The corner store doesn't have the good stuff," Fenna points out.

Hubert, the new family dog, appears in the hallway, carrying his leash, tail wagging excitedly.

Mom and Dad have a brief, silent conversation and it makes my heart hurt all over that despite everything, they couldn't make it work.

"Why don't you go pick some up from the grocery store, and your dad and I will take Hubert for a quick walk," Mom suggests.

"I'm going with you to get ice cream because you always get the wrong kind." Fenna heads for the front door.

"You mean I always get the kind I like instead of the kind you like," Ties says, following her.

"Phillip and I will get the table ready," I offer.

I'm sure my mom is doing this to give us a few minutes to

ourselves, which is kind of her, but I'm worried I'll break down the moment they leave.

Two minutes later, Phillip and I are alone in the house.

He moves to stand in front of me, hands sliding up my arms, palms coming to rest against the side of my neck. I need the contact. Crave it. He's everything, and I'm so freaking scared of how I feel and how he feels and all the things we haven't said.

"Did your mom say something?"

"Not something bad."

"Why do you look like you're on the verge of tears, then?" His brow is furrowed, his eyes slightly frantic.

"Can we have a serious talk later, because if we have one now, I'll start crying and Fenna will call me out for having puffy eyes, and it'll be embarrassing."

He swallows thickly. "Are you breaking up with me?"

"No." *I love you. I'm head over heels for you. I'm so deep it terrifies me.* "That's the last thing I want. It's just been intense, and I wanted tonight to go well, and for it not to be an interrogation and make it even harder."

He wraps his arms around me and pulls me against his chest, lips at my temple. "We're almost through it. When we get home, I'll take care of you, okay? We can check another fantasy off the list."

An idea hits. Is it a good one? Probably not, but I also don't want to get up in my head or for Phillip to ask more prying questions and end up in tears before dessert. I glance toward the stairs leading to the second-floor bedrooms. "What if we could check a box on my fantasy list off now?" I swallow down the anxiety. I desperately need the connection with him.

He nods slowly, eyes darkening. "How long will your parents be gone?"

"At least fifteen minutes."

"Ties and Fenna?"

"Probably the same." Fenna always needs to walk through the snack aisles even if we're only there for one item.

"Do you want to show me your bedroom, kitten?"

I nod, body already warming with the promise of intimacy.

"Take me there." He curves his hand around mine and I guide him to the stairs.

My heart is racing, my mouth already dry. Phillip in my bedroom is one of my top five ever fantasies. I want it to make us better, to erase the uncertainty eddying between us.

My name is still fixed to the door in vinyl letters. Nothing in here has changed since I went away to university, but everything about me and my family has.

I step inside and flick on the light. I try to see it through Phillip's eyes, but it's impossible. Posters of my favorite dancers adorn the walls, along with a collage of Terror photos from my high school internship. This room belongs to a past version of me. One where my family was still intact, and I believed my parents' love was forever.

"This is exactly what I would have expected from high school you." Phillip's gaze skips over the space and lands on my bed. It's a twin, the comforter dance-themed, like the rest of my room.

"I'm that predictable, huh?"

"Not at all, but this matches the version of you I knew back then." He pulls me toward the bed, gaze moving to the Terror collage, which is positioned so I had a perfect view of it while lying in bed.

"There's a lot of me in those photos," he observes, lips ghosting the edge of my jaw.

"I've always liked looking at you." I tip my head and close my eyes, trying to focus on the feel of his hands, and not get lost in worries or memories. "Especially when I was alone at night." Part of me wants to hold back the way he does, but the admission pours out of me, "You were responsible for my first orgasm."

"I'll be responsible for your last one, too." He spins me around, my back to his chest, erection pressed against the small of my back. "If your dad catches me up here, he'll end me."

"He'll never know." Anxiety makes my voice tremble. I focus on sensation, on the quiet of the house, on the memory of wanting him exactly as we are now.

"He can't. He'll take you away from me if he does." He eases a hand under my sweater, sliding up to cup my breast. The other trails down until he reaches the hem of my skirt. I shiver when his fingers graze bare skin, the fabric bunching as it rises.

I moan when his fingers skim my clit.

"Shh, shh." He kisses my cheek. "I need you to stay nice and quiet." He cups between my legs. "Can you do that? Can you be my good girl, Tally?"

"I'll be quiet," I promise.

"I'll be so good to you," he murmurs. "So good for you."

Something feels…off. Like we're wearing masks and not quite present in this moment. I push the fears aside. He's doing this for me, giving me the fantasy I've always dreamed of.

He walks us forward until my knees hit the edge of the mattress. "On your stomach, kitten."

I stretch out across my comforter, eyes on Phillip's reflection in the mirror on my closet door. His belt buckle clinks as he unfastens it with one hand and flips my skirt up with the other. His nostrils flare, and he sucks in a breath. I'm wearing a thong. White with little pink hearts on it.

I bite my lip and watch his reflection as I press my hips up. His pupils dilate as he takes in my bare ass.

He tucks one finger under the thin string and drags it down the divide. "So fucking perfect, and you're all mine, aren't you?"

I nod, nipples tight, body humming with need.

"Say it, Tally." He slips a finger between my thighs. "Tell me you're mine."

"I'm yours," I moan as he pushes inside.

He withdraws immediately and slaps my ass cheek. Not hard, but it startles me.

I shriek, and suddenly he's blanketing my body with his, lips at my ear, voice shaking as he growls, "I can't fuck you if you can't stay quiet, Tally."

"I'll be good."

He kisses my cheek. "Promise me."

"I promise."

"Good girl. You're so fucking sweet." He lifts his head, eyes meeting mine in the mirror across the room. "Promise you'll always be mine." The same desperation I feel is echoed in his voice and his gaze.

"I'll always be yours," I whisper.

I turn my head, trying to reach his lips, but like everything else, he's just out of reach.

"I want to feel you." He bites the shell of my ear, cock rubbing against me. "I need you."

"I need you, too," I whimper and press my ass against him.

He slips a hand under my cheek and turns until his lips touch the corner of my mouth as the head nudges my entrance. "Tell me if this isn't okay. Tell me if you're not okay with this."

It takes me a moment to catch up. He wants to go bare. And I'm so frantic for any piece of him, that I'll take whatever he's willing to give. "It's okay. I just need you in me."

He groans with relief as he pushes inside. Filling me. Pressing me into the mattress as he bottoms out. "You feel so fucking good, kitten. You always feel so fucking good." He nuzzles my neck. "I can't get enough. I'll never have enough."

I bite the inside of my cheek and whimper softly.

Phillip tips my chin and presses his cheek to mine as our eyes meet in the reflection across the room. "Your parents will be back any minute."

I clench and shudder as he rolls his hips, fear and pleasure merging.

"You're being so good." He kisses my cheek. "You feel so good." His hips pull back and he slides back in. "I want you to come for me."

"Oh God." I grip the comforter and bite my lip to stifle another moan.

"And as soon as they walk through the door, I'll fill you with my cum. I wish I could watch it drip down the inside of your pretty legs, but then I'd never get to do it again," he laments. "I'd never get to keep you if they knew the truth." He pumps into me, the bed creaking with every rough thrust. "You're not their good girl anymore, are you, kitten?" He kisses my neck. "You're mine."

It feels like neither of us is really here. We're bodies moving, panted breaths, desperately seeking a connection we can't hold on to.

I say the words and try to make them true. "I'm yours."

"Mine." He props himself up on one arm, the other sliding under my hip. He slips his hand inside my panties and rubs circles on my sensitive clit. "Tell me again. Say it, Tallulah."

"Only yours," I whisper.

"All of you. Every part." His lips brush my cheek, hot eyes locked on mine. "Any second now, they'll walk through the door."

"Phillip," I whimper.

"I need you to come for me. I need you," he begs.

My stomach tightens, and sensation rockets through me as I unravel. Phillip covers my mouth with his, swallowing my moan. His hips slap my ass, hard and fast, the bed groaning with the force. If they walk through the door now, they'll know. He pushes in deep and goes rigid above me, a snarl of satisfaction humming against my lips.

He lies there for a moment, his full weight pressing me into the bed. The sound of Hubert barking outside my window, which faces the front of the house, has him quickly withdrawing.

I feel the emptiness everywhere. He grabs tissues from the nightstand and gently wipes between my thighs. I roll onto my back as the code is punched into the door.

He quickly tucks himself into his pants and fastens them. "I'll go down, take a minute to catch your breath."

He kisses me on the cheek and leaves me lying on my childhood bed, that emptiness spreading through me. I wanted this to bring us closer, but it feels like it's cleaved us in two instead.

CHAPTER 52
TALLY

It was a close call with my parents. Phillip made it to the kitchen before they walked through the door, but we didn't set the table for dessert and I needed a minute to collect myself before I came downstairs. I brought my high school photo albums, and hoped it was a good enough decoy.

Mom and Dad seemed a little preoccupied, though, so if they noticed the vibe between me and Phillip, no one mentioned it.

My exams start in two days, so I should have Phillip drive me back to my apartment after dinner, but he leaves tomorrow morning for an away series, so I want to sleep next to him tonight.

"Are you okay?" Phillip asks on the way back to his place.

"I don't know," I answer honestly. "The whole night was… awkward?"

"Should I have handled things differently?" Anxiety seeps into his tone. "Was it the sex?"

"The sex was part of it. I wanted it, but it felt like it happened and we weren't really there." I wring my hands. "I wanted to feel closer to you, but I didn't." I don't want him to leave on an away series with a chasm between us.

"There's a lot going on. With us, with your parents, with school and dance." He covers my hand with his.

"I know." I want things to be stable, but I don't know how to achieve that.

We arrive at his place and take the elevator to his apartment. It's not even ten, but I'm exhausted, and his flight leaves early tomorrow morning, so we get ready for bed. At least there's comfort in the domestic routine.

He gives me privacy so I can use the bathroom on my own. My favorite tumbler sits on the nightstand on my side, and Phillip is perched on the edge of the mattress, shirtless, wearing his typical pajama pants. He reaches for me and I slip my hand in his, letting him pull me between his thighs.

"I want us to be okay," he says softly.

"I want the same thing." I settle my hands on his shoulders, seeking comfort in the contact. This feels like the most natural part of the entire day. I wrap my arms around him and tuck my face against his neck. For a minute we just breathe.

"I'm terrified of losing you," he admits.

"Same," I whisper. "I just need you to keep being honest with me, even when it's hard. Especially then."

"I know. I'm working on getting better at it. I'm sorry I've made things so difficult for us."

"You're trying and that's what matters." I want to be able to tell him how I really feel about him, but I need it to be because we're in a good place and not desperate to connect.

We climb into bed and he tucks me against him. I want the physical closeness to be enough, but the emotional distance is an uncrossable bridge, and I don't know how to fix it.

I wake alone the next morning. Phillip had an early flight, so it shouldn't be a surprise, but I sort of hoped he would wake me up and say goodbye.

I roll over, my chest already tight with his absence. I rub it, hoping to ease the ache, then glance at the nightstand. Sitting next to my phone is a flower made out of pipe cleaner and a note.

> Tally,
> I miss you already.
> I'll message you when I'm on the ground and settled in the hotel.
> Xo
> Yours,
> Phillip

I run my fingers over the lines. I want him to write the words I feel in my heart. I leave the warmth of his bed and get dressed. The flower and note are tucked in my bag, as well as the hoodie that smells like him from the front hall. I pour myself a mug of coffee—he brewed me a fresh pot before he left—and take the subway back to campus. I get in half an hour of study time, so at least it's not time wasted.

I meet Arya and Charles at the theater for our first dress rehearsal slot. It does not go seamlessly. "I'm sorry I'm so off. This is all me." I kept flubbing the routine, and every screw up feels insurmountable. We only made it through once without any issues, but even then, it still wasn't perfect.

"It's okay. We have two more rehearsal sessions on stage to get it all down. You're under a lot of pressure, Tally. We will get it right and everything will be fine," Arya assures me.

"You're right. We have time. We know this routine." I'm so on edge, struggling to keep it together.

I drop them off at their apartments, but have to circle back to the studio because I forgot to leave the key in the lockbox for my classmates. Normally I'm not this scattered. Once I'm home, I settle in to study for my written exams. My marks aren't quite as strong as I would like, so again, the pressure is on. The swirling anxiety over how Phillip and I left things makes it tough to focus.

I drink chamomile tea and do a calming meditation, but I'm so wiped out from the stress of it all that I fall asleep and don't wake until midnight.

The apartment is dark and quiet. My door is open enough for Parsnip to come and go as he pleases. He's currently lying on my Phillip pillow, paw over his eyes.

I reach for my phone and see that I missed three video calls and several messages from Phillip while I slept.

FLIP

> Landed. I'll message when I'm settled in the hotel.

> Had to get on the ice basically right away. Sorry it's been a bit. How are you? Did you get the flower?

> Everything okay? Message when you get this.

> Cammie told me you were passed out hard with a textbook on your chest. I'll try to message before your exam tomorrow. I sent over some East Side's in case you need study fuel. Heading to bed because we're on the ice early tomorrow.

The missed opportunity feels like an omen that sends me back into a worry spiral. Little things feel huge. Once I'm calm enough, I heat up some of the food he had delivered while reviewing notes. It's not exceptionally productive since I'm still drowsy from my four-hour nap. After my exceptionally late dinner, I try to go back to sleep, but I'm wide awake. Staring at the ceiling won't help, so I study until three in the morning, then force myself to close my eyes. My exam is at eight thirty, and I can't risk conking out in the middle of it because I pulled an all-nighter. Besides, I have dance practice in the afternoon and more studying in the evening for exam number two. I set my alarm for seven thirty, and toss and turn for a while. The last time I look at the clock, it's just after five.

"Talls?" Fee shakes on my shoulder. "You have to wake up! Your exam is in less than half an hour."

I sit up in a rush. "What? I set my alarm for seven-thirty." The clock on my nightstand doesn't lie, though. It's after eight.

I throw off my covers. "Fuck. It takes fifteen minutes to walk across campus."

"What if you drive?"

"Parking will eat whatever time I save."

"I'll drive you over. Get dressed, and I'll make you a coffee and bagel."

"Fuck!" I'm so sick of being on the emotional ledge.

"It's okay. You have time. You won't be late."

I shove the panic down, throw on jogging pants and a hoodie, brush my teeth, pull my hair into a topknot, and ignore my puffy eyes. There's nothing that can be done.

Fee meets me at the door with coffee, a bagel, writing implements, and my phone, which I apparently forgot in my room. "Deep breath, you'll be okay."

She opens the door and we nearly trip over a takeout bag from my favorite bakery. Fee thwarts a Parsnip escape, grabs the bag, and ushers me down the hall.

"Do you want to talk or will that just make it worse?" Fee asks.

We hop in my car and I check my alarm. "I set it for seven thirty p.m. instead of a.m."

"It's happened to all of us. You'll be okay," she reassures me.

"I'm so glad you were there to wake me up."

"Me, too." She thumbs over her shoulder to the backseat where the breakfast takeout sits untouched. "You should send Flip a message."

"Crap. Thanks."

I quickly message Phillip while Fee drives across campus. She drops me at the back of the building. "I'm going to park in the closest lot and drop a pin so you can find the car after your exam." She passes me the second set of keys.

"What about you?"

"It's a fifteen minute walk back to the apartment, and I'll stop and say hi to Enid on the way. Good luck this morning."

"Thank you." I kiss her on the cheek and rush inside, making it with only a minute to spare.

I'm scattered, and I can't get out from under the mountain of worry. I have to rush through the essay question at the end, and I don't have time to go back and check my multiple choice. At least half a dozen are guesses. This course was already borderline for honor roll, and I can't really afford for this mark to slip.

I have new messages from Phillip asking how my exam went. I desperately want to lie, but know I can't. So I reply with honesty and tell him I think the exam went okay, then head to the studio, grateful all over that Fee left me the car. I'm in no better form today than I was yesterday, and the worry on Arya and Charles's faces when I get the sequence wrong for the third time in a row spikes my already out of control anxiety. I don't have time for a break down.

"I don't want to come across as like, mom energy, but have you eaten today?" Arya asks.

"Of cour—" I stop, bite my lip. Fee made me a bagel, but I left it on the dash. And the breakfast Phillip sent is still in the back seat of my car.

"Let's get something from the café, even a muffin and juice would be good, so your sugar isn't crashing," Charles suggests.

"I have food in my car. I'll run out and get it." The bag from Phillip is full of all my favorite things, including fresh squeezed juice. I'm in much better form and far less shaky after I eat. Practice goes better. It's not perfect, but we still have two stage rehearsals left, and that's a comfort.

By the time I get back to my apartment, the guys are already on the ice. This is the last away series of the regular season, and these games will impact where they start the playoffs. If they aren't on the right side of the points, they could end up being out of town during my final showcase of the year.

I heat up my leftover East Side's and settle in for another night of studying. I try to stay focused, but the broken sleep, anxiety, and the adrenaline crash hits hard and I'm struggling to stay awake.

I set my timer for twenty minutes and close my eyes. I crash hard, my timer going off for a full two minutes before I rouse. But at least I didn't sleep through the game. Which the Terror lose.

The weight of everything comes crashing down. Exams, my final performance, my family, my relationship with Phillip.

I know better than to text him when I'm elevated, but my phone is already in my hand and my worries spill out of my fingertips.

CHAPTER 53

FLIP

We were tied until the last thirty seconds of the game. And then fucking Vegas stole the puck and game. It shouldn't feel like the kiss of death in this series, but everything good seems to be slipping through my fingers. The loss means we have to work that much harder over the next three games. And I hate that I'm away while my girlfriend is writing exams.

I avoid answering interview questions, aware they'll bring up my ex-wife and my relationship with Tally because they can't fucking help themselves.

Vander Zee and Forrest-Hammer give us a post-game talk before we change and head back to the hotel. I just want to talk to my girlfriend, see how her first exam went and make sure we're okay.

But when I finally have a chance to check my phone, the messages make my stomach sink. She almost missed her exam this morning.

TALLY

Are you okay? Is the team okay? It's only one game.

You can still be home for my showcase.

Not that this is about me.

I don't know how to make this better. I'm so sorry about the fame.

I just miss you. It's so hard to focus and I wish everything had gone differently after dinner at my parents' house.

I don't want to blow up my life in the eleventh hour.

Everything is overwhelming.

You can't be in a relationship with someone who flunked their final semester of university.

I hate being like this.

I just want us to be on the same page, and I don't know if we are, and I feel like I'm barely treading water.

I want to be supportive but I'm such a mess.

I just need to get through exams and then my showcase.

I just need to take something off my plate. It's too full.

Oh my God.

This isn't what you need right now.

Just erase these.

My stomach knots and the feeling that everything good is slipping away grows.

FLIP

What do you need from me?

TALLY

I don't know.

There's a long pause in which the dots appear and disappear several times. *Please don't break up with me.*

TALLY

I'm really overwhelmed. I'm trying to keep it together.

I'm putting too much pressure on you. On us.

I feel like I need to hit pause.

"Fuck." I drop my head and breathe through the ache in my chest. I should have told her how I feel about her before I left. But I didn't want those words to be tainted with fear and uncertainty, and that's where we've been sitting for a while now. I did this to us. To her. To me. I can't lose her but telling her now won't be helpful. I'd only be adding another weight to carry when her focus should be on exams and making it through the end of the semester.

The only thing I can give her is the space she's asking for. I can take myself off her plate temporarily, even though the thought alone eviscerates me. I type the message with shaking fingers.

FLIP

It's okay if you need to hit pause on us.

TALLY

I don't want to lose you, though.

FLIP

I don't want to lose you either. You are far too important, and you mean way too much for me to let you go without a fight. But forcing this won't make anything easier. So if you need a pause to get through exams and your showcase, then I can give you that.

TALLY

Just a pause, not a breakup?

FLIP

Just a pause.

TALLY

Just until I'm through this.

My hands shake and I can barely swallow as I type my reply.

FLIP

As long as you need.

TALLY

Okay. I should study. Thank you for understanding.

FLIP

I'm in this with you, whatever you need.

She hearts the message and then sends me another heart, and I send her one back before I set my phone on the bed and stare up at the ceiling. I could lose her, all because I couldn't give her the honesty she deserves.

Tristan knocks on my door and lets himself into my room. "You all right, man?"

"Tally asked me for a pause."

He's silent a beat. "Is that college speak for breaking up?"

"No. It's not a breakup." She was clear about that. "It's a pause. She's overwhelmed, she almost missed her exam this morning. She's under a lot of stress and I'm adding to it. I should have fucking told her I'm in love with her before I left, but I didn't want it to seem like I was saying it out of desperation, and things were already messy with the shit that happened at family dinner."

"What happened at family dinner?" Tristan sits on the edge of the other bed, looking concerned.

I tell him about the sex in her childhood bedroom, minus any actual details.

"Holy fuck, dude. While Vander Zee was there?"

"No. There was a short window of time when we were alone." I side-eye him. "Don't get any ideas."

"Too late for that." He blows out a breath. "That was ballsy."

"I know. And maybe under different circumstances it would have been fine, but what I should have done is been honest about my feelings. Instead I defaulted to sex, like a fucking idiot."

"You're learning that lesson a lot faster than me, so don't be too hard on yourself."

"Hindsight is an asshole."

"Don't I know it," he sighs.

"I can't lose her, Tristan."

"You won't. Write it all down, so you can give it to her when you're off the pause. Give her space now, and when she can handle it, give her all your thoughts and feelings on paper. You can take care of her, you can buy her the world, but it's not a replacement for telling her how you feel about her, so start now."

CHAPTER 54

TALLY

I have three exams under my belt and one more to write tomorrow. The last two were much smoother than the first, with no alarm glitches, panic attacks, or falling asleep when I'm not supposed to. I'm also grateful that the Terror have won their last two away games, with Phillip scoring three goals. Their final away game is tomorrow night in Chicago. If they win it, they'll have home-ice advantage for the start of the playoffs. My written exam will be over before the game, so all my focus can shift to my showcase and hoping my boyfriend will be in the city when it happens, rather than on a plane to somewhere else.

My textbook is open in front of me, a selection of high-lighters, sticky flags, and flash cards surround me, as well as a bag of dropjes sent two days ago from Phillip.

Parsnip hops down from his perch on the cat tower and bumbles down the hall at the sound of the door opening.

"Escapee on his way to you!" I shout.

"All good!" Fee calls back.

Yesterday, he slipped out, and we spent fifteen minutes luring him back with treats.

She appears a moment later carrying a box. "It's from Roman

and Lexi." She sets it on the counter. "And Rix." She holds up the card attached to it. "And apparently Flip."

I abandon my textbook and cue card making to check out the contents and the note.

> *Fee and Tally,*
> *Sending you both tons of love on your finals. The balanced meals are from Roman, the cream puffs are from Lexi, and Black Forest-inspired food items and the cherry chip cupcakes with cherry icing are courtesy of my brother. ;)*
> *Love and hugs,*
> *Rix*

I hug the card to my chest and bite my lips together.

Fee wraps her arms around me. "Got a case of the big feels?"

"Yeah." The pause felt necessary, essential even, so I could focus on exams and dance, instead of my relationship and all the fears and hopes that come with it. Phillip has been giving me space, which I need, but he's still taking care of me from a distance. A comfy new hoodie arrived two days ago, and now the study snacks. He's telling me he's here for me. In return, I overnighted one of his t-shirts I've been sleeping in to his hotel in Chicago. It's a little thing, but I want him to know I care.

Fee and I send a message to the Babe chat with a picture of our box of goodies and a thank you.

RIX

Happy to help with brain fuel.

ESSIE

Oooh. Those cupcakes look delicious.

> RIX
>
> There might be extras if Tristan hasn't already found the ones I hid in the freezer.
>
> HEMI
>
> Hammer, have you left for the office yet?
>
> HAMMER
>
> I have not. 👀
>
> RIX
>
> LOL. I can meet you at street level in ten with office fuel!

A photo of a plastic container full of cupcakes follows.

> SHILPA
>
> I'm so glad I'm in the office today!
>
> LEXI
>
> I will be stopping by for lunch.

A slew of good luck messages and *can't wait to see you dance this weekend* follow.

Fee and I heat up one of the dinners and settle in to eat while studying. My phone buzzes with messages from my parents, checking in. I told my mom about the pause, but with my dad out of town and also my boyfriend's coach, I felt like I should leave that alone.

I scroll back to the last messages from Phillip.

I'm in this with you, whatever you need.

I know in my heart this was the right decision. As soon as I made it and put it out in the world, I felt lighter, even though it makes my heart hurt. But after nearly a week of separation, the pull toward him is undeniable, maybe because the stress of exams is lifting.

My fingers hover over the keys for a few seconds before I type the message and hit send.

CHAPTER 55

FLIP

My anxiety has been tough to handle the last few days. My stomach is in my throat as a message pops up from Tally. I take a centering breath and send a silent plea to outside forces to please not fuck with me today before I click on it.

TALLY

I miss you. 🤍

The wash of relief is overwhelming. Saying yes to a pause was the single most difficult thing I've ever done, and that's saying something since I filed for divorce and forked over my entire first-year salary to get Fiona out of my life. But giving Tally space to breathe has been infinitely more challenging. It's been good for me, too, though. Separation brings perspective. I respond right away.

FLIP

I miss you, too, kitten.

She hearts the message.

TALLY

I needed the space, but I don't like the space.

The relief almost takes me to my knees. She's one exam away from being finished, and then it's just her showcase. The pressure of school will be off soon, and then we can focus on us.

FLIP

I know, and same.

She's opened the door and I don't want her to question where I'm at. She's had to do that for far too long.

FLIP

I don't like being away from you. But if I was home and we didn't take a pause, I'd either be sleeping in your bed, being a distraction from your studying, or you'd be sitting on my couch, probably wearing something you think is cute and comfy, and I'd be struggling to keep myself in check because you in one of my hoodies does things to me. And then you wouldn't get the studying in, and neither of us would get the sleep we need because I'd be looking to fulfill a fantasy for both of us. Plus, there's clarity with space. Being separated from you has made me painfully aware of how much I care about you, and how much better my life is when you're close to me.

I want to lay it all out for her, be completely honest about my feelings, but that needs to wait until we're together again.

TALLY

I didn't realize how much I needed to hear that from you.

Or read it, actually.

FLIP

Whenever you need a reminder that I'm in this with you, and that you mean the world to me, all you have to do is open your text messages.

TALLY

I can't wait until you're home.

FLIP

Me, too. Not long now.

In the meantime, I'm thinking of you.

Get back to studying 

TALLY

Diving back in. 🖤

FLIP

🖤

I grab the journal from my nightstand. I have practice in an hour, but it's more than enough time to put my feelings on paper.

Tally,

Being away from you feels like half my heart is missing.

I wanted to call you so badly after you texted to tell me you missed me.

I miss your voice and your laugh. I miss hearing my name on your lips.

I miss the smell of your cherry blossom shampoo.

I miss the way it feels to wake up with you wrapped around me.

I miss the softness of your lips.

I miss making KD with you.

I miss watching you dance.

I miss all the things that make you uniquely you.

There are so many things I can't wait to do again once we unpause.

I'm making a new fantasy list, but this one isn't X-rated. It's all the things I never want to take for granted.

I want to take you to the Dutch Toko and watch your eyes light up when we buy all your favorite treats.

I want to go shopping with you for new lingerie and have you edge the hell out of me the entire time.

I want to cuddle on the couch and read together.

I especially want to read Cammie's fic updates with you and then re-enact the scenes (but we might have to improvise with those why-choose moments because I was ten thousand percent serious about no one ever touching you again but me).

I want to build furniture with you. I don't know why, I just do.

I want to take you to a carnival and eat funnel cake and make out with you in the fun house.

I'll keep adding to the list, but those are a few of the things that have made it onto My Life With Tally fantasy list.

But the one thing I want most is to finally to tell you how I feel about you.

I love you.

Everything about you.

I love your smile, the sound of your laugh, the way your eyes light up when I've done something nice for you. I love the way you smell, how dedicated you are to your craft, how supportive you are of me, how patient you are. I love that you're the kind of friend who will always step up for the people you care about.

I love you with every ounce of my being, and when we're finally together again, I will tell you exactly how much every single day for the rest of our lives.

Love,

Phillip

CHAPTER 56

TALLY

"How does it feel to be ninety-five percent done?" Mom asks as the server drops off our drinks.

"Amazing and a little scary." I sip my Shirley Temple. I would love a margarita, but I still have my showcase, and our final dress rehearsal is this afternoon, so the celebratory drink will have to wait another twenty-four hours.

"Big changes are coming, huh?" She smiles empathetically.

"Yeah. I'm excited, but I'm nervous about the unknowns."

"You've had a lot of those this year." She pokes at the ice in her club soda with her straw.

"Our whole family has," I agree. "But I see how this is better for you and Dad." I don't know if I'm ready for them to start dating other people, but it's not my choice, either. I just want them to be happy, however that looks.

"How are you and Phillip?" Concern laces her tone.

"Still on a pause." Their last away game is tonight. "But that will change when he's home."

"He's serious about you."

"I'm serious about him, too."

"Serious enough to consider moving in with him?" she presses.

I blow out a breath. "I mean...eventually I think that's a possibility." Probability even. I summon my courage. "I've been thinking a lot about where I'll live after graduation." I have my apartment until the end of April. Even if Phillip and I were in the best possible place relationship-wise, we've only been dating for a handful of months. I don't want to move too fast. I want sleep-overs and time to enjoy dating without the pressure of cohabitating and learning each other's quirks and habits.

"Do you want to live with your dad?" Mom asks.

"It's not because I don't want to live with you," I say quickly. "I'm not angry or upset with you over the divorce. I feel like you and I are in a good place, and like our relationship is healthier now."

"We needed a reset and university helped with that," Mom says softly.

"We did, and it did. I like this a lot better, where you're still my mom, but we can be friends, too." A piece of me worries that if I moved back in with my mom and my sister, we would fall into old habits.

"I feel the same way, honey."

"Dad and I need time to work on things. I know he's not perfect, but he and I need the most healing, and living with him could help," I explain.

She smiles, and it isn't sad or disappointed, it's full of pride. "I think that's a good idea, sweetheart, and your dad will be ecstatic. Have you told him yet?"

"I wanted to talk to you first."

She reaches across the table, and I slip my hand into hers. "You've had so much on your plate, and you're over here worrying about how I'll feel."

"That's the thing, Mom. I wasn't worried. I knew you would be supportive and that you would see exactly why I was making the choice." It won't be long-term. Eventually I'll move in with Phillip, but in the meantime, I'll work on repairing my relationship with my dad, and this is a start. It's the right thing to do. I feel it in my heart.

"He and I need this more than you and me, and Fenna deserves a chance to build the same kind of connection we have, just with a little more balance."

"I'm so proud to be your mother."

"And I'm just as proud to be your daughter."

CHAPTER 57

FLIP

Tally,

I'm nervous.

So damn nervous.

Tonight's game is a big deal. If we win, we start the playoffs in Toronto, and you'll be able to come to the first game, which I desperately want. More than that, though, I want to be at your showcase.

You are magic on stage. There is nothing I love more than watching you dance.

Well. That's not entirely true, but watching you dance is definitely in my top five. Right up there with playing hockey and being close to you.

I want my cake, and I want to eat it too. So I'm manifesting a win tonight so I can sit in the audience and watch you own the stage. And then I'll finally be able to hug you again and tell you how much I love you.

I'm going to be really honest.

I'm kind of obsessed with you, Tally.

I printed out your favorite fic, the one with all the highlighted passages, and I read those parts before I go to bed every night. I also maybe borrowed one of your well-read books from your shelf and compulsively read the dogeared pages when I miss you the most.

I packed the pillowcase that you sleep on at my place so I could put it on the hotel pillow and hug it.

I borrowed your travel lotion from your backpack so I could sniff it when I'm desperate, which is really fucking often.

I bought myself some of those salty dropjes that you love and tried to eat them because they remind me of you. I'm still not a fan, but I'd suffer through them just to be close to you.

One more confession, and this one is a little filthy.

I found a pair of your panties on the floor before I left for the away series.

It was the night you stayed over and we made grilled cheese and canned tomato soup and cuddled on the couch. And then we started kissing. That's another thing I can't wait to do again, by the way. And you climbed into my lap and made those sweet little sounds and one thing led to another because one thing always leads to another, and I couldn't get you naked fast enough. I just wanted to be surrounded by you, feel the warmth of you under me, swallow up your pretty moans.

Sorry. That got heated.

Anyway. I found your blue Terror cheekies. I packed them. And last night I fucked them and I don't even feel a little bit bad about it.

So yeah. I'm a little obsessed with you, Tallulah

Vander Zee.

With your sweetness and your sass.

With your beauty.

With your talent.

With everything about you.

I love you.

I'll win the game for you tonight so I can tell you that in person.

Phillip

I set the journal aside. Tristan will be here in a few minutes, and we'll head to the arena together. I grab my phone just as it buzzes with a new message.

TALLY

Good luck tonight! 🩶

FLIP

I'll bring home a win just for you. 

An hour later, Tristan and I are taking the ice. It's a high-stakes game for both teams, and we're playing against the Chicago Rage tonight.

"All we need is the win and three goals and we start the play-offs at home."

"We got this." I fist-bump him and we get into position.

Chicago wins the faceoff, but we gain control of the puck within the first minute of play.

Shots on net are plentiful in the first period, but nothing gets past the goalies. Ryker is holding strong, and our enforcers are playing smooth with a side of grit. Romero can't help it. That's who he is, and Grace likes to push buttons. As long as they stay out of the penalty box, we're good.

"We need a goal on the board before the end of the first period." I chew on my mouthguard, following the puck as Bright and Palaniappa pass back and forth, looking for a hole in the Rage's defense.

"Same." Stiles taps his stick on the floor.

"I want my kids at my first playoff game," Grace adds.

I smile. Those adopted twins have made him a different man.

"We'll make it happen." I need my girlfriend at my first playoff game this season and I need to be at her showcase.

The Rage's lead scorer was injured last week, and he's still favoring his left side. At shift change, Romero bolts down the ice, Grace at his side, and I move in to steal the puck from a Chicago right wing. I send it to Grace just before I hit the boards and a Chicago player slams into me. I shake it off and get into position as Stiles, Grace, and Romero keep the puck away from our opposition. Stiles passes to me, but there's no open shot on net, so I pass back to Grace. Behind him, Romero is getting up in a defensive player's space.

I scoop the puck while he's distracted and pull one of Kodiak Bowman's moves, flipping it into the air before I tap it, arcing it over the goalie's glove. It hits the back of the net, and my teammates converge on me.

"One down, two to go." Stiles bumps my shoulder.

The Chicago player tries to grab my jersey, but the refs pull him off. We end up with a powerplay, and we take full advantage of that precious time, setting up for another goal in the last minute of the period. There are only fifteen seconds left on the clock when I take the ice again. Stiles passes to me, and Grace moves into position, ready to take a shot. It goes wide, but Stiles catches it and tips it back to me. I fake the shot, then pass to Grace, who slips it through the five hole.

The buzzer sounds, and a fight nearly breaks out, but we keep our cool and leave the ice without throwing punches.

During the second period, we maintain the lead, but Romero ends up with a penalty for roughing, giving the Rage a powerplay. Grace and Palaniappa help Ryker keep the puck out of the net.

In the third period, Chicago is looking to close the gap, but Romero won't make the same mistake twice, and Grace is playing clean. Bright scores a goal five minutes in, extending our lead with the third goal. But Chicago finally puts themselves on the board two minutes later.

We fight to keep the puck in their territory. The hits keep coming, and Chicago earns another penalty for high-sticking. Romero is forced back to the bench so the doctor can look at his bleeding eyebrow. The powerplay is the advantage we need, though, and I score again with Grace as the assist.

We win 4-1. It's the best game of my career, and it puts us exactly where we want to be for the start of the playoffs, giving us home-ice advantage.

The mood in the locker room is buoyant. Some of the younger guys make plans to go out to celebrate, but Quinn has three stitches above his left eye and a killer headache.

"Oh my gosh, Quinn, what was that even?" Lovey, his long-time friend who has attended several events with him over the last couple of years, takes his face in her hands and inspects his eyebrow. "Do you have a concussion?"

"Loves, I'm fine. It's just a few stitches." He jams his hand in his pocket and lets her mother bird him.

"In your head!" She props a hand on her hip then inspects the wound again. "I'm staying with you tonight."

Quinn glances past Lovey, to where a guy leans against the wall, looking hella uncomfortable. Quinn arches a brow. "Really? You and your boyfriend are going to stay in my hotel room with me?"

"He can drive home. I'll just stay." She bites her lips together.

He says nothing, just continues with the arched brow.

"I'm worried about you."

"I have a whole team of guys who will make sure I'm fine. But thanks for coming to the game. I'm sorry we can't hang out."

"We'll make plans in the offseason." She fiddles with the lapel on his suit jacket.

"Lovey, babydoll, we should go," the boyfriend calls out.

Quinn's nostrils flare.

Lovey sighs. "Text me tomorrow so I know you're okay." She hugs Quinn, and he makes awkward eye contact with the irritated boyfriend.

They leave and Quinn rubs the back of his neck. "I fucking hate that guy."

"I thought you two were maybe a thing," Connor says.

"No, man. We've been friends our entire lives."

"I've known Bea my entire life," Tristan points out.

"Maybe she'll break up with the loser," Dallas says helpfully.

"One can only hope. Anyway, I need a couple painkillers and a bed."

"I can't wait to sleep in my own tomorrow," Ash says with a sigh.

"I can't wait to sleep beside my wife," Tristan adds.

"Same, and to hug my kids," Connor agrees.

I can't wait to see my girlfriend, hit unpause, and tell her exactly how I feel.

CHAPTER 58

FLIP

Tally,

Tonight's the night.

I get to see you perform.

I get to hug you and kiss you and feel your warmth.

I get to tell you all the things I've been afraid to say.

When I think about what the future looks like, it's full of you.

I love waking up next to you and I'm excited for the moment you decide you're ready to move in with me. While I wait for that day to come, I'll keep filling drawers with clothes for you. I want the comfort of domestic bliss. I want to find your hair ties all over the place, and your dance tights drying on the rack in the laundry room.

I'm already thinking about how I'll propose, when and where and the kind of ring I'll buy.

I want a family with you, Tally.

I want kids, at least two, but more if we think we can handle it.

Before we get married and have a family, I want time with just you. I want to watch you grow in your career. I want vacations together, travel to new places, but also to build our own cottage on the lake so we can escape up there and fulfill fantasies and just have time and space to love each other. And we'll invite our friends too, but half of them already have cottages in Muskoka, so it won't be hard to find privacy.

It's not just the big moments I'm looking forward to.

It's not just all the firsts, although I've loved having so many of those with you.

It's the little things, too.

I want to make all our favorite meals together.

I want to go on adventures.

I want to take care of you when you're sick.

I want to grow old with you.

I want sunsets on porch swings and sleepovers with our grandkids.

I want a life with you.

I want to love you every single day for the rest of my life.

Always yours,

Phillip

I stick the photo my sister took when we were playing *the floor is lava* on the page beside the letter, then tuck the journal into my breast pocket, grab the flowers from the passenger seat, and head into the theater.

My teammates, their wives and girlfriends, and Tally's Tilton friends are all in the bar, enjoying a pre-showcase cocktail.

"There you are!" Rix flits over and throws her arms around me and murmurs, "I was getting worried." She pulls back and takes in the flowers. "Oh, those are stunning."

"They're all her favorites."

"She'll love them, and the journal."

"That's what I'm hoping."

She smiles up at me. "I'm really proud of you. I hope you know that."

"Thanks, sis. That means a lot." I turn to Fee, Cammie, and Enid. "How's she doing?"

"Excited," Cammie says.

"A little nervous, but her dress rehearsal went well yesterday, so she was feeling good about things this afternoon," Fee adds.

"We had to take her dropjes away, so she wasn't retaining two pounds of fluid from all the salt." Enid makes a face. "But you probably didn't need to know that."

"She wake up with lines on her face?" I ask.

"Like two days ago. Hence the confiscating." Enid opens her clutch and shows me the evidence. "I promised I'd have them for her after the performance."

"I have a bunch waiting at my place for her, too."

Enid grins. "Of course you do."

They give us the fifteen-minute warning over the PA and we file into the theater and claim our seats. I secured us tickets in the first two rows, so we have an unobstructed view. Tally's parents and brother and sister are already seated when we arrive.

"Phillip, thank you so much for getting such great seats for us." Her mom stands and hugs me.

"Honestly, it's my pleasure. I want Tallulah to feel supported." And I want us to be the first people she sees when she steps onstage.

"You were great last night on the ice," Ties says.

"I had some serious motivation and a lot of help from my teammates."

"You really pulled through, Madden." Vander Zee claps me on the shoulder. "It's an honor to have you love my daughter."

"Thanks, Coach. She means the world to me."

We take our seats and the lights go down. The first number is an entire class ensemble. It's incredible to watch twenty dancers move as one. My gaze stays locked on Tally, who twirls across the stage with ease and grace. Even as part of a whole, she stands out. After the full class ensemble, they break off into small troupes of three to six dancers.

I'm on the edge of my seat as Tally, Arya, and Charles take their places. There are scouts from local theaters in the audience, and tonight could see her courted by some of her favorite dancers.

The lights come up with the first strains of the song. I've heard it plenty of times. It's on one of Tally's playlists. She's front and center, poised and still, one hand reaching for the stars, the other extended toward the audience. I can't take my eyes off her as she moves, completely in sync with her troupe. It's a beautiful piece with compelling choreography, telling a story of love, loss, and rebirth.

Charles and Arya perform their solo pieces, and Tally finally takes the stage again. The music is moody and sensual.

Her eyes find mine as she unfurls and suddenly the world melts away. There's no one but us. Because this song, this dance, it's for me. And she is glorious. I'm transfixed, enraptured, as she spins across the stage, emotion pouring out of her. I could watch her for hours and never get tired, but the song eventually comes to an end and the theater bursts into applause. I whistle and cheer right along with everyone else. I'm so proud of her. So proud to be hers.

Tally's performance is the last of the night, and the rest of her class joins her onstage for a standing ovation.

"God, I'm in love with her," I say as I whistle and clap.

Dred squeezes my arm. "You can tell her that soon."

It feels like it takes a million years before we file out of the theater. All I want is to see my girlfriend and congratulate her. Finally, we're back in the foyer with all the dancers still dressed in their costumes.

Tally's eyes lock on mine from across the room. She touches Arya's shoulder and then she's heading for me. I stride to meet her, arms open as she launches herself at me. I hug her tightly and lift her off her feet.

She pulls back, eyes searching mine, hands on my face. "Unpause."

"Unpause," I agree.

She presses her lips to mine. It's a balm to my soul. Her hair creates a curtain around us, and I angle my head, lips parting to let her inside. I just want to get lost in her.

"I missed you so much," I whisper.

"Me, too. Let's never pause again."

"Never," I agree.

I want to whisk her away and keep her all to myself, but her family and friends deserve a moment with her first. I set her down. "You were otherworldly up there. I couldn't take my eyes off you. It felt like you were dancing just for me."

"I was, and I will again, when it's just us."

"Can't wait." I pass her the flowers. "These are for you."

"They're beautiful." She brings them to her nose and sniffs the blossoms.

"Not as beautiful as you." I pull the journal from the inside pocket of my suit jacket. "And this is also for you."

She runs her fingers over the leather, then opens it, eyes flipping up to mine. "What is this?"

"It's my truth. All my hopes and fears. All the things I've wanted to say but have been afraid to."

"And you want me to have it?" She hugs it gently.

"I want you to have all of me."

CHAPTER 59
TALLY

My anxiety melts away with his admission. I'm through the hard parts, exams are finished, my showcase is over, the Terror will start the playoffs at home, and Phillip and I are unpaused.

My family converges on me. I'm showered with hugs and congratulations while Phillip watches wearing a proud smile.

"You were amazing up there. Just so incredible." Dad squeezes my shoulders, emotion shining in his eyes. "I'm so glad my team pulled out a win so I could be here."

"Me, too," I agree. "One of your players had a lot of motivation."

"It rubbed off on the rest of them." Dad winks. "They're all here for you."

"Like a big, extended family." My Babes are like sisters, the Terror guys like big brothers, and my Tilton crew are an extension of that.

"You were phenomenal." Mom steps in next to hug me, followed by Ties and Fenna.

And then I'm pulled into a group hug with my Babes and Tilton friends.

Once I've been squeezed and congratulated by all the people I love, Soraya, my dance instructor pulls me aside to speak briefly with the casting director at En Pointe Theater.

"I know you've already submitted an application, but we'd like to extend a personal invitation to our first round of auditions next month," Kenzie says. "You were flawless up there tonight, and we would love to have you with our company."

"It would be an honor, truly. I've followed your dancers for years, and I love how innovative and creative you are with choreography. Your productions have hugely inspired me."

"Well, you inspire us. We look forward to seeing you next month. I'll let you get back to celebrating with your family and friends." She squeezes my shoulder and moves on to another group of dancers.

Soraya beams. "It has truly been a joy watching you grow as a dancer. I can't wait to see where you go from here."

"Thank you for always pushing me to be creative and step outside the box. I am so grateful for your guidance."

We're called to take a group photo and then we head backstage to collect our things before I return to Phillip, who waits patiently for me in the nearly empty foyer. Fee took most of the flowers with her back to our apartment, so all I have are the ones from Phillip and his journal. He links our arms and guides me out into the cool April night to his car.

"My place or yours?" he asks once he's behind the wheel.

"Yours, please." Tomorrow is game one of the first playoff series, and his bed is a king versus my double, so it will be more comfortable, plus there's guaranteed privacy.

"I saw you talking to the casting director from En Pointe. How was that?"

"They invited me to audition for their fall production next month."

"That's amazing, Talls. And not a surprise."

"It feels like everything is falling into place now," I admit. "Like the weight has lifted and the way forward is clear."

He laces our fingers. "Sometimes we need to take a step back to gain perspective."

"I hated the pause, but I needed it," I confide.

"Me, too, on both fronts. But it gave me a chance to really focus on what I want for us in the future, and it forced me to put all my energy into securing home-ice advantage for the beginning of the playoffs."

"I'm really glad that happened, and that you could be here for my showcase and I can be there to watch you play tomorrow."

"The last thing I wanted was to miss it because I had to be on a plane."

He pulls into the underground lot and parks in his spot. We take the elevator up to his apartment.

He turns to me once we're inside. "Why don't you take a quick shower? I have a few things I want to set up, and then you can read my journal and we can talk?"

"That sounds perfect."

Everything is already set out for me in the bathroom. I shower quickly, moisturize and brush my teeth, pulling one of Phillip's comfy shirts over my head, excited to be surrounded by him again soon.

The living room has been transformed when I come out of the bathroom. Glasses of champagne and a spread of all of my favorite snacks, including cherry-chip mini-cupcakes, are laid out on the coffee table next to his journal.

He meets me halfway across the room and I let him guide me to the couch, where I tuck myself into his side. Phillip passes me the journal, expression nervous and expectant.

I open it to the first page, which boasts a collection of doodles and a heart with my name written inside it. The pages that follow contain collages of photos, some just of me, others with the girls, and more still of me and Phillip, often caught candidly by whoever took them.

And then the letters begin.

Tally,

We're on pause.

Even writing those words terrifies me. I understand why you need it, and maybe I need it too. All I want is to fix things. To go back in time and be honest with you about Fiona, about everything, about the way I feel. But I can't, so I'm putting it all down here, and when you're ready to unpause, I can share this with you the way you keep sharing yourself with me.

It's time for some real honesty.

I've been fighting this attraction since Dred and Connor's wedding.

I just never believed I'd be worthy of you.

I never believed I'd be able to let someone into my heart again.

But you are everything I could ever want in a partner.

Kind, intelligent, ambitious, supportive, independent. Adventurous. ;)

You gave me back so many firsts.

Reframed them.

You make me feel worthy of love.

And no matter what happens from here, you will always have my heart.

Yours,

Phillip

Some notes are just a few lines, scrawled in messy cursive, like he had a thought and just wanted to get it down.

> *Tally,*
> *Today I went to the Pancake House and ordered your favorite meal just to feel close to you. God, I miss you.*
> *Yours always,*
> *Phillip*

> *Tally,*
> *I used your expensive conditioner for not condi-tioning purposes and I'm not even a little sorry about it. When you're mine again, I want to make it mandatory that we shower together at least once a week. Also, that we read in the tub together.*
> *Yours until the end of time,*
> *Phillip*

> *Tally,*
> *Today we lost a game and all I wanted was to lie with my head in your lap and feel your fingers in my hair.*
> *I miss you.*
> *Phillip*

Tally,

I have watched the video you sent me of you dancing an unreasonable number of times. It's the first thing I do in the morning and the last thing I do at night. I'm wildly obsessed with you.

Obsessively yours,
Phillip

Tally,

Would it be crossing the line to have a 3D replica doll made of your significant other for away games? Asking for a friend.

Seriously in need of therapy and okay with it,
Phillip

Tally,

I'm jealous of my body pillow. The one you're probably sleeping next to every night. So I went ahead and had a picture of you printed on a body pillow and then had the brilliant idea to take it with me on away games by putting it in a vacuum sealed bag. Except I didn't pack a vacuum in my suitcase so I had to call house-keeping and pay some woman a hundred dollars to help shrink you down again. I would have just owned it, but the picture I used isn't fully PG and if your dad saw it I might not make it home with all my teeth.

Best laid plans and all.

Still obsessed and okay with it.
Xx
Phillip

PS. Even pillow you is sexy AF.

A picture of Phillip hugging pillow me is taped to the opposite page, along with another of him glowering at my body pillow.

"Oh my God. How did you find out about the body pillow? When did you find out about it?"

"Remember the day your bathroom was converted into a spa?"

"The one day I forget to put him away!"

"I love that you sleep with it when I'm gone and also that Cammie bought that for you." He kisses my temple.

"He's a decent stand in, but he has nothing on the real thing." I kiss his cheek.

"Pillow Tally is the same."

I keep reading the notes, some sweet, some filthy, but mostly emotional, until I reach the last one. I climb into his lap, straddling his thighs as I read it aloud.

Tally,
I'm hiding out in the bathroom, writing this. You were magnificent tonight, but I knew you would be.
I'm so proud of you.
You worked so hard for this, and your talent is mind-blowing.
I can't wait to hug you, kiss you, hold you, and tell you how special you are.
I can't wait to give you this journal and share all

my thoughts and feelings for you, about you, about us
and our future with you.

But most of all, I can't wait to tell you I love you.

Always and forever yours,

Phillip

A TEAR ESCAPES AS I SET THE JOURNAL ASIDE AND CUP HIS FACE in my hands. He looks so earnest and beautiful and mine. I press my lips to his. "I love you too. With all my heart."

CHAPTER 60

FLIP

"You own me, Tallulah. I'm yours."

"That's all I've ever wanted." She sucks my bottom lip, dragging it through her teeth. "Now take me to bed."

I grip the back of her thighs and stand, leaving behind the untouched champagne and spread of snacks as I carry her to the bedroom.

Tally kisses my neck, biting her way across my jaw. "I need you inside me."

I climb onto the bed with her still wrapped around me. "What if I want to take my time with you?" I gently lay her on the cool sheets and settle in the cradle of her hips.

"You took your time with me for months. We have the rest of our lives for sweetness and romance." She rolls her hips and kisses my chin. "Show me how obsessed you are with me."

I cover her mouth with mine, pressing her into the mattress. She moans and our tongues tangle as she pulls at my shirt, trying to free it from my pants. We part long enough for me to get it over my head.

"I need these off. You can take your time with me later.

Tomorrow. After the game." She yanks the belt free and pops the button on my dress pants. I shove them down my thighs and rid her of my shirt.

Before she can pull me down on top of her, I loop my arms around her thighs and lift her hips off the bed. She grips the sheets, shoulders and head still resting on the mattress as I bring her to my mouth and lick up the length of her.

"Oh God."

I groan as I latch onto her clit and suck roughly. "Fuck, I missed the way you taste." I bite the inside of her thigh. "Tomorrow night I'll edge you for as long as I want, kitten. I'll have you creaming down my throat, begging for my cock."

"I fucking hope so."

"I'll make this pussy rain for me." I bury my face between her thighs, devouring her like a starved man until her legs quake. I can't get enough of the taste of her, of her deep moans and needy whimpers. I can't get enough of *her*.

Before she tips over the edge, I un-suction my mouth from her and lower her to the mattress.

"No!" She grips my hair and tries to guide me back to her center.

I press a soft kiss to her swollen clit and untangle her fingers from my hair as I prowl up her body. My cock drags along the inside of her leg. "You wanted me to show you how obsessed I am," I remind her.

"I'm so close, though," she whimpers.

"I know." I suck her nipple, following with a gentle graze of teeth.

She arches under me and tries to snake her free hand between us.

I drop my hips, blocking her attempt.

"Phillip," she groans.

"I love my name on your lips." I gently lave the other nipple.

"Please."

"Say it again." I kiss over her sternum and up her throat. "Please."

"Not that." I shift until I'm positioned at her entrance. "Phillip."

I brush my nose against hers. "I love you, Tallulah."

Her eyes soften. "I love you, too, Phillip."

I push inside in one smooth stroke.

Tally's mouth drops open and she shudders violently, clenching around me as she comes.

"You're so beautiful." I cup her face in my hands. "I'm going to love you every day for the rest of our lives."

She nods and her arms tighten around me, feet hooked at the small of my back.

I roll my hips and her eyes flutter closed.

"No, no, kitten. Eyes on me. I need to see you."

She pries them open, fingers shaking as they trail over my cheek.

"Only I get to see this side of you. It'll only ever be me filling you." I pull back and snap my hips forward. "Making you come." Slide out. "Fulfilling every fantasy."

"Only you," she agrees.

I tug on her ankle, and she uncrosses her feet, allowing me to hook my arms into the crook of her knees, pushing them up until they meet her ribs. I move over her, sliding in deep, fucking her into the mattress, bodies slick with sweat, her moans whispered across my lips.

"I'm keeping you," I whisper.

"Forever," she agrees.

I drive into her, the need for her overwhelming. We cling and caress, push and pull, love and fuck. I'll never get close enough, have enough of her. We come in waves, our eyes locked, all the feelings we kept hidden from each other laid bare.

I roll us to the side, still inside her, and hold her close while we kiss. "This is just the beginning."

"There is no end to us," she promises.

Eventually I pull out and clean her up, then tuck her against me and we fall asleep intertwined. In the middle of the night, we reach for each other at the same time and I fill her again, slow and sleepy.

My alarm clock goes off at a miserable o'clock in the morning.

Tally makes a disgruntled noise as I uncurl myself from around her.

She rolls over and tries to grab for my arm. "Stay with me."

"I have practice."

She blinks blearily at the clock. "We stayed up way too late."

"I'll be fine. I'm high on love." I kiss her temple and her cheek. "I'll see you tonight at the game."

Her eyes flare and she's suddenly far more alert. "It's the first playoff game. We had all that sex."

"It's a good warm-up." I pull on a pair of joggers and a T-shirt, then give in to the urge to go back for another kiss. "I love you, Tallulah."

"I love you, Phillip."

It feels like a superpower.

CHAPTER 61

FLIP

TALLY

How are you feeling? 😬😬🫣🫤

FLIP

Tired and nervous, but no regrets.

TALLY

Same, and same. Except I'm a spectator and not a player tonight. 😬

FLIP

I'm riding the high of having my girlfriend tell me she loves me. 🥹

TALLY

We're twins. I'm riding the high of my boyfriend telling me he loves me, too.

You'll be great tonight.

FLIP

I'm playing to win for you.

TALLY

I love you.

I slide my phone into my bag and take a deep, steadying breath.

"You all right, man?" Stiles asks as he hangs his suit jacket carefully in his cubby.

"I'm fucking awesome."

He grins. "Yeah, you are."

"Better stay awesome so we can win this game," Grace says as he passes.

Nothing phases me. I'm on cloud nine. "You have just as much on the line as I do."

"I need to win this game for my wife and my kids," Grace agrees.

"And I need to win this game for my girlfriend, who fucking loves me."

Romero laughs. "Dude, you are a sappy fucker."

I turn to find him videoing me.

"No cameras in the locker room." I lunge for him.

"You'll thank me when we play this at your wedding." Romero tosses his phone to Ryker.

"You know what, you're right." I shrug out of my button-down and hang it in my cubby.

"It's been a long time coming," Palaniappa says. "Shilpa has been waiting for this for nearly four years."

"Tally was only a first year."

"Yeah, but she was already tuning into your vibe. You just took a while to catch up with her," Bright says.

We suit up and I take the ribbing good-naturedly. Tally loves me and I love Tally and the future looks fucking amazing. A win tonight will set the tone for this series. I'm just grateful we're not up against New York this round.

The arena is humming with excitement as we take the ice for

warm-ups. I spot Tally in the box with the rest of her friends. It doesn't matter that the world is watching. That there will be articles about it tomorrow that have nothing to do with the game. I drop my gloves and make a heart with my hands. Tally laughs and mirrors the action.

"Seriously, man, this is beautiful," Palaniappa calls as he passes.

I toss her a wink and focus on the warm-up.

"It's different, eh?" Stiles says as we stretch our inner thighs.

"Having someone to play for?" I clarify.

"Yeah. It changes things. You're not just playing for you anymore, or your team, or whatever the arbitrary goal is. You have someone rooting for you and you want to make them proud," he says. "I play for me, but I play harder for Bea. I want her to be proud of my game. The stakes go up with every person you add to your life, right? I want to make my dad proud, I want to be a role model for my brothers, especially Brody, who will be one of us next year, and eventually, I'll want to make my kids proud."

"It's big, isn't it?"

"Yeah. But it's not pressure in the way we're used to. It's like we're living inside the best version of ourselves." He claps me on the shoulder. "You're going to make her real proud tonight, man. I know it."

The buzzer sounds and we move to the bench. I take my childhood best friend's speech to heart. He's right about all of it. I want to win this game for my team, for myself, my family, for Dred who's married to the sandwich fucker, but mostly I want to win to make my girlfriend proud.

I carry that energy into the game. It's contagious. We're on fire during the first period. Romero is killing it on defense, so are Palaniappa and Grace. Ryker is protecting the net like he was born to do, and the offensive line is tight and strong. We have decades of experience between us, years on the ice together, and we're all playing with the same grit and determination.

I score a goal five minutes in and then Stiles jumps in with one of his own. We keep the lead all through the first period. In the second, Boston gets on the board with a goal, but Grace and Romero push the defensive line and help Ryker keep the puck out of our net. Bright manages a sweet goal off a rebound at the end of the second period.

We start the third with another goal, Stiles the assist and Grace with the point. And then we crush Boston, adding two more goals, giving us the win 6-1. It sets us up for an intense start to the series. They'll need to work hard to keep a positive headspace with such a rough loss in game one.

We're all pumped on adrenalin as the sportscasters come at us with questions.

"Madden, you've had a tumultuous season, but this was arguably the best game of your career. What do you attribute your stellar game play to?"

"My girlfriend is my inspiration. She's had to deal with a lot this season and I'm grateful for her unwavering support. And the support of my team. We're in this together, and I think tonight we showed the hockey-watching nation that we have each other's backs. But honestly, every goal I scored tonight was for Tallulah. She's incredible and I'm lucky to love her."

"That's a bold statement. How do you think your teammates feel, knowing you prioritize your girlfriend over your job?"

"Feel free to ask them, but I'm pretty sure you'll get the same response as me. You said it yourself. I'm playing the best hockey of my career. I'm also the most settled I've ever been, and I have a person in my life I can rely on and who relies on me. Love makes it easier to thrive. And Tallulah, well she has my whole heart."

CHAPTER 62
TALLY

"We have so much to celebrate." Phillip frees my hair from my jacket and kisses the side of my neck.

"You should kiss me right here." I point to the hollow just below my ear.

"I'll kiss every inch of you when we get home." His lips ghost along the edge of my jaw. "But right now, we have to leave, or we'll be late."

I sigh. "You're going to edge me the entire time, aren't you?"

"If you want me to." He smiles against my skin.

I turn in his arms and loop mine around his neck. "I love you."

The way his face lights up never stops making my heart squeeze. "I love you, too, kitten." He kisses the end of my nose, my chin, and then my lips. "And I'll show you how much *after* the party."

"I'm very excited for that."

Phillip opens the door and ushers me into the hall. He laces our fingers as we wait for the elevator. It's not empty, so we make polite conversation with the older couple on the way down, then walk the short distance to the Watering Hole.

All our friends are already there when we arrive. Balloons and party hats proclaiming congratulations are strewn across the table. So much has happened in the past few weeks. Toronto won the first series after game six, then went on to take the second series in four games. They have a few days off while Vancouver and the Seattle Storm fight it out for their place in the conference finals.

"Ah! Talls! Congratulations!" Fee hops off her stool and rushes over, throwing her arms around me. Cammie and Enid follow, and then the rest of the Babes.

"Thank you!" I absorb their affection and their love, elated all over.

"I cannot wait to see you onstage in a professional theater!" Hammer gushes.

Yesterday En Pointe Theater offered me a place in their dance troupe for their fall production. "Me either."

"You must be so excited!" Hemi beams.

"It's a dream come true."

Today we're celebrating our university graduation, my first ever adult job, and the Terror making it to the conference finals.

The past month has felt like the best kind of dream. Phillip and the Terror guys helped me move out of my apartment into my dad's place. He's only a couple of blocks from the Terror office, which is also very close to Phillip's apartment and En Pointe Theater is only a twenty-minute subway ride away. When Phillip isn't on an away series, I spend most of my nights in his bed, but I always try to keep a night open for my dad. Our relationship feels more stable these days and moving in with him has helped. When the Terror are away, I'll spend time with my mom, Ties, and Fenna. We'll have our own family celebration in a few days, once the guys are on their way to either Seattle or Vancouver.

We gather around the table, pour drinks and order food. Phillip stretches his arm across the back of my chair.

I glance around the table, smiling as I take in the second family my dad created for me. Ariel and Pavin are side by side, Pavin trying to feed her his fries, but mostly sticking them in her hair and ear. Hammer is sitting next to her little sister, wet wipe at the ready, her smile wide and full of joy. Hollis watches his wife, eyes full of warmth. I won't be surprised if they announce a pregnancy of their own soon.

Brody sits between his brothers, staring longingly at Enid at the other end of the table.

"We'll be celebrating you soon enough," Roman says to Brody.

"Huh?" He drags his gaze away from Enid.

"You'll be signing a contract soon," Quinn says. "The Rage are interested in you, right?"

"Oh, yeah." Brody runs a hand through his hair. "Chicago would be good."

"They could use a Stiles out there," Tristan adds.

"I wouldn't mind ending up back out that way again eventually," Quinn muses.

"Dude, don't say shit like that." Kellan elbows him.

"I said eventually." Quinn rubs his arm.

"Well, the universe might hear you and think eventually means now."

"Mac would happily take your spot on defense, so would Gage," Brody adds.

"For fuck's sake, stop!" Kellan throws his hands in the air.

"Goalies, always so superstitious." Phillip shakes his head while smiling.

"You should see some of the stuff Roman does before his team plays." Lexi hugs his arm.

"Does he still insist on an apple every game?" Hammer asks.

"I like apples." Roman smirks down at Lexi. "Especially with caramel dip."

"Please don't look at each other like that in front of me," Hammer jokes.

Roman arches a brow.

Dallas clinks his knife against the side of his pint glass.

Hemi widens her eyes at him. "Thunder stealer!"

"Honey, I can't hold it in."

She rolls her eyes but gives him the go-on motion.

Shilpa grins. Hammer bites her lips together.

I already know what they're about to tell us.

"I got my wife pregnant!" Dallas is absolutely beaming as he hugs Hemi to his side.

The table erupts in excited chaos. I jump up to hug Hemi, along with the rest of the Babes, while the guys congratulate Dallas on his virility.

We lob questions at her, like when is the baby due, how far along is she, and does this mean her brothers will finally settle down and have a baby-making competition where they try to pop out the most babies in the shortest span of time.

"You know Samir will try and get his wife pregnant with triplets just for bragging rights," Dallas says.

"He would absolutely do that," Hemi agrees. "He just needs to find someone to marry first."

"Those two as uncles will be something," Phillip laughs.

"I would pay money to see Sam hold a baby," Brody says.

Tristan snorts a laugh. "Can you imagine how protective those two would be if they end up with a niece?"

The table erupts in chatter and laughter.

I hug Phillip's arm and kiss the edge of his jaw.

He gazes down at me. "What are you thinking about?"

"Just how amazing it is that we get to be aunts and uncles to all our friends' babies."

"We'll have lots of practice by the time we're ready for our own," Phillip agrees.

I smile up at him. "I'm excited for us."

"Me, too, kitten."

I can see our future taking shape and I'm in love with all of it.

CHAPTER 63

TALLY

"I can't come into the locker room with you."

"I mean, there is no real rule." Phillip keeps our fingers laced.

The media snaps photos as I walk down the hall with him toward the locker room in question. It's game five and Toronto is up 3-1 in the series.

"Do you really want me to see your teammates' junk? I could find out if Quinn really does have freckles everywhere."

Phillip narrows his eyes while I grin up at him.

The media goes wild, flash after flash going off.

"You know that'll be some kind of headline later tonight."

"We can do better." He wraps his arm around my waist and dips me backwards as he kisses me senseless.

"I see you're taking a page from my book these days," Connor says dryly as he passes. "Your coach is watching, by the way."

I glance over to see my dad standing with Lexi and the other coaches.

"You're going to be amazing tonight." I smooth my hand over his lapels.

"Bringing home the cup for you," he promises.

He kisses my nose, my chin, and then my lips before he disappears into the locker room.

"Everything okay with Madden?" Dad asks.

The only downside of living with my dad is that he knows when and where I spend my nights, so I slept in my own bed last night. Not that we didn't have post-dinner, pre-me-going-home sex, but at least he had a solid eight hours of sleep. "He's in a good headspace."

"This is his best season, by far," Dad says.

"He had a lot of motivation to play well," I agree.

I see what Phillip means now when he says he's not just playing for his team and himself anymore. It was the same for Connor when he married Dred and they adopted the twins, who are starting university next year at Tilton. He suddenly had a reason to play better. He wanted to make the people he loves proud, and Phillip is the same.

I kiss my dad on the cheek and leave him to strategize, while I join the Babes, my Tilton friends, and my mom and siblings in the family box. The little ones are here, too. Callie is attached to Victor at the hip, and Everly is wearing a Grace jersey, but she has a Ryker cuff on her wrist.

"Everything okay?" Mom squeezes my arm.

"Everything is great. I'm glad you all could make it tonight."

"It's a big deal for your father, and for you," she says. "We all wanted to be here to support you."

"I want this for them." I'm nervous but excited. Winning the Cup this season would feel particularly gratifying, especially with how much focus there was on my relationship with Phillip. We're still a highlight, but the negativity has finally shifted. Pictures of us with our Terror friends and their families keep popping up, and now the question is who's getting married next and when will there be more babies.

Mom surveys the group. Ties and Victor are chatting, Fenna

has been pulled in with Callie and Everly, and the littles are gathered around Brody, who doesn't seem the least bit bothered by all the attention. He's been coaching special needs hockey since he was in his early teens, so it tracks.

"They're like a family, aren't they?" Mom muses.

"Yeah, they really are," I agree. "They're like a bunch of older siblings."

"It makes sense. You were always taking care of everyone, and you found friends who take care of each other."

Hemi and Shilpa call us over and we join the rest of the group as the game gets underway.

They're all playing hard, but the Seattle Storm went to seven games in both series before this one. They're tired, and the Terror had some downtime to recharge before the final series. Time off can go either way. Sometimes it causes a team to lose momentum, but in this case, it rejuvenated the Terror and added enough fuel to their tanks to make them a formidable opponent.

In the first period, Grace and my boyfriend score a goal together. Seattle tries to even the score, but defense is playing tight, and Romero and Palaniappa are working hard to make Ryker's job easier. Bright scores a goal at the end of the first and we keep that lead through the end of the second period. In the third, Stiles scores with Phillip as the assist. Seattle finally puts themselves on the board with ten minutes left in the game. They try for another goal, but Phillip gains control of the puck and scores again for Toronto.

The last ten minutes of the game are intense, with lots of hard hits into the boards, but the Storm can't recover, and the Terror bring home the Cup.

It's a glorious win.

A perfectly epic end to an epic season.

And a beautiful start to the next chapter in our lives.

EPILOGUE
FLIP

THREE YEARS LATER

"Phillip? Baby? Are you ready to go?" Tally calls from down the hall.

"Coming!" I flip the tiny velvet box closed and tuck it into my pocket.

"Not without me, I hope." My girlfriend (soon to be fiancée) pokes her head in our closet. We've been living together for two years, now, and I'm more than ready to make it permanent. "What are you doing in here?"

"Grabbing my wallet." I nab it from the dresser and tuck it in my pocket as well. "Ready to go?"

"Do I look ready?" Tally does a full-body shimmy.

She's wearing the dress I bought her, her athletic dancer's body stunning in the flowy, clinging fabric. "You look incredible."

"Incredibly edible?"

"Don't start." I wind an arm around her waist. "I will spend all night edging you."

"It's my birthday, though."

"You think that gives you a free pass from the edging?" I kiss a path up her neck. "We need to go, or we'll be late."

"You're terrible," she grumbles.

"You love it." I bite the edge of her jaw.

"I really do," she agrees.

"When we get home, I'll fulfill whatever new fantasy you come up with," I promise.

After three and a half years together, we long ago exhausted her original list. Cammie's fics-turned-published works definitely keep things creative these days.

"Will you at least give me a hint about where we're going tonight?"

I gaze down at my girlfriend. "No hints."

"Obviously we're having dinner somewhere."

"We are definitely having dinner," I agree.

"And then what?" Tally fingers the hair at the nape of my neck and bites my chin.

"And then it's a surprise."

"I'll try to swallow your whole cock later if you just give me one hint," she bargains.

I snort. "Nice try. It's like your favorite fucking pastime."

She huffs, then sighs. "It's true."

The elevator doors slide open, thankfully, because I can see my girlfriend's wheels turning. We hold hands as I guide her to the car and drive the short distance to the restaurant. It's her favorite place, and I've rented it out so we can celebrate her twenty-fifth in style.

"Oh my gosh! This is perfect! I wonder what their special will be. Maybe they'll have lobster ravioli. Oh! And the panna cotta with sour cherries. I love it when they have that!"

"It's a favorite for sure." They'll have all of Tally's most loved dishes, of that I made sure.

The host greets us, and Tally is too busy being excited to

notice that the restaurant is deserted as he guides us to the main dining room.

The lights come up as we round the corner and all our friends and family shout, "Surprise!"

Tally turns to me, already overwhelmed with emotion. "You are the best." She cups my face in her palms and brings my mouth to hers. "How did you plan this without me finding out?"

"I had help from some friends."

"I love you. You're amazing."

The restaurant is decorated in her favorite colors, and a banner that reads Happy 25th Tallulah! is strung across the back wall. A photo booth with a stage backdrop takes up one corner of the room.

It's full of all the people we love and who love us. Quinn even managed to make the trip out from Chicago. Kellan wasn't wrong about manifesting a trade. Gage Steele, one of Tilton's enforcers and Tally's friends, was picked up by the Terror, and Quinn went to the Rage, along with Kellan. It all worked out the way it was supposed to, though. Quinn is close to his family again, and finally got the girl he's been longing for. Steele and our new goalie have been a great addition to the team.

Tally is engulfed by her friends, and I smile as she flits around, introducing some of her troupe mates to the Terror group.

"You bring the ring?" Tristan asks quietly.

I pat my pocket. "It's right here."

"Good man."

"Dada!" My nephew bumbles over, falling twice on his way, Rix following behind him, a wide smile on her face.

"You got this, little man!" Tristan crouches and holds his arms out while his son wobbles into them. He showers his little face with kisses and picks him up, then bends to kiss my sister. They jumped on the baby train after Dallas and Hemi had their first. It started a trend. And my parents finally moved back to the city so they could focus on being grandparents and be closer to us.

Tally and I aren't in a rush. Her career is taking off and I want her to enjoy it. She's been dancing for En Pointe and this year she has a lead role in the fall performance.

In the meantime, we love being Uncle Flip and Aunt Tally.

"You've outdone yourself, Phillip." Tally's mom hugs me. She's dating a guy who works in tech and leaves his job at the office. She's happy and that's what matters most to Tally.

"She deserves the world."

"She's lucky to have you."

"And I'm lucky to have her."

She moves on to chat with Tally's friends and Vander Zee comes over. "This is a great party, Phillip. Thank you for celebrating my daughter."

"I live to make her happy," I say.

"I know you do." He smiles fondly and claps me on the shoulder. "I'll be proud to call you my son-in-law."

I asked him for permission a while ago, knowing eventually we'd be in the right place to take the next step.

We mix and mingle, chatting and catching up, and sit down to a huge, chaotic family dinner. Ties is heading into his final year of university, and Fenna is attending Tilton for music in the fall. Dallas and Hemi have two kids, Ariel is growing up way too fast, Callie is in high school, and Everly and Victor have one more year of university to go. Dred confided that they want to wait until they're finished before they jump on the baby train with everyone else.

I have a five-year plan that includes retiring from professional hockey and shifting gears so I can be home to raise our kids with Tally. I want a house full of love and kids and memories. And I want to be present for all the important moments.

After dessert, I stand and offer my hand to Tally, who rises with me.

"Thank you, everyone, for celebrating with me today!" Tally turns to me. "And thank you for being the best boyfriend in the world."

"Thank you for being mine." I take a deep breath, reach into my pocket, and withdraw the velvet box as I drop to one knee.

Murmurs and excited gasps come from our friends and family.

"Phillip," Tally whispers.

I open the box and she sucks in a gasp.

"I love you so much, Tallulah."

"I love you too, more than anything."

"I want to spend the rest of my life waking up beside you. I want a house full of love, and kids, and big celebrations. I want to take our nieces and nephews to the theater to see their aunt perform, and one day I want to do the same with our kids. You are my future, Tally. You have my whole heart."

Tears spring to her eyes. "And you have mine."

"Marry me, Tallulah." I squeeze her hand. "Keep me."

"Forever." Her smile lights up the room. "My heart is yours. Of course I'll marry you."

I slide the ring on her finger as our friends and family cheer and whistle.

I rise and wrap my arms around her, kissing her tenderly.

She's my home.

She has my utter devotion.

Her happiness is mine, and my heart is hers to keep.

Need more Flip & Tally? Subscribe for instant access to a bonus scene!

ABOUT THE AUTHOR
HELENA HUNTING

NYT and USA Today bestselling author, Helena Hunting lives on the outskirts of Toronto with her amazing family and her adorable kitty, who thinks the best place to sleep is her keyboard. Helena writes everything from emotional contemporary romance to romantic comedies that will have you laughing until you cry. If you're looking for a tearjerker, you can find her angsty side under H. Hunting.

OTHER TITLES BY HELENA HUNTING

THE TORONTO TERROR SERIES

If You Hate Me

If You Want Me

If You Need Me

If You Love Me

If You Claim Me

If You Keep Me

I Could Be Yours

TILTON UNIVERSITY SERIES

Chase Lovett Wants Me

Mac Meyer Needs Me (coming June 2026)

THE PUCKED SERIES

Pucked (Pucked #1)

Pucked Up (Pucked #2)

Pucked Over (Pucked #3)

Forever Pucked (Pucked #4)

Pucked Under (Pucked #5)

Pucked Off (Pucked #6)

Pucked Love (Pucked #7)

AREA 51: Deleted Scenes & Outtakes

Get Inked

Pucks & Penalties

Where it Begins

ALL IN SERIES

A Lie for a Lie

A Favor for a Favor

A Secret for a Secret

A Kiss for a Kiss

LIES, HEARTS & TRUTHS SERIES

Little Lies

Bitter Sweet Heart

Shattered Truths

SHACKING UP SERIES

Shacking Up

Getting Down (Novella)

Hooking Up

I Flipping Love You

Making Up

Handle with Care

SPARK SISTERS SERIES

When Sparks Fly

Starry-Eyed Love

Make A Wish

LAKESIDE SERIES

Love Next Door

Love on the Lake

THE CLIPPED WINGS SERIES

Cupcakes and Ink

Clipped Wings

Between the Cracks

Inked Armor

Cracks in the Armor

Fractures in Ink

STANDALONE NOVELS

The Librarian Principle

Felony Ever After

Before You Ghost (with Debra Anastasia)

FOREVER ROMANCE STANDALONES

The Good Luck Charm

Meet Cute

Kiss my Cupcake

A Love Catastrophe